Made in United States
Troutdale, OR
04/29/2024

# Similar Series by D.K. Holmberg

## *The Dragonwalkers Series*

The Dragonwalker

The Dragon Misfits

The Dragon Thief

Cycle of Dragons

## *Elemental Warrior Series:*

Elemental Academy

The Elemental Warrior

The Cloud Warrior Saga

The Endless War

## Series by Jasper Alden

The Lost Riders

The Golden Fool

The Binding Trials

To L²

Although Hal and Keershan's hearts would always be in Malarsan.

---

That's all for The Lost Rider (for now!), but we think you'll love our next series.

**Don't miss book 1 of The Binding Trials**, The Shadow Elemental!

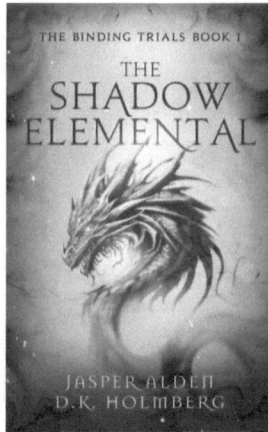

# Chapter 1

**D**eath is seldom dignified, but as a private investigator, he some times overlooked how personal it could get. This time it blind-sided a lot of people, including Craige. During the annual Board of Directors banquet, CEO Llewyn Royce Sedgewicke died in front of God and all his fair-weather associates. He took what little decorum he ever had with him when he foundered like a tuxedoed, beached whale across the formal dining table. His obese carcass shoveled cups, plates, silverware, floral centerpieces and assorted crystal into a tangled heap. That mess was bad enough, but he left a bigger one behind. The death certificate said heart attack—it wasn't. Craige yawned, stretched, scratched his day-old, reddish beard and stared out across the yard toward the splash of the river against his dock. The night's heavy river fog was still so thick he couldn't see the far curve of the river toward Silver Bluff Point. It blanketed the yard, beading the screens of his dogtrot-sleeping porch with shimmering water droplets.

Lucky, his German shepherd, slurped his ear to wake him; otherwise, he won't budge.

"OK, go ahead," Craige mumbled.

Lucky nudged open the screen door and was gone by the time he remembered his tendency to chase Mrs. Courtney's chickens. She's a nice, old lady who lives several miles down from me, and that day, he couldn't blame her being a touch beyond upset. Craige's Grannie

7

would've laid a load of buckshot into any four-legged mutt bothering her Rhode Island Red settin' hens. He would have to do some sweet-talking to Mrs. Courtney about those chickens.

The sheet felt cool against his bare skin. He buried his head in a goose down pillow and tried to break years of up-before-daybreak routine, but the yen for a jolt of thick-boiled Turkish coffee wouldn't let him be. He ruffled his hair with both hands and felt the tangles from yesterday's quick skinny-dip in the river. He needed a haircut, but with no bow tie socials on the immediate calendar, putting off the barber a couple of days wouldn't matter. He should've known something was cockeyed with the grayish daybreak and when the mockingbirds weren't raising their usual morning ruckus.

"Forget it, Ingramme," he muttered and threw back the sheet.

He blamed it on jetlag. Even for a long flight, piloting his new TranStar jet from eastern Siberia had been a snap, even though being the only one aboard cut down autopilot and shuteye time. With all the cockpit whistles and bells, there wasn't much to do other than punch in coordinates and keep her belly full. Having his own wings handy was the main reason he hired a topnotch mechanic like Hank full-time. His new bird was always A-one ready for up and away on a moment's notice. The Kamchatka roundtrip flight came off a lot different than his last Siberian cat-and-mouse covert junket when Operations Section made sure none of their SEAL insertion team took any ID—no papers, no passports, nada. On his last Kamchatka trip he'd shelved stopovers in New Zealand and Tasmania with ex-navy buds he hadn't seen since their last recon. He hadn't given anyone a heads-up, and it wasn't his style to show up unannounced unless surprise was part of the OpsSection plans.

*****

After his parents were killed in a botched California robbery and his other grandparents returned to Europe, he went to South Carolina to live with Grannie. Mom had been Catholic, and Grannie held a wake for her in the front parlor. It was the first time Grannie let a priest set foot on Moccasin Hollow since the time she shoved the business end of her shotgun in one priest's face.

"No papist is buttin' in twixt me an' Jesus," Grannie ordered. "Now git!"

8

After the wake, Grannie pulled Craige on her lap.

"Things gonna settle down now," she said.

He snuggled closer. "Grannie, someday you gonna be gone like Mom and Dad?"

As she rocked him slow and quiet, she answered, "We all go someday. Grannie gonna be around a long time." And she pulled his head onto her bosom, hugged him close and kept rockin'.

He didn't like thinking about it then and still don't. Grannie had a heart full of love, and there were times he must've taken most all of it. In the stillness before sunup, he can still hear her quick footsteps squeaking the wide "Heart of Pine" floorboards on the way to fire up her kitchen stove.

Right soon he'd hear, "Git out'a bed. Breakfast is ready." With a frazzled sweet gum twig in the corner of her mouth, she'd continue, "Day's not waitin'. There's chores to git done."

She'd stir herself a small pot of grits with dark ham gravy, and make him a bowl of corn meal mush to go with her cured ham, cream gravy with hot biscuits, scrambled eggs and fresh buttermilk. It sure tasted good.

Years later, Grannie's death turned his world upside-down. He still remembered watching her coffin sink into the ground next to Mom and Dad's and the terrible time he had afterwards. It wrenched his butt out of the Naval Academy, but Grannie was right again—she believed things happen as they should.

After several months of brooding, his high school bud, Graysen MacGerald, and he enlisted. He went through navy SEAL BUD training where he learned a lot about himself, met some great people and acquired some bad habits, which he still has. Heavy sack time wasn't one of them, unless he had a tequila hangover or was snugged next to a hot body. That never happened on base—well, almost never.

*****

Investments have paid off nicely. He'd added several large sections to Grannie's place. She'd had a tough fight keeping her land with speculators pulling tax schemes to force it to auction. Some were her own kin. It wasn't the first time Ingrams and Graemes faced that, and it wasn't the first time backbiters reckoned wrong about Corinthia

Ingram being easy pickings. She logged enough timber to pay the taxes and made damn sure riffraff, Ingram or otherwise, never set foot on Moccasin Hollow. Water and mineral rights were worth plenty then, and they're worth more now. Now and then, kaolin conglomerates pinged Craige about long-term leases, but it's not happening on Ingramme land.

His broker almost choked at his idea of investing in Russian timber commodities. The seven figure chunk of negotiable paper made him nervous. It wouldn't be the first time he'd done business with them, and Craige didn't tell him they once had standing orders to shoot him on sight. For a minute, he thought he was going to have to administer CPR to this man.

He said, "You could lose it all, and they can be mean as snot."

"Sometimes they have a right to be," he said.

He looked at Craige like he'd lost his mind and made the arrangements. Craige hadn't planned on inspecting the properties till spring, but absentee landlords make for easy skimming. By being there he could make sure the cuts were from the selected sections. He won't be partner to slash and stripping whole mountains. Even with his inside contacts, it was a real eye opener. It's never all about the money.

*****

He steamed another cup of gritty Turkish and opened the paper. Sedgewicke's death made the front page in big, black letters.

"In his tux, all dressed for the coffin," he chuckled.

Sedgewicke was none of his business—or so he thought. Besides, he didn't respect the way he did business. In short, he didn't like him, but the article reminded Craige to make an appointment to finish the McGiffern estate business. Ignorance is bliss—it can also kill you.

He skinnied into his denim kick-abouts and shoved the cell phone in his back pocket. He hadn't made it across the yard to his machine shop before his phone rang. Few people had his unlisted number. When it jangles, odds are it's business.

He answered, "Ingramme."

"Hope I didn't catch you at a bad time," Gray said, "but any chance you'll be on my side of the river this morning?"

Even with his high-pressure, police job, ex-SEAL ComOfficer

Graysen MacGerald was usually laid-back, but he could be bulldog tenacious. He claimed Craige was worse, but as his SEAL CO, that was just one reason Craige wanted him in the unit. Gray doesn't make social calls in the middle of a workday.

"Was planning on it," Craige said. "As soon as I get in touch with the bank."

"Interesting you'd mention the bank," Gray said. "I need to pick your PI brain."

"Something urgent?" Craige asked.

"Your nose has always been good at sniffing trouble," Gray remarked. "Right now I could use that."

"Been a time or two that wasn't true," Craige said.

Memories of some of their tight spots flashed, and anytime Gray needed help, the particulars didn't matter. They both preferred playing things low-key, especially when his snooping became police business. It kept any flak about his going outside the department to a minimum. Gray had put together a topnotch investigative support team in his homicide bailiwick, and with Coroner-Medical Examiner Fred Dinkins at the head of the forensic team, it made a strong department. Between them, there's not much they didn't ferret out.

"You smell a rat?" Gray asked.

"I've got a few things that aren't cozying up quite right."

"Pick a time. I'll be there."

Craige asked, "How's the wife?"

"Sybil's doing fine," he answered. "She asked about you the other day."

Gray always liked talking about his true love, and as far as it was any of his business, Craige thought Sybil was one of the best things that ever happened to him.

"The daughter's discovered boys, which scares the hell out of me," he continued.

Of all the guys in their unit that got tangled in woman trouble, Gray was one of the few that never let it happen. His daughter was his heartstring, and Craige pitied boys if he ever had daughters.

"Don't worry, Daddy," Craige kidded in his bar-cruise voice, "she won't do anything you haven't done."

"Jezus!" Gray exclaimed. "You could've gone all day without saying that."

Craige laughed as he said, "I have to tie up some loose ends for Theosia's estate—mainly paper shuffling."

"She the McGiffern the paper did a spread on?" Gray asked. "Lived in Ardochy Manor and buried in the family mausoleum at Silver Bluff?"

"One and the same," Craige said.

"You attract women like flies."

"My natural charm and good looks."

They both laughed. Their navy gang had worn out that line.

"What you need checked out?"

"Fred pulled an all nighter." Gray stated. "Had the Sedgewicke autopsy prelims ready by the time I got here this morning."

"Which is your way of saying there's a rat in the corn crib,"

"Which is my way of saying he didn't die of natural causes." Gray didn't mince his words. "But for the time being, that's off the record."

"There've been rumors that the bank's talking merger. Wouldn't be the first time money paved the road to a kill," Craige said. "If Sedgewicke was a problem, getting rid of him was one way of handling a road block."

"Interesting way of putting it," Gray replied. "From what I hear, bank officers deny any merger talks are in the works."

"Sedgewicke may have wanted the merger kept on the QT," Craige said. "'specially if he's got some kickbacks in the works with offshore cash or stock options. Any leads about who might've had it in for him enough to take him out of the equation?"

"I'm not finding much love lost for the bank's late prez. Anyone who did the deed would likely get a medal from the others."

"I've met most of the bank officials. I can think of a couple who didn't like Sedgewicke, but that doesn't mean they had enough guts to kill him. Besides, if every motive had a dead body, the human race would be extinct," Craige said. "What about employees or the possibility he was involved with someone?"

"There's plenty of scuttlebutt about girlfriends," Gray replied, "but nothing about who'll be the next CEO."

Craige had seen less trigger a lot of hate.

Gray continued, "The word is that Sedgewicke had a lot going on besides offshore bank accounts and foreign stock trades. There's questionable campaign donations from some of his pet politicos. A few of those have already bent my ears."

"I'd expect as much from some of those freeloaders," Craige said. "They don't want their shirttail to get smuttier than they already are. Most politicos haven't done an honest day's work in their life."

"The longer I can keep the lid on, the more breathing room we have before hemorrhoids tighten up," remarked Gray. "I don't want the rats to start covering their tracks."

"Any lawyers knocked on your door inquiring about the details?" Craige asked.

Cynicism about his second least liked profession doesn't take much to get under his skin. Craige guessed that's just one of his bad habits. He shouldn't judge a whole profession by a scurvy few, but somehow they seem to have more than their fair share.

"I figured it wouldn't take long for you to get around to that," Gray chuckled. "Mabel said a few law offices already made inquiries."

Craige made a guess. "For incident reports which you made sure haven't been filed."

"And won't be for as long as I can keep it that way," Gray said.

Craige never forgot an SOB who sneaks behind anyone's back. He wish he had more of Gray's patience. He'd always believed the success of their SpecOps unit was more his doing than mine. Up front might be rougher and not nearly as neat, but in the long run, it's a whole lot cleaner—better too.

"Dirty money always keeps its big guns on the ready," Craige said. "Any of Sedgewicke's family object to the autopsy?"

"I've only dealt with his wife," he said. "I explained that under certain circumstances state law requires an autopsy."

Craige was curious. "She didn't ask what circumstances?"

"No, and I couldn't tell," he said. "She's one cool lady."

Craige said, "That's about what I'd expect."

Gray asked, "You know her family?"

"I've met them on occasion," Craige said.

"I figured as much, considering the circles you move in," Gray said. "Her only question concerned the death certificate having been signed by Royce's personal physician." Suspicion was part of his job.

"The female is always the deadlier," Craige stated, "but I can't see someone with her background having anything to do with murder. The money angle won't fly. Her family is old money, more than Sedgewicke ever thought about having."

"Class has nothing to do with money, and it's never been a barrier to murder."

"True," Craige agreed, "but they go about it with a bit more finesse." He then tossed in another wild card, "How about his doctor?"

"The man's eighty-two, married to the same woman for fifty-two years, lived here all their lives, practiced nowhere else, has three grandchildren, travel some, don't gamble, house and cars paid for and no outstanding debts."

Craige juggled other angles. "Suppose the physician is hiding something to avoid a scandal—protect his wife. Fear can make people do things they'd otherwise never consider. They'd both seen killing for less. Blackmail has a way of spicing things up."

Gray was silent for a moment. In a deadly serious tone, he then said, "I want this kept between you and Fred and me. That's where I can use your help. Once the killer knows we're looking into it as a murder, the next step will be to get rid of evidence and any witnesses before we find them."

It was a point well taken. He'd grown up with these good ol' boys, some of them are the finest people I've ever known, but there are a few rotten apples in any bushel. Some weren't so damn good at all.

Then Craige rained on Gray's parade when he said, "Suppose we're already past number one. Suppose Sedgewicke wasn't the first kill."

"That crossed my mind," Gray said. "'Specially with this merger business having to do with more than money."

An indefinable premonition yanked at the bottom of his stomach, the kind Grannie never ignored. Bottom feeders play for keeps, and the fact that Gray was a cop wouldn't matter. Craige said, "My business at the bank shouldn't take long."

"I'll be here." With that, their conversation was over.

Craige stood there, the day more off keel than when it started. My first impulse was to skip the bank. He wasn't in the mood to dicker with paper shufflers. He called them instead. Craige should've waited, but he didn't, and it didn't get any better.

"Landmark Trust Department," the receptionist answered. "Can you hold, please?"

The singsong elevator music in his ear didn't help his attitude for a host of maybes that had nothing to do with banks, and Gray's ticklish situation was at the top of the list. Craige grumbled something

disparaging about secretaries and hung up.

Craige hit the bathroom. Electric is OK for hit-and-run, but a straight razor kept his five o'clock shadow from showing up by noon. He whipped up a hot lather, smeared it on, stropped the blade and straightaway nicked himself. He let it trickle while he scraped but with a bit more caution. He buried his face in a steamy towel, wiped away leftover lather, jumped in the shower, got out, toweled his hair, slapped on after-shave that stung like the dickens, put on some clothes, climbed in his rebuilt World War II Jeep and crammed it into gear.

The nondescript, red brick building was your typical '60s three-story box—small, white windows in a row, painted so many times you couldn't pry them open. Sooty smudged scorches showed through the roof-line paint and tar from the big downtown fire decades ago. On the street front, a pair of squat brick posts topped by large, white globe sconces sat on granite tops stenciled with large black letters—PO-LICE. From roof to basement to steel door holding cells, John Q. Taxpayer had gotten his money's worth from this one. The building needed replacing. A new law enforcement center had been budgeted for the last 7 years, but city council freeloaders kept siphoning monies off the budget for their "pet" projects.

Craige pulled into the EMPLOYEES ONLY parking lot and parked next to Gray's beat-up old sedan, in its usual spot. Gray routinely arrived early—hours before things get in their morning scurry and scramble and regularly dings his already dented front door on the light pole.

Gray claims that he gets more done in those two hours than he does the rest of the day."

Mabel is never far behind. She keeps things even keeled.

A Jill-of-all-trades—whatever Gray needed—secretary, assistant, receptionist, stenographer, gopher, watch schedules and shift changes. Mabel played no favorites—well, maybe Craige and Gray, which was OK with Craige. The lot was never full, but pencil-necked whiners groused about his parking in "their" lot. His fuse was way too short when it came to the do-nothing gripe and snivel crowd. With Gray in a bind, it got even shorter.

As Craige came up the steps to the rear entrance, Mabel spotted him and popped the security code to open the rear steel door.

She gave him a wicked smile. "Good morning, good-looking." She

15

had a big heart that she rarely let show.

"Morning to you, too," Craige said.

There was something different this morning about Mabel—she had a new perm.

"I like your new do," Craige said.

"You know how to perk up a girl's day," she blushed.

"I've been known to try," Craige grinned.

"I'll bet you have." Mabel smiled right back at him.

Mabel and Craige enjoyed the banter and tease. Nothing serious, well, not that serious.

"It's the old-is-new-again Gibson look I've always liked," she said.

It did look good. At forty-five Mabel was a striking woman. Craige had often wondered what she was like in her heyday. Hell, for all he knew she was still in it and more than a match for any man, including him. Main thing Craige liked about her was her passion for guarding Gray's flanks. Anyone dumb enough to be pushy dealt with iceberg Mabel and found out jiffy quick she wasn't bluffing. If she thought you were trying to pull a fast one, there was no warning, just a chunk ripped out of your nearest body part. Trying the ploy "me and the mayor went to school together" never worked either. Her soft-spoken "I don't think Lieutenant MacGerald would approve of that" was the only warning to tread no further. She knew enough about the locals to hang any troublemaker. Craige made no bones about anyone knowing Mabel was one of his favorites.

Just then, Gray opened the door of his office with its crooked "E" HOMICIDE sign. "Come on in," he said. "I thought you were going by the bank first?" His bushy brow was in a wrinkled frown.

"They're busy," Craige said. "Instead of cooling my heels and watching fish in an aquarium, I detoured here. I'll catch them later."

"Take a look at this," he said.

He handed Craige a thick folder with red letters blazoned DEPT CPY—EYES ONLY/MacGERALD. Gray slouched back into his worn leather swivel chair with its tattered padding poking out one edge and waited. The solitary overhead ceiling fan creaking away as Craige settled into the matching frayed sofa and did a quick read-through with special attention to Fred's notes scrawled in the margins. Fred's notes often contained more than the official report.

"Quite a dossier for a prelim workup," Craige said. "How come

16

there's all these photos of the banquet area when everyone thought it was a heart attack?"

"With a high-profile incident, it never hurts to cover all bases," Gray said. "Any criminal attorney worth his salt knows Fred does his homework."

Gray wasn't the only one who knew they could bank on Fred's rock solid nit-picking the minutia.

"Sedgewicke certainly made an exit," Craige remarked. The photo was a doozy.

"In more ways than one," Gray said.

Gray fixed him with a serious "there's more" look and shoved him a stack of body shots taken from different angles.

"Looks like he took the tablecloth with him," Craige said as he thumbed through them.

"And about everything else."

Craige winced when he came to the photo of the shattered, Baccarat decanter and several Waterford goblets. The next one was a close-up of Sedgewicke's hand, a frozen claw entangled at his belly roll cummerbund. A third was a face shot, his purple tongue bulged from a sickly blue-mottled lips, the floral centerpiece formed a halo star burst of torn petals and shattered cobalt blue fragments of a wine bottle.

"One sure way to highlight a banquet," Craige mused.

Gray sighed, "He made quite a media splash when he built his new bank building and made it the centerpiece of downtown revitalization."

"Yea," Craige snorted. "Without mentioning his private penthouse and Pinnacle Club on top with a view of land along the river he wanted to own."

"Royce Sedgewicke was no different than his forefathers who were working this river before Farmer George wore the crown," said Gray as he leaned back and locked his fingers behind his head. "With redcoats in Savannah, Sedgewickes did their patriotic duty for king and country.

A few cannons for the colonials, the rest of the cargo was geegaws and bootlegged firewater to trade with the Indians, then switched sides when it pinched the pocketbook. Royce liked to brag how without his family's ships Fort Cornwallis couldn't have survived."

"I doubt Royce Sedgewicke knew enough history to know there

was a Fort Cornwallis," Craige remarked.

The part of Craige that couldn't tolerate people like Royce was at odds with the other part that knows he can't change the world. The more the Sedgewicke type has, the more they want. It wasn't the first time old-fashioned greed pushed his buttons.

"Word is Royce dipped into discretionary funds to bankroll construction of the new bank," Gray said.

"I wouldn't be surprised," Craige replied. "And all the time making sure the old bank property never came on the market until river front values dropped, and he could snap it up for next to nothing."

An angled photo of a silver wine label caught his eye, a splayed grape leaf logo clinging to what was left of the bottle. Craige wasn't familiar with the label.

"Why a picture of the label?" Craige was intrigued.

"The banquet was catered but not the wine," Gray said. "It came from Royce's private stock."

"Cabernet Sauvignon, special selection," Craige said. "Cabernet grapes make some fine wine, but for my money, Sauvignons belong in salad dressing. Never one of my favorites."

Gray grinned. "I buy mine in jugs."

"Some highbrows don't know enough about wine to order anything but a Sauvignon," Craige said.

Craige flipped to a picture of the fleshy blimp in garish white, patent leather boots and a sequined cocktail dress, which was not only out of place but way too tight. If her intention was to be noticed, she had achieved it with unqualified success.

Craige asked, "Who's this buxom number who looks so pissed? She's not Royce's wife. Lavenia Preston wouldn't be caught dead in an outfit like that."

"Leah Rea Covington Marshall," Gray answered. "Only daughter of bourbon swilling real estate tycoon Brightton Covington. She's a bona fide chunk off the old block, and you're right, she is pissed. She was digging out a glop of banana pudding with whipped cream that somehow landed down her hefty cleavage and raising the devil about how Royce ruined her new gown. She probably intended wearing it that night, return it the next day and mad because she had to keep it. I don't think she knew Fred took that photo."

"She married to Nathan Marshall?" Craige asked.

"Yep." Gray gave a nod. "The bank's executive VP, Donnie Marshall. His family calls him HughDon. Supposedly in line to fill Royce's shoes."

Craige didn't miss Gray's "supposedly."

"I doubt the Board will let him step into Sedgewicke's position," Craige replied. Donnie-Boy hasn't made a decision since he was weaned. Breakfast scuttlebutt at Duke's is that if he became CEO, the bank would be in a deep cow patty. Besides, his mother's a McHugh. She runs the McHugh family. Together, she and Lavenia Sedgewicke hold a controlling block of stock, much more than Royce. She's not about to let Donnie ruin a good business. The two wives could clean out the whole Board, elect who they wish, which makes a nice motive except for one slight detail—HughDon's mother and Royce's widow have enough of their own money to buy and sell the bank several times over."

Gray asked, "Don't both of them contribute to some of your favorite charities?"

"Big time!"

"Lots of folks wonder how Royce lucked out marrying a Preston."

"Might be as simple as someone you can't live without."

"For which one?"

"Far as Royce was concerned, he couldn't live without her money," Craige said. "All he changed was the price of his suits. Far as the wife was concerned, I can't say, but I can't see a Preston connected with anything like this. Theosia sure had a big dislike of Sedgewicke. The day she and I came in to sign some papers, we hadn't been with the lawyers ten minutes before Sedgewicke bulled right in. Walked straight to her. Theosia couldn't abide rudeness, and she never got rattled. She slowly sat her teacup down with an imperious 'we are not pleased' look, gave him a requisite 'nice to meet you,' then ignored him. I'll never forget the startled look on Royce's face." Craige flipped through several pages, then asked, "Wasn't the bank's annual stockholders meeting the week before this banquet?"

"That's what the big banquet shindig was about," Gray answered. "Promotions were to be announced that night."

Craige thumbed some more. "Sedgewicke's medical file shows he had bypass surgery two years ago."

Gray nodded. "Just before Royce collapsed that evening, he complained of feeling light headed, that his fingers were numb and couldn't

get his breath."

"And everyone assumed he had a heart attack."

Craige looked where the cause of death had been entered—myocardial infarction.

# Chapter 2

A testy Barry Jamison Peters sat at his desk in the bank, nervously folding and refolding a once immaculate handkerchief. At forty-two, Barry looked haggard way beyond his years—the prep school and college gridiron hunk long gone to flabby chunkiness, a once pleasant face was drawn with a perpetual chip on his shoulder. Like he'd done all his life, he waited, listening as the workday ended. The ebony-glass high rise became still and quiet as the five o'clock hired help scurried to the suburban parkway. Breaking routine attracted attention, and he sure didn't want that.

Math whiz nerd Barry liked numbers.

"You can trust numbers," he once told a new teller.

Barry didn't mind working late, the solitude was warm and familiar. He glanced at his Carrara marble clock that graced his orderly desk.

"Thirty more minutes," he murmured.

At breakfast that morning, he played with a slice of crisp scorched toast. His puffy eyes in a sagging puffy face buried in the morning paper hardly glanced in the direction of his frumpy wife.

"I have to work late again," he said.

She tugged at the waist of her soiled sloppy nightgown.

In more ways than looks, she matched him dull for dull.

"What's so different?" she said grumpily. "When you're around, we never talk."

In that moment, his look glittered on the hate side of disgust. She'd served him divorce papers three times, stopping when her checking account bottomed out. She never paid any of her lawyers, and the last one lost the papers in the bank's parking deck where the idle-talk crowd found them.

At the half hour, on the mark, Barry took the elevator to the main floor. His steps quickened through the red marble foyer with its malachite green columns and tall, ornate clock beneath the enormous oil of the Steamship Company's first steam locomotive. The duplicate master keys seared his sweaty palm. He unlocked the steel-barred grill into the safety deposit vault, inserted both slender keys and turned them at the same time. He pulled out the long, flat box, raised the lid, pocketed the small, velvet satchel from inside, replaced the box, removed the keys and made sure the grill locked behind him. His heart drubbing faster—anxious to get to Royce's secret place and the vintage collection of Cabernets in the cellar beneath the street. He took the elevator to the fourth floor, then the parking garage connector and the fire stairs down to the street. He scuttled across McIntosh, turned down the narrow alley with its unused railroad siding, brushed beneath the tangle of overgrown Virginia Creeper and slipped the new key into his new lock. He stepped inside, made sure the door locked behind him and the stale, dank air closed in around him. He was safe. No one could find him here.

He pulled out the wrinkled handkerchief, dabbed his face, took a deep breath and listened to the muffled street sounds above. His fingers fumbled for the tarnished, brass light switch that was old before Barry was born. He pushed the round button with a white-circled top, and a single bulb glowed feeble in a once ornate fixture—tulip shades long gone, clogged cobwebs in two empty sockets.

The meager light danced frail apparitions that followed him to the bottom of the foot-worn marble steps and the scrolled, bronze door of the old vault. The massive door opened easily as Barry shoved against it. On racks Royce built, the rows of dust-covered, neck-down bottles queued like ranks of toppled toy soldiers. Beyond the racks, massive brick arches blurred into shadowy lower levels echoing with the gush of underground water spouting from cracked clay pipes and flushed into the silo-sized cess pit. Collapsed side tunnels held the smell of vague shapes and soggy rot, wooden brewing vats, rusted turning wheels

and moldy gunpowder grinding stones abandoned when the levee buried Front Street. Barry took the list from his pocket, squinted in the feeble light to make sure he had everything he needed—2 by 6s and 4 by 4s, nails and bolts, electric wiring, breaker boxes, camcorder, tripod and cables. He would make this all his, this secret place of scurrying night creatures beneath a world that was always against him, always giving others credit for the things he did.

*****

Terri Wofford Stanley cleared away the evening dishes, spread the canceled checks and bank statement on the kitchen table. Making ends meet was a monthly stretch, even with Paul's insurance and death benefits, it hardly left anything. Her eyes stared at the figures, but her thoughts were elsewhere.

"Oh Paul—" a murmured *cri de coeur.*

No matter the reality, her heart wanted to reject those unspeakable, awful days. Paul's sudden death had shredded her world and brought back the loss of her father, that solemn finality when she saw him in his coffin. At night her pillow was often damp with the soft tears she made sure she kept silent, their soon-to-be-college son, Jeff, hurting as bad as she. Little things kept reminding her. The time of day he usually pulled into the drive, picking up his dirty socks, the smell of him in bed nestled next to her, listening to him breathe, the utter contentment of being held by him, safe and content in his arms, the cares of the world in a far place somewhere else as he kissed her eyelids shut and made tender, while at the same time wild, love to her.

She remembered that time at her father's grave.

"One simply gets on with it," her mother had quietly said.

Stockton Banker Halbert Wofford had doted over his only daughter, but it was her mother, Emilia Wofford, who made sure their daughter was grounded with a solid measure of level-headedness.

Between college classes, Terri worked part-time in her father's bank. It was there, in her junior year, that she met Paul David Stanley. The rugged marine fell head over heels for the raven haired, pug-nosed, California, Napa Valley beauty. It was the first year of the rest of their lives. Terri loved the way Paul pampered her—the times he would surprise her with a single yellow calla lily, her favorite flower, a what-

not maudlin trinket in pink or blue or some expensive bauble to go with her steal of a designer dress she'd found at Seconds N' Things.

He would plant a quick kiss on the tip of her nose, "You never buy yourself anything."

"You spoil me—don't stop," she would smile. "Edward's wife was fussing how I never go shopping with her."

His touch never failing to thrill her, his kisses lingering along her neck, her ear.

He would hold her closer and spoke, "Who wants to talk about other men's wives when I have the best one of all."

She shivered at his touch, at his nibble. One hand tenderly cupping one breast, kissing one rosebud nipple, as she held his head tight, never wanting him to stop the wonderful things he did that made her body sing in a thousand unnamed ways.

"You are so bad," she said as she reveled in him.

Through muffled lips, Paul murmured, "You make me want to be bad."

Lost in his arms, caring only that he was here. Terri adored this gentle man, this hard-bodied marine with a heart as big as Texas, who blazed her universe, made her feel protected and marvelously loved. She never doubted she was the luckiest woman in the world.

Down the hall in his room, Jeff sometimes caught the muffled sounds of his mom and dad. He could tell the mornings after his dad and mom had made love—his mother humming as she made breakfast, his dad not quite so rough-and-ready as he put on his uniform, the way they looked at each other in that moment before Dad pecked her cheek and left for his command. Jeff thought about it all the time. Seeing his mom and dad sure made him think a lot more about what it was like doing those same things with a girl. Jeff knew he had the best parents in the world. He could talk with his dad about anything. Paul was a big part of his son's life—Cub Scouts, Little League, hiking, kayaking.

It was Jeff's job to check under their battered red canoe and flip it over to make sure no moccasins were curled under it.

"Canoe's clear!" Jeff would call out.

They'd head out before sunup or late twilight, clean and gut their catch, then go for a skinny dip while the fish baked. They'd go hunting, crabbing, frog gigging, overnights and weeklong camp outs—

Paul as much the kid as his son. He remembered he and his dad messing around, hiking, poking under fallen logs along the sandy banks for Diamond Backs or Canebrake Rattlers. If the weather turned wet, his dad would show him how to set a camp site so it drained well, not have water get into their sleeping bags and get a roaring fire started before the wood got soaked. They would roast marshmallows or wieners, fresh fish if they got lucky and listen to rain patter their tent. Blue smoke would rise from the outdoor grill in the early, dew-touched sunrises, with the smell of eggs, griddle-hot jonnycakes and skillet ham or fresh bass or catfish.

Sometimes Mom came along, sometimes his friend Byrd, but the best times was when it was just the two of them.

His dad would call out, "Breakfast is ready."

Jeff kept up with the hardware his dad used.

"There's a new website with the latest marine choppers." It mentioned several choppers, reeled off specs, airspeed, weight, range, mid-air fueling. The kid knew his choppers. "You ever ride on those?"

Paul said, "Couple of times."

Or man-to-man, he would hesitantly ask, "Dad, can I ask you something? It's kinda personal." His curiosity outweighed uncertainty.

Night sounds croaking and snapping in the underbrush thickets surrounding them.

"What's bothering you?" Paul asked.

"Some of my soccer teammates never talk with their dads," Jeff awkwardly replied.

"About what?"

"Girls." The word came straight out like his dad said a real man did.

"What about girls?" Paul's face was painted by the orange and yellow flames.

Jeff quietly said, "Some of the team keeps rubbers in their wallets."

Paul answered, "Guys do that." Voice quiet. "I did. Mostly for show-and-tell, brag talk. I never used mine."

"Gosh …" He was unsure if he ought to ask more. "Some of the guys do it after school before their parents get home."

His dad said, "Any idiot can act like a wild dog and knock off a quick piece. And it's not just guys either. I've known some women who were worse gangbangers than any man."

"Wow." Jeff stared into the fire. "You know women like that?"

"Son, there's people like that everywhere."

"We call them birthday players," Jeff said.

"Birthday players?" Paul hadn't heard that one.

"Yeh—" Jeff blushed. "They have a gang over for their birthday, and everyone has sex with everyone else. Those are the kind of parties I stay away from."

"That's smart," Paul said.

"You ever do anything like that?" Jeff inquired.

"No," Paul said. "But, in my case, I suppose it was more luck than good sense. I kept the Big Guy upstairs busy watching out for my backside."

"Dad, is there something wrong with me?" Jeff asked.

Paul remembered those kind of growing-up doubts. "Why would you think that?" he asked.

Jeff tossed a branch into the fire, as he said, "I've never done much with a girl. Other guys seem to know so much."

"They said the same about me in high school. You don't have to prove anything."

"You don't have to prove anything."

"Wow!" Jeff felt good knowing he was like his dad. "They sure razz me. Some say it feels better without a rubber or how I'm missing the best fuck years."

"That's just plain crap. Screwing doesn't make a man out of you." Paul poked the logs, red sparks flurrying into the dark night. "Jerks like that think with their balls, don't care who they're pounding and make babies nobody wants. Those blockheads are sleeping with everyone their partners have slept with, sharing diseases. The lucky ones end up dead, and those who don't die, wish they had." His eyes blacker than night. "You want to get naked with all the girls your buddies share?"

"No way!" Jeff said. "Some of the girls they pass around aren't even good to look at. They sneak into the locker room, get naked with the whole team."

"I have nothing against singles getting together and having fun, but once a guy has a wife ..." Paul didn't finish, his face sad. "Some wives of men in my command mess around when their husbands are off on assignment."

"The husbands know?" Jeff asked.

"Some of them don't care," Paul answered. "In some cases I suppose it's true about ignorance being bliss." He fell silent for what seemed like the longest minute. "Your mother found some of your clothes, and it was obvious you'd been taking care of business." He tossed another log on the fire.

"Oh crap! Mom knows?" Jeff gulped. "How'd you find out?"

"Your mom and I talk about everything," Paul chuckled. "'Specially if it concerns you."

"Dad!" Jeff blushed. "She asked you about what I'd been doing!?" He blushed harder.

"Your mother didn't have to ask, she knows. We've watched you become a young man. She's glad you and I can talk guy-talk. It's nothing to be upset about."

"It's kinda private," Jeff replied.

"Yes, it's private," his dad said. "It should be. What a man and a woman do in bed, what your mother and I do, is private. The same goes for you, but you be more careful where you leave your clothes. Don't get the wrong idea, I'm not saying it's OK to nail every girl you can." Paul thought back to his high school times—wild times that seemed another lifetime ago.

"I don't know anything about what you and Mom do with each other," Jeff said as the fire danced across his face.

"I guess we do get sort of loud sometimes," his dad said.

"Yeh, sometimes you sure do," Jeff stammered. "But I don't listen on purpose."

Paul jabbed the glowing embers. "I was the same when I was your age."

"You ever get a girl in the back seat?" Jeff asked.

"I didn't have a back seat," Paul said, the corners of his mouth in a slight smile. "I had a secondhand pickup."

Curious, Jeff asked, "With a mattress in the back like Byron's?"

"No," Paul chuckled. "I let the tailgate down."

"Gosh!"

"My first time going all the way was the week after I got out of boot camp." He leaned forward, elbows on his knees.

"Really?"

It felt good to Jeff, his dad talking with him like a grownup, and

he didn't feel like such a nerd for being virgin. After all, his dad said that was OK, and his dad was an 'oorah leatherneck.

"The guys say blow jobs feel really good." Jeff stared into the dark.

"Girls were all I thought about," Paul interrupted, "wondering what they were like, all soft and wonderful. I didn't know what I was doing, couldn't think of anything else, couldn't sleep, and couldn't wait to do what I didn't know anything about," Paul smiled. "I didn't have a clue."

"I thought maybe I was weird or something or that I didn't like girls," Jeff revealed. "After practice when we shower, the guys always check one another out, calling each another fags and making fun about each other being too small."

"Guys always call each other names," Paul laughed. "Son, I'm not laughing at you, but those kinds of games are older than the hills. The guys doing the most talking are the ones who know the least. Blind loud mouths leading the blind."

"Even marines?" Jeff said sounding surprised.

"'Specially marines," Paul said. "Me included." The darkness hid the faraway look on his face. "Remind yourself every chance you get how being young is fun, and no matter what a woman tells you, they enjoy the boy inside the man."

"The guys rag on me when I don't go to some of their parties," Jeff revealed. "They have liquor and drugs and lots of sex."

Paul frowned, "Where are the parents while this is going on?"

"They're never around," Jeff said. "I guess most of them don't care."

Jeff was glad he wasn't any different from his dad. He was lucky. His parents actually liked each other instead of fighting all the time or getting divorced. He was proud of his dad—his dad was "The Man." He could tell his mom missed his dad the times his dad was up and gone before daylight. He did, too. Like his dad said though, some nights when he thought about girls, and that was about every night, it sure wasn't easy to get to sleep.

"Dad, what's it like … being with a girl?" Jeff asked.

"Son, there's no way to describe it." Paul had often wondered the same thing. "There's lots of ways of doing the physical bit, but with someone you love, like with your mother and me, it's more than sex—a lot more. That's what horn-dog players miss."

They both fell silent. Jeff felt closer to his dad.

Paul broke the silence, "Sure, sex feels good, but with someone you love, it becomes a lot more, sometimes even funny."

Jeff asked puzzled, "Funny?" He never thought of it being funny.

"Your mother and I often laugh about some of the things we do," Paul said. "When she found your clothes."

Spark of the father in the son's quick, "I don't think it's so funny." He was glad it was dark so his dad couldn't see him turn beet red embarrassed.

Paul's death shredded a raw hole in Jeff's world. At the graveside, Jeff choked back the lump in his throat, stood ramrod straight next to his dad's flag-draped coffin. The men in his command formed an Honor Guard as their flag bearer folded the flag.

"Ma'am," the soldier said as he handed it to Terri, "Major Stanley never asked us to do anything he wouldn't do. He died saving one of our guys."

"Yes—" Terri struggled to keep her words steady, "My husband was like that." Her thin, pale lips and chin quivered.

"He was a fine officer." The young man came to a square-jawed spit and polish attention. "Respected by everyone in his command."

"Is the young man going to be all right?" Terri asked.

"Yes, Ma'am." He snapped a smart salute. "It was an honor to serve with Major Stanley. One of the best."

Terri choked, then swallowed, "We thought so."

Jeff remembered his dad saying, "If you wear the gold, you face what has to be."

Jeff knew protecting the men under his dad's command was part of that. The air was still as the young Marine dropped his salute, about-faced and smartly took his position. Jeff stepped up to the coffin.

His voice steady and hardly above a whisper said, "I sure miss you, Dad."

He unclenched his fist and let the soft earth dribble onto the coffin as it sank into the dark-red earth with his Annapolis Ring Knocker father, Marine Major Paul David Stanley. Later that day, Jeff carried the box of insignias and medals into the den.

"Mom, I want to keep Dad's stuff in my room."

"Of course." Terri said. "There's other things in his footlocker in the garage. The key's on the pegboard by the kitchen phone."

Jeff stopped in the middle of the room, "Mom, why do bad things

happen to people like Dad?"

Terri said, "I don't know." Silence closed in around them.

"But I know your father was doing what he believed in."

Jeff quietly said, "You think Dad knew he was going to die?"

Terri fought a surge of emotion. "Your father wouldn't have thrown his life away." Solemnly, she added, "He loved us too much to do that. Honor and loyalty were two things he truly judged a man by, and I loved him the more for it, but honor means facing choices. There's worse things than dying."

Jeff mumbled, "I sure miss him." Tears gathered around his eyes.

"Me too," Her words choked.

Terri put her arms around him and held him, wanting to take away his pain more than anything, knowing that only time could dull it. In that moment, the room with its memories was their whole world.

After a bit, Terri said, "You haven't eaten all day. You want anything?"

"I'm sort of hungry, but not really," Jeff said. He ran his fingers through curly black hair. "Mom, are we going to move to California?"

"Jeff, why would you think that?" His question completely caught Terri off guard. "This is our home," Jeff said. "Sometimes you look sad." He looked at his mother from big, brown eyes that were carbon copies of Paul's.

"Sometimes I am," she admitted but tried to give him a fresh smile.

"I thought you might want to move back to where you grew up," said Jeff. "I'm glad we're not 'cause I sure didn't want to be in a new school for my senior year."

She didn't tell him the thought had crossed her mind, but Terri knew the memories that are part of a house being "home" were here. Especially for Jeff, perhaps for her as well, but Jeff didn't need to be uprooted. Besides, this was a banking town, perfect for what she had in mind.

A few weeks before school was to start, Terri waited till Jeff and Byrd sat down for dinner to tell them her surprise. It took a few minutes for what she said to sink in. The two boys gawked at each other.

Jeff looked at his mother, and slowly asked, "You mean me'n Byrd can take Dad's car to Six Flags?"

"You'll have to get it checked," Terri cautioned. "It hasn't been driven much in the last few weeks."

Jeff jumped up, sloshing his glass of milk, "All right! Not a problem. Get it serviced, the brakes, transmission, everything." He was so excited. "My own wheels! Byrd can help me drive," he quickly added.

"You two have talked all summer about wanting to go to Six Flags before school starts," she acknowledged. "I was thinking about selling the car, but you could use one once you start college, and you might as well have it now. You'll have to be careful, Atlanta traffic is terrible, and before either of you ask, you're not inviting any girls to go with you."

Byrd said with a big grin, "I got my license."

It was all Jeff and Byrd talked about the rest of the week—how they'd be on their own, the girls they could meet. Both doubled after-school job hours for more spending money. Byrd slept over at Jeff's the night before. They got up early the next morning, wolfed down breakfast, packed and were ready to go.

"Keep that in case of an emergency." Terri handed Jeff extra money. "Did you check the car?"

"Mom—" Jeff said and rolled his eyes, "That's the third time you've asked. The service guy at your filling station looked over everything—adjusted the brakes, flushed the radiator, checked the battery, the lights, replaced the engine belt and put in a new water hose, and last night, after we got back from the food market, I checked to make sure there were no oil leaks. Everything's fine."

Terri asked, "You have the cell phone?" She tried not to show how nervous she truly was.

Jeff looked at his mother and said, "Mom, I have the phone and its car charger."

"My mom's the same," Byrd said as he shut the trunk. "She called twice this morning."

"You be sure and call. Let me know you got there OK," Terri reminded them. "And call me when you start back."

They climbed in and buckled up—eager to be gone. Jeff blushed as Terri kissed him in front of Byrd then waved as they drove off. Terri was not nearly as calm as she pretended.

She watched until the car was out of sight then went back inside. The house seemed so still and quiet, but with no distractions, it was a perfect time to finish what she'd started. She had enjoyed being the stay-at-home mom and having a new baby, then a toddler, preschooler, first grader and up. Switching from housewife to working mother would

take some getting used to.

"Terri Stanley, you're acting like a mother hen," she muttered. "If those two wanted to look for trouble, there's plenty right here at home."

She fired up her laptop and tried not to think about Atlanta with all its temptations two boys could find. Before they made it home, she spent the weekend putting the finishing touches to an updated résumé.

The following Tuesday, Terri dressed, fit to impress, in one of her designer Seconds N' Things finds—a strictly business ensemble with her favorite off-white blouse.

Her phone was ringing by the time she got home from her interviews. She was offered the assistant to the Administrative Secretary position in the prestigious downtown bank's Trust Department and a good salary.

*****

The morning of her first day, Terri found herself more than a little anxious. Her hair refused to cooperate, she smeared her makeup, burned the toast, and Jeff couldn't find his shoes. She'd forgotten how crowded rush hour could be, and to top it off, there was an early morning wreck on the Riverwalk Parkway. As Terri pushed through the double glass doors into the reception area of her new office, her secretary, Irene Rozkovsky, looked up from her desk.

Irene stood, gave her friendly smile and said, "I'm so glad you're here. I keep getting questions I don't have answers for," she added as she followed Terri into the inner office. "I put the layout of our files on your desk."

"Thanks," Terri said. "I'm sure it won't take long to get the feel of things."

As Terri set her purse on her desk, she looked at the stack of memos, letters and folders smothering her in-box.

She could just imagine her e-mail clutter.

Irene brought a steaming cup. "I made a pot earlier. Would you like some hot tea? I remembered from your interview, you said you liked it with lemon."

Terri accepted the cup and took a sip, "Thank you."

As Irene started out, she said, "If there's anything you need, just buzz. Will you be going out for lunch?"

Terri said, "I brought a chicken salad sandwich."

She took a deep breath, nothing like jumping in to get back in the groove. It felt good. Just then, their department head walked in. She was a striking woman with a pleasant confidence without being intimidating, carrying herself as though she was in charge.

"Good morning, Mrs. Stanley," she said. "I see you're getting settled."

"Good morning," Terri replied. "Yes, Irene has everything organized."

"I apologize for not meeting with you longer during your interview, but that was a somewhat hectic day. I'm so glad you decided to join us. We've been short-handed and snowed under with this merger. Now this audit, and here I come with more work for you on your first day. I picked these up from legal." She then laid several thick files on Terri's desk. "We've managed McGiffern investments for a number of years, and with Theosia McGiffern's death, we want to make sure all trust account portfolios are in order. I'd like for you to look through them before we meet with the successor trustee. The accounts are all there—somewhat extensive, stocks, bonds, mutual funds, real estate holdings including Ardochy Manor at Silver Bluff. If there are any loose ends, I'd prefer we catch them."

"More families should use *in vivo* trusts," said Terri. "They can be excellent for estate planning."

The woman's expression quickened, relieved she didn't have to train another novice. "The trustee's address and unlisted phone are also there."

Irene's eyes shimmered. Unable to contain herself, she remarked, "I met that one the time he came in with Theosia. He's quite rich."

Terri thought it a crass remark. The woman was obviously enamored with money. To Terri, it was somewhat tawdry as well as in poor taste.

"I'll get right on these," Terri said.

Later that evening, as Jeff cleared the kitchen table and washed the dinner dishes, she took the files into her dining room and spread them on the table.

Jeff came into the study and smiled. "Looks like I'm not the only one with homework."

Terri took a sip of tea. "Like your father said, the job's not done till

the paperwork's finished."

Jeff gave his mom a goodnight peck on the cheek before heading to his room, his headphones and his books.

"Sleep tight." Terri called after him. "See you in the morning."

Terri turned back to the pile of timeworn papers and spotted a few minor things. Unless this Ingramme trustee wanted to make changes, she couldn't see any reason for this to involve more than a short conference. She finished the folder containing the McGiffern overseas holdings, leaned back and finished the last of her tea.

*Enough for one night,* she thought and pushed back from the table. *Let the legal eagles cross the "T"'s' and dot the "I"'s.*

She could tell she was going to like this job. That evening, she brought the accumulated work home for a one-time catch-up was OK, but Terri decided she would never become a workaholic briefcase junkie. The next morning, she wheeled her sports convertible onto the freeway earlier, missed the traffic and made it to her office 30 minutes earlier. Irene was already at her desk.

"Good morning, Irene," she said.

Irene gave her a cheery, "Morning, Mrs. Stanley. You certainly sound chipper this morning." She already liked working with Terri Stanley.

"It is a beautiful day," Terri said. "I almost let the time get away from me while having breakfast, watching two hummingbirds squabble over the Franklin Magnolia." Terri stopped at the door to her office and said, "Irene, check with Legal this morning. See if we have anything pending with the McGiffern trust. If not, set up an appointment with the trustee. His number's in there."

Irene said, "I'll get on that right now."

Her mascaraed eyes were wide, she smoothed her polka dot yellow blouse. Just thinking about talking with Craige Ingramme gave her the flutters, even if it was business.

\*\*\*\*\*

Craige leaned down, doused his hands in the river and washed off the mud—didn't want to get any grit in the lines when he bled the air out. Once he had the siphoned flow going good, Craige switched on the new pump he'd mounted under the dock and let it run. The hose

gurgled, and a gush of water spouted between the rows of new tomato plants. He'd had his fair share of dumb luck while installing the pump.

He named him "The Duke," a smoky, thick-bodied handsome cottonmouth who made his home under where the dock wedged into the graveled bank of the yard. Nothing could get at him except straight on, and head-on is no way to prod a moccasin. Craige was just glad the king snake in the barn hadn't found Duke. The "King" would win. He didn't want to lose either, both are good for keeping down rats and mice. Moccasins are shy. They don't strike unless some idiot pokes at them. He'd worked the whole morning with Duke curled up not four feet from his rear. Never bothered Craige if one dropped off a branch into the skiff, but he didn't like being surprised by one. He was gathering his tools when Lucky got wind of him—sniffing, growling, pawing, raising a general ruckus. He's been bitten several times and has a thorough dislike of any snake. Duke coiled and puffed up, flicking his tongue, all set for business. All he wanted was to get away or be left alone. Still, it was a bit disconcerting when he saw how his backside made a perfect target.

"Sure forgot about you, big boy," Craige muttered.

He headed inside to check the bass he'd set baking. He was digging in the fridge for the bones Mae Ruth brought for Lucky when the phone rang.

"Ingramme," Craige answered.

"Good morning, Mr. Ingramme." Irene's eyes were coquettish. "This is Irene Rozkovsky in the Trust Department ... Mrs. Stanley's secretary. We've spoken before."

Irene was nervously twiddling with her scarf as though a famous heartthrob was standing in front of her in the flesh.

Craige said, "Yes, the McGiffern matter."

"Mrs. Stanley wanted me to set up an appointment with you," Irene said.

Craige's first impulse was to give her a white lie excuse. He didn't want to shoot the rest of the day. Then, he had second thoughts. So much for getting both skiffs moved up to his big lake for their annual charity outdoor cookout. On the way through the den, Craige grabbed a grannie apple and ripped a chunk out of it. Munching it in her ear was rude. Its tart sweetness tasted good, like an almost ripe persimmon. His patience with pencil pushers was never strong, and he had

35

gotten out of bed with an attitude. Theosia would've understood, but he could hear her "tsk-tsking" him for taking it out on some secretary who was probably doing the best she could. Craige thought to himself, *Get a grip.*

Craige said, "Is it possible to mail the papers?"

"Perhaps you should speak with Mrs. Stanley," Irene said. "One moment, please."

Terri picked up her extension and answered, "Good morning, Mr. Ingramme."

I'd half expected to be stuck on hold, this seductive voice flip-flopped everything.

"Uh—good morning," Craige felt semiliterate as he stammered. "The originals and my signatures are on file." It wasn't his dumbest comeback but close.

Terri said, "We prefer originals be signed in the presence of a notary and two witnesses."

Terri could tell that this one obviously knew nothing about the legal "ins and outs" of a trust. Terri recalled her father's premise: "side-tracking trouble is easier than cleaning it up." She continued, "It would be best if you came to the bank."

Craige could've listened to her recite the alphabet, but with his luck lately, she was probably double ugly. Craige squeezed down on what Gray called his short fuse. Maybe it was hormones, but bad habits can trip a body up, and he'd collected a bunch of them. It wasn't her, she just happened to be there.

"Is there any way they can be delivered to me?" Craige asked.

His demeanor made Terri think of ill-mannered officer wives. Trying to be reasonable with those types seldom worked. She refused to let him ruffle her. Not about to let him call the shots, she cleared her throat, "Mister Ingramme, I'm sure both of us wish to resolve this matter."

Knowing that would be all-around simpler, Craige said, "I'll be glad to come in."

Terri said, "Tomorrow at nine will be fine. Thank you." And hung up.

After she hung up Craige grumbled, "You know it's not her voice."

He wondered what else he might discover about her. He punched in Mabel's number. It was one of those times when he was glad he had

Mabel's brain to pick.

Mabel never let the phone ring twice, "Metro Law Enforcement. I.S.T. Lieutenant MacGerald's office."

"Morning, Mabel."

"Good morning, you want to talk with the boss?"

"No," Craige answered, "I need you to find out about someone for me."

"That's a turnaround. You're usually the one doing the digging." Mabel didn't hesitate, "You have a name for me?"

"Terri Stanley." The name made him almost want to keep the bank appointment.

"I wondered how long it'd take you to zero in on her." She spoke in an come-hither tone. "She recently joined the bank's trust department."

"I just got off the phone with her."

"You certainly didn't meet her at any happy hour social. She's not the type."

"I've never met her, but I have a meeting with her tomorrow, and I acted like a complete idiot."

Mabel gave out a throaty laugh and said, "I've seen both you and Gray pull that a couple of times, but you do it really well. Considering your weakness for a well-turned ankle and Terri Stanley's penchant for good manners, I'd say you pretty much screwed that up already."

"It's business," Craige retorted.

"Sure it is," She said with her put-on motherly tone. "If it's all business, you wouldn't be on the phone with me. Besides, where women are concerned, with you, it's never just business."

"OK, you know me way too well," Craige said.

"Terri Stanley comes from a California banking family. She's nice looking, good taste, stays to herself, recently widowed with a teenage son. Her husband was a Major Stanley, killed in a some sort of training accident."

"How do you women find out warts and all about everything?"

Sometimes Craige thought Mabel knew everything, and he'd never bet against her.

Mabel chuckled, "We have our ways. Sort of like you have yours, but women do it more easily. We tell one another everything, but we're better at it. And Craige Ingramme—" In her serious voice, she said, "Terri Stanley is very nice, so you be nice, too."

"I'm always the gentleman."

"Sure you are. That's what I'm afraid of."

Craige's mock surprise never came off with Mabel, and they both knew it.

*****

It was straight up nine when Craige pushed through the doors of the trust department. He figured after the way he'd behaved, he'd get the brush-off from Ms. Rozkovsky but knew he was wrong the minute she looked up at him. She didn't stare, she ogled and promptly dribbled her coffee. Craige figured if he said anything too pleasant, she'd spill the whole cup, but he decided to risk it.

"Good morning," Craige said. "I have an appointment with Mrs. Stanley."

The blistering instant he spoke, Irene went deaf and numb, swallowed into those gorgeous, green, scintillating eyes, wishing this stack of a man would do everything to her she'd ever wanted a man to do. She scrutinized every scrumptious imagined morsel she could just taste under his casual Madras cotton shirt.

Having not heard one word he had said, she stuttered, "Can I help you?"

In her mind, she was already peeling away the faded cords pulled across his thighs, that marvelous face with its strong jaw and hint of heavy beard. She wanted to run her fingers through those curly brown locks, shaded tawny gold like a male lion's mane. Every unmentionable she'd ever had swirled in her dizzy head and gave her tingly goose bumps. She didn't care what he said as long as he kept looking at her.

Craige repeated, "I have an appointment with Mrs. Stanley."

Irene blinked and blinked again as though she had no idea who he was. She then stammered, "What's your name?" Courtesy such as "please have a seat" shot to hell.

"Craige Ingramme," Craige answered.

"One moment, I'll tell her you're here," she gasped.

Irene's heart was in a pitty-pat dither. Her bra squeezed so tight, it was hard to breathe. She stumbled around her desk and hurried into Terri's office and somehow managed to shut the door somewhat quietly.

In a butterfly falsetto and a hand at her throat, she said, "He's here!"

Terri thought Irene meant Accountant Ben Harrell or the bank examiners that had everyone so jittery.

Terri asked, "Who?"

"Craige Ingramme," Irene blurted and rolled her eyes. "He's gorgeous!"

The scatterbrained silliness of a grown woman acting like some goggle-eyed schoolgirl struck Terri as hilarious. She'd seen that sort of Junior League titter before, and her father's "don't mess on your own doorstep" came to mind except he'd put it a bit stronger. She suppressed the urge to laugh. It was not the time for humor. Irene wasn't infatuated, she was in heat.

Terri smiled and reached for the McGiffern files. "Ask him to come in."

"He is to die for," Irene said with an excited gush. "And he has the cutest butt."

"For goodness' sake, Irene. Don't keep the man waiting." Terri stood, straightened her chic pale linen suit and said, "Show him in."

Irene fluffed her hair, pasted on her idea of an alluring smile and opened Terri's office door.

"Mister Ingramme," she said, "please come this way."

As Craige came through the door, on the prowl Rozkovsky stayed rooted in the door like some addled, lonesome crane. She wasn't about to move.

Craige said, "Excuse me." He would have had to be dead not to smell her heat, rubbing against him was precisely what she wanted. He wasn't one to object to a female in heat, but when Terri Stanley came around her desk the rest of the room went empty. He forgot all about secretary "what's her name" who reluctantly, ever so slowly, closed the door.

"Thank you for coming," Terri said and extended her hand. "I do apologize for the confusion. It's been somewhat hectic around here."

It was Craige's turn to try and not rubberneck. She was stunning, and the touch of her hand scalded like steam and ice water at the same time. His mouth became cottony dry, and he forced a smile which in reality wasn't that forced. Mabel had been right—Terri Stanley was a looker, but he hadn't been ready for just how right Mabel was.

Craige somehow managed to stammer, "Theosia would appreciate your being so particular."

Something about him caught Terri off guard. Irene was right. Who could miss the devil in those ruinous eyes that somehow reached deep into her as though he could almost read her thoughts. His incredible smile would disarm any woman. It was an uncertainty Terri wasn't prepared for.

"Everyone has bad days." Her voice became softer. She was unsettled by her attraction to this man.

The last time Craige had been this tongue-tied was in the fifth grade when he stole that first kiss from Peggy Cowan under the bleachers.

"May I start over?" Craige asked.

"That isn't necessary." Terri tried to shake away feelings she thought she would never have again.

"I would feel better if you'd accept." Craige couldn't take his eyes off her.

"Of course." Terri was glad Irene wasn't in the room.

There was no one thing about Terri that stood out—well, aside from a knockout figure from earlobe to ankles. He'd always been an ankle man, and hers were perfect. The elegant loose blouse and the fit of her tailored skirt were absolute wonders to behold. Any man could drown in her fluid chestnut eyes, the loose wave of soft black hair barely brushed with a hit and miss of grey, her full lips and slender neck, her peach radiant skin. Her smile pitched his stomach in a free fall. Terri Stanley would wake a dead man. Craige tried not to be so bloody overt, as though he were appraising a young filly at some county fair. He managed to partly recover, like a giddy-headed, mush-mouthed schoolboy begging for a sign that she knew he existed.

Craige continued, "Please, call me Craige."

"I'm Terri," she smiled. "I'm sure you would like to examine the estate records. I reserved our conference room for you. Take as long as you wish, and if you have any questions, please let me know."

Wishing he were the folders she gathered in her arms, his nonplussed thoughts tried to make up questions just to keep her here with him. That's when it hit him—*God, Ingramme, you have been out on the ranch too long.* Craige hem and hawed, finally saying, "This will be fine. Thank you." And he followed her into the conference room.

He would've followed her anywhere.

She asked, "Would you care for something to drink? Coffee? Per-

haps a soft drink?"

"Irish breakfast tea, if you have it."

"I'm sure we can find that." She smiled right at him.

As Craige watched her walk out of the room, his mind was far from the moldy bank records. What he thought had nothing to do with banks. He sat down, fiddled with pages without reading, got up, ambled to the tall windows with their ceiling to floor drapes and stared beyond the river toward Moccasin Hollow. He thought how Theosia would chuckle that warm, soft, quiet chuckle if she could see him—or maybe she wouldn't. Theosia had known him too well.

A knock on the door and Rozkovsky-in-Lust came in with a Styrofoam cup of tea, the paper tag of the tea bag stuck to the outside.

"I hope I'm not interrupting," she said.

As relentless as a jet jockey widow on the prowl, it was obvious she was hoping just the opposite. Give her an inch, she'd take it all and often.

Craige took the cup of steaming tea. "Thank you."

At least it was hot. Craige should've known better than to ask for hot tea. Plastic ruins the taste of good tea. He supposed Grannie taught him what lots of folks call being a snob, but it's real simple—do things right or don't do them. Propriety seems to have fallen out of fashion in their light-speed Internet world. It's no wonder people go crazy.

She lingered. "Can I get you anything else?"

"This is fine, thank you. I've marked several pages I need to look into. Could you fax them to this number?"

Craige wanted to talk with Terri Stanley again before he left, but her office door was closed. Irene wasn't the only one pawing the ground.

# Chapter 3

Terri finished the dinner pots and pans and cleaned the stove. Jeff dried and put away the dishes, as the kettle began to boil a steady whistle.

"Got to hit the books. Math exam day after tomorrow. Night, Mom—" He kissed his mom and headed to his room. Terri called after him, "Sleep tight." And poured steaming water into the teapot.

As it steeped, she pulled a chair out from the breakfast table. Her day at the office had flown by, five o'clock rolled around before she knew it. Terri couldn't shake her distaste for Craige Ingramme being so short with Irene, yet her resolve to have as little to do with him as possible wasn't working quite as she expected. He refused to leave her thoughts, that dazzling moment she first set eyes on him. Paul was there as well. She tipped the warm tea cozy and filled her teacup. The aroma of unsweetened tea prickled her nose as she sipped. Her mother's aristocratic Castilian features flashed across the daughter's face.

"Terri, you're being silly," she muttered.

She sat her cup on the saucer. Her brief office encounter with Craige Ingramme piqued a vexation, which Terri couldn't quite put her finger on. Besides, Paul and the self-possessed imperturbable Mr. Ingramme were not the least alike.

"Mother?" Jeff's voice broke her thoughts.

"I'm in the kitchen," she called out.

As he came in, he said, "I called you three times."

Terri smiled, "I must have been daydreaming."

"About Dad?" Jeff asked.

"I suppose so, but the office, too. My job is taking some getting used to," she smiled. "We had a busy day."

Jeff said, "I sure miss him."

Terri looked at this son who was growing up so fast and more like his father every day.

"Mom, can I ask you something?" Jeff said.

"Of course. Sit down." She put her cup down. "Something bothering you?"

"Sometimes you seem so far away, even sad," he said with youth's clear-sightedness. "You ought to get out more, meet new people. Have some fun. You deserve that."

Terri felt herself blush. "Whatever in the world gave you that idea?"

*****

Running from something wasn't like Craige, but he needed to get away, think some things over. He headed up to the AmPhib Base at Little Creek for a throw away weekend of parasailing and good times with a few East Coast SEAL buds from their unit, who'd stayed in for the career-haul. He was back home the following Tuesday, killed more time doing things he'd put off—piddled at fishing, finished putting in the new posts. It was too hot and sticky to fire up the chain saw and thin scrub brush from the section of pulpwood pines, but he did it anyway. Craige came in thirsty and sweaty, and the full slug of bourbon and branch water on the rocks tasted better than good. He should've stuck to hot tea.

Craige took a long swallow as he scratched Lucky's ear, "That feel good?"

He wouldn't mind having someone scratch his ear. It had been a long dry spell since Reba, and the getaway trip to Little Creek hadn't gotten Reba or any of the others out of his mind. He knew exactly who he wanted to do the scratching.

Craige refilled his bourbon and water, strolled barefoot out to the dock and watched a fading summer Grand Canyon sunset merge with far-off smutty thunderheads. The sun squashed fatter, a sinking lemon-gold orb skipping behind broomtail clouds, turning the flat river sur-

face into a plain of placid undulating mercury. Green underbrush and trees along the river turning that brilliant yellow-orange that seems to happen in autumn. It matched his feelings. He emptied the glass, tossed the cubes into the water and plodded back to the house as early night breezes picked up. He noticed the fax light blinking as he mixed another drink. He guzzled a swallow, remembering other faces, different countries, hump-hump-and-run, any port-in-a-storm, one-night stands. Fixation on Terri Stanley took root marrow deep. The last thing he remembered was stretching out across the sofa.

Her phone call came early. Two documents needed retyping. At least he'd get another chance to see her, and he'd make sure that was the end of it.

*****

The minute high school rugby jock, chip-on-his-shoulder Eric Stompfer walked through the door of the U.S. Marine recruiting office, the recruiter saw bonus money rolling into his pocket.

He said, "Get your college education paid for and get to see the world." He promised him the moon, signed him up and shipped him off to boot camp, Marine Corps Recruit Depot (MCRD) Parris Island. Eric Stompfer wasn't short on brains, but he seldom used them for the right reasons. He picked up the Corps' "getting by" habits jiffy quick. After boot camp, he made a convenient pastime of comforting lonely sea duty widows who needed urgent R&R loving while their marine pilot husbands were off protecting God and country. Nothing better than this latest sweet, young midmorning delight as she reverently rolled a fresh rubber over his primed marine staff.

He looked into her eyes and said, "Careful, that thing's locked and loaded."

He spent the rest of the morning grinding her into dreamland with his "Eveready." Her husband's ribboned dress uniform hanging over the closet door, the medals glinting bright and shiny in the sex smell half-light of the bedroom. Eric took pride in a job done thoroughly. She was smiling when he sneaked out early the next day.

Eric didn't like being in the ooh-rah, gung-ho mah'rines, but at least he knew what to expect. It was better than working the streets for spending money like he did during that summer after high school,

but he sure liked marine benefits. He served his time, got his discharge, and his older brother, Landrom, waited for him when Eric stepped off the bus.

"There's plenty room at my beach house," Landrom had offered. "No point spending money for an extra place."

Landrom always looked out for his kid brother and cocky go-with-the-flow, 22-year-old Eric liked being taken care of. Landrom's latest grocery market check out sweetie watched Eric in the outdoor shower as Eric stripped out of his trunks, rinsed the saltwater and dune sand off and wrapped the towel around his waist.

As Eric came through the kitchen, she came up from behind, "Nice," she commented as she squeezed his ass.

When Landrom came in from work, Eric grinned up from their tangled arms and legs and said, "We've been waiting for you." And didn't miss a pump.

As he unbuttoned his grimy shirt, Landrom replied, "I'm gonna jump in the shower."

In a few minutes the shower cut off, and Landrom scooted in with them for a tandem threesome. It made a smooth arrangement until she tried pitting brother against brother and ended up with her conniving ass out the door. It wasn't long before a different face became the salami in the Stompfer brothers tried and proven sandwich.

Eric soon picked up where he and high-school fuck partner Beth Cobbin left off, cruising familiar stomping grounds for quickie diversions—the med school student center, juke joints and interstate clubs for fat cats with nose candy party favors. Beth hadn't been lonely while Eric was off playing marine, and Eric learned she'd made contacts he could put to good use.

One night at the Tip Top, she remarked, "Landrom's not bad in bed."

Eric laughed and said, "Want me to ask him to join us?

Landrom knows how to give a woman what she wants, too." Later that spring during the big golf week, Beth and Eric worked their rent-me matters with a rent-for-private-party shuffle.

Eric pulled up one day in a fancy new set of wheels, and Landrom asked, "That Beth's new Jag?"

"Daddy gave it to her," Eric said. "Might as well be me helping her spend Daddy's money."

Without taking his eyes off the television, Landrom asked, "Word is Beth got engaged. Hubbie-to-be Gordon Pilgrim know about us?"

"Intern Gordie does what Beth tells him to do," Eric said as he came out of his bedroom. "She asked me to go on the honeymoon with them."

Landrom guffawed, "Threesome honeymoon ought to be a hoot."

"Be a good chance to work me up some lonely rich contacts—I got what they like," Eric said, hiked his crotch at Landrom and walked out.

While Beth was on her honeymoon, used car mogul Daddy Cobbin had everything set to go. He'd done the manager of the prestigious sedate George Harrington Apartments a "good deal" trade in return for jumping the waiting list for the first available penthouse suite. It sat on the "Hill," first settled above the Yellow Fever ridden trading post waterfront.

Beth didn't know plywood from Sheetrock, but when she saw her favorite colors she said, "Ooo, Daddy, it's nice."

Corpulent Daddy bragged as he jammed the unlit Cuban cigar between stained teeth, "That red granite come all the way from Egypt, and the green stuff is cipolino ... something like that. Comes from an island by the name of Euboea. One day we'll get us a yacht and visit that place."

Heart of Pine board floors, wood paneled walls and massive sliding doors joined spacious dining rooms to Victorian parlors. Daddy's old-is-new-again interior decorator made sure the layout made the Sunday edition social section. The Harrington had aged gracefully, one of the few structures to escape the fire of '26.

Daddy pursed his lips, strolled out onto the terrace, fired up his cigar with his gold plated lighter, sucked till the end glowed cherry red, blew a mouthful of blue smoke in the still air and peered down at the city.

"Blackball my daughter from a sorority. All you hypocrit' do-gooders tryin' to close down my pinch gut businesses," he sneered and blew a blue, smokey puff. "Who's on top lookin' down on you pissants now?"

*****

46

Eric stepped inside the mildewed trailer and sniffed the stale smell of old tobacco smoke blasting out of the rattling, single window unit. The body with its mussed, brown hair sprawled across a sheetless mattress. One of Eric's "associates" had warned him about Todd, but Eric needed bodies. A few more here and there, and he'd have himself a nice stable. He looked at Todd's skewed boxers and wondered if this package looked any more promising once it was cleaned up.

\*\*\*\*\*

"Advertise it tonight!" Eric said to himself as he strutted in front of the mirror suited up in his idea of looking cool—black baseball cap swung backwards, black shades, sun-yellow tank top cut to the waist to show belly skin, no shorts, the tight pants leaving nothing to the imagination. A honk came from the curb, and Eric was out the door.

Todd scooted out of the driver's seat. "Hot set of wheels."

Eric gave a snort, "Keep them happy, they'll give you anything."

Beth's directions were good. Didn't take long to find the place. Shrubs and trees studded the yard jammed with cars, SUVs and pickups parked along the highway.

Todd swaggered straight to the kegs, topped off a full cup, slugged it down and refilled. He then cruised the cruisers splashing around the pool, sniffed and wiped his nose. His nooner fix was gone, but it didn't take him long to score freebie snorts along with some nice skin and grind in the crowded hot tub. He noticed a fidgety man near him but paid no attention to him. That is until the man said, "Want to make some good money at a real party?"

The cash-in-his-pocket offer hooked Todd, and as soon as he saw the Mercedes with its expensive leather interior, he decided jiffy quick—taking this one back to Eric's dump of a trailer might scuttle the deal.

As they pulled onto the highway, Todd said, "I don't have a place."

The Mercedes picked up speed and Barry smiled, "I do."

Todd felt good. He finally got a break, wouldn't have to hit the streets tonight and, best of all, wouldn't have to split his take with some sleazy night manager. Play this right, he might have him as a regular, a bed of his own and new set of threads. He thought it kind of strange when the Mercedes wheeled into the downtown bank's parking ramp, climbed four decks and pulled into a reserve slot.

"Thought you said we were going to your place?" Todd asked.

"I park here while my new garage is being resurfaced."

Todd followed Barry across the empty parking deck. He was going to treat this one right.

"I'll have me a big car one day," Todd said.

Barry used his elevator key, punched "EL" for the private executive lobby, no guards and no witnesses. Once outside, he gave an anxious glance up and down the deserted street, hurried across toward the building that glowed saffron yellow in the flickering of the street's Victorian gaslights. He unlocked the door, stepped inside, made sure the door locked behind them and then punched the light switch.

"Want to make a hundred bucks?" Barry asked.

"Yeah!" Todd said excitedly.

This was a big payoff. He'd thought of charging fifty. A hundred was more than he had in a long time.

"Down those stairs," Barry pointed.

Todd started down ahead of Barry. This guy sure had a weird place, but he'd partied in worse. He then spotted the rows of neck-down dusty web-covered bottles of wine.

"Wow, that's a lot of wine," Todd said. "What is this place?" He heard the faint splash of water.

"My wine cellar. Get the shirt off." Barry said as he thought how dumb this one was.

As Todd slipped out of his shirt, he asked, "What do you do with all this wine?" The damp, cool air felt good on his skin.

"You drink wine?" Barry asked, giving Todd a cobra stare.

"Yeh, I like wine," he answered, the crumpled shirt in his hand. The camera was now visible.

Todd knew this was no different. One more rich man's party place. At least it was better than doing videos in seedy motels and strip joints. For a hundred bucks he would play whatever "Sugar Daddy" liked.

"What you want me to do now, Sir?" Todd asked.

Barry liked being called "sir."

"Get your pants off," he ordered.

"Yes sir," he said as he kicked off his shoes, then his jeans. Todd was glad he'd dressed bareback free-hanging with no shorts, this way he could get right down to it.

The veins in Barry's forehead throbbed. He felt better than he had

the whole week, and now he could be sure everything worked.

"Get up on the table," he ordered.

"Yes sir." Todd submitted.

Todd had partied with freaks and their toys. It was the only time most of them got to play at being boss.

"Have some more wine." Barry topped one goblet full.

"Thank you, sir." Todd took the glass.

"Pour it on your chest," Barry commanded.

Todd said, "Sir?" He wasn't sure he'd heard right. Didn't want to piss this one off and lose a hundred bucks. For a chubby man, Barry moved quick, both hands at Todd's throat, he choked him till Todd's bloodshot eyes bulged and his tongue gagged.

Through clenched jaws Barry said, "I'll show you whose boss." then loosened his grip.

Todd coughed before he finally could say, "What else, sir?"

He quickly sloshed the blood-purple liquid down his chest and watched Barry refill the goblet.

"Drink all of it!" He shoved Todd toward the bench. "And lay down!" Barry said as he switched on the overhead lights.

Todd gulped it all, crawled onto the table and stretched out as Barry focused the blood-red spotlights on Todd. Todd knew this one liked making kinky videos so he could play them down here at his private parties.

Barry said, "Put these on." He handed Todd the clanking medieval-looking manacles. "And make sure they're tight."

Todd said, "Yes sir." He snapped the metal cuff around one wrist.

Barry became impatient. This was taking too long.

He groused, "I'll do that."

He yanked both wrists behind Todd's back and snapped the second cuff.

"Sir—" Todd grunted as the metal pinched harder. "That hurts, Sir." He winced at the pain and decided he was charging more next time.

Barry knotted a fist in Todd's hair. "I'll hurt you more if you don't keep quiet." He then jammed Todd's head against the board. "You got that!"

"Yes, sir."

As Barry locked down the strap across Todd's chest, he caught the

sour odor of Todd's breath. Whore boys were filthy. He ratcheted the table, the spotlights were centered. The faint whir of the camera was barely audible. Barry switched on the motor drive and stepped back. He waited until the first bayonet of pain hit Todd.

Todd's mouth flew open and he shrieked, "Oh, God …" in a choppy, raspy gasp.

Barry's eyes grew wide forming black pits. The skin of his face and neck became moist as he watched Todd strain away from the grinding pain. His mouth gaped open, frothing in a drawn incoherent wail. Bubbly spittle foamed the nostrils, lungs rasped as the auger gristled through his chest.

Barry was spellbound by the stringy flecks of steak-red muscle and bone dragging along the emerging spike. He curled his nose at the smell of bowels and bladder and waited for the body to quit jerking. He then reversed the motor drive, unbuckled the strap and cuffs, turned on the hose and washed the bench with its gawk-eyed corpse. He unsheathed the heavy blade and diligently sliced the joints of the wrists, shoulders, knees and ankles. He reached for the hatchet and guillo-tined the neck in one clean chop. The raw neck muscles still squirmed as he set the severed head on a clean white cloth. Next, he slit open the belly and chest. The steamy guts and liver reminded him of gutted deer kills.

Pressure washed the jumbled body parts into the cesspit and hauled down on the handle. The holding tank emptied with a cascade roar into the black, brick-lined pit. The swirling, greasy slime of chunks and scurrying roaches sucked in a whirlpool down the funnel of the storm sewer. Scavengers would feed well tonight.

As the tank refilled, Barry scrubbed his hands and arms and used a clean towel to dry. He remembered his wife's Fourth of July barbecue party, wondering if human flesh really did taste sweeter.

Barry sneered, "With all this fresh meat I ought to make a real special BBQ."

As he cleaned his nails in a silence, broken only by the trickle of water, the arches of bare, brick walls seemed to close around him. Barry knew exactly what he wanted.

*****

The curator opened the catalog. "Not many people request early Flemish masters. I believe you'll find what you're looking for here, but with measurements that large, it will have to be special ordered."

Barry placed his order. Putting up the scaffolding, he dropped a plumb line to make sure the marine plywood backing would be straight and rewired for the track lights. When it arrived, he made sure to hang it just so. He smoothed the last panel to place, removed the scaffolding and switched on the lights. In the soft illumination, Bruehgel's 1562 somber *Triumph of Death* with its skeletal hordes and rapier scythes seemed alive—a grand masterpiece created just for him.

*****

Terri couldn't put her finger on why she felt the need to go through the files again but she did.

She buzzed Irene, "Reschedule my morning, make my apologies and hold my phone calls."

She closed herself in her office and started page by tedious page through dog-eared codicils, money market funds, outdated balance sheets, timeworn stock certificates, real estate, property deeds and a glut of lesser holdings. Most of the documents were years out of date, and she assumed the files would have been computerized or at least updated. She was puzzled why hardly any records had been entered. Most were scanned copies of originals, the latest dated four years ago. Her fingertips grazed an unsealed envelope, no stamp or address. Tucked inside a quarterly report were handwritten notes, no names and no dates except for one. It was a brief notation of a six-figure payout, and at the bottom, the scrawled initials "LRS" with the scribbled note "deadline on the 30th" below that.

She muttered, "Why would anyone ..." Her words were stopped by a tiny, inner voice. She buzzed Irene.

"Yes, Mrs. Stanley?" Irene answered.

"Irene, does our department prepare quarterly reports?"

"Not unless there's a specific reason. Each section prepares a department report at the end of the fiscal year. Those are collated in the president's office before the annual stockholder's meeting. Individual department summaries are prepared by specific accounts and only at closings or liquidations."

Terri said, "Come take a look at this."

Irene looked at the paper and said, "Those are Mr. Sedgewicke's initials, and it looks like his handwriting. The last time Theosia McGiffern came in, I know she met with Mr. Sedgewicke, but that was several years before her death. Perhaps he made a note about their meeting."

"This was paper clipped to our last quarterly report," Terri said.

"It couldn't have been written very long ago," said Irene. "Maybe he forgot about it. About six weeks ago, I was getting our files ready for the merger audit and the examiners, and I couldn't find the McGiffern folders. I asked Mr. Marshall's secretary about them. She said Mr. Sedgewicke had them. I told her we needed them, but I don't recall receiving them. By the way, don't forget your noon luncheon with the downtown Rotary."

"Thanks, Irene," Terri said.

Irene closed her door. Almost an hour passed when Irene knocked and stuck her head in.

"It's 11:30, I'm headed to lunch. Anything you need before I leave?"

"Nothing I can think of." Terri added, "When are the auditors due to start with us?"

"The first part of next week."

"Who has access to our accounts other than bank officers?"

"Anyone authorized by legal."

"What about computer access?"

"They'd need account passwords and work station access."

"Maybe it's sloppy record keeping." Terri stared at the spread of papers.

She locked the files in her desk and reached for her purse. She called out to Irene, "If anyone asks about the McGiffern files, tell them I have them. That'll keep you from ending up in the middle. Maybe it's time we did our own audit."

Irene gave her a bewildered look as Terri headed into the powder room, slipped on her light jacket, refreshed her lipstick and made sure her hair was OK. She dug in her purse for her car keys, hurried up the stairs to the roof parking deck and into the bright sunshine.

During the Rotary luncheon, Terri tried not to let her preoccupation show when she was introduced as a guest. She wanted to believe it was nothing more than careless posting. The likelihood of it being

calculated seemed too far-fetched, yet doing nothing could be worse. Terri didn't quite know when the idea first crept into her thoughts. The applause startled her, she hadn't heard a word the woman said.

Back in her office, Terri mulled whether or not to follow her intuition. The next morning, she was in her office before anyone else. Before her nervousness churned out an excuse not to do what intuition said to do, she took a deep breath and dialed.

Craige answered, "Ingramme."

"This is Terri Stanley." Her words sounded rushed. "I apologize for calling so early, but would it be much of an imposition if I changed our appointment? There are some details I'd like to look into."

"Not a problem." The sound of her voice brightened him right up. "Something wrong?" Craige asked, not telling her he wouldn't mind making a trip for her. "Any way I can help?"

Terri wondered if she were leaping from frying pan to fire.

She said, "I dislike being so vague, but I may need some help. Can I get back to you?" She felt more nervous this time.

"Of course," Craige said.

She could've asked Craige for anything, and he would've agreed. It wasn't so much what she said as the way she put it. Her conversation was too short and anxiously quick. He locked down on his paranoia, but he didn't lock it down tight. Unless he'd badly misjudged her, this phone call was totally unlike the confident Terri Stanley he'd met, and it left him with the feeling that something wasn't right. He wasn't sure if he was glad the meeting was canceled or glad he would see her again. It finally hit him that he wasn't glad at all. He thought of Gray and how often he'd laughed at some of Craige's predicaments where women were concerned, that his hormones often overloaded his brains.

Later in the night, Lucky brought the skull back to his pallet. He gnawed on the sun-bleached pieces, then curled up and went to sleep. It was one time Craige should have paid more attention to both her and the dog.

# Chapter 4

**B**arry picked the trendy, live entertainment lounge.

With the convention in town, he figured the bar at the Riverside Suites would make better pickings. But it was a slow night. The Snake Lady's boa constrictor was tired, and the drinks were watered. Only a few stools were occupied by retread barflies with tired eyes and hairspray wigs. Barry wasn't interested in tight, leather, short-shorts that off-season prostitutes trucked from convention to convention, desperate enough to skip the motels for sleazy rent-a-trailer quickies.

The strangling halter tops didn't hide turkey skin nor the overdone makeup. Most of them useless for Barry's nightscape foraging. He tossed a ten on the table for the drink and tip, then headed toward the interstate. He ruled out the malls, they were mostly jailbait. That kind of meat could be dangerous—security guards might remember a face.

The new bar off the interstate was full. Friday night army weekenders were packed belly button to crotch, parking lot jammed dent-your-door tight. Things were looking up. Barry parked, lifted the lid on the shoe box, its goodies better than any nickel and dime buy, snugged the lid back to place, shoved it behind the passenger's seat and headed inside. Music and voices boomed a muffled smoky din, predators and prey on the hunt. He hated the smoke. He would trash the clothes he was wearing.

*****

As soon as they got off duty, they'd changed into civies and left out from Beaufort. The drive took little over an hour. They checked into a cheap motel, then hit the liquor store. Couple of bottles of Southern Comfort, one Oso Negro Tequila. Could've gotten liquor cheaper on base, but their gunny would bust whatever stripe they had if they got pulled over again. Between Beaufort's double-ugly ex-marine sheriff and bull gunny, there was no way they could have any fun. Beaufort was a real quiet town.

That night, Shane and Leigh never made it out of their motel room. Empty bottles, aspirin and a near-noon wakeup slug of warm beer took the edge off the hangovers.

Shane was out of bed first and said, "Get up." He shouldered Leigh awake. "We gotta get more liquor."

"Take no time to spend what little money we got." Leigh's words were dragging.

Shane, bare-assed, towel in hand, said, "I'm hittin' the shower." and disappeared into the bath.

Soaped from top to bottom, he tilted his head into the spray, let it rat-a-tat-tat his face as he lathered a scalp stubble of once wavy, black-brown hair. His stomach felt kinda funky, but he sure was looking forward to tonight. He leaned against the shower wall and let the water splash away the soap. He then shut off the water, grabbed a towel and dried all under as he walked to where Leigh's groggy arm hung off the bed. During their last party, Shane watched Leigh pound some new one half the night, then fall asleep on top of her. Rousting Leigh was useless unless Gunny was on the growl. Shane grabbed his hot dog trunks, headed toward the pool, hit the chilly water and did several laps. He had a quick poolside rinse-off before heading back to the room where he stretched across the bed and rumpled the sheet around him. Neither moved till the sundown witching hour.

Strapping, big-boned Shane Knuckles was a 6'2" squared-away Marine recruiting poster—proud of how his daily gym workouts made him look good in his uniform or in a tight pair of chinos. He foamed what was left of the pitcher into his mug, gulped a big swallow, wiped off his beer-fuzz mustache and lifted the pitcher high. The barmaid swung by, her back to them, as she thudded two full pitchers between

the rowdies at the next table.

Shane nudged Leigh and said, "Look at that." His eyes zeroed to her mini-skirted thighs. "Think of the good times we could have." He already had a good buzz going.

Leigh, a boot camp moniker shortened from Burleigh, said, "Yeh, and this time, you take seconds. Told you this place would be jumping. I'm sure ready." He hiked his crotch and gulped a big swallow.

Both had looked forward to this all week—their first long weekend pass since posting guard duty at Beaufort's Marine Corps Air Station.

"Check the fancy suit-and-tie dude," Leigh said, nodding toward the man. "He's been shoveling ten spots to her for the last hour."

"Women go for rich fuckers," Shane said, acting world wise. "Whoever she can get the most out of." He guzzled and shifted for a better look. "Wish I had a roll like that."

Leigh said, "You get pissed at big spenders 'cause they have the money and you don't." Leigh's mug was empty. "Last time, you almost got us arrested. This weekend, I'm keeping the car keys. You're not costing me another stripe plus a month's pay."

Shane gave a boisterous laugh, "You were having just as much fun." He took a swig. "You're a wuss."

Both marines were surprised when moneybags and the woman came up to the table.

She said, "Mind if we join you?" Her big tits on a five-foot frame goggling right in his face.

Shane gawked, almost tongue-tied. "Sure!" He sputtered and kicked out a chair.

"What you two drinking?" the man asked.

Shane found his tongue, "Beer." If they play this right, they could have all the booze they could drink and not pay for it.

Barry asked, "How about a round of Wild Turkey for everyone?"

Shane said, "Yeh!" The pitcher was quickly abandoned.

Sweet Thing was getting friendlier, even if up close she didn't look so young.

Barry said, "My friend here wanted to meet you two, but she was too embarrassed to ask. I told her you were probably soldiers from the army fort."

"Marines," Leigh said.

Not havin' anybody think they were run-of-the-mill anyone-can-join army.

"Oooh, Marines," she squeaked. "I love big strong marines." With that, she scooted closer.

She let her eyes rove and made sure they noticed. Her thighs made contact, nudged against a leg that didn't move away. It was grope time.

Barry said, "Good duty?" Out-of-towners made it even better.

"They depend on us to make sure the heavy ordinance is secure," Shane bragged. "That's bombs and bullets." He liked what her hands were doing.

More rounds of drinks were ordered, conversation became more bleary eyed and neither Leigh nor Shane were holding their liquor well. The woman's smile was pasted in place, her attention never wandering, her tongue played with the rim of her glass, and Shane and Leigh were eating it up. The night stretched longer, the liquor making her better looking. Barry bought one last round of drinks—he didn't want to be the last to leave. That would be too noticeable.

"My friend and I are headed for a little party," Barry said. "You two want to join us?"

Leigh was quick, "Hell yeah! We were about to blow this joint anyhow."

"We'll take my car," Barry offered and pushed back from the table.

Shane gulped his drink. "Never leave good liquor," he said as he wiped his mouth with the back of his hand.

They piled in, she in the back with Leigh and Shane sideways in the front seat watching Leigh maul her tit. He knew if they didn't get somewhere soon, Leigh would bang her right there. It wasn't long before Barry pulled up the ramp into the garage. Leigh grappled his zipper closed. They crossed into the main building, took the elevator down, the shoebox tucked under Barry's arm. He'd timed it right—the guards were on their rounds, the lobby was empty. The woman threw a furtive look across the dark narrow street, but said nothing. She wasn't about to jeopardize four, crisp hundreds stuffed in her purse. At the foot of the stairs, Barry pulled open the vault door and stepped back.

"Wow!" Shane goggled at row after row of wine. "This all yours?"

Barry unlocked the door and cautioned, "Watch your step."

He then lit the candles, their flame the only light dancing off the faceted, long-stemmed goblets and white tablecloth. He popped the wine corks, poured and said, "A toast to a good party night." And raised his glass.

Both marines chugged while the woman sipped.

Bluntly, Leigh asked, "Where's the bed?" He could hardly see anything.

"We'll get to that," Barry said.

Leigh moved against her, "Looks like we're gonna have our own party." His arm was around her waist, his tongue in her mouth.

Barry sat the shoebox on the shelf, checked the video camera and let the marines get busy with the woman. Her storefront expression never wavered as Shane pulled off his shirt, more than ready for a double buddy ride. Leigh was already out of his pants, shorts around his ankles. Her dress hit the floor. Barry opened another bottle, filled the pressed glass candy dish with multicolored glitter from his box.

"Have some," he said and held the dish.

Shane reached in, fished for Ecstasy, some champagne heavens and black beauty go-fasts and gulped them down with a wash of wine. Leigh threw Shane a leer, crawled on top of her. There was no holding back—no stopping for a damn rubber. Besides, one time didn't hurt. He'd wash it good back in the room. This was their best weekend ever.

Barry, pleased, walked toward the shelf and said, "You two want a real turn-on? Toys for the videos," He pulled out leather. "Make copies of the tape for you to take back to your buddies. Show them what a good time you had."

Leigh said, "Never wore anything leather before." He picked up one of the harnesses. "Always wondered what it was like," He added with a grin.

Shane blustered, "That looks weird." He emptied his glass.

Leigh untangled the straps and put it on.

"That looks hot," she said and flicked a long, red nail across his nipples that were framed by the crisscross leather.

Barry said, "Try these." He brought out handcuffs.

"Go ahead," Leigh said and stuck out his wrists.

"Behind your back," Barry said. "More fun that way."

Leigh adjusted the straps, and with a silly grin said, "Leather feels cold between my legs."

She caressed his belly as she said, "I like a man all trussed up."

The lights played across Leigh's spread-eagled body. Barry handed a bottle of wine to Shane, "Pour it over your buddy, slow and don't get in the way of the camera."

"That all you want me to do?" She asked as she sidled up to Barry.

"Wait for me up front," he said.

She picked up her clothes, and Barry went with her through the wine cellar, closed the door and came back to Shane and Leigh. Camera running, he came up behind Shane and smashed an unopened bottle across the back of his head. Shane dropped like a stone.

Barry knelt, quickly snugged gray duct tape across Shane's mouth and crisscrossed wrappings around his wrists and ankles.

Leigh craned his neck, "What'choo want me to do now?" He felt woozy.

"I want you to shut the fuck up." Barry slapped duct tape across Leigh's mouth.

He made sure the tape on both of them hadn't worked loose, then hurried to where she waited. They then walked to the parking garage. He was slightly behind her as they crossed the deck. He was nervous that she might panic, so he made certain no guards had seen them. He gave one last quick look before he whipped the cord around her neck, avoided the frantic claw of her nails and swiftly cakewalked her into the dark corner and twisted the cord tight till she stopped struggling. He let her body sprawl onto the concrete, unlocked the trunk, reached for the bat and clubbed her head till he was sure she was dead. He grabbed her purse, slued the contents across the deck and retrieved the four bills he'd paid her—muggers didn't leave cash. He ripped her dress and popped a couple of buttons. While breathing heavy, he gazed at the body and turned up his nose at the smell of blood mixed with her bladder. Should've used his fist more, he thought, but that was too risky, she might've screamed. He wanted this to look like a hit-and-run,so he scattered a few pretties from his shoebox, couple under the body, then hurried back across the street, down the steps and found Leigh struggling. The side of his face rubbed raw where he'd pushed loose the tape.

Leigh yelled, pissed, "You sonuvabitch! what the fuck you doin'?"

"Shut your mouth!" Barry backhanded him. "You pervert shit!" And hit him again.

Barry liked the feel of it and liked the trickle of blood from Leigh's split lip even better. Barry made himself calm down, unseemly to let white trash see him upset. He half rolled Leigh to face Shane and made sure his wrists and ankles were still tight.

Barry said, "It's fun time now ... and not goddamn much left of yours."

Fear washing his gut, Leigh said, "I thought you wanted to take pictures."

Shane struggled, arched his body and struggled harder, "What'cha gonna do?"

Barry had enough of this. He had wanted this to last, but they were pissing him off. He grabbed Shane's chin, forced the head to one side—neck muscles strained—and slashed the blade along the jugular. Shane's eyes fixed on the crimson gush of his own blood. Barry became excited by the look in Shane's eyes and at the sight of blood, but the pleasure was soon gone. The only thing left for Barry to do was clean up. As Shane gurgled and choked on his own blood, Barry rolled up his sleeves, took out the hunting knife, wrestled Leigh's head to one side and relished the fear that welled out of Leigh's eyes—knowing Leigh knew. Barry forced Leigh's chin up. Leigh's eyes followed the blade as Barry drove the point into the bony notch at the base of the neck. Leigh jerked, his eyes lurched wide as his mouth worked through a soppy froth, and his legs jerked with spasms. Barry pushed and sliced through leigh's spinal cord. His body was left jerking as he hurried to an unconscious Shane. Barry dribbled his fingers in the syrupy warm clots and wondered if it was true that human blood tasted sweet. He let the tip of his tongue touch lightly across his gory fingertip and shrugged. It didn't taste sweet to him. He bent Shane's head to one side. He wasn't about to wait. He sliced the neck clean through, rinsed it before the blood clotted and sat it next to Leigh's. It took the better part of an hour to degut the headless corpses, slice a few prime filets of liver and made sure not to nick the greenish gall bladder and leave it bitter. He thought about saving a nice rump roast, wrap for the BBQ, keep it in freezer—some honey, brown sugar, a few pineapple slices, new potatoes and marinate it overnight. The pig-eyed SOBs would be stuffed with nature's best. When he was finished, Barry tumbled the heap of bones, torsos, arms, legs, hands and feet into the cesspit, hauled down the handle and flushed the catfish and turtle chunks riverward.

He soaped his hands and arms and rinsed, soaped again. After he dried and fastidiously put each cuff link to place, he slipped into his suit coat, turned out the lights, locked up and left.

As he drove home, Barry thought about the evening. This woman had been the best one—a whore deserved killing, spreading her sinful legs every chance she got. He rubbed his knuckles where her nails had clawed. He liked the push of her butt against his belly as she fought, remembering the twisted cord burying deep in the flesh of her neck. Doing two guys was a kicker. He would have to try a double again. His euphoria abruptly dulled as images of his long-dead mother watching with her burning eyes and pulled-back hair, caught him playing with himself. She told everyone at Sunday school what a nasty little boy he was. Barry threw a glance into his rearview mirror, expecting the ghost of his pucker-lipped Aunty to be glaring at him from the back seat. The lust for killing rose and left him alone with his craving demons. Faces from the bank were like Aunty—the in-crowd, beauty queen cliques and their boyfriend jocks made his pimply teen years a chronicle of putdowns. His gut churned in a blizzard of hate. They were going to pay.

He pulled into his garage, the door lowering behind him. His wife was in her bedroom by the time he got upstairs. The next morning, she was her usual, snarly mood. She lumbered her bloated ass around in her bedroom to slumber the day away. He looked at the time, showered, dressed, shoved down a bagel and cream cheese, left for the office, and another dreary morning.

As he pulled into the parking garage, he broke out in a cold, nervous sweat. Flashing blue lights and yellow "crime scene" tape sectioned off parts of the lot and cops were everywhere. He eased passed his reserve spot, parked up top and knew he should've pulled into the spot he'd finagled and AKed to get. He decided never to break routine again.

From his desk, he could hear secretaries gossip the whole day.

"Just terrible," one said.

"Poor thing," said another.

A third asked, "She have any children?"

"Of course not," eyes rolled. "Her kind never do."

"The parking deck never had enough lights, and we need more security guards," big, red glasses griped. "Always takes something like

this before they do anything."

More guards were hired, and Barry decided the deck wasn't the best place.

*****

Terri finished her sandwich, then asked Irene to buzz auditing.

"If it's for the McGiffern Trust, Ben Harrell is probably more familiar with it than anyone," Irene suggested.

"See if he can spare me a few minutes this afternoon."

"I'm sure he can." Irene's expression said it all.

Terri brought up her screen, retrieved the McGiffern files, the accrued portfolio, the impressive assets, plus real estate, timber, land, commodities and mineral rights. Most of the transactions she'd understood and the market values and total fund shares seemed straightforward. Treasury money funds showed good improvement even during the downswings, yet there was something peculiar with the treasury notes—the dividends showed random deficits. A crosscheck of quarterly tax reports showed steady decreases in some balances and lump sum direct transfers into a recent cash management accounts. She knew the inconsistencies might've been for any number of reasons, but the IRS reports had more than a few CMA rollovers. Some withdrawals had incurred heavy penalties, or hadn't stayed ahead of minimum inflation rates, and lucrative purchase options had not been picked up. From what Terri heard about Theosia, it didn't fit. Recent 1099 DIV and INT and 1099Bs showed the same. It left Terri with a needling caution. She needed to talk with someone more familiar with the details.

Irene buzzed, "Line six, Ben Harrell from Accounting."

"Thanks." She punched the small, blinking light. "Ben?"

"Irene said you had some questions on one of our accounts." Ben said in his usual peacock tone.

"Your terminal up?" Terri asked.

"Yeh," he answered. "Just got off with the corporate big boys in Atlanta." He wanted the Stanley babe to know he had connections. "What file you working?"

"The McGiffern Trust," Terri answered.

"I heard about that," Ben said.

Terri, curious, asked "Heard what?"

"That you were given that account," he said. "Quite a feather in your cap."

Terri detested office magpies and their prattle. She decided her best bet with Ben Harrell was to let his remark slide.

"That's what I wanted to talk to you about," she said.

"Has that account audit I requested been completed?"

"Atlanta put that on the back burner," he said. "With the merger in the works, they've ordered updates on all accounts."

"Really," she said, wondering how much more this how-important-I-am one would brag. "Do me a favor?" She knew she could be asking for trouble.

Ben said, "Sure kid, anything. I'll be right over."

Terri bit her tongue. His familiarity left her uncomfortable. He might be a good accountant, but Benjamin Harrell had a philandering rep, and he certainly hadn't waited for her to ask him to come to her office. He was there in less than ten minutes. Terri kept it strictly business. She'd known too many officers like that. One couldn't trust them, especially behind closed doors.

Half an hour into the files, Ben said, "I'm not sure about the holding companies or where the CMA transfers took place."

"Can you find out?" she asked.

"It'll take time," he said.

Terri said, "I don't want this to drag on till Christmas next year." She wouldn't put it past him to string her along. "I need answers, and the trustee certainly will."

"I'll get right on it," Ben said. "Just for you."

He straightened to his near full six feet and flashed his killer smile as he looked her up and down. It was Ben Harrell's weakest point, where he'd screwed up with lots of people. He was convinced that all he had to do was ooze his charm, women liked attention. There was certainly no woman alive who could resist the pale azure eyes of handsome, sport-stud Benjie Harrell—classic features with a Mediterranean skin tone made his teeth incandescent.

After the door closed behind him, the thought hit Terri, one she hadn't considered. What if she was meant to find something? At first, it struck her as ridiculous. It would mean someone in the bank had picked her as the newcomer, a patsy to take the fall if McGiffern assets

came up missing. A quick shiver iced through her. She balked at taking a rumor to her boss, as though she couldn't handle it. After all, it was only a hunch. Terri clicked her mouse, brought up the menu, selected trustee, and then personal and saw his legal name for the first time—typical southern name, probably one from each generation.

INGRAMME, Craige Howelle Graeme Roynane
Occupation: Private Investigator

She swiveled her chair and gazed out the window toward the promenade. After wrestling with several choices, the one she preferred meant stepping outside office protocol. The account was hers. It wasn't like she was bringing in an outsider. Trustees had a right to know. Her intuition said yes. Personal feelings contended with emotions shouting "careful,"—Ingramme was dangerous, but she already knew that. For a moment she wondered if she was doing the right thing. She didn't buzz Irene. Instead, she picked up her private line and punched in the Silver Bluff phone number for Moccasin Hollow.

# Chapter 5

As Terri held the phone and listened to it ring, she pushed aside a fleeting impulse to hang up before Craige Ingramme answered. She wasn't sure about this, but as the trustee, he needed to know. Her palms moist, this man was affecting her in ways she had not expected. She heard a faint click as though an answering machine was rewinding and decided she was not leaving a message. She was about to hang up when he answered.

"Ingramme."

Hesitant, she said, "This is Terri Stanley."

"I recognized your voice." He was pleased it was her.

"I thought perhaps we had a bad connection," Terri said.

"I call-forwarded my phone here to Ardochy Manor. I wanted to get started with the inventories, get ready for the appraisals."

"We need to talk," she said.

"You need me to come in again?"

Terri paused, "I'd much prefer not to discuss it over the phone. There are enough rumors without my causing more. Inquisitive eyes and ears are quite ready to do enough of that. I can meet you somewhere."

That surprised him. More than taken aback, for an instant Craige said nothing. Her voice reminded him of other indolent dawn-breaking mornings, melted honey tones among the pillows. He thought of that moment in her office, when he first saw her, a "well-cut jib" ap-

praisal made him think of the rest of her—the tilt of her extraordinary head, the impertinent nose, listening to her speak, not caring what she said. Her saffron gold eyes had bored into more than a few of his nights. She was all business, and Craige—he just wanted to keep her talking. Terri Stanley fits none of his good time molds. He couldn't see her being like so many others, business was a convenient excuse to orchestrate her own diversions. His gut feeling told him he was way off base with this one.

She broke his train of thought when she asked, "How do I get to Ardochy?"

Her question caught him off guard again. She was full of surprises. His dumbfounded reflection came back at him from the baroque, high-drawer, mirrored chiffonnier of Theosia McGiffern's bedroom.

"You know how to get to Silver Bluff?" Craige asked.

"Yes."

"When you leave Silver Bluff, stay on the Charleston Highway. Don't take the fork. It goes to the bomb plant, and the next turn-around is thirty miles at the main gate of the Savannah River site. Stay on the main road. In about fifteen miles you'll come to Redcliffe Plantation. The main property lines of Ardochy and Redcliffe adjoin one another. Ardochy is a couple of miles beyond Redcliffe. You can't miss it. It's a large, two-story, white stucco and brick, Georgian-style manor house. It sits up the hill about three miles beyond the Old Yard."

"I'm leaving now." Terry madly scribbled the directions.

After Craige hung up, he started second-guessing himself. This had come out of the blue, seemingly too deliberate to be hanky-panky, or was she one of those aggressive types who wanted to keep the office out of the loop. The thought of a quick roll in the hay made a pleasant prospect—long legs and well-turned elegant ankles had always yanked his anchor. Had he read her wrong? The core, deep-hot-heat country boy in him didn't buy it. There was more—something about the way she spoke ...

*****

Before the Forensic Team videoed the kill zone, they took pains-taking wide-angle photos and close-ups, made a detailed sweep of the area, packaged possible physical evidence and tagged the zip-locks.

The heavy, thick, plastic, body bag zipped shut. The woman's remains hoisted into the van with County Morgue stenciled on the side—slaughtered meat on a gurney. It was ready for storage and probably a pauper's grave.

In one desolate corner of the garage, beyond the yellow marked area and oil splotched parking slots, the two bag ladies tried to be inconspicuous, waiting where they'd been told to stay. Her drab, gray-blond hair twisted in a bun, Sallie Mae Drutherferde darted distrustful glances at the clusters of police. She squinted a sky blue eye, didn't like cops one iota. She gave a dubious, all-knowing look at Agatha Ruth. Together, the two are often pushing their rickety grocery cart with its one lopsided wheel.

Sallie Mae asked, "A'gatha, you not gonna tell 'em anything?" Her eyes were cocked big and round.

Sallie Mae always called her A'gatha 'cause that's the way Agatha Ruth Hutchers said it. Didn't matter what others said. A'gatha nervously adjusted her dumpster-discard, hairbare, blond wig twisted askance, which made her look like she were staring sidewise.

A'gatha said, shaking her head, "Ain't sayin' nuthin' 'bout nuthin'—'bout no big, show-off, black see-dan automobile that pulled in here last night. Right off the bat, they'd be askin' why we was where we didn't supposed to be. We end up havin' to find us another place to skitter in out of the weather. No sirree. Ain't sayin' nuthin'."

"Gonna have to find another place anyhow," Sallie Mae muttered as she crooked one finger to scratch her curls. "'Sides, I didn't hear no scuffle."

"Whole lot of 'em drunk as hoot owls," A'gatha said. "Was all set to have a wing-ding party long 'fore they showed up here. Poor thing yonder in that amb'lance wadn't no innocent church mouse. She was more'n willin'." She then added with a snap of her head, "Lordy mercy. Tsk-tsk. More'n willin' and a cagey type, too. The type who makes sure to be paid 'fore puttin' a foot in anyone's big, long car. Scandalous, tight dress showin' off her wares, and a skimpy blouse didn't hide nothin'—poochin' out her chest for any fancy man long as they brung money. Even if she was a harlot, ain't no bizness of our's." Her face softened. "Ain't tellin' nobody nuthin'. You know how cops be."

"The likes a her endin' up dead in some alley don't surprise me none," Sallie Mae said.

"Sallie Mae!" A'gatha eyed her. "You hush up 'bout us seein' them in that alley. Bankers that works in this building won't bat nary an eyelash payin' some low life to dump us off the Fifth Street pier. We end up gator bait stuffed amongst swamp sycamore tree roots." Truth glimmered from her eyes like a cornered rabbit. "Them kind got money to buy their scutwork done."

The police finally got around to them.

"What were you two doing in here that hour of the night?" the beat cop asked.

"Passin' through." Sallie Mae said, her head up proud.

"Passing through …" the cop snorted. "Up here on the upper deck?"

A'gatha scowled, "We got lost." Her lips were tight as she glowered, "We ain't done nuthin' wrong."

"This is private property," he said. "Nobody's supposed to be in here unless you got business with the bank, and nobody's supposed to be in here at night."

"We didn't bother nuthin', didn't see nothin'." Sallie wasn't about to let any cop push A'gatha around.

He knew he was getting nowhere. He'd dealt with these two before. They were never arrested except when some owner found them sleeping in his garage or in the back of an unlocked delivery van. They were tough and not about to crack, but finding them here meant an extra patrol for him and his partner. He knew there was no point in pushing further, so he closed his notepad, and shoved it in his pocket.

"You two can't loiter here," he said. "The bank don't like it."

A'gatha bristled, "Ain't loiterin'." She wasn't going to put up with being called a bum neither.

"Don't let me catch you two in here again." And he walked away.

They hurried away. A'gatha knew they didn't amount to anything to any of these cops. They were nothing more than dust in a world that passed them without ever seeing them.

"Might be a good time to take a vacation to Florida," A'gatha said. "Ain't never comin' back near this here place." She could feel the spirits hovering about. "Not ever."

"Cops don't scare me none," Sallie Mae said.

"Tain't the cops," Agatha said and kept looking around.

"They's a smell to this place, a hoary breath of death abouts. I can tetch it. You best listen t'me. Be like about that other time when I said

things wadn't safe," she said, directing a sidewise glance at Sallie Mae
and sensing the murky gloom behind the midday brightness. "I'm rollin'
the bones this night. Death be here." Her eyes were big with fear. "Ain't
stayin' where demons walk the night mist."

"A'gatha, you stop now." Sallie Mae sidled closer.

"You givin' me shivers." She knew A'gatha was born with the gift.

"Shivers be good, when the Devil goes walkin'," A'gatha said. "Long
as a body stays right with Jesus, Devil cain't get'cha." Her toothless
mouth drew narrow. "Sweet Lord done protected us one more time this
night, and this body don't have to be told more'n onct. Evil be here. Yes
sireeesir, an' I ain't tellin' no cops neither."

"Me neither," Sallie Mae mumbled.

Sallie Mae's rheumatism had gone achy. She gave a strained look
behind her, made sure nothing was creeping up on them. She was sure
she could hear ghostly movings. It didn't matter if the new street lamps
burned bright. Sallie Mae knew that the God of Abraham, Isaac and
Jacob protected them, didn't matter that no one believed. He warned
her more than a few times about danger. She done give her soul to the
Lord—Satan's hoards always ready to snatch it back. She had her worn
leather "Good Book," Yahweh, her keeper against Satan's fallen archan-
gels. Fear stabbed her belly deep. The black Beelzebub had come to
town. She had seen his hunched silhouette across the street in the night
shades. Her poor sinner's eyes sometimes didn't recognize corruption,
but the Lord of the Israelites protected her from what she saw in the
alley. Shadows couldn't hide the profane, big houses, fancy cars, hoity-
toity fresh paint and bricks. None of that could ever wipe clean the
blood curse on this place.

*****

Terri had no trouble with Craige's directions. A half hour later, she
turned into Ardochy's meandering, white-graveled drive and spotted
Craige waiting on the steps of Ardochy's columned porte-cochère car-
riage porch. Terri thought of her father and his brushy-browed scowl at
her for breaking his business rule. Once, her father learned of her infatu-
ation with a teller at his Napa Valley Bank, and he said, "Never mix
business with anything else, and never on your own doorstep." He didn't
mention it again.

As her car pulled up and stopped, Craige hurried down the steps. Craige opened her door and said, "I see you made it."

As she stepped out, his eyes followed every turn of the shapely ankles. "I had no problem," Terri said.

Her thoughts cluttered as the feelings she'd had since that first time they'd met surged, somehow stronger, with his nearness. Terri would never have believed her good sense could be so altogether rattled, and she tried not to think about what Irene had said. In the private sanctions of her heart, Terri tried to keep her mind on why she came—it wasn't working.

"Come on in the kitchen," Craige said, holding open one of the double-carriage, porch doors. "I iced a fresh pitcher of tea." He led her through the Butler's pantry into the sedate library.

"Oh my, all these marvelous books ..." Terri murmured.

"It's my favorite room," Craige smiled. "All for the enjoyment of reading. Theosia left me several first editions. Sit down, make yourself comfortable."

The soft leather chairs, Tiffany lamps and comfy reading niches made the high ceiling expanse of shelves somehow cozy. She looked around the library with its frescos in delicate pastel blushes, intricate friezes and matching tiered chandeliers heavy with Austrian crystal drops. Without seeming out of place or time, she thought he seemed to belong to this refined, patinaed ambience of high ceilings and ornate carvings. He filled the Chippendale chair as though he belonged—male supremacy without being rawboned.

Terri sat as she recalled private times with her mother, of parlor rites and playing dress up that wasn't all play-act—learning to sit, stand and walk properly; how to set an afternoon high tea, finger cakes and scones. Terri wished she hadn't hurried her makeup that morning. Had she used too much perfume? Did he find it pleasant? She'd refreshed her lipstick before she left to come here—what if it was on her front teeth? She found herself acting like a high-school subdeb.

"If you prefer, there's unsweetened tea." Craige iced his glass with the tongs from the silver and crystal ice bucket.

"No," she said. "It's fine."

His devil-may-care, rakish smile, the dark auburn reflections from his hair and the fiery golden flecks in his green eyes kept getting in the way of why she came.

"With so little to go on, I'm not sure where to start," Terri began. She tried to soothe her jitters.

"About what?" Craige asked, picking up on her nervousness.

Terri knew she was taking a risk. He could be part of it, yet some inherent trust told her different.

"Perhaps I'm overreacting," she said. "Several of the portfolios don't quite add up. There's stocks, mutual funds, international oil, precious metals, grain futures, money markets. Some of it's over my head."

She looked straight at Craige without wavering. He jigsawed any number of reasons she might have for coming out here. Her eyes seemed to swallow the room. At least he was lost in them. He wanted her visit to be more than just business.

"An audit should take care of that," Craige said.

"There's been some foot dragging," she replied. "Enough to leave me somewhat uncomfortable."

It struck Craige as an odd remark for a bank officer, even more so about her own bank. He studied the bottomless eyes of this wholly female creature, and his gut feeling told him this visit wasn't a concoction.

She continued, "I conferred with our accountant before I called you. He made the excuse that he didn't have time to go through the accounts until the audit was complete. I didn't particularly care for his lack of interest since it involved the bank as much as the estate. It leaves the bank and the estate vulnerable. Some would say it's my grandstanding to make a name for myself, making noises about things being amiss, when it's simple bookkeeping errors. Nevertheless, the discrepancies need looking into."

"And you don't want to use the bank's resources?" Craige asked.

Terri paused, then said, "I see possible conflicts of interest."

"You might say the same about me," Craige said. "I'm one of the bank's major stockholders."

"Your interests aren't quite the same as the bank's, even if you do own bank stock."

Craige smile at the way she put it.

After scanning several pages, Craige said, "On the face of it, I see a few things but nothing that would justify an independent audit, much less an investigation."

The remark left Terri feeling exposed, but he was right. Craige

followed as she moved to the massive library table and spread the paper trails of Theosia's investments. She pointed out one item, then another. Balances didn't balance, and there were disjointed transactions. She'd done her homework. There were some glitches. Her perfume was intoxicating. He rationalized that she came to him because she trusted him to help. How could he do anything else?

"I've turned this all manner of ways," she said, her fingers pressed at her forehead. "Suppose ..."

Craige interrupted, "Someone at the bank is involved?"

"I'm glad you said it," Terri sighed. "I've tried to make myself believe that there had to be a perfectly good explanation, but this is one of the bank's most important accounts."

"I can see where it would upset middle management," Craige said.

He wasn't sure he wanted to open a can of worms with what he was thinking, but he did.

"What if you were hired as a stopgap convenience?"

"What?" A flare of anger crossed her face.

"A ready pigeon in case someone needed to smoke screen a problem without upsetting the apple cart?"

His words punched Terri in the stomach, and a deadly stillness invaded the mahogany and black cherry wainscoted library.

"It crossed my mind," she said.

"There's a nastier possibility, one potentially more dangerous." His tone was steely. "Flip-flop the looking glass to the other side. Suppose you were the trigger without meaning to be. Let's assume you were hired to fill a slot, the off the street patsy, your résumé never read, your desk backlogged with files, no one expecting you to dig into the accounts."

Her eyes fluttered, "That's not very flattering."

"Trouble is never flattering," Craige said, "especially when it blindsides you. Anyone know you brought these to me?"

"No, I didn't even tell Irene," she said. "Originals aren't supposed to leave the bank, but you are the trustee."

Craige liked the way she'd seen a problem and started trying to handle it. It was the mark of a winner, but in this instance, it could spell trouble.

"I won't tell if you won't," Craige reassured her.

For the first time since she'd started this, her anxiety seemed to

lighten. Terri couldn't deny being drawn to him. For a moment she forgot she was at Ardochy—the splintered half-light blazoned from behind him sheening his auburn hair red-gold as it curled behind one ear. He had the most beautiful eyes she'd seen in a long time. She'd tried to deny it was happening, but she knew it was.

Yesterday Jeffrey had flustered her when he asked, "Mom, you got a boyfriend?"

Her train of thought snapped when she realized Craige had asked her something.

"I'm sorry," she said. "I was thinking of something else."

"You mind if I keep the copies?" He repeated.

"I'd prefer you did." She reached for her purse. "I must get back to the office."

Craige watched as she drove away and wished she hadn't. The more he weighed what she'd brought, the more it took on a bitter color. Theosia and Terri Stanley were a lot alike. He shut down the main breakers except to the kitchen, the outside safety lights and the security system; gathered the McGiffern portfolio and climbed in his Jeep. Lucky burst out of the bushes when he fired up the engine and followed alongside until he turned onto the highway. By the time he reached the house, some of the details were bugging him even more. He flopped down on the sofa. He couldn't keep her out of his mind.

Craige needed a woman, needed to be alone, needed to go fishing, needed to think straight. That night his fitful dreams weren't of old girlfriends like Reba, but of a black-haired, uncompromising mother with a brain to match and a knockout body that refused him any tranquility. If pucker-minded bible thumpers could have seen the skin flicks dancing his thoughts, he would've been damned to hellfire. He rolled and tossed the entire night. It was filled with haunting chimera and an obstinate pounding woodie refusing him any serenity. His brain clustered around one, long, exhausted, passionless, Technicolor night. It had been a long time since he'd had a wet dream, but last night came close. He lurched out of the sack before sunup. A raging erection would drill a smile into any partner hungry for lovemaking instead of a quick, wet hump. He tossed yesterday's sausage to Lucky. Something about Terri devoured him. He finished a lean breakfast—toast, no butter, smear of his blackberry, homemade no-sugar jam and forced himself to one cup of staggering, turkish coffee that tasted more like syrup

than anything. Instead of going down the drive, he jogged a winding roundabout to the highway newspaper box for the morning Herald Gazette. Lucky was lopping along beside, stopping to sniff and mark spots. He then caught the scent of the bull coon Craige had heard raiding bait buckets last night and was off again.

He sat down on the porch swing, skimmed sections of the paper then tossed it aside. He couldn't dodge a bird-dog sense about the things Terri showed him. It badgered him more than her sneaking into his fitful night. He went inside to where he'd spread Theosia's files on the dining table. His attention sucked to the same snags Terri had noticed, the arbitrary transfers, rollovers that weren't due. No one thing stood out till he followed the CMAs consolidated in non-McGiffern offshore accounts, which led him to electronic transfers to diverse Caymen Brac Island banks—none of it with Theosia's signature. He'd worked with DEA, ATF, CIA and ReconOps ploys. The Caymen's were infamous for being a ready laundering interchange. Wall Street and Toronto were neck-to-guilty-neck right up there with South America. His appetite whetted the further he picked at the tangled trail, most of the documents were dated well before Terri came on the scene. It could be more circumstance than design, her being in the right place, a too convenient way out for the wrong people to pass up. By prying into a trail of monies siphoned from McGiffern accounts, Terri might've uncovered more than she realized. It could force who-ever was behind this to change plans and set Terri square in a bull's eye.

That didn't make him feel one bit better. That kind of panic can churn out a killing before anyone knows there's a storm coming. Craige sat down and painstakingly went over everything again. Hours later he slumped back, his fingers locked behind his head, as he stared at a carefully disguised deception and the possible connection with Sedgewicke. If Sedgewicke discovered the fraud, was he killed to keep it quiet? Craige had known murder for less. The first kill is the hard-est—more often than not followed by more. He put the brakes to his runaway PI suspicions. He could be overlooking the simple. First thing was to check who was sleeping around—emotions make powerful se-ducers—blackmail is even more of a motive. Money was not nearly so strong as a blistering, blood, bone-deep fear topped off with rage.

Several about-town double-crosses came to mind, some of them

already boarders in the federal pen, but none of the other shady characters had connections to the bank except Garland Holton. He was thickheaded and not gifted with a whole lot of sense. That often caused its own set of problems. If blackmail was at the bottom of this, Craige had seen dishonor among thieves twist into stalemated murder. Whoever shuffled the accounts had kept it low key. If Holton was part of it, it meant going against some of the town's influential old families. If reputations and pedigreed bloodlines were involved, things might've turned rough and nasty.

Craige would bring Gray up to speed on what he had found, but for anything to stick, Gray would need proof, names, dates, all the trivia. If it came to a jury trial, Craige didn't want any circumstantial inference giving a defense attorney the opening to poke Gray's case full of doubts.

Craige had some pavement pounding ahead of him—interviews, record searching, digging among family closets. Sometimes the only way to unmask rot was pick a spot, dig till the pig squealed, and there was no time like the present to get started. The CMA transfers were as good a place as any.

Craige retraced all entries. It didn't take long before he had a potpourri list of names with access to several accounts, including Theosia's. The list was a humdinger of bank officers and two law firms. The list alone made nitroglycerin waiting to explode. His best bet was to dig into Royce's dealings to see if he could find what had set it off. That would ruffle some feathers.

Right then, the ugly thought hit. If Theosia's accounts weren't the only ones involved, suppose Royce wasn't the first kill. That could call for his disinterring Theosia for a thorough autopsy to confirm if she died of natural causes. That didn't sit well with him. He wouldn't want that for anyone he cared about, yet he refused to live with doubts of her having been murdered. Craige could depend on Fred for straight answers. Screw jurisdiction. He'd make sure the river border between the two states wasn't a problem, at least till it was over and done with, and he had his answers. Any legal rumbles never stopped him—get it over and done before anyone was the wiser. Easier to get forgiveness than permission. He had the keys to the granite and marble McGiffern Mausoleum. He could remove the coffin and haul it to the morgue himself. It would be hell to pay if he got caught crossing state lines

with a corpse. He shouldn't tell Gray till the deed was done. There was no need putting his butt at risk.

Craige couldn't see any point in dragging it out. He roamed through names for helping him get from mausoleum to morgue and back. He'd rubbed elbows with dictators on horseback and assorted gutter sickos and never had a problem as long as they knew he was the alpha male with eyes in the back of his head for keeping track of vermin. He hated crude methods, but if you're going to swim in the gutter, you better approach things the way those types do, or you'll get your throat slit from not covering your butt in case of a bushwhack. Let your guard down at the wrong time, and you end up fighting consequences, which is no way to win a chess game. He wouldn't say anything to Terri till he had something definite. He reached for the phone and dialed Garland Holton's law offices.

"Holton, Holton and Crayes," the soft-spoken voice said. "May I help you?"

"Garland in?" Craige asked.

"Mister Garland Senior has left for the day."

"Garland Junior," Craige corrected.

"May I say who's calling?"

"Craige Ingramme."

"One moment please." A faint click-click, then elevator music in his ear.

Garland picked up, "Craige, ole boy!" It was the same old convivial smoke screen bullshit. "Haven't heard from you in a while." his fakeness was second nature. "How you been?" His tone was condescending. "When we gonna do some fishing?"

Envy akin to hate for Ingramme bubbled fresh inside Garland Holton—he'd locked horns with this country boy and lost. His jealousy for Ingramme stemmed from everything Ingramme had that he did not—reputation, social position, his innate culture and polish but mainly for his money investments that made Ingramme more filthy rich with each day—bank stocks, Kamchatka-Quebec Timber Limited, Middle East and Okhotsk oil leases, Gulf Coast Kaolin & Shipping Inc., European pottery, Skye and Hebrides Scottish wools, iridium and platinum mines on three continents. Holton complicated his own life with the cardinal stamp of being a spoiled fool.

Craige answered, "Just moved the boat down to the new lake I

dammed on that 300 acres."

"Word is you picked up those kaolin leases," Garland said.

"Only way to shut down mining upstream of my properties," Craige continued. "I may have to buy two other sections. I don't want them, but slurry runoffs can ruin artesian springs."

*You arrogant ass,* Craige thought. He knew he was twisting Holton in his tender parts, but an angry adversary is already off balance.

Craige bullshitted, "You should come over sometime. Catfish are fat for the frying."

There was no danger of his accepting. Tailored, air-conditioned Garland would never muddy his handmade Italian shoes or get far from his Jag.

"Have to check my schedule," Garland said.

He didn't have much of a schedule, and Craige started to make a "have your people beep my people" crack, but he wanted to keep him on the defensive.

Craige cut to business, "I need your help with something confidential." That was all it took.

"Sure thing," Garland said, pretending disinterest.

Craige baited him with some names.

Knowing fear ruled his world, Craige added, "I have a feeling I might be dealing with dummy holding companies."

"Dummy corps for what?" Garland asked.

When he said that, Craige knew he'd set the hook.

"Let's just say loose ends I'm looking into." A PI's reputation has its moments.

"Who about?" Garland sounded canebrake rattler curious.

"That's where I need your help," Craige parried.

"Where'd you come up with the names?"

"Can't say."

"You mean won't." Garland's buddy-chuckle was almost ugly.

"OK, won't." Craige admitted. "Client privilege, you understand." Craige was enjoying this more than he should have.

"Confidentiality doesn't exist, not in this town," Garland said.

"That's true in any town." Craige knew it needled him.

"Any of these names come from the bank?" Garland sounded a bit too eager.

"I figured you'd recognize them," Craige answered. "That's why I

came straight to you. Those are families who never like to see their names bantered about."

"That's for sure." Garland had more than enough to choke on. "I'll keep this quiet," Garland replied, "but I know for a fact two of your names are involved in merger talks."

"You handling the negotiations?" Craige asked.

"Some."

That came as no surprise. Holton could never resist the call of money, and their brief one-on-one had answered one question—Terri had a right to be suspicious. Garland was smack dab square in the middle.

Craige asked, "Merger going smoothly?"

"If we can iron out some minor points."

Garland's "iron out," meant "run over," and it reminded Craige of Grannie's scuffle to save her land. She held a religious distrust for any lawyer.

Then Garland asked again, "Where did you get those names?"

His question told Craige a lot. Holton never had been a good poker player, he never knew when to shut up.

"Like I said, a client. I need the info as soon as possible." Craige responded.

Garland was too dumb to work something like this alone, and Craige's swamp fox rocking of their boat had to be done carefully. He'd meant to upset Holton when he phoned, and it had mainly because it came with a where-there's-smoke-there's-fire intimation. Craige was raking open a buried stench. His backroom associates were where the powder would be, and it wouldn't take those types of cronies more than a heartbeat to consider making sure mouths stayed dead shut ... including Terri.

Holton interrupted his thoughts, "I'll get back to you."

Garland was fuming after he hung up. He remembered his English Aunt Mildred saying, "Uppity Ingrams, Grannie Ingram keeping her name with one "m" and no "e" like it was something to be proud of." And with a turned-up nose, she continued, "Their Queensborough Town kin no different from the ones from Moccasin Hollow. Bad blood always tells, even back with that scoundrel, Roynane deWorthe Ingram. Throwbacks, ever last one of them. The Greshams as well as Grannie Ingram's grandson. Craige Howelle Graeme Roynane

Ingramme is no different. One simply can't trust highlanders."

"Kick your fucking ass." Garland Holton was seething. "Before this is over, I'll kick your ass."

Garland punched in the number on his private line, his fingers nervously drumming as it rang.

When the other phone was picked up, Garland said, "We got to talk." He paused. "I don't give a crap whether you like me calling you there or not. You'll like the phone call I just got even less. We got a PI problem. Craige Ingramme is poking around, asking questions about several holding companies. You realize what this could do to us if word gets out? Meet me in twenty minutes." He listened, then frowned and began shouting, "Make time!" he snapped. "I'll play along, find out how much more Ingramme knows. He wouldn't tell me where or who he got his info from, but no private dick is messing this up, not after all that I've put into it."

*****

Even with Valium, Barry couldn't sleep. His nights were long, restless catnaps followed by groggy, morose mornings merging with greyer, ambiguous days.

"You feeling all right, Mister Peters?" his secretary asked.

Without answering, Barry slammed his office door and surrendered to the cravings. He knew it was time for another.

With the parking garage off limits, there were no more older ones, and no doubles, even though doing two had been a real kick. He had to figure how he wanted this one, maybe this weekend. If only he could get some sleep.

# Chapter 6

Craige had to be careful not to overplay his hand by spooking Garland Holton too much. He was a mover-and-a-shaker, a legend in his own mind, and Craige wanted him to keep believing that. With his overconfidence, Craige wanted to add a touch of fear on top of his being short on street smarts. It was ready-made for the kind of blind spot he could use. Garland enjoyed using his blow-hard law degree mouth to intimidate, as well as being ugly just for the fun of it. Craige had dealt with better BSers. Over the phone he'd sensed Garland Holton was agitated and way short of keeping his cool. He was hiding something or he wouldn't have been fishing so hard, which he wasn't any good at. A string of what-ifs squeezed him and brought a wicked, low snarl from his need to know first rule of co-vert—never trust anyone. "Dartman" Darrell had ignored that and ended up dead. The more Craige mauled his little talk with Holton, he couldn't twist it any way that felt any better. Too congenial, good-ol'-boy Garland was a wily hallmark of the whole Holton Family—friendship and business associations grounded in ready cash changing hands.

Grannie never liked the family, and Craige didn't have to ask why. The Holtons had practiced law in this city for generations, and marsh-bottom Ingrams and their cotton-belt Ogeechee River, Queensborough Creek cousins weren't acceptable in those lofty circles of the Bourbon

Holtons. One of Garland's great-Grandsire had been the youngest and readily took any sucker ripe for plucking. He pushed his trade routes across the Savanno Indian's Isondiga River and into colonial Savannah Town. He then came up river to the Carolina Silver Bluff trading post-settlement as the Revolution heated up. It didn't take long before the whole of East Central Georgia and piedmont South Carolina knew about "them old line Charlestonian geechee aristocrats." Holton straddled the fence till the winning side came up and would have gotten his ass shot if he hadn't run. It was a good time to be scarce. Afterwards he'd pushed his first mill south of Brier Creek and built Holton's Trading Post. He opened another one a "fer piece down the road" near old town Galphinton, piled up a fortune in the doing and bred up a gang of half-breeds, which he never claimed nor took care of.

Squire Holton married a Marshal and got rich. His later genera-tions got richer, but they never changed. Scion Garland was no better, no worse and still managed to be disgustingly ill-bred. Being known for what they "wuz" was a lurking fear that yanked Holton's balls tight against his crotch. Holtons never concerned themselves with whom they hurt, which ran counter to everything Craige held of value. Deal-ing with Garland's type is a fact of life. They're everywhere. Garland Holton was crass because he liked it, and letting him know Craige knew about his low-bred background was one sure way to keep the bastard in line. Craige had tangled with fatback establishment, his blinders long gone. It works for any snob.

Still, Craige wasn't handling the churn in his belly well. It irri-tated him for letting the likes of Garland get to him, but Holton was on the bank's advisory board. He had contacts who Craige wanted stirred, and he wanted his hand to do the stirring.

Daddy Holton's circle in Hilton Head were old hands at covering their butts, a nice way of saying they'd let Terri spin in the wind. If he hadn't already, Craige could see Holton running to check who the McGiffern executor was. It never surprised Craige when stump-dumb screwed up their own doings, and Garland made the perfect doer. Craige tried to offset his bad taste at money's golden canon "who has the gold, makes the rules," but murder fits too snug and easy into that. It was easy enough to make one woman disappear, mix the kill in with a run of DOA convenient accidents, and have no questions asked. Craige decided to sleep on it and see if he felt any different in the morning,

but he quickly changed his mind. He dialed Terri's office first thing.

Irene answered, "Good morning, Trust Department. Mrs. Stanley's office. May I help you?"

"This is Craige Ingramme," Craige said. "I need to speak with her." Craige was unsure who to trust in the bank, and it would be Terri who paid for his misjudgment.

Irene melted at the sound of his voice.

She stammered, "Mrs. Stanley stepped out for a moment." She would just die if he ever wanted to talk to her. "May I have her return your call?" She tried anything to keep him on the line. "She shouldn't be much longer."

"Have her call me as soon as she returns," Craige replied.

"I certainly shall." Her eyes were limpid.

Craige turned back to the spread sheets on the table. Less than fifteen minutes later, his phone rang.

"Ingramme," Craige answered.

"Irene said you called. You find something?" Her feelings were ambiguous. She wondered what he had discovered.

"Not over the phone," Craige said.

One of the cloak-and-dagger main rules—never discuss business on open lines. Aside from other things, it was one reason Craige trusted her.

"Can you get away?" Craige asked.

"Yes," Terri said. "Where?"

"My place," Craige said. His seriousness caught her by surprise.

She glanced at her watch, "Forty-five minutes?" She bit her lip.

"Don't tell anyone, not even Irene."

She listened to directions to Moccasin Hollow—take Middleton-Heyward Boulevard and the Old Jackson Highway. He hadn't wasted any time. His words had unnerved her.

"I'll be back later, I've got something I must take care of," She hollered to Irene over her shoulder.

Irene didn't have to be told. She could tell that they were having an affair, and she was pea green with envy, wishing she was the one.

As Terri drove, she bit her lip between her teeth. Irene would wet her pants if she knew Craige was meeting her for the second time in as many days. Terri tried to push away the parts of her life he had awakened, parts that she'd pushed into their own compartment that be-

longed to another life. She couldn't unsnarl the spinster-think of thinking of both men at the same time. She and Paul had talked about what
the other should do if either were gone.

She murmured to herself, "Why shouldn't you enjoy the company
of a man ... especially this one?"

Yet guilt stood there and wouldn't move. A tide of Paul fluxed
through her on shimmering iridescent hues. She missed him dreadfully.

*****

As Craige arranged the clutter of McGiffern papers according to
certain dates, all sorts of weeds took root in his suspicions.

It finally got through his thick skull that he was deaf, dumb and
blind. Craige was making this an uphill tackle and even dumber by
doing it alone, especially with some of the best help he could want
right at his fingertips. He flipped through his dog-eared phone book,
came to Frank's Stone Mountain name, main number and his fax. Craige
then fed the papers through his fax and grabbed the phone, hoping his
SEAL buddy lawyer wasn't wrapped up in court. The slow tock of
Grannie's grandfather clock by the front door marked the time that
had gone by as he listened to his phone ring.

It was answered on the third ring, "Fescher Law office."

"Is Francis in?" Craige asked.

Officious, the voice on the other line didn't recognize his voice nor
the name, she asked, "Who?"

Craige asked, too brusquely, "Is this Francis Fescher's office?" Rush-
ing in when he wanted to get something done fast was one of his bad
habits, which made people break against him.

Accordingly, the receptionist asked, "May I have your name?"

"Is he in?" Craige pushed.

"He's with a client," she said. "May I take a message?"

"Put me on hold. Ask him if there's a better time for Peadinger to
call back."

"Pardon?" She sounded puzzled.

Agitated, Craige repeated the name and said, "Just tell him."

Craige knew he was being pushy, but he didn't need to give his
creepings more time.

She balked. This certainly wasn't a client, and she wasn't about to permit some screwball to pull a fast one. Handling situations was part of her job, yet something about this one told her it was neither nut nor joke.

She said, "Hold please." And punched the Intercom.

Frank grabbed it and answered sounding gruff, "Yes?" He had left instructions not to be disturbed.

"I apologize, Mr. Fescher," she said, "but there's this gentleman on the line. He insists I ask you. It's a funny name, Peadinger ... something like that. I told him you were in conference. He wants to know when to call back. Would you like for me to get any further information?"

"No," Frank chuckled. "I'll take it." He excused himself from the couple sitting across the ornate, carved, oak desk. "This won't take long," he added before jabbing the small blinking light.

"You ol' scudder!" He said with a big grin. "You stayin' out of trouble?" The ever-honed, cultivated, upcountry, affable talk was a smoke screen that disarmed more than a few courtroom adversaries.

"Trying not to get caught," Craige said. "I faxed you some trust documents, copies ought to be getting there about now."

Craige spotted Terri's yellow sports car easing up the drive.

"I've already looked at them," Frank said.

The scheme he laid out gave Craige a chuckle and took his breath away. It would jar a lot of jaws.

*****

Lucky was already sniffing Terri's car by the time Craige came out onto the porch. She opened her door, her skirt stretched up as one foot and well-turned ankle stepped out. Who could miss the long, well-shaped legs? As she petted Lucky, Craige's gaze slid to her waist; her slender neck; the light suffusing a haloed, golden, glow of her aquiline face; full, pasteled lips; a long-legged, sensational creature promising the world. He was having all manner of uncivilized thoughts about her. He gripped the wood railing hard—a forked-horned urge squeezing his guts, stripping away everything, wanting to inhale everything about her, his whole body engorged with a life of its own. He tried shoving his feelings to the back burner and wished he hadn't slipped

into his lounge-about denims. Pressing against the porch railing, he prayed to heaven that he could stop it before she noticed. She was a bright sun ray in his hustle-n-bustle universe. He dredged up what determination he could muster, his night-mulish phantasm intertwined with her.

She stopped at the bottom of the wide steps and scuffed Lucky's chin. "You are a nice one." His long, wet tongue was slurping her hand. "Wish I had a place big enough for a dog and a horse. I miss having horses, and Jeffrey's always wanted a dog."

Damn, a husband, boyfriend ... Craige didn't like that. He questioned, "Jeffrey?"

"My son," she said, ruffling Lucky's ear one, last time. "A high-school senior soon to be off to college. Sometimes more than I can keep up with and never boring."

Craige held the door open. She didn't look old enough to have a son ready for college.

In the kitchen, Craige asked, "Coffee?" He was already refilling his cup from his well-used aluminum perker.

"No," she said. "Thank you." She put her purse on the sofa. "Coffee gives me jitters. I drink it much too strong." Then she spotted the papers spread on the table.

"Me too," Craige said as he took a swallow.

"After Paul came back from Greece, he taught me to like strong coffee," she stated.

She slipped off her grey suit jacket, straightened the sleeves and laid it over her purse. She'd shopped six months trying to find the simple, straight, two-piece suit, which she could dress up or down, perfect for the office or evening socials.

"Paul?" Craige asked.

He'd been right—this one couldn't be alone, not a looker like her.

"My husband," she answered.

His heart plummeted right through the floor, yet Craige caught a sudden sadness in her eyes.

"I'll never forget the first time I saw him in his dress uniform," she winsomely continued. "The picture of a Marine recruiting poster. He was a Major ... killed during special operations."

"Sorry to hear that," Craige said. "Lots of good men die for the right cause but the wrong reasons."

Craige poured another cup of reboiled brew from the unwashed pot that was off limits even to his maid—she even badgered him about not letting her clean it. He leaned against the counter top, eyes over the cup rim as he sipped, couldn't take himself away from her. Her pale cream, raw silk blouse softened the lines of her suit, brought out the color of her hair and her elegant, simple, straight skirt suggested but didn't reveal.

She radiated class, always one of his turn-ons. His gaze traveled from waist to butt to calves carved by the not-too high heels and finally to legs molded by perfect curves that begged to be stroked. He could dream of her skin that promised much. His imagination gained momentum. He slowly set his cup down, senses turbulent with the utter mystique of her. From experience, he knew it was the quiet ones where rip tides ran deep and fast. Was it the mother in her that made her so poised? Perhaps it was being the widow of a uniformed man who died for his country? He wondered about her husband, and at the same time, felt the impulse to gently encircle this exquisite persona, pull her into me, take her lips with mine and discover all of her. She noticed.

"What was your 'don't tell Irene' all about?" Terri asked.

"Sit down." Craige pulled out a chair for her. "Hear me out on this." He sat and leaned toward her. "You may have a problem that's my fault. You'll be receiving a court order by special courier."

Her lips parted. "Court order?" Her words were more of a gasp.

Craige continued, "From a Stone Mountain lawyer." The room grew quiet. "No later than tomorrow, if Frank works as quick as usual."

"What about?" Terri asked. This legal dodge surprised her, and coming from him didn't soften the abrupt bluntness it would have at the bank.

"The order will cover all McGiffern Trust documents, assets, cash, and every investment Theosia had," Craige said. "Certified copies will be left with the bank, but the bank will no longer be involved in day-to-day management of McGiffern assets."

The news took her breath away. "My boss will hit the roof," She said, startled by his swiftness.

"It's likely to get more than your boss's attention," Craige said. "The bank has its own legal staff to cover their backside. You don't." His night-stalker, cunning intent was to protect her. "And you're the

one who needs a safeguard. This way, it's out of the bank's hands."

"It will look as though I went behind their backs," Terri said. "I simply don't do things that way."

"It will have my name on it as trustee. That way, the proverbial cat's out of the bag, and if there's a problem, there's no way it should be kept quiet. I don't want anyone tampering with evidence, and I'd rather apologize for being hasty instead of regretting that I had. I don't want anyone destroying any smoking guns or making the paper trails disappear. If you were picked to be the pigeon, the court order gives you legal protection. Anything done will be over my signature as trustee, the accounts stay in your department, but all fiduciary transactions will undergo an audit independent of the bank, which means all past or present monies moved or converted will be looked at. The bank doesn't have to like it, but it safeguards all trust assets, and as acting-executor, I've authorized Theosia's will to be placed into an ex-officio probate with you appointed as the bank's co-executor representative. Frank said he'd fax me the details. He's always been a good sounding board. Anytime any of their guys ended up in a tight spot, he always came up with ways to get us out of it. He suggested this, said it's seldom used. It gets everyone's attention, keeps everything on the up-and-up, makes me the patsy and gets you out of the line of fire."

Terri said, "It will certainly give everyone something to talk about." She was not happy with it, but she understood.

"They'll do that regardless," Craige said.

"My first big account, a legal mess." Her eyes flashed. "I'm not sure whether I'm relieved or upset at what you've done, maybe a bit of both."

Craige said, "You did make sure my signature was on file as trustee?"

"Yes," she answered. "The bank was interim executor until your signature was submitted at probate." She was uncertain where this was taking them. "I want to see that audit."

"Me too," Craige said. "Only thing the court order does is ..."

"Did you have to get a lawyer?" She interrupted, trying to stay calm.

"Without a court order," Craige said, "the bank could've claimed confidentiality, prevented access to any material or worse, could've shred-ded documents."

Craige hadn't wanted to upset her, but he'd known it probably

would. Having done this didn't make him feel good, but he wasn't sorry it had been done.

"That's one reason I wanted you out of the office," Craige said.

"One reason?" Terri asked. "I'm not sure I want to know the others."

"I didn't want you in the bank when the court order was delivered, where someone might have wanted to question you," Craige flushed. "I didn't want that happening, and the best way to prevent that was to get you away from your office."

"I haven't been comfortable since I began digging into this," Terri said. "The whole situation seems so underhanded."

"Bastards count on honest folks playing by the rules," Craige said, cutting to the bone of it. "It gives them a free pass at your jugular. Let 'em squirm, it makes them more vulnerable."

"I have a son to raise and debts to pay," Terri said. "I need the job."

"With your background you could have any job you wanted," Craige assured her.

Craige was trying to make her feel better, or maybe he was trying to make himself feel better about his tactics.

"I wish I was sure of that," she said.

Craige replied, "Using lawyers may not be the most harmonious way, but it sure as hell is the safest. Always keep a crook off balance. Give them enough rope, they'll laugh at you for being stupid."

His counterterrorist training stirred his paranoia with all the nightfire if and maybe recon reasons he had seen go wrong. His heart begged that she understood.

Terri sounded irritated as she said, "I don't know whether I should thank you or punch you in the nose."

"Why did you decide to let me know?" Craige asked.

Craige could always fall back on his doing this because of his commitment to Theosia, but it was that and more, much more, and they both knew it.

She said, a bit too quickly, "You were the trustee." She caught the quick wince at the corner of his eye. Then quickly said, "That's not true, and I shouldn't have said it. I'm sorry. You didn't go behind my back, and I did ask you to help. Theosia McGiffern used the bank her whole life," she said, knowing she was waltzing around her heart-truth. "Oh, I don't know." She was flustered. "I needed someone who wouldn't

turn queasy if things got difficult."

Very quietly Craige said, "Frank doesn't think you're wrong about the accounts, but—"

"But what?" Terri said.

"Theosia had recently changed some of her accounts," Craige said. "She told me she wanted to show me what she'd done. Anyone else would've made sure they got with her, but we both let it slid. No one expected her to die, least of all me."

"She was ninety-three," Terri interrupted.

"A young ninety-three," Craige smiled, remembering some of the talks between him and Theosia. "I hope I'm doing that well at ninety. I should've gotten with her." Melancholy painted his heart. "I intend doing what Theosia wanted, and I'm faced with what could happen to you. Without proof we have nothing, the ones behind this are no amateurs. Without the court order they had a wide-open playing field. The threat of exposure can drive a wolf pack to take some desperate gambles, and money can buy a powerful lot of truth and death. Garland Holton's partners wouldn't bat an eye burying any proof along with any incidental problems. Lives could be in danger, yours and anyone close to you or anyone who knows too much. Going to Frank was the best protection I could give Theosia and you. I've trusted Frank Fescher with my life more than a few times." His eyes were on her. "Anything's possible." Craige took a slow breath. "When you first talked to me about this, like you, I assumed it was sloppy bookkeeping. It's not." He watched the color drain from her face. "When I talked with Garland Holton, he got real uncomfortable, and it left me feeling he wanted me to think it was all routine. I didn't give him your name, but it won't take long to figure it. My guess is he's in this up to his walnut-framed law diploma, and I'll stake my hide it involves Theosia's will and her properties." His green eyes were battlefield luminous. "Just a hunch but a damn strong one. There's lots neither of us thought about."

Terri shivered as if some child's bogeyman had sneaked full-blown into the daylight. A mother's protective ire rose, Jeff had lost enough.

She said, "You have a reputation for being rough if you have to."

Craige set his cup down. "My reputation is that I splurge on imported Scotch." He said, trying to lighten the mood. "I've had good training by some of the best, roughest, dependable professionals who I

wouldn't want to go up against." The air was thick between us. "I can hold my own." He was wondering if he should tell her. "It's not my style unless I'm left with no choice. Brute force in its way can be effective—makes backbiters run for cover—but it's not as useful as the step-by-step drudgery of good planning. People shy away when they see push-and-shove, rough stuff, none of us care for that, but it happens." His expression was Stone Mountain hard. "No telling how far this reaches." Sinewed wrists and corded arms and shoulders gave the impression of primed and loaded power. "No outsider could pull it off. It was done over an extended period by party or parties with access to Theosia's records. Either no one looked or didn't care and just maybe could be the reason Royce Sedgewicke is dead."

"I thought he died of a heart attack," Terri blanched.

"That's what everyone was supposed to think." Craige's voice dropped. "I just pray Theosia's death was natural. If not, I really let her down."

Terri's hand trembled at the soft skin of her throat. The throb at her temple was barely below the crisp edge of pain.

"I shouldn't have snapped at you," she said. "What do you want me to do?" She asked, brushing back her wavy, black hair.

Craige said, "Make sure you're safe. You have glass in your front and back doors?"

Terri frowned, "The patio French doors and the top half of the front door are glass."

"What about ground floor windows?" Craige asked.

"You're serious." Terri was unnerved. "You believe they'd go that far?" She instantly knew it was a dumb question. He reminded her of how impatient Paul would get when his deployment orders came down the pipe, and he was going to be away.

Craige said, "Make sure all doors are key-locked inside and out with double-length key dead bolts." His eyes locked with hers. "Change the locks if they're not, and make a habit of never leaving the keys in them. Check all windows. The house have a security system?"

"It was already there when we bought the house." Terri said. "But I've never used it."

"Get it checked," Craige said. "And make sure Jeff uses it."

"That could be a problem," she said, "'specially when he's home alone. He trusts everyone."

Harshly, Craige said, "Make sure. And be prepared for something else."

Terri stammered, "What?"

For the first time in her life, Terri felt exposed with no way to protect her son, instinctively she moved into Craige—his shoulders stretching so wide, so protective. Terri felt she was looking up the side of a living cliff.

"If Holton contacts you," Craige said with his arms around her, "I want to know."

His breath caught. She felt like molten fire against him.

*****

Verging on a double-barrel, caffeine-nicotine fit, Irene pushed through the door into the employee smokers lounge. Cigarette and lighter ready, she stopped at the coffeemaker.

Beth was fiddling with the TV as she said, "Hi Irene. You almost missed our soaps."

"Hey, Hallie Beth," she said as she flicked her lighter and sucked the glowing red cigarette. "How's your day going?" Her eyes squinched in the smoke as she poured half-and-half into her cup.

"This economy kick has everyone uptight," Beth said.

"You don't see the fat cats cutting their expense accounts. Got everyone edgy not knowing what to expect. Who needs this crap? I'm thinking of looking for another job."

Irene sipped, "Heard you got married." Commercials blared on the TV. "Congratulations." She added and took a drag off the filter tip. "Married life treating you OK?" She took a swallow of her cream with a little coffee.

"Going great," said Beth.

"Med school rough on Gordie?"

"Lots of things are rough on Gordie," Beth offhandedly said. She was catty-snippy as usual.

"You and new hubby doing all right?" Irene finished her cigarette and drained her coffee.

"Never saw anything so great about being married," she answered and flicked at her mascara.

"Gotta go." Irene crushed the lipstick-smeared butt in the over-

flow ashtray. "See you later." She didn't like this soap anyhow.

"Yeh," Beth called over her shoulder, "Later."

On the elevator, Irene thought of Beth's daddy and his two-state automobile dealerships—all that money to buy anything Beth's heart desired—new car every year, new wardrobes. Somehow, Beth never seemed happy. Irene had heard how Daddy was keeping them in spending money.

*****

Craige sat in his 4by, windows down, hardly noticed the oppressive mugginess beading his chest and trickling down his neck. He'd skimmed the death certificate the clerk had just handed me, hoping against hope he didn't face the prospect of Theosia's murder.

DECEDENT'S NAME: Theosia Ambarella McGIFFERN. He browsed her death certificate—time/date of death, the coroner's signature. Uneasiness flailed at him. At least he'd found no Department of Health red flag on her case. Someone hadn't bothered to find out that Theosia named him as trustee 17 years ago in her last codicil change. Craige's inbred dislike for Holton jumped right up in front of his brain. Probate court was an estate lawyer's pet turf. He was perfectly capable of trying some shenanigan to call her will into question, submit it to probate and alter the trust documents. Holton's clients were mainly corporate cases with little to do with wills or estates, but he had plenty law school classmates who could handle anything for him.

The clerk took the original death certification and made copies. Craige had noticed smudged entries across some dates and several blank entries. The smudges weren't apparent on his copies but the names were. He'd talk to Fred, but for the moment, keep it between them so as not to tip his hold cards, keep them on the razor's edge.

# Chapter 7

**B**arry decided it had to be away from downtown, no crowds and no bars. He finally settled on the airport. He parked on the far side of the three-story, buff, brick hotel with its squat, brick columns and open-air veranda, a safe walking distance from terminal and security patrols. Predawn, ground-hugging, night fog rose out of the river bottom bayous and settled in thick blankets across the runways, around hangars and service buildings, smothering the parking lots in smoky, thick mantles of grey mists. Flights were already delayed, the runway lights were only hazy, fuzzy blobs. The night shifts were changing—coming and going in ones and twos. Try as he might, Barry couldn't shake a nagging barb akin to boredom, like it was one more plodding day at the office. He watched several, picked an older one and waited till she crossed the lot toward her car. It was too risky to draw this out. He took solace in the misery he was saving her. He didn't want to see her eyes, so he came from behind with his baseball bat.

In that split, final instant, she must have sensed something as the bat was raised. The only sound was a soft, mushy thud, and her body folded onto the ground. Her cares were gone forever, but Barry couldn't stop hitting, again and again, her legs wouldn't quit jerking. He pummeled her until bone, flesh and hair became indiscernible marmalade. He scattered rainbow capsules, one near her loose shoe and its splayed

foot, poked two under her shoulder and another next to her purse.

"That's enough," he muttered. He didn't want the cops to think the drugs were planted.

He'd enjoyed doing that harlot in the parking deck, she needed killing, but it pissed him off when her picture appeared in the paper for everyone to see. She hadn't rated headlines or a picture. He looked at the grisly club in his hand, the meaty flecks on his collar and sleeve and decided this had not been done right. Now he'd have to do another one till he got it right, but from now on, he'd do it in front of his "Grim Reaper" with its skull and gleaming lipless teeth. Besides, it didn't matter. No one cared what happened to a riffraff cleaning woman.

Next morning's headlines were more to his liking. WOMAN BEATEN TO DEATH filled the top half of the front page. Barry drank his orange juice, munched his toasted bagel and smiled, thinking how he might work in his carping wife. Breakfast tasted better than it had been in a long while. He relaxed during a leisurely drive to the office and strolled to the deposit box, the small round vial a beckoning starburst beacon. He'd show them.

*****

Eric was in the shower. Beth stretched across the bed and sulked. She couldn't forget that pair of oval, garnet earrings Mrs. Uptown Terri Stanley had worn that night, taking over like she was bitch special.

"Piss on her and her elegant designer gowns," Beth grumbled. "I'd like to smack her across her smart mouth. I'll fuck her Carolina boyfriend, show her who's top of the heap." She tossed and turned, madder than ever.

She dug the checkbook out of her purse. Daddy had put money in her checking account yesterday, but she might have to call him again. Those two new outfits hadn't made her feel a bit better. Daddy would have to get her another charge card, her others were maxed out. When the shower cut off, she lazed onto her back in the grayness of the bedroom. Her manicured nails idled the frill of her peignoir, its lace prickling her nipples. Eric came out, his head buried in the towel shuffling it through his hair. She said in her baby doll wheedle, "I told Gordie to come here." Her hands were busy running up Eric's thigh.

Eric let his towel down and slumped across her. "Gonna be a great weekend."

*****

Traffic was light, at least leaving the office late avoided rush hour. As she drove, Terri's thought turned to her misgivings about Craige's Stone Mountain lawyer friend and the court orders. She punched the automatic garage opener, the door rose as she pulled up her slanted drive and noticed the flower beds and splotches of lawn needed water. In the kitchen, she spotted Jeffrey's scrawled note clipped on the fridge.

"—gone water skiing with Byrd. Can he eat supper with us? His mom said it was OK but to ask you."

She knew the two would ski till the last glimmer of daylight, likely as not hit one of the burger hangouts on the way home and still be hungry when they rolled in. She took a large package of ground meat and a package of burger buns out of the freezer, shoved the meat into the microwave and punched defrost. As she spread the buns on a cookie sheet, ready for the broiler, she questioned if one package was enough for the pair of bottomless pits.

An hour later, Jeff and Byrd roared in and scarfed down on her Sloppy Joes. Terri smiled, Paul liked them too. She went to her bedroom and started folding the load of clothes from the dryer. Through the open window, she smelled the faint fragrance of the Confederate jasmine Paul had planted. It reminded her of his lean form stretched next to where they slept and the last time she and Paul made love. Craige's towering, inexorable maleness abruptly rose before her. Her feelings became mixed, feelings she wished she wasn't having. In a wash of guilt, she shook Craige's image away and walked into her bath.

She murmured to herself, "Terri Stanley, what is the matter with you?"

She heard Byrd leaving as she turned on her bath water and added a splash of lilac bath oil. She slid into the soothing, hot water; rested her head against the tub; basked in the steaming, nosegay immersion and let the day's quandaries never-never land waft gone. Except it didn't work. Her hands played with the soothing, fragrant lilac bubbles and her skin heated where Craige's touch had scorched her. Terri's cheeks were blushing beet crimson as Craige's Michelangelo-likeness rose naked. Her gaze riveted to his stout thighs, to every glorious inch of him. Terri's universe hushed, expectant, spinning with two faces to the im-

maculate maleness coming toward her. Her nipples puckered, first Paul, then Craige. Her fingers dallied with the bubbles, pitapatted them in her belly button, but the face she kept seeing was Craige.

She blinked, "God, Terri Lee, get a grip. You have a grown son, and you're acting like some—" the word "schoolgirl" almost whispered across her lips.

Her sleep became a fitful dream, a fractured phantasmagoria of uniforms and funerals, of getaways and furtive rendezvous that wouldn't go away.

The next morning, Terri hardly settled at her desk when Irene buzzed, and said, "There's a Mister Holton with Garland, Garland and Crayes on line three. You want me to take a message?"

"No," she said, "I'll take it." Her stomach quivered, as she punched three. "Good morning, this is Terri Stanley."

Holton said, too pleasant, "Good morning, Honey. Craige Ingramme stopped by my office the day before yesterday."

He paused, expecting a response and got flustered when she said nothing.

He then asked, "You know anything about that?"

Terri's intuition jangled loud and clear, knowing she shouldn't have been taken aback by his patronizing, cheap familiarity or his total lack of manners. *You sonofabitch,* she thought, *most certainly did not like his "honey" one bit.* Bad manners may be more habit than deliberate, but in his case, it was considerably more of the latter. There was something in his voice, it was more than his doing his job, but her best gambit was to listen and find out what Holton was after.

She said yes in her best business voice—two could fish in the same pond.

Her one word answer rattled Holton's good, old charm approach.

Holton said, "Ingramme wanted me to look into some things for a client."

"How may I help?" Terri asked, bull's eye legal. She'd never met Garland Holton, even if half the cocktail talk was part truth, she didn't particularly want to. It was no secret she was in charge of most of the bank's trust business, but Garland Holton was after more, he was on a meddling expedition. Terri continued, to the point, "If he's the same Ingramme you're talking about, I believe he's one of the bank's customers."

Holton's silence lengthened. She wasn't about to tell this mealy mouth anything and sure glad Craige had warned her.

He finally said, "His answering machine is on at his home. I thought maybe I might catch him at your office. You expecting him any time?"

She said, "I'm not aware of any appointments," thinking you pompous ass. "One moment, I'll have my secretary check."

Holton had seen Stanley, she was one of those real lookers with no brains, got where she was with a toothy smile and a promising Marilyn Monroe wiggle. Scoring with that type was never a problem. He knew what those kind of bimbos wanted and how to give it to them.

Holton said, "If it's no problem, I'd sure appreciate a little help from you, Sweetie."

"Certainly," she said.

Terri stabbed HOLD. "Honey" was coarse enough, the "sweetie" about ripped it. She tightly screwed down her social niceties, wanting to shut him up with a "hold it right there" in his ear, then hang up. She remembered Paul laughing once after they returned from some on-base affair and her gentle but pointed honesty to some wife.

Paul had said, "Honey, you knew she couldn't handle the truth."

"Well," Terri had replied, "she asked, and there was no point in cream coating words."

She left Holton on hold as she dialed Craige, got the machine and left a message. She waited a few more minutes, then came back on line.

"Mr. Holton," she said.

"Right here, Honey."

"Mister Ingramme isn't scheduled with anyone in this office." Holton's familiarity was still grating. "May I help with anything else?"

"Nope. Maybe me and you'll talk later, Honey." He hung up.

Terri buzzed Irene.

"Yes, Mrs. Stanley?" Irene answered.

"Irene, has anyone requested the McGiffern files lately?"

"Funny you should ask," Irene said. "A request came in last Friday." Terri heard papers rustling. "I meant to tell you."

"From whom?"

"I never saw her before, probably a temp hired till we get through this audit," Irene said. "She did have an interdepartment routing chit, but when I told her you had those files, she didn't say anything. She just left."

"And there was no follow-up request?"

"Not that I know of. At least not with me." Irene continued, "Want me check on it?"

"No," Terri answered. She thought for a moment, then said, "By court order the McGiffern records are to be kept locked in my private office. If anyone wants to see them, I want signatures, a valid ID and written permission from the trustee. They can use our conference room, and none of the portfolios are to leave this office."

Irene stammered, "What do I say to them?"

"Tell them to see me," Terri said. "The files stay in this office."

Troubled crow's-feet furrowed at the corners of Terri's eyes. Her dislike for Holton rapidly became a strong distrust. He was digging for answers, but more important, she wondered who he was digging for?

Irene interrupted as she said, "Don't forget the Staff meeting this morning. You want the restrictions on the McGiffern accounts added to the agenda?"

"Not for this meeting," Terri said. The situation was sticky enough.

Late that afternoon Jeff called. "Mom, Byrd and me are going water skiing at Clark's Hill."

"You two be careful out on the river this late." Terri cautioned as she glanced at her desk clock. "It's nearly five."

"That's still more'n two hours of daylight," Jeff said. "Byrd's dad left their ski boat at Modoc. It'll take us less than thirty minutes to get there."

Terri said, "Tell Byrd I said to be careful."

"Mom!" Jeff protested and rolled his eyes. "Byrd doesn't drive that fast."

"I didn't say that," she said, imagining Jeff's look. "Byrd and you get to talking, your CDs turned up so loud you couldn't hear it thunder. It's other drivers that worry me. Besides, it will be dark by the time you two get back."

Jeff asked, "Can I stay the night at Byrd's?"

"Has he asked Marlene? Or is this you and Byrd's idea?" She inquired.

She and Marlene often felt amused on how their sons tried playing them off against one another.

"His mom said it was OK if it was OK with you."

"I suppose," Terri answered. "You be sure and call me when you

get back to Byrd's house. I'll have the whole South Carolina Highway Patrol out looking if I don't hear from you."

"Mom—" he said like he was still a kid, "we can take care of ourselves."

She said, "Yes, I know, but I won't be able to shut my eyes till I hear from you. Neither will Marlene. I want to know you're both safe."

She wanted to tell him she loved him, but he was at that shying away stage—wanted none of Mom's mushy stuff. When she did give him a kiss, he'd cut his eyes at her and mumble, but she could tell he liked it.

Jeff said, "I'll call."

As he hung up, Jeff thought how Mom trusted him—that he already had a lot of independence, his set of keys, and she didn't pick if he came in a little late from a Friday night date or middle-of-the-week team practice. She had let him know that if he ever needed the emergency $100 mad money, it was under the jardinière. Jeffrey David Stanley knew Mom and Dad loved him. Some of the kids at school weren't so lucky. Their parents were never home. After school, they engage in sex, drug and parties, while their parents didn't care where they were, what they did or who they did it with. Word was out around school. Some of his classmates were bragging how their dads were renting them motel rooms for after-graduation parties.

Jeff missed going camping, fishing, soccer or ball games with his dad, their man-to-man talks. There were a lot of things they talked about. He missed those times with his dad, but his mom was extra special.

*****

Irene stuck her head in. "It's quarter after five. You intend working all night?"

"Jeff's off skiing with a friend," Terri said. "It made a good time to catch up. I seem to get more done when there's no hustle and bustle distractions. I won't be long. See you in the morning."

"I'll tell Mitchell you're here," Irene said. "He's on lobby night shift this week. He'll check on you. 'Nite." She grabbed her purse and ran to catch the elevator.

Terri returned two calls, then noticed one of the office Stenos at

the coffeemaker changing the filter and adding coffee and water for tomorrow. She initialed the routing slip with the attached photocopies for the auditors and then emptied her e-mail inbox. She was signing the last of the letters Irene had left for her when the corner of her eye caught one of the phone lines blinking and then ringing on Irene's desk. After a bit, it stopped and almost as soon started again. It did the same thing a third time. It wasn't Jeff, he had her private number. Then she realized one line flashed busy, and a few seconds later the second one on the same trunk began to ring. Her first impulse was to let it ring, probably some arrangement to get around the "no personal calls" rule, a husband, boyfriend or both. It kept ringing. Terri picked up.

"Trust Department, Terri Stanley," she answered.

There was no answer, only a still silence except she could hear someone breathing. At first she figured it was a phone prank until she realized it hadn't come in on an outside line.

It was coming from inside the building. The skin on the back of her neck tingled, the sounds of the empty offices and vacant halls somehow edged with a penetrating keenness, the rush of air from the vent became louder to her ears. Answering with her name was second nature, but she wanted to kick herself for doing it.

"May I help you?" she asked.

There was an abrupt click, the line disconnected, the dial tone buzzed in her ear. An oily seed of fear sprouted, the dark center of her pupils grew wide. She reached for her keys, walked passed Irene's desk through the reception area and made sure the outer doors were locked. She went back to her office and found herself staring at the closed supply room door in Irene's office and wondered what lurked behind it. After a while, she felt truly silly. There were no phones in there. The call could have come from any office. In that moment she wished Craige were there. She looked at her phone but fought the impulse to call him. She pictured herself all alone in the emptiness of the tall, black, mirrored building.

"Damn if I'll be boxed in," she muttered and dialed the lobby.

Mitchell Worley picked up. "Lobby."

"Mitch, this is Terri Stanley up in the trust department." She threw quick glances toward the empty foyer.

"Yeh, Mis' Stanley," he said. "Mis' Rozkovsky said you'd be working late."

"Has anyone checked into the building since five?"

"Not unless they used their key and come through the parking deck on four."

Spidery tentacles webbed around her. Terri found herself wanting out of the grating, murmuring building with its invisible soughing bumps. A child's moment crossed her mind—sheltered inside Daddy's strong arms, huddled against him, listening to gales howl off the Pacific, whipping through the valleys, filling a seven-year-old girl's night dreams with wailing ogres lurking to snatch her away to secret lairs.

She continued, "Mitchell, I'm finished up here." She forced her wits to move slower. "Could you walk me to my car?"

"Be my pleasure," he brightened. "You stay right there, Mrs. Stanley. I'll be right up."

Everyone talked about how special Mrs. Stanley was, always polite, spoke to everyone. Not like some of the others, and she sure was a fine-looking woman. Mitchell couldn't wait to tell everyone she asked him to walk her to her car. He straightened his collar and tie, adjusted his official guard's cap above his bushy eyebrows and grizzled, round face.

Terri was truly relieved to see his salt-and-pepper hair when she heard him pecking his ring of keys on the outer office, glass door.

He stuck his head in and said, "You're sure working late, Mrs. Stanley."

"Mitchell, I certainly appreciate this," she said.

"No problem," he answered with a big smile. "Other guard is spotting me at the lobby station." He was pleased as all get out to help Mrs. Stanley.

"Nothing here that can't wait till tomorrow," Terri said.

"One thing at a time. Only way a body can work, one thing at a time," He agreed while locking the outer door behind them. "Now'days folks don't take enough time to look around and enjoy how much we got to be thankful for." The elevator he'd locked open for her was standing ready. "Too much TV, rush here to yonder so they can hurry somewhere else. Don't like that no better when they get where they think they wanted to go." He inserted his key, and punched 4. "I'm not so sure modern is a bit better."

He hefted his uniform britches, last night's catsup spot still on one leg, a burly steak and potatoes stomach straining at his belt. The elevator opened into the big, spooky parking deck. Terri was thankful

her car was just across from them.

"Thank you, Mitch," she said as she unlocked her car.

She climbed in, rolled down the window and said, "See you to-morrow," and locked her door.

"Yes Ma'am," he said. "You have a pleasant evening, Ma'am."

As she navigated the dwindling traffic, she tried to reason away letting herself get so rattled. Amused by her silliness at nothing, she was almost calm until she walked into her kitchen and froze. With keys clutched in blanched knuckles, she couldn't believe the disar-rayed chaos of shelves, books, papers, drawers, dishes, cushions, clos-ets, towels, kitchen, dining room, bedroom, mattresses, pillows and towels from the bathrooms. She sensed a noxious, prowling nearness ready to pounce. She slowly backed out through the laundry room, through the open garage and onto her driveway.

Neighborhood kids played down the street. Fading dusk light grew dim as her eyes fastened on the dark rectangle of the laundry door in the cavern garage. She was relieved that Jeff was at Byrd's. This was no kid's prank. Terri sat in her locked car. As daylight faded, she thought about going to a motel but discarded that idea. She couldn't leave the house open. Besides, being in a motel alone, in a strange place, was not something she wanted. Fury went side by side with her battered peace of mind. Her privacy was violated. Anger grew, the calls at the office, whomever had been on the line was making sure she was still in the office. Someone had been watching or following her. Holton popped into her mind. She didn't want to think what could have happened if Jeff had been home. A sigh of relief escaped through her that he wasn't as she pulled out her cell phone. She refused to give way to tears as she phoned Craige. She prayed she wouldn't get his answering machine.

"Ingramme," Craige answered.

"Can you come to the house?" Terri sounded disturbed.

"What's the matter?" Craige could sense trouble all over her voice.

"You'll understand when you get here," she said.

"Are you all right?"

"I'm not hurt," she answered. "I'll be in my car. Please hurry and don't hang up, I need the sound of your voice."

"On my way."

Soon after Craige said that, he bolted out the door. He broke a few speed limits, pulled in behind her and was hardly out of his "four-by"

before Terri was in his arms, shivering as she clung to him.

"I'm so glad you're here," She said as she held him tighter.

"From your tone on the phone, I knew something was wrong."

Craige tried to keep his thoughts aboveboard with this whirlwind of a woman pressing into him. She calmed down, and after she explained, he felt guilty. His dodge and feint strategy with Frank had upset someone.

"You call the sheriff?" Craige asked.

"No," she said. "I wasn't thinking straight."

"Stay out here, I'll check inside," Craige said.

She watched him disappear into the house, and the shocking dread oozed back. Someone could be waiting inside. She felt relieved when he came out.

"No one inside," Craige said. "But the place is a mess. You don't need to stay here tonight."

"Jeff expects me to be here," she said. "He's spending the night at Byrd's."

"You should call him, let him know," said Craige.

"He'll know something's wrong, and he's going to be upset," Terri said. "Some of the things they got into were Paul's."

"Of course this will upset him, but he deserves to know."

"Yes ... I want to stay here tonight. I won't be run out of my home."

The whole incident—the phone calls, the break-in—twisted inside her.

Craige said, "After you call Jeff, let's at least get the big pieces out of the way."

Terri pushed away her anger, followed Craige inside, went through the house and turned on every light. She then headed back to the kitchen and called Jeff.

She said to Jeff, "Nothing bad. I'm fine. I'll see you in the morning." She didn't tell him everything.

After she hung up, she said, "I think I'll have a glass of hot milk. Would you like some coffee?"

"Coffee would hit the spot," Craige said.

She added fresh coffee and water. In no time the pan of milk was steaming, and she filled her glass.

She took a sip, softly laughed and said, "It's not funny, but look-

ing around at this mess, the only other thing to do is cry. You think they'll come back?"

"That depends on what they were after."

A moment's frown wrinkled above her eyes.

She said, "I'm glad you're here."

Craige put his arms around her, held her, hadn't intended anything more or maybe he had. He tipped her chin toward him and stopped her words, as their lips met. She tasted wonderful. There was only a moment's resistance on her part.

Something about his gentleness, the softness of his words, his eyes, made her feel safe. Terri melted into the strength of this man. Her arms slid under his, around his shoulders, pulled him tightly to her, then tighter. She lightly caressed the dark russet curls at the nape of his neck, surrendering to whatever he wanted, to what she wanted.

Her touch was like luminous, fragile, summer lightening ripping through him, pulling him deeper, churning his guts with a fire only one thing could extinguish. Craige held her against him, swung her slowly around and laid her across the sofa, his hand flailing to find the lamp switch on the end table. The coffee gurgled, filling the house with its pungent vigor, quickly followed by the red "ready" light. Her warm glass of milk cooled, and the other rooms in the house blazed with light.

# Chapter 8

**W**ho are you!" Jeff Stanley's words thundered.

The gruff, loud words yanked Craige awake, addled his reflexes and wrenched him straight up. He was sprawled awkward on the sofa with blankets slumped away from his bare chest and clumped around his waist.

"What you doing in my house?" Jeff demanded. "Where's my mom?"

Craige's brain sleep fuzzed, night specters snapped his eyes wide open. He was confused. The room was strange, sofa too, besides being the wrong color, wrong lumps—wrong house. Craige was uncertain for that moment where he was and who this was yelling at him. It didn't match anything. His mind scrambled through flashback, jubilee skin romps, except he wasn't hungover. His bare feet hit the floor as he tried to get his bearings. He faced a sun scorched, irate, tousle haired, glowering intense face scrutinizing him like he was his worst enemy.

Jeff Stanley repeated, "I asked you where's my mom? What you doing in my house?" He meant to have his answers.

Craige stood, "Morning." The blanket slouched to the floor, pants, Jockey shorts twisted. He muttered, "You must be Jeffrey."

"I know who I am," man of the house Jeff bristled. "I live here." His fist clenched around a bat.

He glanced around at the disarray from the break-in, then back to

105

this stranger asleep on the sofa where he didn't belong.

Again, Jeff asked, "Who are you, and where's my mom?"

As Craige ran his fingers through tousled hair, he stifled a yawn and noticed the bat Jeff held, remembering how Craige was about Grannie. He decided he'd better do some fast talking. Just then, he was saved by the bell when Terri came into the den in robe and slippers.

She said, "Jeffrey, I didn't hear you come in." Her remark sounded worse than it was meant.

The night came back to him in waves of heat and skin, her lips quivering against his, both of them battling some kind of frenzied resistance as it got hot and hotter for more and more.

A blush flooded her face and neck.

Jeff glanced between me, a half naked outsider asleep in the middle of their plundered home, and his mom.

Craige said, "Excuse me while I freshen up." He grabbed his shirt and headed for the bath.

Craige could almost read Jeff's thoughts. Right now, saying anything more was pointless.

Terri said, "I laid out a new toothbrush. Fresh towels are behind the door, and there's a razor, top drawer on the right."

"Mom, that's where I keep Dad's razor and stuff. Who is he?" His brown eyes flung a ferocious blaze down the hall toward Craige. "What's he doing here? He's acting as though he was right at home. He stay all night? What happened?" He asked without pausing as he looked around at the disarray.

"Someone broke in. They went through everything," Terri said. "It was like this when I got home yesterday from work. I've never felt anything like it, and I was afraid to be here alone."

Jeff sounded hurt as he said, "You could'a called me."

He felt passed over in his own home. Without Dad it was his to protect. His buddies were right when they said he just lived here till he was old enough to move out.

Terri realized how it looked to Jeff. She was caught somewhere between being surprised and the shock of seeing Paul's glowering face in her son. At the time, it had seemed like the best of poor choices. In hindsight, she shouldn't have let it happen but it had.

She said, "I didn't want to stay in a motel in case you called."

With tight jaws, Jeff said, "You could've called Byrd's. You could've stayed there."

This interloper didn't belong in his dad's house. He felt that his father was betrayed. He was Dad's only defender. Jeff somehow sensed it was none of his business, yet somehow it was.

With a forlorn look, Terri found herself uncertain with a son who'd grown into a man without her quite realizing it. She felt a little scared how quick this man-child from her body became the full-blown man with his father's temper. Jeffrey was pulled between his dad and his mom, acting like something he'd never seen before.

"Who is he?" Jeffrey asked once again with another glare toward the bath. "They trash the whole house?"

"Pretty much," Terri said.

"The cops find anything?" Jeff asked.

"I didn't call them."

"But you called him?" Jeff's jaw was tight. "They take anything?"

"Nothing," Terri said. "At least as far as I can tell."

The bathroom door was ajar, and the whine of the razor and the aroma of steam, soap and shampoo filled the air. Terri had never seen such irate rancor in Jeff. She was proud of him and, at the same time, a little unsure. It was her fault. She should have known. He was so much like Paul—testosterone guardian of hearth and womenfolk. It was her place to reassure him, and she wasn't exactly sure how to do that.

Jeff was upset finding this man. He could tell his mom was upset too. He looked around at the clutter and began to sense how this had frightened her. He was certain that it would've been all right if he hadn't gone skiing, hadn't left her alone.

Jeff said, "They hurt you, Mom?" All kinds of feelings stirring.

"I'm fine," she said. "I knew you would be staying at Byrd's, so I worked late. I wasn't here." She tenderly touched his face. "When I came in on this mess, I was upset and angry that anyone would do this, all at the same time. The more I saw what they'd done, the madder I got." Her eyes glittered. "Then it dawned on me how lucky you and I had been. What might've happened if they'd come when you were here alone?" Her fist clenched, nails stabbed her palms. "That's when it frightened me." Her lips became deathly pale. "If anything ever happened to you ..." she stopped. "I didn't want any more strangers

in my house, not the police, not anyone asking questions, making reports, all of this a public record. Didn't want you here because I knew you'd be upset, too." She sighed, "So I called Craige."

Jeff said, "You should've called me, too." The brittleness was gone from his words. "I needed to know."

"You're right. I should have," Terri agreed. "But, if you'd been here, you would've reacted exactly like your father. You've a temper like his, impossible to stop once it's loose." She suppressed a deep shudder. "You could've ended up in the hospital or worse. Nothing in the house is worth that." She fell quiet. "I didn't intend leaving you out. I just didn't want you in harm's way."

"Dad used to say that," Jeff said.

"What?" Not realizing what she'd said.

"Going in harm's way. Dad used to say the same thing. Maybe you didn't call 'cause you didn't want me around." He gave another glance toward the bath.

His true bred Stanley face graded with a slight smile hurt as only love can hurt. Still, she could tell his anger lessened.

"Jeffrey!" Terri said feeling his pain. "You know that isn't true." It wasn't the time to say more. "You're the most important thing in my life." A woman's—a mother's tenderness softened the wounded male. "I miss your father as much as you do." An ache that more than hurt stood between them. "Your father was in the delivery room the day you were born." She smiled with an engaging softness as she continued, "He was so proud he had a son. His whole world brighter." Her words paused. "Jeff, I don't quite know what I'd do if anything—" She stopped, the deadly possibilities too monstrous to put into words.

The shower cut off.

Jeff said, "It surprised me finding a stranger sleeping here."

Terri hugged her son and kissed his cheek, just as Craige came into the room toweling his head. The father's brown eyes in his son glanced between Mom and this man. Jeff blushed, not about to be babied in front of some stranger. A man doesn't show they like stuff like that, but Jeff remembered his dad always seemed to like it when his mom got in that kissy mood. His dad would kiss along the back of his mom's neck, which always meant that they'd go to their bedroom early that night. He'd seen them a couple of times in the kitchen or late at night on the sofa. He never let on. He knew he shouldn't have watched but he had.

Terri caught Jeff's look as a barefooted Craige came into the room.

Craige continued to dry his hair as he said, "That feels better."

Terri said, "Craige, this is my son, Jeffrey. Jeff, I'd like you to meet Craige Ingramme."

"Morning, sir," Jeff said politely and extended his hand. His upbringing denied being rude.

"Morning, Jeff." Craige shook his hand.

Terri said, "Let's see what we can find for breakfast for two hungry men." She headed into the kitchen.

Jeff nodded, "Mr. Ingramme." His grip was firm.

"Call me Craige," Craige said. "Your mother's told me a lot about you."

The firm handshake told him lots about the young man, and it didn't take a genius to figure this son hadn't liked finding him here.

"My dad said I'm not to call grownups by their first name," Jeff said.

Jeff's remark reminded Craige of what Grannie once said, "These ol' bones love you to death, and no matter how many times I have to tan your hide, you gonna learn proper manners."

"Now I do feel old," Craige smiled. "I'm sure your father wouldn't mind if you and I made a deal ... just the two of us."

"I suppose," Jeff said. "My friends call me Jeff."

"Least they didn't wreck the pantry," Terri hollered from the kitchen. "We have homemade maple syrup and fresh butter." The griddle was already sizzling. "You two jump on these pancakes before they get cold. Let's enjoy a good meal. The mess can wait."

The two men chowed into the steaming flapjacks, syrup and butter. Craige topped it off with Terri's strong coffee as he studied the strapping son. His parents had raised a good one, which said a lot for Paul Stanley. He wondered how it was to have a son.

Craige looked across the table at Terri. "Maybe we should do some digging of our own. I'll go home, pick up a fingerprint kit. There's a chance we might find usable prints. Won't hurt to check."

"You a cop?" Jeff asked, pancakes midway between plate and mouth.

Craige shook his head. "PI."

"Wow!" Jeff said. "A real private investigator?"

"Now and then," Craige said and smeared on some butter and raspberry jam. "I don't do it full-time. I've picked up a few tricks along

the way." Terri's hotcakes were as delicious as Mae Ruth's.

Jeff said eagerly, "Wow!"

"I doubt they wore gloves," Craige said. "We might find prints from window locks, door jambs, the edge of a counter, draw pulls, and if we get real lucky, we might make a match in the FBI's IAFIS system."

Jeff asked, "You work with the FBI?" His fork plopped on his plate.

Craige said, "I know a few."

Jeff asked, "What's IAFIS?" His questions came faster.

"IAFIS stands for Integrated Automated Fingerprint Identification System," Craige said. "It's an on-line ID system."

Eager and more interested, Jeff asked, "You think you'll find prints?"

"There's a good chance," Craige replied. "Every room was ransacked. That's the mark of a hurried job. Whoever did it didn't find what they came after. If they had, they would've stopped in that room. I could use the help. You like to fish?" Craige looked at Terri, then back to Jeff and added, "If it's OK with your mother." He asked Terri. "You be all right with that?" More than words passed between them.

"I've got to get ready for work," Terri said. "Since it's not a school day, I'd feel a lot better knowing Jeff wasn't here by himself."

Jeff exclaimed, "All right!"

It was a for real blood sport—getting the bad guys.

Terri said, "Jeff, go get dressed and don't forget to brush."

Jeff raced upstairs toward his bedroom.

Terri said uneasily, "You don't think this is finished, do you?"

"No." Craige shook his head.

"We both know—" Terri started to say, then stopped. Last night was still too fresh.

Craige wanted to take her again, right then, right there.

Craige said, "I didn't want to say anything in front of Jeff."

"The break-in makes me feel so damn helpless," she said.

Her look said it all.

"Jeff was upset finding I'd been here all night," Craige said. "Give him time. He's got a good head on his shoulders. It's natural for a son to feel it's his place to protect his mother. He wouldn't be much of a man if he didn't feel that way. You and his father wouldn't want him any other way."

"You ought to tell him that," she said.

"I will," Craige said. "When the time is right. Right now, he's still not sure about me and shouldn't be."

Terri's feelings pulled her in opposite directions—for Jeff, the house, and emotions she swore she would put away when Paul died, which Craige unleashed. She was resolved not to give in to sniffles and go to work puffy eyed. Office gossips would have a real wag with that. This irrepressible man already knew too much about the way he made her feel—schoolgirl hot flashes, sweatiness any time she thought of him. She forced her mind to the tedious grocery shopping, laundry, bills, oil and lube due, but she still couldn't get away from last night. With his arms around her, self-control seemed to have flown like thistledown on the wind. She had even thought of her honeymoon with Paul, the glorious things Paul did to her that two lovers do for one another—that Craige had done. Guilt and longing joined in battle. Guilt lost as Jeff came bounding down the stairs.

"I'm ready," Jeff said, raring to go.

"Jeff, I need to make a phone call," Craige said, "then we're gone. Terri, there's no signs of forced entry on any windows or doors."

The implications were something she didn't want to hear. Craige had questioned the use of a second garage door opener, and she couldn't remember if she locked the laundry room door yesterday when she left. She wouldn't forget again, but it scarcely mattered. Hollow core doors were good for privacy and nothing else.

"You have any spare time today or tomorrow?" Craige said to Gray. "I need to pick your brain." Craige listened and then said, "Six is fine. I'll meet you there."

Craige hung up and said to Jeff, "Ready?"

Jeff said, "Yes sir."

Jeff swore a silent heart-secret oath to keep his Dad alive even if Mom did have a boyfriend. The minute he walked in the house, he could tell. It wasn't so hard figuring out women. Just as she gave him privacy, she needed her own. Mom deserved a life. It wasn't his business, and in that moment, Jeff knew his time in this house was drawing closed. Part of Jeffrey, the child, was left behind. Jeff, the man, was taking its place.

"Grab an extra pair of jeans or cutoffs in case we decide to do some lake fishing," Craige said. "Might hook into a big one and have to get in the mud to haul him out. Lake can be cold. Dry pants can sure feel good."

"You two be careful, there's moccasins," Terri said.

Jeff rolled his eyes and exclaimed, "Mom!" Women were so squirmy

about snakes. "Snakes don't hurt anyone."

Craige said, "Terri, don't touch anything till Jeff and I do the fingerprint thing. We'll be back here before you get in from work."

"Can you stay for supper tonight?" Terri asked.

Craige gave a quick look to Jeff and hesitated, "Let's see how things go."

\*\*\*\*\*

Surrounded by Ingramme land, fishing rods and tackle boxes in the skiff and a full cricket bucket, they headed to the oldest of his fresh water lakes 10 miles from the house. Bobberfished for Bream among shady, ebony-orange roots of moss-hung Spanish Cypress until the sun pushed high, and the day turned tropical. Craige enjoyed it, and so did Jeff, romping with Lucky. After they swam, they went back to the house for sandwiches and iced tea. Jeff was on the dock skipping rocks across the river when he spotted the dusky brown, thick-bodied Cottonmouth draped on the swamp magnolia branch hardly three feet from their boat.

Jeff said, "He always stay there?"

"Pretty much," Craige said. "Snakes are territorial. Once you spot them, leave 'em be. You'll always know where they are."

Jeff baited his hook and plunked it right under the overhang not a foot from the snake. The snake never moved the entire afternoon. They banked the skiff, gathered handfuls of ripe blackberries, left the skiff, grabbed their rods and tackle and took the turkey trail back to the house.

"When we get to the house, peel off all your clothes," Craige said. "Dump them in the washer, shower and check everywhere. Woods are full of deer ticks and limes infection. Wouldn't want to face your mom if I let that happen to her favorite son."

With no warning and with youths instant insight, Jeff asked, "You like Mom, don't you?"

His remark, straight from a son's heart, caught Craige off guard. The worldly sailor in him should've seen it coming. I'd had enough hot to trot, navy, raunchy weekends of "hump-hump-switch-around girlfriends" foursomes. It wasn't a time to be equivocal. This one was up front, bone honest.

"Yea," Craige answered nodding slowly, "I do."

Jeff never mentioned it again.

*****

Before six o'clock the next morning, Craige hung a left into the parking lot of the city-county law enforcement center. Gray had just pulled up.

"Mornin'," Craige yelled across the top of his car.

"Must be important," Gray said. "Fine day like this and a country boy like you coming into town."

Some rumored Gray had his eye on the mayor's chair. They discussed it once. Gray dismissed it saying, "Never understood anyone wanting to go into politics."

"You're already in politics up to your neck," Craige said. "What's a little bit more?"

"Politics brings out the worst in lots of folks," he replied. "I like to think I'm making a difference here. I think I'd miss that in politics."

Gray would make a good mayor or governor. His laid-back attitude belied the bulldog cop and one damn fine detective.

Gray said, "Mabel will have a fresh pot brewed, and she'll be glad seeing you drag in with me." They grabbed cups and filled them. "Woman takes care of me better'n my own mama." Gray slipped off his jacket.

Mabel called out from the outer office, "Don't think you had a mama." And to Craige she said, "And how is my favorite South Carolinian this fine morning?"

Craige called back, "Doing fine." As he stuck his head around her partition, he asked, "How's my favorite Georgia peach?"

Mabel flashed her big smile, gray eyes peered at him over the top of black wire rim glasses. She'd always had the hots for the grace and charm of this born gentleman and never hid it. She never discussed it with anyone either.

Gray kicked back, cup in hand, "What's eating you?"

"A hunch," Craige said.

Gray's steely eyes zoomed into Craige as he sloshed his coffee.

Gray sputtered, "Oh shit! I get jittery when you get one of your feelings."

"For starters," Craige said, "two murders don't add up to two murders."

"Which ones?" Gray left his coffee untouched.

"Two women, maybe more," Craige said.

"You know something we don't?" Gray asked.

"Nope," Craige said, not missing Gray's switch from "I" to "we."

"I've seen you play hunches like a pole-axed snapping turtle," Gray said. "Everyone thinking you're up the wrong tree when you're headed in some other direction. Spit it out."

"Right now it's just theory." Craige took a mouthful of coffee and swallowed.

Gray got up, closed the door to his two-by-nothing back hall office with its water stained ceiling tiles.

"Two dead women," Craige continued, "one mugged and killed in the parking deck, the second at the airport."

"Cause of death, dissimilar backgrounds, different MOs, *modus operandi* weren't even similar." Gray frowned. "Only similarity was the times of death."

Craige edged forward. "Drugs don't fit. Stay with me. I checked the autopsy reports. Neither victim tested positive for drugs and only a trace of blood alcohol with the woman in the garage. The pills were a plant ... meant to be found."

Gray said, "It could be a drug deal gone sour."

"I could accept that with the younger one," Craige said. "A high stepping lady of the evening, easy-come easy-go money, tacky but expensive tastes. Her roommate said she had a list of well-heeled repeat clients who didn't mind opening their wallets, but I can't make drugs fit the woman at the airport—widow helping a son through college, barely could pay her bills, a car that won't start except on a good day."

"Dealing would've made a ready shortcut to extra cash for her," Gray said. "Maybe she cut herself a little share under the table and got caught."

"Again," Craige said, "I could buy that for the woman in the parking deck—roll of big bills, nothing smaller than twenties, paid cash for a five-bedroom, three-car garage house in Westlake. She and her roommate partners in a competition with suburban wives turning afternoon tricks during Masters Week, but there's way too many 'ifs' with both killings. I have no evidence they're connected, but dammit

Gray, it smells rotten. As if we're supposed to buy a few scattered pills as proof of what went down."

"Could still be drug related," Gray said.

"Maybe, but I don't buy it," Craige replied.

"Drugs make for a lot of freewheeling cash that flows like water," Gray said. "That can buy an awful lot. Both of us have seen killing for less."

"Take the money out of the equation, and it don't feel right," Craige tried to persuade him. "The victims had several things in common— killed in public, bodies not hidden. The killer or killers either didn't care or were sending a message."

"The message bit goes with drugs." Gray held fast his beliefs.

"I know," Craige said. "It still doesn't fit the psychological profile of a blackmailer. Blackmailers want to keep their secrets not trumpet them with a bloody kill." Craige leaned forward, elbows on knees. "The ugly part comes in if it's not drugs. If we have two killings as covers for a murder that hasn't happened or ones we don't know about."

"I think you get more devious every time the sun comes up," Gray said.

"So I've been told," Craige agreed.

"I learned not to ignore your hunches," Gray said. "That's why most of us in our SEAL unit are still alive, but I don't like thinking we're facing cover-up killings."

"I wanted to bounce it off you," Craige said. "See what you thought."

"And pick my brains for what CI division hasn't released to the media," Gray grinned.

"That too," Craige admitted.

"I called in and told Mabel you'd be coming by this morning." Gray reached for the RESTRICTED—CONFIDENTIAL file and handed it to Craige. "She made sure these copies were up-to-date just for you." Gray pulled out a sheet and shoved it toward Craige. "That's pertinent stats on one pissant dealer trying to be a big wheel in East Central Georgia, coastal South Carolina. Minor problem. Not only was he not in town when the parking deck victim was killed, he was in jail in Savannah when the widow woman at the airport got hers."

"So some muscle cretin did the job for him." Craige skimmed the sheet. "Gives himself an airtight alibi." The name on the sheet was familiar.

Gray said, "Neither victim has any connection with dealers or book-ies."

"You convinced it's drugs?" Craige asked.

"No, but right now nothing else fits."

"That may be what the killer intended." Craige gritted his teeth.

"How come you're so against it being drugs?" Gray asked.

"As I said, just a hunch," Craige answered. "But the whole layout is screwy. If it's not drugs, we're stuck with no motive, and I don't quite buy it being random. If we are dealing with opportunity killings of unconnected bystanders, those that aren't dead soon could be."

Gray said, elbows on his desk, "You got the damndest way of making a straightforward case all knotty."

"It was knotty from the git-go," Craige said.

"Get me some proof," Gray continued.

"Yeh," Craige said, laying the file on Gray's desk, "For sure what's in there is not the whole package by a long shot."

"Your client, who is she?" Gray asked.

"I didn't say it was a she." Craige's quick glance at Gray told him he was right.

"I've seen you heat up for a woman," Gray chuckled. "You snort and paw like a bull in heat. I'll bet a day's pay it's a woman. Always was, always will be. You're one hard-as-nails loner, but you couldn't turn down helping a nice-looking woman in trouble if you tried."

Craige said, "Not very confident in what you believe if a day's pay is all you'll ante." Gray had been around him too much.

Gray said, "You know how we overpaid public servants are." He gave a quick look at his watch. "Gotta run. Got a court appointment in five minutes." He grabbed his coat, and with one hand on his shoulder, he continued, "If you come across anything I ought to know ..."

"You'll be the first to know," Craige said. "Count on it."

"This time, try to keep the body count to a minimum."

"I never carry a weapon," Craige rebutted.

"With what our hands are trained to do, you don't need a weapon," Gray said. "Least you never waste bullets. Make sure your license is in order. I know a few malicious knot heads who'd love to stir trouble for you."

"They've tried before," Craige said.

"And they will again," Gray added.

"Whatever jerks their chain," Craige answered, shrugging.

Craige never liked mixing in drug money, and he liked it less where it might involve Terri. The bank could take care of itself. Craige's restless boogeyman curled through his mind and loosed a wormy conviction that drugs weren't it. The parking deck was a peculiar kill site, but so was the airport. Murder usually has some element of panic. Scattered, random murders gave Craige the creeps—no common MO, a masquerade of the unrelated, the real victims pigeonholed among random dead. Was that why the drugs were made obvious? It fits. The victims didn't know one another, and if all the targets hadn't been taken out, they were unknown victims in a silent plot. Machiavellian thoughts coiled, zigzagged. Were the killings premeditated or psychotic? He'd seen minds unhinged in combat. Reality was a homespun term, and it fits a damn few. A calm exterior on a Jane or John Doe meant death was a hair's breath underneath. Madness had its own reason. His mind stitched at flimsy strands of a killer's blueprint with more killings cocked to happen. Gray was right, it went nowhere without proof.

\*\*\*\*\*

Barry remodeled his entrance downtown paying no attention to the rotted, weeded-up jumble of freight docks and narrow cobblestone alleys. He hired a fly-by-night, cash-only carpenter to re-roof the old, leaky shed by the side of the abandoned spur, a perfect place for the car. He rewired interior outlets, eager to try the electrodes.

The next day, he headed for the deposit box when the vault clerk took a break. He opened the long, narrow lid and reached for the vial. He would dilute it more and would take only a sip. He could hardly wait to pick just the right pair. The woman at the airport still haunted him. She had been a mistake. He shouldn't have rushed the job. At least it made for a good wild goose hunt for the police. From now on, only the selfish, young ones would be gotten rid of— they make handsome corpses and fresh meat. He finally understood the macho hunter's rowdy bar talk about the gun-toting euphoria of the hunt—sitting in windblown deer stands, icy duck blinds, stalking living things. He was the avenging angel with his very own hiding place. Double-dealing frickers weren't yet afraid enough , but they would be and the wife too.

"They'll pay," he muttered. "Before I'm finished, they'll all pay."

## Chapter 9

Garland Holton was in his office alone, and he was worried. He grouched, "Wasted good money on two punks for a search and snatch of Stanley's place and nothing to show for it. Those papers were probably right under their noses. Now, that prying bitch knows someone is on to her. Damn court order! There's no chance of getting hold of the originals. Ingramme bastard has always been trouble. Stanley probably paying Ingramme off by slipping between the sheets with him." He stared at his phone.

He didn't want to make the call, but he wasn't about to sit still and be left holding the bag, the dog-eat-dog rule. Garland knew better than most. He dialed, listened to it ring and flinched when it was picked up. He explained what happened.

After he listened to the voice on the other end, he said, "Not my fault the papers weren't there."

The voice said, "She has them somewhere."

"Either Ingramme or Fescher has them, but why bother?" Garland asked. "You said there was nothing incriminating in them."

"I took care of the computer files including backups, but those copies in Fescher's office might not be the only problem. If you'd done what you were supposed to do and made sure the paperwork was cleaned, there wouldn't be a problem. Sending those idiots to Stanley's made it worse. If Stanley copied the files to CDs, the question is where she put them. She have a safety deposit box?"

"Probably, but she wouldn't leave them in the bank."

Garland choked. "There's Ingramme's place."

"Those files have to be destroyed, and we can't involve anyone else."

Garland said, "I'm not going out there." His balls pulled tight. "His dog eats strangers for breakfast." Panic rising, he added, "I'm not tangling with either one of them."

"She had a kid? Grab him. That ought to leverage her."

"You nuts!" Garland shouted. "Kidnapping is a federal offense." He wanted out.

"So is bank robbery, not to mention murder. You didn't balk at that," he snickered. "It's too late to get squeamish."

"You said no one would get hurt," Garland said. "I didn't kill anyone."

"Royce got greedy. You're more stupid than your grandmother thinks you are if you think a jury won't believe you helped set it up. Stop sniveling and get rid of the whole damn portfolio."

"You killed Royce," Garland accused. It wasn't any jury that worried him.

"It was a perfect arrangement until old lady McGiffern made Ingramme her executor and that Stanley bitch butted in."

"Stanley would've had nothing if Royce had taken care of things," Garland said. "No one knows I'm involved."

"I do."

Garland felt terror all over him. He didn't have to ask; he knew it was a threat.

He muttered, "What's in those files I don't know about?"

"Mostly your signature on your legal stationery. Use your master key, check and see if Marshall's office is clean."

"You nuts!" Garland yelled. "Someone might see me."

"That's the least of your worries if the auditors start asking questions with Stanley waiting in the wings. Your high and mighty grandmother won't sit still for a scandal like this, and she'll like your undergrad, moneymaking ventures even less." It was deadly.

Garland's voice wobbled as he exclaimed, "What?"

"That was quite a little enterprise you had going at Big Red U. Stealing midterms and lab finals didn't bother your frat brother, but they sure got steamed when you charged them for copies." The threat was enough.

An ashen-faced Garland said, "Leave my family out of this."

His heart beat faster. Goddamn busybodies would spread it all over town.

"I may not have fancy degrees hanging in a big, impressive office, but you better do something about this before it gets any worse, or is that too much to expect from you?"

Garland said halfheartedly, "You the one doing the blackmailing."

"Not yet," he snickered, "but I could."

Garland wished he'd never gotten mixed up in this. It wasn't the first time he regretted being involved with fast money schemes. At least his stock market losses had been legal. Daddy wouldn't bail his ass out of this, and Grandmother hadn't blinked when she blocked his voting the family's controlling proxies in Gulf Oil Limited stock. His grandmother had said, "I own the majority stock." Her obdurate blue eyes would stare out above her long-stemmed, ivory cigarette holder with its imported cigarette. "I will not countenance you squandering the efforts of this family."

He could've swung that deal. Reading the newspaper about the airport murder, he'd thought how nice it would've been if grandmother had been the one to take a walk in that parking lot.

Garland said, "How was I to know the bank would hire some busybody who'd be picky with the trust accounts?"

"That's what you're there for. Bank policy is that no originals are supposed to leave the building. You could've had those files under lock and key where no court order would've ever found them."

"That Stone Mountain lawyer did it," Garland said. "Nothing I could do."

"So a legal eagle colleague of yours got the jump on you." He sounded disgusted.

"It's not the first time one of you lawyers used the law to cover your ass. Seems the vice president isn't waiting around."

"What's Donnie Marshall got to do with this?" Garland asked.

"Something he's not talking much about. He tried to move all McGiffern documents to his office," he said with a big chuckle. "Something you could've done before anyone was interested."

"That why Marshall called a special meeting of the Board to fill Sedgewicke's position?" Garland asked.

"Marshall wanted to make sure no one on the Board got a look at

them because he wants Royce's position."

"He doesn't have the votes to get elected CEO," Garland said. "Sedgewicke deballed ass kisser Marshall long before he made him executive vice president."

"Marshall is smarter than you. If Donnie Marshall could get at those files, he might use what's in them to swing a few votes his way, and there's another complication. After Fescher's court order was delivered, Stanley had new locks installed on all department file cabinets with new passwords for their work stations. Do something!" He slammed the phone down.

The smash of the phone in his ear was like a garrote around Garland's neck. It had seemed so simple. Pissed at Stanley, pissed at a throwback, swamp lowlife, trash like Ingramme. He knew Ingramme contacted Fescher. That roughneck SOB had a nasty reputation of pulling dirty laundry out into the bright glare of publicity. His headache got worse. Garland Holton would've thrown a full-blown cardiac arrest if he'd known how right he was.

*****

Barry was humming his favorite Disney tune, "Whistle While We Work," as he parked next to his spanking-new, white Mercedes inside the shed. He ran his hands around the steering wheel of his freshly vacuumed, freshly washed and waxed, second-hand Mercedes purchase. He had gone on an incognito plane trip with a cheap toupee to cover his bald head; fake name; one-way, cash ticket to Charlotte; changed planes into Richmond; had an alias registration and driver's license; a post office box across the river in South Carolina for them to mail the title; signed an illegible, right hand scribble; and paid cash for the demo model. Salesman nonplus, accustomed to car loan paperwork, never dealt with real money.

Barry drove off the proud possessor of a Mercedes. There was no paper trail, no one alive would ever know. Those bastards in the bank would shit if they knew. His wife would never find out. He wouldn't have to listen to her pester him to get her one. He would be smug in his very own *haute couture*, double-car garage with new, automatic doors closed snug and light tight.

His heart raced. It was retribution time. He thought of all man-

121

ners of things—leave a bloody finger in their glove compartment, a toe or finger nailed to the front door of their house. He nixed that as too chancy but would've been fun. Then it hit him. Didn't know why he hadn't thought of it before. It would be flawless with the merger and the auditors poking around. He liked the idea the more he thought about it. He knew copying and moving those files to his safety deposit box would pay off. He was glad he'd worn gloves; prints last a long time on paper. He used the interoffice mail—a page mailed here, a page mailed there. They'll shit their pinstripe pants.

The next morning, everything was ready. His secretary was on her coffee break, no one was around. He pulled the sheets from his brief-case, headed for the copier and handled only the cover pages. He ran the copies. Then, back in his office, he put the sheets he'd touched into the shredder. The interoffice routing slips were ready. He folded the single sheet with the words, YOU WON'T GET AWAY WITH IT. He buried the envelopes in stacks of outgoing mail. He wished he could see each one opened. The next day would be the best Friday ever.

"You sure are in a good mood today, Mr. Peters," his secretary said.

"Fine day," Barry answered.

He went to lunch, ordered a second sandwich takeout for a stage prop and returned to the office and told his secretary he'd be working late.

After the eight-to-five left for the day, he opened his new, silk shirt bought especially for tonight, put on his favorite cologne and slicked what hair cradled his ears. He had checked the guards' schedules be-cause he wanted to be sure the next shift change saw him come back into the bank with the sandwich. Baggy in hand, he hurried through the covered walkway, took the stairs down and came through the door. He had timed it perfectly.

Barry said, "Evening, Mitch."

Mitch's head came up from the bank of black and white TVs.

"Working late tonight?" Mitch asked.

Mitch thought it odd. It was the first time Peters ever spoke to him.

Barry rustled his paper bag and said, "Paperwork never ends." He punched the elevator.

He hurried to his office window and waited till Mitch's wife pulled

their pickup curbside. Mitch climbed in, and they drove away. Barry reached into his genuine leather brief case, took out the small bottle of pale yellowish powder. He took the garage stairs again, through the street entrance, down the shadowed street and away from the bank. The new shift was getting settled. They'd never see him. He slipped into the alley garage and eased his new vehicle out.

Barry checked out several stale, smoky bars before he spotted her unbounceable, silicone boobs, fuck-me pumps and net stockings. When he flashed his wad of bills, she whispered to her stout, burr-cut, pool partner and asked Barry to join them. They put away another round, while Barry nursed his beer, making sure his fat wallet came out each time they got served. BoobJob kept eyeing the folding money. It was party time. They piled into Barry's Mercedes.

She ogled and said, "You got a nice, fancy car." She cozied both hands around his arm.

"That's not all I got," Barry replied and flipped the console open, rainbow glories beckoned. "Help yourself."

From the rear seat, GuyPerson leaned forward, grabbed a handful and popped a couple with a mouthful of beer from his Styrofoam cup.

GuyPerson slurred, "Gonna be a dreamland night."

Barry asked the cheap floozy, "You like wine?"

She said, "I sure do." She nestled closer.

"I have lots of wine at my place," Barry bragged.

Guy asked, "Got'ny liquor?" He belched.

"Plenty of that," Barry lied. He smiled at her, "We'll have a party, just the three of us."

"I love parties." She flashed a jaded, beauty queen smile for Daddy Big Bucks.

The guy grabbed more purties and sagged back into Nirvana. The speed was quickening with hardly a nudge of gas as she diddled the FM and dropped a CD. She stepped on it trying to pick it up as Barry opened the electric sun roof. She leaned her head back in the cool, humid rush and ran her fingers through her too much hair-sprayed hair as the elegant sedan rushed through the night. Barry slowed, eased into his garage, the doors slowly dropped behind them and closed them into his world.

Barry said, "Exclusive private club." He fastened on a smile for this Jezebel filth. "Rented just for the night. Just we three. No one will bother us."

Her eyes grew big and sparkly. This was just like those pictures she'd seen of movie stars' fancy places. It sure would be nice if she could be a regular for this one and cut out working the streets.

Barry never understood how horny, cannon fodder junkies could stick their tongues in her mouth or on her anywhere.

Barry unlocked the door. "Private entrance. Members only." The guy stumbled behind them. "They have a table all prepared."

"You sure do have a lot of wine," she said staring at the loaded racks. "Never seen this much, even in a liquor store, but the bottles sure are dusty. Don't nobody ever clean this place?"

Barry shoved the man's dead weight to a bench. "Let him sleep it off," Barry said. "You and I can enjoy the evening."

He opened the lower door and stepped back. Beyond was an intimate cabaret table set for two, heavy drapes along one stone wall. With an air of elegance, he lit the candle.

"Be seated." He pulled out her chair.

She beamed, "Why, thank you, sir." Her miniskirt was too snug.

He popped the cork with a snuffed "poof" like she'd seen on TV and filled her glass with amber burgundy then his.

He said, "A toast to the night."

She raised her glass, "This is good." She tasted. "Ummm," she said taking a full swallow. "That's good wine." She took another swallow.

"The proper wine for special occasions is very important," Barry said.

"All them bottles back yonder yours?" She emptied her glass.

"Yes," Barry strutted. "Would you like to look at them?"

"Sure," she said.

She'd had a long, dry streak. Finally, she found a golden goose. Whatever he wanted was fine. After going to the clinic three times a week for a month and taking the cure, she still had spells of being tired. She'd rest tomorrow. At least this one wasn't manhandling her.

Barry said, "Stay right here while I turn on the lights."

He hurried to the breaker box. The fluorescents flickered on dusty, wooden frames in dusty queues. She didn't stare, she gawked.

"Taste for good wine is acquired," he boasted.

He hooked her arm as they strolled between the stacks.

A finger here and there across barely legible labels as though he was examining, checking.

She said, "One bottle don't last very long. That's why I buy mine at supermarkets. You can use food stamps if you know how to work it." She tittered like it was a secret.

Barry said, "I think you'll like this." He brushed grime from one and continued, "Very expensive."

"Sure not the High Valley brand daddy drinks," she squinted. "Labels all faded. Got a funny name."

Barry said, "It's Caymus." Royce's favorite ... now his.

"I once saw some wine in a liquor store window all frilled up with a big, gold frame propped around it," she said. "It had purple velvet draped all around. Cost more'n a $100."

Barry said, "Some of these cost much more than that."

He felt good saying that.

"More than a hundred buck!" She stared at the bottle.

"Why drink something that cost that much? For a hundred you can buy more than one bottle. I heard about folks who buy high-priced booze, but I never knew nobody like that. You sure got a bunch of bottles."

"Pick one you like," he told her and then moved to their table. "We'll open it."

"What if I pick one that cost a lot?" she asked.

Barry smiled, "My pleasure." He watched as she moved deeper in the racks. "Take your time."

He hurried to the guy, duct-taped him across the mouth, put double corkscrews around his wrists, which were crossed behind his back and then tossed the tarpaulin over him. He went back to the shelf for the vial and the box of Q-tips. He swabbed a trace of the pale yellow powder, dusted speckles into her glass and placed it on the table.

She brought him a bottle. "I'd like to try this one."

Barry noticed it was 1975, California Napa Valley, Rutherford Special Selection. He buried a smirk. Royce would shit if he could see this trollop swilling his prize vintage. He plunged the corkscrew, and the cork squeaked. He filled two glasses with the swarthy, burgundy liquid.

Barry raised his glass, "Cabernet Sauvignon."

He knew she had no idea what he was saying. He tasted, she drank. Barry curbed his dislike of harsh Sauvignon and gritted his teeth against

the aftertaste. He wasn't about to let her know he also preferred his wine from the super market.

She emptied hers. "Ain't sweet like most." She said, licking her lips, "Has a bitter taste. I like it sweet." She touched her lips with a finger. "Leaves your mouth sort'a fuzzy. Sure warms up the stomach though. Be good on a cold night."

Her face was garish. "Gracious ..." she said, wiping her mouth with her hand, "expensive wine sure is powerful. Makes me feel all fluttery, but I guess when it cost that much, it ought to have a kick. Sort of high proof like good moonshine."

Barry was pleased, the dose was about right.

Kicking off a shoe, she said, "Makes my toes tingle."

Barry asked, "Another glass?" He was the perfect host.

"I don't think so," she answered, taking a deep breath.

Her eyelids fluttered, her head slumped forward, lips were working and shallow breathing rattled her throat. He half carried, half dragged the bitch to the table and dumped her across it, no need to tie her. He stepped back. Her tits didn't rise and fall. Her belly barely moved with each breath. He went to the guy and pulled back the tarp. The fierce glare from the bound face told Barry the pills and liquor had worn off. It was more fun this way anyhow.

Barry reached down, "Come on big boy." He grabbed his collar. "Your turn."

Barry dragged him to the table and levered it vertical. He manacled the wrists and legs, made sure they were tight against the wooden frame and yanked away the strip across the mouth.

The man yelled, "What the fuck kinda pervert are you?"

Barry smirked, "We're going to have a party."

He yelled and struggled, "Goddammit! Turn me loose!"

"Shutup!" Barry yelled and backhanded him across his face, spittle flew. "Teach you some respect."

"What the fuck you want, mister?" he asked.

Barry said, "That's more like it." He gently reclined the table.

The guy demanded, "Untie me." He struggled, but the bindings didn't budge.

"I'll untie you when I'm ready," Barry said as he filled glasses. "Your lady friend liked this. Very expensive."

He flung the full glass in the man's face. The man's lips

clenched, the face seethed.

Barry sat his goblet down. It was more fun when they resisted. He picked up the sharpened fish knife, watched the man's eyes follow the gleaming tip and let fear take over. He slipped it between his open shirt and collar, and with one swift slice, the shirt split from neck to waist.

Barry, close to one ear, said, "This won't take long." He made savage nicks along the ribs.

The guy whimpered, "Jezus!" He licked at the dribbles of wine. "Tastes like shit." His Adam's apple was working hard.

"I don't like Sauvignon either," Barry said and smiled. "Drink all of it."

The man sensed something not right, as Barry walked behind him. He twisted to see what was going on as Barry drew the curtains back from his mural. There was a dull splash far below. Barry rolled what looked like a body into a God-awful, black pit.

"What the fuck you do?" The man gawked.

Death was coming with a knife toward him.

"Please, Mister …" he singsong whimpered. Spittle drooled from his mouth. "I won't tell."

"That's right!" Barry screeched. "You won't tell! No witnesses!"

He made vicious slashes at the shirt, pants, socks and underwear. No one needed these animals. There was a single, grunted explosion of breath as the knife plunged across the neck. The scarlet fountain finally slowed through the clean throat slice. The big pieces were removed; the head and carcass dumped into the pit. Barry threw the box of pills and capsules into the cess pit, pulled the handle and watched the mass swirl away. His high-school English teacher was wrong. Love wasn't life's driving passion—vengeance served cold was the best of all.

He turned out the lights. Now he was ready for those bastards in the tall building across the street.

*****

Midlife crisis at forty-two, Nathan HughDon Marshall had been pouring over the stack of papers since before sunup. He wasn't supposed to double up on his prescription, much less drive after he'd taken the "no alcohol" Nortriptyline. He'd been doing both for days,

even sneaking his wife's Valium, but it wasn't helping. Nobody understood the pressure. His wife, Leah Rea, didn't give a shit, neither had Sedgewicke. He wanted to change the nameplate on his executive suite from "vice president" to "acting CEO" but didn't care no matter how good it would look on his résumé.

The phone rang. It had to be his damn wife. She was the only one who ever used that number. He put the handful of paper down, wondering what her bourbon guzzling, whore-hopping Daddy Brighton Covington had egged her to do now.

Last Thanksgiving, daughter and Daddy hadn't bothered closing his study door. Old bastard didn't care whether anybody heard.

"Never understood what you ever saw in Marshall," Daddy griped. "He's never amounted to anything."

HughDon punched the speakerphone, "Yes dear?" He sounded humdrum.

Royce Sedgewicke had trained Donnie Marshall well.

"You son of a bitch!" The words blared. "You gave them the deposit box master key."

The words bashed a pantywaist fear through Marshall.

Donnie gripped the phone and spluttered, "Who is this?" His ulcer simmered hotter. He repeated, "Who is this?" He needed a drink. "What are you talking about?" He sensed danger.

"Don't play kiss-ass, don't-know-nothing with me." Garland Holton snarled, "You know what I'm talking about. Sedgewicke had a good thing going, and you screwed up."

Marshall hem-hawed, "I don't know what you're talking about." He never liked Holton.

"Gimme a break, Donnie Boy," Holton sneered. "No wonder floppy titted Leah Rea and you never bred up no kids. You never could get it up, could never give her what she needed."

Donnie said, "You got no call talking about my wife like that."

"Cut the shit," Holton grunted. "Since you two married, I've fucked her as much as before." He was badger mean.

"I nailed her in the kitchen at your bachelor party," he laughed. "And twice the night before your wedding, while the cooks watched. Almost got her again next day in the chapel, but all she had time for was a blow job." He gave a mongoose growl. "She don't suck very good, but it wasn't for lack of trying. What you think we did in the locker

rooms at Buckingham Academy, read Bible verses?" He said this matter-of-factly. "A real locker room celebrity, she was in there more'n most of us. Daddy bought her a couple of abortions," he taunted. "It was that or name a Covington bastard after half the basketball team and two of the coaches. Everybody knows your family expected you to marry money, but your family always was wooden spoons with champagne attitudes."

He enjoyed lording right of the first-born over any Marshall.

"Know something Nate ol' buddy?" Holton said. "She's got cast iron insides. She's a great stand-up fuck, long as you make sure she knows who's boss. Not the best piece I ever had, but there's no such thing as bad. Too bad you don't have a cast iron dick to match. I've been doing you a big favor keeping her serviced. Not many men would take on a cow like her. You know how women are, lay good meat to 'em once a week, keeps them humming along, happy as a jaybird. Don't worry, long as you do as I say, ever'thing'll be cozy. Couldn't ask more from a friend, could you?"

HughDon asked, "What do you want?" He wasn't sure he wanted to know.

"You made a good lap dog for Sedgewicke. Long as Sedgewicke petted your weasel head every now and then, you didn't mind eating his shit," Holton said. "Who's in this with you? You couldn't pull it off on your own, and I'm not sitting still while your dumb butt fiddles and farts till the roof comes down. Got to hand it to your partners, they covered their ass better than you. Paper trail aimed straight up your fanny." He paused. "So, ole Buddy, who's jerking your strings?"

HughDon hated the ring of "ole Buddy" and a child's haunted specter rose. If he messed up, his parents always scolded with "we don't love you anymore."

His brain jellied with fear. Donnie Boy gurgled, "I don't know what you're talking about." It wasn't even a good lie.

Holton growled, "OK, ole buddy—" this gutless chicken shit never could face the truth. "That's the way you want, that's the way it'll play. Feds all over that place, *Herald Gazette* reporter poking around to feed people's itch for dirt." He slammed the phone down.

Immigrant, Southern planters, the Marshals and the Holtons had known one another since before the late, great King Cotton land squabble with those people north of the Mason-Dixon line, but they

survived. Land was money and power, no matter what it took, but they didn't want anyone knowing how they survived. Now HughDon was going to be blamed for losing it.

He slumped at his desk. It wasn't his fault, but Holton was right about one thing, his signature was everywhere. His gaze drifted around his paneled office, rococo side table and bleached purple, raw silk lamp shades that blended with the mauve and pale lilacs. He glanced at his massive oak desk that Royce had specially ordered for his new VP—a symbol of success better than a raise. It's all coming to an end. He would be arrested, laughed at and thrown to the wolves. His family would make sure his disgrace never touched them. It was like thirty-plus years ago was only yesterday, and chubby Donnie HughDon was the brunt of everything that came down the pike, used up and discarded. He wasn't about to live with that again. His parents would be sorry when he wasn't around. His position was all he had.

He unlocked the bottom drawer, the snub-nosed .38 beckoned like a rediscovered mistress. He stroked its clean, blue sheen, fondled its smooth warmth and, for one very short instant, pictured using it on Garland. SOB deserved it. He discarded the idea. It was better this way.

He leaned his head back and pictured his grandparent's spiral staircase. Nathan HughDon, of the McHugh Marshalls, was always the glitch in their unyielding parade. He never would be allowed to join the row of austere family portraits in their tall, gilded frames. He cocked the hammer and made sure the safety was off. He couldn't botch this and face the ultimate indignity of a born loser. He smiled with a moment's satisfaction. His wife would break into a blue-faced howl when they read the suicide exclusion clause in his two million dollar insurance policy. Neither of the Jaguars nor the antebellum mansion were paid for and neither was most of the furniture. She'd have to move back home with Daddy or get him to pay it off. He wondered what dying would feel like, sucked down on the muzzle, winced briefly and pulled the trigger. His frozen, sardonic smile on blood-flecked lips was the only part of his face left.

His secretary recognized it only as a muffled, out-of-place sound. She went to the door of Mr. Marshall's private office. She wasn't sure she wanted to face him if those new shelves had fallen. She knocked, no answer. She knocked again and gingerly opened the door. For a

moment, what she saw refused to register. The purplish clots, the crimson speckles across his shirt, grayish soufflé smears and greasy blobs slithered down the costly wallpaper in knurled, polka dot daubs. Red rivulets trickled down one arm, soaked his gold watch band and chair cushion. It dripped off his fingertips then oozed down the chair leg, pooling graceful, rounded soppypuddles into the carpet. She clutched her throat, giddy, the world spun in a narrow whirlwind. She finally found her breath and screamed.

In less than half an hour, the word galloped beyond the bloody office. All over the hill, phone and whisper from Frog Holler to Pinch Gut and beyond to the Valley. When he heard it, ice-cold, boiling fear flushed through Garland Holton. He decided to avoid any reporters and not let anyone know he knew of any reason a rising, young banker might kill himself. He uttered a silent, baneful prayer that HughDon hadn't left a note or recorded their phone conversation. Garland Holton wasn't the only one that changed their mind.

Homicide Lt. Gray MacGerald kept the volume low on his police scanner, but the string of ten codes plus the location got his attention.

He caught, "Code 3, 10-71, 10-57." He turned up the volume. "Landmark Railroad Bank. Possible 10-56A with 10-54, ME en route." He caught a burst of static. "10-9, 10-9, gimme a comeback. 10-45 en route."

As Gray eased his unmarked car into the bank's parking deck, his conversation with Craige zigzagged his misgivings. He spotted Fred Dinkins talking to a uniform. Gray punched his radio handset. Mabel was not at her desk when he left. The watch officer patched him through to her.

When she answered, Gray said, "This is messy."

"You at the bank?" Mabel asked.

"Just got here. Fred's going to be a while, and I don't want any phone calls here."

"Gossip pot is already boiling about who it was."

"Go shopping. Go home. Just get outta there so you won't have to lie about where I am."

"If I was worried about a few white lies, I would've quit working for you long before now. See you in the morning."

At the door of HughDon Marshall's office, Gray nodded to the young cop, making sure only authorized persons entered. Gray stopped

just inside so as not to step in the pattern of rusty red pieces.

Short, roly-poly Fred looked up, his glasses threatened to slide off his nose.

"Afternoon," Fred said. "Figured a blood hound like you couldn't pass this up."

"Is it Marshall?" Gray said.

"Looks to be," Fred answered. "Fits his general description. Angle of penetration blew away most of the upper face." He matched a fragment to the shattered soup bowl that had been a skull. "Marshall's secretary said he was in here on the phone when she got back from lunch."

Gray said, "Anyone pay him a visit?"

"Not that she knows of," He said, nodding toward the door. "And that's the only way in and out of his office." He retrieved another glossy fragment. "I figure it's Marshall, but for now, that's between you and me."

"I'll get with you later," Gray said.

Gray sat in his car. He'd gone to high school with HughDon Marshall. Everyone knew of the old money, Summerville Marshalls, HughDon never more than a name in the year book. Suicide never made sense to Gray, but it wasn't the first time he'd seen privilege come with an awesome price tag, too much too soon on a silver platter. HughDon had a reputation in town, never proved himself to himself, couldn't live up to expectations—his own or the family's. Position never kept anyone from doing themselves.

It looked like Craige had hit it right on the nose. Two messy murders plus this didn't square with it being coincidence. Was Marshall in this up to his gullet, maybe being blackmailed, or had he stumbled onto a third party killer? He'd wait for Fred's report, but he made a mental note to pay a visit to the med school's Department of Psychology to get some info into psycho profiles. That might be a wild goose chase, but it wouldn't hurt. Craige hadn't bought the drug squabble. Neither did the street cop in Gray. This was way too tidy, but if he and Craige were wrong and this turned out to be a drug turf war, he could easily be facing a rising body count. Being SEALs, neither of them were shocked by the mayhem people did to one another. He pushed by-the-book aside, reached for the radio phone and dialed Craige.

*****

Sweat broke across Garland's forehead and ringed his armpits. He was worried about that moron Marshall having left anything connected to him before he blew his head off. He was glad he did a good job and wished he'd done it sooner. Garland's first impulse was to call the bank. He nixed that. He needed a drink. He buzzed his secretary.

"Yes Mr. Holton?" she answered.

"Cancel the rest of my appointments today," he said.

"Mr. Holton, you have clients waiting," she said.

He groused, "Just do it!"

"Yes, sir," she said.

His mind was clicking as he drove. He was plotting how to window dress his being a legal counsel to Royce Sedgewicke. He didn't care whether anyone believed him. Image was all the State Bar Association cared about, to hell with truth. His garage door swung up, and he eased his sleek badge of success, freshly washed, foreign, four-wheel into his basement garage and saw his wife's car wasn't there. He hurried into his study, set his briefcase down, poured a double shot of bourbon, no ice and drained it. He was pouring another when he noticed a message on the answering machine. He pushed PLAY as he gulped a swallow.

"You're all going to die." The words were plain enough.

The house balefully shushed. The late afternoon splendor burnished a deathly hue. Garland choked at mid-swallow. He looked bugeyed at the malevolent machine. He didn't recognize the voice. His savoir-faire self-control vanished with a panicked thud and a lump in his throat. No one knew except HughDon. What if it wasn't suicide? What if someone was in the office with HughDon during that phone call? He snatched the tape out of the machine and started to call the police. But fear got in the way, leaving Garland cornered in the middle of his study, his choices dwindling.

*****

Predawn risers were at Duke's breakfast diner in booths and at tables. The aroma of fried eggs, pancakes, grits, bacon and country ham filled the air. Gray caught Craige up on Sedgewicke's autopsy

reports—chronic degenerative heart condition, sky high cholesterol and arterial disease.

"His heart wasn't what killed him. Got us a crafty one here," Gray sighed. "CDC Atlanta verified Fred's gas chromatography runs on the poison."

Gray handed Craige the folder, and his eyes zeroed to the big, bold word—ACONITE.

"Lethal dose of aconite in Royce's tissues," Craige said. "Gives the how but not the way it was slipped to Sedgewicke." He looked through the rest of the toxicology report. "Not very original. Rome's Julio-Claudians treacherous family of brigands was in some ways a lot more honest than most of us and far more sophisticated with aconite. They called it wolfsbane and used it often. Old Octavian Augustus had a determined wife, the Empress Livia. It was reportedly her favorite method for eliminating rivals. She kept her supplier on call. Augustus wouldn't eat anything except food prepared by his own slaves. Livia wanted her son Tiberius to succeed to the purple. She was afraid Augustus meant to be rid of Tiberius, so she dusted her husband's figs with the bane. People do get away with murder and simple makes for better odds." Craige glanced at the next page. "This gone beyond your office?"

"Only CDC," Gray said. "Your crack about possible killings we don't know about keeps troubling me." He scratched his wiry mustache. "Marshall's suicide, Sedgewicke murdered, two women dead, the Stanley break in."

The waitress brought their orders. Craige dumped more syrup over his hotcakes than he needed, but it sure tasted good. He drained his coffee, and she refilled him as soon as the cup hit the saucer.

"Wolfsbane wouldn't come from a local pharmacy. Aconite monkshood is used in vet medicine," Craige said. "Grannie used to doctor her mule with what Mountain Tobacc. Would've skinned the hide off my backside if she caught me messing with it. She showed me how to mix it and paregoric, how much to use, when to use it, when not to. I remember her saying that wolfsbane tobacc'll kill you dead if it was too strong."

"Reckon our killer is a vet?" Gray asked.

"Either that, knows one, has a vet in the family or with the state line right here in the middle of the river, an out of state vet supply."

"Wholesalers keep records," Gray said.

"A small satchel of wolfsbane could easily be smuggled in on a freighter, in military cargo planes, MATs flights or a diplomatic courier," Craige said.

Craige drained his cup. They both knew more than a few of those kind.

"Eight of the bank employees have passports with visas dated within the last three years," Craige said. "Two tellers, one in mortgage and loans but none with access to trust records or Sedgewicke's private files."

"Anyone skimming accounts would have a field day with any inactive ones," Gray said. "You ever think about that?"

"Yea, I had and possible real estate rake-offs could even be bigger," Craige answered.

"That might fit real neat into some of Sedgewicke's deals," Gray said.

"It sure would," Craige said. "What bugs him though, is why anyone smart enough to set up a rake-off with this many accounts would be crude enough to bash in a head."

"Unless it wasn't about money," Gray said, playing devil's advocate.

"I get the feeling we're being force-fed," Craige said.

"Me too," Gray agreed. "At least Sedgewicke's exhumation is a done deal. The judge was the only one who knew I cordoned off the area, hired the hands to dig him up, rode with the body to forensics and waited while the tissues were taken. Fred did an outstanding job. We had Llewyn Royce Sedgewicke in the hearse and reburied before anyone knew. I met with Sedgewicke's wife after it was over. She only asked why, as next of kin, she hadn't been notified beforehand. I told her felony cases don't require that. She seemed to accept my answer, but it was plain she wasn't too happy."

"Rumor was she wanted him cremated," Craige said.

"That's true, and a cremation was planned," Gray confirmed.

"It's a good way to do away with evidence."

"'Specially if the ashes are scattered," Gray added. "There's just one slight catch to that angle." He took a swallow of black brew. "Sedgewicke's youngest sister objected on religious grounds, and the wife didn't push it."

"What about insurance?" Craige asked.

"There was a life insurance policy, a big one," Gray said. "And just as big a snafu with it being a motive."

"How much was the policy for?" Craige asked.

"Three mil," Gray said.

Gray saw Craige's eyebrows go up. Three million was a big motive.

Gray continued, "Sedgewicke's life insurance doesn't pay if a crime is involved in the insured's demise or if beneficiaries are convicted of a said felony."

"There's other motives beside money," Craige said. "Some of Royce's partners filed unpaid claims of a million two against his estate."

Gray asked, "You don't think she did it?"

"Nope."

Craige drained his coffee. The pompadour sprayed, stiff hairdo waitress was right on him with a fresh pot and a come-on big boy smile.

"Thanks," Craige nodded to her then said to Gray, "Lavenia Sedgewicke had nothing to gain. She comes from old money. Hearsay was he married her for position and security. He wasn't the one in love."

"She had opportunity and means," Gray said.

"More than most, but so did a lot of folks Sedgewicke dealt with. The real question is if she did it with his medical history, why would she kill him in public when offing him at home was easier and more private? Their acquaintances filled him in on ten years of their separate bedrooms. Craige didn't understand that kind of marriage, but couples do have that kind of arrangement for whatever the reasons. With aconite, she could've done him at dinner, got him to his bedroom and conveniently discovered him next morning too late for 911. No witnesses and no headlines with plenty time to tidy up the leftovers containing the poison. Neat and done with, a brief note in the obits and no questions asked. No, I don't believe she did it."

Gray smiled and said, "I like it when you agree with me."

"Whoever did Sedgewicke wanted it public," Craige said as he finished his ham. "Either that or had their hand forced. Either way, we keep digging."

They paid their tabs and walked out to their vehicles.

Gray got in and rolled down his window. "I'll keep you posted." He drove off.

After Gray left, Craige sat in his car and rolled down his window in the early cool of morning. He was not sure if he should tell Terri what Gray had found, and more importantly, what he hadn't. Maybe Craige had moved too quickly with the court order. No matter how he looked at it, he had a big part in putting Terri's life on needles and pins, but he was convinced Frank had done the right thing by protecting the originals. He went over the banquet guest list in his mind and got to wondering. Beside those who were there, who was supposed to be there and wasn't? Without being noticed, how do you poison one person at a sit-down banquet while making sure no one else is?

A car door slammed, wrenching him back to the parking lot. No matter how the cards stacked, it came to someone in the kitchen, and he'd overlooked the simplest thing—bank employees with previous records. Craige hit the ignition, shifted gears and hurried toward Gray's office. He needed Mabel's help.

"Good morning, good-looking," Mabel said in her usual, cherry greeting to Craige.

"Got a minute?" Craige asked.

"Anytime for you," she beamed.

"Your StateNet connect to NCInfo Center on-line?" Craige asked.

Mabel said, "You're serious." She brought up her screen.

"Can you log it to Gray without anyone but him knowing?" Craige asked.

Mabel gave a wicked chuckle, "What you need?" She would make it happen.

"Priors on those." Craige handed her a list of names.

"Whoa!" She exclaimed, her eyebrows shot up. "You're digging in some uptown stink."

In no time she had his info.

"Thanks," Craige said.

"That all you need?" she asked and smiled. "Have a good one."

"You too." Craige glanced at the printouts.

He pushed out the rear door of the precinct and spotted no apparent red flags on the list. He would go over it later. As he pulled onto Walton Boulevard, he couldn't stop wondering how the poison got to

Sedgewicke and no one else. It really ate at him. He shoved it to the back of his mind, looking forward to Terri's dinner invite for tonight.

*****

Jeff met Craige at the door, "Mom's upstairs, I'll tell her you're here. You like spaghetti? I just put on the pasta."

Craige patted his stomach, "I'll race you to see who gets to scrape the sauce pan."

Jeff grinned and called his mom from the foot of the stairs.

"Craige's here." He turned to Craige and said, "Be ready in no time."

Dinner was nice.

Afterward Craige said, "Jeff, that's some of the best spaghetti I ever had."

During the meal Terri didn't mention how Paul liked spaghetti. This morning as she dressed for work, she'd wondered if she was becoming one of those lonely widows, jumping at the first man who paid her attention. The idea aggravated her, and she was almost able to dismiss it.

She pushed back from the table and said, "I just happened to stop by the ice cream shop on the way home." She went to the fridge and continued, "I couldn't decide which one, so I had them wrap both ice cream cakes."

Jeff exclaimed, "All right!"

"Not too much for me," Craige said. "Pasta about did it."

Terri pushed hers around her dessert plate, while Jeff finished off a big piece and went for seconds.

"Jeff, you and Byrd are bottomless pits," Terri smiled.

Craige said, "Enjoy it while you can, Jeff."

As Jeff cleared the table, he said, "Mom, I'm running over to Lawton's. He's got mine and Dad's sleeping bags, and Byrd and I need them to go camping."

"Mom, we're leaving early tomorrow." He started up the stairs.

Terri called after him, "You didn't tell me about a camping trip."

Jeff stopped mid-landing and said, "Mom, I told you last week."

"How long will you two be gone?" Terri asked.

"Couple of nights. Outside Asheville."

"Does Marlene know you two are going that far?"

"Mom, it's a national park." He came back down the steps. "Byrd's dad let us borrow his Bronco." He gave a quick peck on her cheek and hurried upstairs to pack his duffle bag.

Terri said, "Those two are together all the time." She caught Craige's look. "I suppose you think I'm being overprotective?"

"You're his mother. You're concerned about him. My Grannie was the same. Nothing wrong with it," Craige said. "And it's good he has a close friend. I still have friends from elementary and junior high. I'm glad Jeff's going to be away from the house, but I don't think you should be here alone either."

"Let's not hash that all over again," she said.

Craige told her what he had found and said, "You're not safe here."

"You don't have to scare me any more than I already am," she frowned.

"I'd rather have you a bit scared than risk something happening to either of you," Craige admitted.

Terri turned away, gazed out the window, one hand to her breast, her fingers rested at the base of her throat. Brutal uncertainty and a savage fear possessed her home. Her golden brown eyes washed with determination. She felt squeezed between the break in and this man yet could not deny that his being here felt terribly reassuring.

"It all seems so impossible," she murmured. "How did it all become so complicated?"

Craige went to her. "Marshall may have been killed to shut him up." Craige put his arms around her.

She turned into him. "I thought Marshall killed himself."

Craige said, "It looks that way and probably is, but with what's been going on, nothing's certain. Whoever's behind this wouldn't hesitate making sure you and Jeff were out of the way." He wanted to protect her, wanted more than that.

Terri said, "Don't talk like that." She was trying not to let fear fasten her in its grip.

"It's no longer a matter of what either of us like." The skin of her neck was soft and warm.

"I didn't ask to be in the middle of this," she said.

Craige said very softly, "No, you didn't." Guilt chewed on him. "'Specially since it's my fault, but I want you and Jeff away from this house."

For some time he had sensed powerful shades hovering to strike, not knowing where or when and, worse, no idea why or who.

"My place is safer with a big dog that tolerates no strangers," Craige said. "And not that many know how to get to Moccasin Hollow."

She tilted her head up to Craige and said, "Safe from whom?"

Craige stopped her words with a finger across her half-parted lips, "Whoever trashed your place may be waiting, picking their time. If you or Jeff were here …"

Their faces were nearly touching. Fear filled her eyes. Craige took her lips, took her soul, into him. Her eyes blazed incandescent as she resisted for a moment, then her eyes shut as she bent into his arms. Her arms encircled his shoulders, grasped him to her, her touch rippling through him. He felt his desire between them blaze with her own torrid, white heat. He felt her stiffen and pull back. He looked at her, her eyes open where they had been closed. She looked past him. He turned. Jeff was standing at the foot of the steps. The look on his face was a mixture. None of them were quite sure about anything.

# Chapter 11

Jeff came through the kitchen, started into the den and stopped. Craige's arms were around his mom. They were kissing. He hesitated. He felt embarrassed. His feelings were all mixed up. He felt he was intruding. He started to leave, determined to be cool. Terri saw her son and caught his scowl toward Craige.

"Jeff—" she said. "Don't go."

"You don't have to explain to me," Jeff said.

"I don't want you to leave," she stated.

Craige interrupted, "Jeff, I'm glad you're here."

Craige knew what her son must have felt—the loss of his father. He had felt the same with the loss of his parents. Jeff found Craige here with his mother, where memories of his father were everywhere. Those kind of prickly pear edges can only be tackled man to man, face-to-face.

Craige said, "Jeff, you need to hear what I told your mother." He laid it out. "There's plenty of privacy at Moccasin Hollow, bedrooms with their own baths."

"What would the bank say?" Terri asked. It was a lukewarm excuse for her real reason. Terri closed her eyes, "What an unbelievable thing for me to say." She slowly shook her head. "Our lives could be in danger."

Craige lifted her chin up to him, "For a sophisticated, California woman, you are way too concerned with what other people say. It

won't interfere with Jeff's school." Craige looked at Jeff. "He can finish the year where he is. No one has to play taxi. You have your car for work. Jeff can use one of mine."

Jeff burst out, "All right!" The thought of his own set of wheels excited him.

"Jeff!" his mom declared.

"Mom, I have my license." He eagerly looked back and forth between his mom and Craige.

Craige looked at Terri, "Give it some serious thought."

"Yea, Mom," Jeff said. "Be great out in the country." He turned to Craige and asked, "Could I get a horse?"

Terri exclaimed, "Jeff!" The two were boxing her in.

Craige grinned. "I'd been thinking about getting a quarter horse."

"Quarter horses are the best," Jeff said. "Not so inbred, good blood lines, but you better sit the saddle good. They're quick. Get out from under you if they cut sharp, and you're not paying attention."

"How you know so much about cutting horses?" Craige asked.

"Last couple of years I worked the Futurity for free tickets," Jeff answered. "Cleaned stalls, shoveled manure, walked cool-downs for horses coming out of the arena."

Terri said, "I'll think about it."

She felt as though the two of them had already made the decision, knowing she ought to be pleased Jeff was comfortable around Craige. She knew Jeff had worked the Futurity but had no idea he was so interested in horses. She could understand his drawing close to Craige— the two were a lot alike.

As Craige started toward the door, he asked Jeff, "When you and Byrd leaving?"

"Tomorrow, before daybreak," Jeff said. "Maybe this isn't a good time to be gone. I don't want Mom here alone."

He was looking forward to camping with Byrd, and his mom was safe with Craige around.

"We'll talk about horses when you get back," Craige assured him.

Craige leaned forward, kissed Terri lightly on the lips, pulled the door closed behind him and drove away.

"You like him, don't you?" Jeff said.

"What you need is a good breakfast." Her face blushed hot.

"I mean you like him a lot," Jeff persisted.

"Go brush your teeth while I get dressed," she urged him.

Her face grew more red.

Jeff watched his mother disappear into her bedroom.

He picked up one of his father's pictures, took it to his room and laid it on his bed. He looked at his dad's face as he slid into a pair of checkered boxers and kicked into his jeans. He found he wasn't so upset about his mom and Craige. He remembered evenings when Mom and Dad would tell him to go to his room. They'd start that mushy stuff, which meant sex. Sometimes he could hear their murmurs and moans as though they were hurting one another. Once they left their door open, and he'd peeked in. Shadows undulated across his dad's shoulders, Mom's ankles locked around Dad's waist, sheets and pillows pitched cockeyed, while he heard soft, muted giggles. He could never figure why grown-ups got so uptight about sex. Same kind of thing when he walked in just now. The look in Mom's eyes, trying to make it seem as if that wasn't what they were doing. Some of his soccer team and their girlfriends did it everyday after school. There was locker room talk, centerfold magazines, and he and Byrd swapped stories in their tent, their sleeping bags or bedrooms. By the time Jeff was 16, there were jerk-off sessions at his house or Byrd's and summertime skinny dipping on the slippery rocks of the Savanno rapids. Cold lake water gave them goose bumps and made their dicks look like wrinkled-up prunes. He couldn't wait till he had a girl he really liked. Watch out world, he'd munch her real good. He looked forward to his birthday—watch out world, the stud buddies Jeff and Byrd about to arrive.

He and Byrd double dared one another to a switch-off, flipping coins for who got seconds. It never got further than back seat fumbling of cramped arms and legs though. He didn't cotton to hurry-up hotties just to get off. He had thought about asking a Southside college freshman a year ahead of him for a date and a good deal more. Byrd had the hots for her too. He asked Jeff if it was OK, then asked her out.

The next day Byrd told him, "Man, it was outta sight!" "She's a lot of woman." He acted as though he was some big expert.

Jeff had two dates with her but never did get beyond grub and suck face. The next week, on one sultry, cutting-edged afternoon, he and Byrd basked on the bright sunshine rocks of the river rapids.

Jeff said, "No telling where she's had her tongue."

"Who cares?" Byrd said and flicked water out of his ears.

"You better watch out," Jeff cautioned.

"I used a rubber," Byrd said.

"That don't always take care of things."

"College is gonna be fun," Byrd said. "You wait and see."

"Too much party and your grades will slide," Jeff replied.

"Plenty time for that. You still going to the party?"

"Yeah. You?"

"You asking her?"

"Nah, you go ahead."

"Lots of babes out there," Byrd said. "Do as many as you can."

"Don't want to do all of them," Jeff said.

He thought of his dad and mom, and from the way Craige was built, Jeff figured Craige could really pound a woman. He thought of that saucer-eyed, sharp-looking cheerleader and her jock boyfriends, after school sport fucks for rides home or a new varsity jersey.

They would say "I love you" to one guy, then throw their heels in the air with the next one.

All women weren't like that. His mom wasn't.

*****

Even after Craige got home he couldn't keep Sedgewicke's autopsy report from digging at him like a clump of hungry maggots. He stripped off his shirt and pants and put on his favorite washed-soft cutoffs. His fingers were idling his chest as he set the pot of coffee on the burner and sat at the kitchen table. The single overhead spot glared long into the unending night. He retraced every scrap of the investigation, court documents, exhumation and autopsy. He plundered the gallery of plausibles looking for crannies and chinks he'd overlooked. Was he too close or was his interest in Terri sidetracking him? Where was the elusive trigger to who or what precipitated Sedgewicke's death? His gut kept saying something wasn't quite right. Had it started with intimidation? Was Royce's murder a backfire to shut his mouth? The papers stared at Craige—the trail had to be there no matter how well camouflaged. He was convinced the killings weren't finished, but where was the key to the watershed instant that ended up with Royce dead?

Money was the most conspicuous, power and cash were two things Royce lived for. How or where he had gotten it was messier. Unease

laced at Craige that he was not seeing something plain as day. Was Sedgewicke's killer the same one who pushed Marshall over the edge? No matter how he curled the facts, there had to be a double-deal tangle among Theosia's estate, embezzlement, CEO and boardroom politics. Sherlock Holmes' "Sign of Four" hammered him and eliminated the impossible. What's left has to be the truth.

The money angle was the most seductive, but it chafed Craige to accept Royce's well-known greed as the cause. It was a ready-made reason for anyone wanting it to appear that way. It may have started there and blackmail right with it, but it was a slippery *modus operandi*. Other emotions could be just as deadly. Jealousy didn't seem one of them unless there was a girlfriend or friends. Sedgewicke was cut from the robber baron mold. He hadn't gotten where he was without stepping on toes, including Marshall's. Had Marshall been an unwilling accomplice, or had he tried to blackmail someone, hadn't covered his ass and took the easy way out? Craige had dealt with murderous hands too often to discount the cornered rabbit possibility. Corner any animal, and you sometimes get an unexpected explosion. Maybe that's why looking for a motive kept eluding him. Maybe there wasn't one. Maybe he had a dead body that was never planned, money no part of it.

An inner voice warned not to discard the obvious. If there could be two killers, why not three or a psycho killer posing as two? It made a sick kind of sense since the victims didn't know one another, either compulsive kills or indiscriminate victims so the real target would be lost in the serial kills. The idea wasn't new.

Craige didn't like where Conan Doyle's logic was taking him. He went to the liquor cabinet, to the lower shelf in the back and lifted the dusty bottle of his favorite Royale Salute blend. It was the last of the case he'd picked up last spring from Chivas Limited distillery, Aberdeen. For him, Royale Salute was more apéritif than liquor. He broke the seal and took a gentle sniff of the twenty-one-year-old, eighty proof bouquet. He then poured a generous shot into an antique-pressed, glass liqueur goblet, scowled at the paper-laden table, slouched down in the chair and took a slow, connoisseur sip.

Past BlackOps and Broken Arrow botches forced him to start over. As Craige retraced each file and reread each tedious page, a chilled notion hit him that it wasn't what was in front of him but what wasn't.

He halted the goblet with its last swallow in midair, not liking his thought one damn bit.

Craige needed a brain-flush. He ambled out onto the porch, his eyes straying to the nail where Grannie's fern once hung. His mind retraced the bullet's trajectory. Fate pivoted on the unexpected as Lucky picked that moment to slurp his hand. As he bent down to pet him, the fern pot above his head shattered in a cracking thunk shower of dirt and shards. Another half second and he would have had a hole in what would've been left of his head.

The rasping of twilight crickets brought him back to the porch. Craige finished his scotch and hit the sack for a restless night's sleep. Early the next morning, he untwisted the sheets from his nakedness and rolled out of bed. His early morning impatience greeted the sun as it sliced through the overcast. He reached for the cordless and punched autodial.

When she answered, Craige said, "Sorry if I woke you." He enjoyed hearing her voice and tried to sound calm.

"You didn't," Terri said. It was a lazy moment. "You call earlier?"

"No," Craige said. "Why?"

"I've been up since before five helping Jeff pack. He and Byrd just left. I was in the shower, and I thought I heard the phone," she said. "Why, what's the matter?"

"I thought about you all last night," Craige said.

"How nice." She cozied tight into her cotton robe. "Knowing you, I'd guess you spent a sleepless night going over all those papers." She was safe with the distance between them.

"You mess with my head," Craige said in a low voice.

Terri chuckled an infuriating beckoning in his ear.

"I'm serious," Craige growled as he recalled the faint smell of her perfume on the pillows.

"I would like to think you called just to talk," Terri said. "It's not too early, but I know you well enough to know you called about something else."

"Maybe you know me better than I think," Craige said. "But this morning I feel even stronger about you and Jeff not staying in your house. Pack your suitcase."

"Craige, there's lots to consider."

She wasn't about to tell this amazing man her entire night had

been bewitched with his image in and out of her own night dramas, fixations she didn't want to stop.

"Then I'll stay there," Craige said.

"You know that would complicate things."

"I was hoping it would," Craige said, half teasing.

"You're being just short of pushy," she said.

"I'm not being short of pushy. I'm being pushy on purpose. I don't like frightening you, but I'm not comfortable with you or Jeff staying there. You're using him as an excuse to avoid the issue."

"Jeff isn't an excuse," She said sharply.

"He's more mature than you think," Craige said. "Why are you afraid of committing to something that might be good for both of us?"

"You're a fine one to say anything about not wanting a relationship," Terri said. "How would you know, you don't have any children."

Terri regretted the words the moment they were out of her mouth.

"I'm sorry," she said. "I shouldn't have said that."

"My feelings about you are personal, but wanting you out of there has nothing to do with anything except you and Jeff being safe. I'm not his father, but that's not the point. If something happened to you whether he's there or not, he'll end up blaming himself his whole life. He's got this idea that it's his place to protect you, and I can't fault him for that, but with a killer on the loose, he could die trying to do that."

Craige was crowding her hard. He knew Terri wasn't thinking only of Jeff but neither was he. He couldn't deny what he felt waking up with her, having her in his arms. But motel rooms, even with him in an adjoining room, was ridiculous, not to mention having no security, which left him jittery.

"All of this takes some getting used to. Then you come into my life like a Kansas tornado," Terri said.

"I thought it was sort of nice," Craige remarked. "I even hear it's rumored we sailors have a girl in every port."

Terri said, "You take a lot for granted."

Craige muttered, "Dammit!" He never liked cat and mouse sparring. "You have me so wrapped up."

He was probably saying too much, but it was exactly the way he felt.

"No one bent your arm," she said.

147

"I swear," Craige sputtered, "you're as hard-headed as Theosia."

"Me, hard-headed?" She let out a quick chuckle. "Now that is the pot calling the kettle names."

She pictured his green eyes flaring with that touch of bronze.

"This isn't the time to be stubborn." Fear coated his words. "How many times do I have to repeat that neither of you are immune to what happened to Sedgewicke?"

A shapeless, wintery thing hovered somewhere in a bright sunshine morning that no longer seemed so tranquil, random exterminations in a game with no rules.

Craige said, "I'm not exactly happy admitting it might've been better for you if we'd left the originals where they were."

Terri interrupted, "Being at your place probably would be safer." She tried to make her heart be calm. "There's only the sofa bed here."

"The sofa's not the problem," Craige said. "It's the layout of your house."

"Jeff already believes we're sleeping together," she said.

Her directness shouldn't have startled Craige, but it did. Still, it wasn't as though he hadn't thought about it the first time he laid eyes on her.

"So Jeff saw me kiss you," Craige said. "The idea has its appeal." Craige was trying to make light of it.

"That's the most backhanded compliment I've ever received," Terri said.

Craige said, "I doubt I'm the first man the thought ever occurred to." As though handling some rare piece of crystal, he told her, "You are a very desirable woman."

"Why, thank you Mr. Craige Expert Ingramme," Terri said. "If you ever saw me in the mornings in my robe, you might have second thoughts."

Craige said, "I'd rather see you without your robe."

"Now I am blushing," she said.

He changed the subject. "I'll pack a few things. Call me before you leave your office. I'll wait for you at your place."

Terri started to object, but instead she said, "All right." Her thoughts were all messed up.

"I'll call you at work." Craige then hung up.

She thought of Craige and knew she had no handle on the whole concoction.

"It's all moving so fast," she mumbled. "How can I love someone I've only known such a short time?"

She glanced at the clock; time had flown. She snapped on her shower cap, pulled out some fresh, silk lingerie and noticed the mauve, lace trimmed piece with its glare of red. She remembered the day she bought it and Paul's look that evening when she slipped off her dressing gown. She'd been surprised that next morning that it had survived Paul's robust rampage. They had gone shopping together, and she liked the color. She loved silk but hated synthetics. For being a bit of nothing, it had cost a fortune. Paul made sure the saleswoman was out of earshot when he nuzzled her ear and said, "Let me squander some money on my favorite wife." When the woman returned, he said, "We'll take the red one."

Terri buried her face in its softness. She could almost smell Paul in the faint fragrance of her sachet. She held it a moment longer and remembered the splendid, virile beauty of PaulBeast striding toward her, the marvelous things his body promised—his laughter and giddy sense of fun, times he'd surprise her with little things, his gentleness when they cuddled in that lingering world between wake and sleep.

She was sure no other woman could possibly have what she had—endless, wonderful warmth when he made love to her, his stalwart, male strength reared upon her, into her, his power dispensed untold pleasures. From day one, they worshiped one another body and soul.

They had wanted a child. Paul was in the delivery room with her. They were both unbelievably delighted in the bouncing, healthy, squalling Jeffrey David who wanted to nurse almost before the cord was tied. Terri smiled, recalling the spread of delight that took his face when he saw his son. Terri's hand caught at her throat as Paul's face abruptly morphed into Craige's. She tried to deny what lay quiescent within her yet wasn't sure she could risk the pain of such loss again.

*****

Irene was not yet in. The first thing Terri saw as she walked into her office was Beth. She still hadn't put her purse down and gotten her jacket off when twenty-six-year-old, going on baby talk two Beth Pilgrim bobbed and flounced through the double glass doors of the reception room and straight into Terri's private office.

149

She strutted in with a giddy, chirped "hi" like they were bosom buddies. "Wasn't the weekend great?"

Beth uttered "great" at least once every time her mouth opened. Terri was taken aback. She had seen Beth just more than a few times, but she wasn't about to ask her what she wanted. She knew Beth was angling for something. Terri slipped off her jacket and put it on a hanger.

"Good morning," Terri said.

Rolling her eyes, Beth said, "Weather was great, cooked out, went water skiing, had a great weekend. We were all at the lake, and I got to thinking …"

Terri refused to be drawn in by this petulant woman-child. She buried her sarcastic impulse to say "you had a thought?" In a way, Terri felt sorry for Beth Pilgrim's pretentious social climbing. She was a mill hand's offspring who knew exactly what she was but desperate to be more than she ever could be, more than the town would let her be.

Beth said, "There's lots of new faces here." She plopped her overextended rear end on Terri's desk. "Before the weather gets too chilly, wouldn't it be great to have an office party at the lake. There's some great looking guys here, and since you never go across the street to the pub for our 5 o'clock happy hours, everyone's sort of got the idea you're being standoffish. Be a great chance for you to meet guys who're just dying to meet you." She showed her best grin as she slid off the desk. "I'll ask around, let you know what weekend's best." She headed toward the door.

Having a matchmaker try to fix her up was all Terri needed, especially from this wanton woman-child who did her personal phoning at work with no care about the bank's "business only" phone policy. She'd heard of Beth's escapades, and apparently, this was Beth's way of concocting intimate parties.

"How's married life?" Terri asked.

With a flip of her hair and a pasted on smile, Beth said, "Great." She hesitated at the door. "Really great. I'll give you a buzz. Be great to chat."

Beth could tell from the highfalutin look on Stanley's face she was being given the brushoff. This one thought she was better than everyone else. Get Miss FancyPants Stanley to bring that Carolina buck up to the lake, show her what a real woman can do with a man.

"Morning, Beth." Irene greeted as she came in. "Morning, Mrs. Stanley."

Terri said, "Morning, Irene."

Terri closed her door, left Beth to Irene, read her messages, returned her calls, then opened the dossier Irene had pulled last Friday. Later, she walked to the window, looked down on the placid sparkle of the river. What she saw was thoroughly contrary to what was stirring deep in Terri Stanley's heart.

# Chapter 12

Craige paced the floor. Frustration bumped into overdrive with too much of his turkish brew. He didn't know how many more nights he'd spend on Terri's sofa. Most times, anything is better than waiting—he'd seen sitting and waiting get men killed. It was never his strong suit. Playing defense boxed one in. It lets an opponent take the high ground, success thrown away before the fight starts. In a friendly game of chess or hot-fire entanglement, offense always has the edge, but he'd learned to mull over his ideas real good before kicking them into gear. A well-laid plan was the key to a good shadows onslaught. The only other option was to wait, and he was in no mood for that. He didn't discuss what he had in mind with Gray. If he got caught he'd have the out of deniability, besides there was Terri. She didn't need to know. She was already upset. It wasn't a good plan, but it was the best he had.

That day in the outer reception area when he was waiting to meet Terri for the first time, he happened to notice the open interoffice phone book on Irene Rozkovsky's desk. Ever since then, it had nibbled a slow spark in his mind. In the KISS "Keep It Simple" rule the second "S" stood for stupid. Dropping that last "S" is a lot better, but there'd be hell to pay if his hair-brain chance backfired, and he got caught.

Someone was keeping tabs on every move made inside the bank and a few outside as well. He doubted Gray would find any record of

poison purchases. His plan was playing a hunch, FieldOp rule number one—one step at a time. Familiar faces among the bank's personnel was as good a place to start as any. He would've preferred a more subtle ambush—tailing a few leads for several days to see where they led him—but time wasn't on his side, and he damn well wasn't giving an SOB a chance to cover their ass. At least, not if he could help it.

Craige had bought a pair of jump coveralls that matched the bank's housekeeping. In his "BlackOps" room off his bedroom, he opened the humidity-proof case, unwrapped the silicon-impregnated cloth, the miniature, oblong oval snugged in his palm as he loaded the cassette. He pushed the release and heard the imperceptible click. It was ready to go. Even if office, overhead lights were off, he'd need no extra light, ambient would be enough. The only glitch might be was if employee records had been digitally stored and originals discarded. He grabbed a couple of mini CDs. If he couldn't photograph the files, he'd tap their mainframe, his decrypt systems could handle the rest. On the insulated case, he pressed both thumb-plates simultaneously, the lid slid open, and he flipped through backups till he found descramble programs courtesy of E-Corp Executive Outcomes. He hoped he didn't have to deal with any networked stations, but odds were he would. He preferred to avoid security systems, plus the time it would take to track and erase any date-time logs.

Quick in-out, tried and true best for success. Anything more, the chances of being caught zoomed up, which could put the screws to a lot of people he was trying to protect, not to mention himself.

Over the next week, Craige reconnoitered Terri's building—outside, inside, service elevators, maintenance passages and peak foot traffic times. Housekeeping shifts left at three, secretaries between four and 4:30 and department heads by 5:30. He engaged his ring-and-search program and let it random dial between four and nine—not too early, not too late. The phone picked up only once. He would enter before the close of business hours to minimize dealing with after-hours security. Daytime was chancy but still the best disguise. No one paid attention to a uniformed body in a busy corridor or office.

He headed across the river. His heart raced as though he was snorkeling toward the beach about to rise out of sea foam, from an airborne HELO or a silent panther stalk of a target marked for "resolve with extreme prejudice." He parked in the BANK CUSTOMER PARK-

ING ONLY section of the garage, avoided the fourth floor connect and took the side street toward the rear service loading docks. Unnoticed and with his toolbox in hand, he caught the freight elevator to the brightly lit halls on the floor above personnel. A shapely looking thing gave him an interested haven't-seen-you-before look. The wall clock stood at a few minutes before five as he headed down the steps.

Craige stopped at the door marked PERSONNEL, fiddled with his stage prop utility belt to look busy and listened for any voices inside. He heard nothing, took a deep breath and, as though he belonged, pushed through the door. He thanked his lucky stars everyone had left. Most desks and file cabinets were unlocked and the director of personnel's office was straight ahead. He found the files he wanted, spread them out and rapidfire photoed what he needed, plus a few other interesting tidbits. He made sure the files were placed back exactly where he found them and got out and back in traffic in under an hour. No questions, no notice and no complications.

In his dark room, Craige removed the film strips from the cassettes, developed and double washed the negatives, carefully shook them free of excess water, squeegeed each strip with a soft sponge for no smudges, and weighted each strip so they hung straight. He never did like digital or automatic developers. Digitals can trip you up, and autodevelopers don't wash out all the fixative, the negatives turn brown and, eventually, become useless. He plugged in the blow dryer, set it on low, air-dried each strip, duplicated blowups of several frames, then onto the drying drum and timer. He turned his attention to a couple of misdemeanors—traffic incidents that had showed up among his list of names. After some later footwork, he found the misdemeanors to be another dead-end, leading to no prison records.

After the timer on the dryer dinged, he trimmed the excesses off the prints, then pegged the photos to the corkboard. He thumbtacked Sedgewicke and Marshall side-by-side at the top with the garage and airport victims underneath Sedgewicke. Craige stuck possible connections of missing persons to one side and left blanks for pictures for what bothered him most—victims they didn't know about.

Craige stepped back and studied matches to misfits, the indiscriminate MOs, predictably unpredictable patterns, isolated kills or serial. The brutality of the women's mangled faces tugging at him because they seemed so out of place. A single killer eluded him no

matter what sort of twist he put into it, rogue cop, lawyer, banker, grudge kill, drugs, heat of passion. Too much scotch and too many hours, and he was still at zero. No one suspect knew all the victims. An icy, summertime shudder hit him—the warren of halls in Terri's building. Aside from the public areas of offices and meeting rooms, there were the fire stairs, lounges, storage areas, a basement power plant of catwalks, boilers, pipes, countless cubbyholes, niches, nooks and crannies to hide in. He got up, walked away, made some turkish, came back to his pegboard and stretched his imaginings around any bizarre niches, any possible leg up on their faceless exterminator.

Craige's checkerboard of photos was screaming that circumstances were playing their own rules, which jolted him into seeing that the different MOs was the pattern, obvious from hindsight. What he liked least was that it made a twisted kind of sense. Gray always had an uncanny nose for where to look. Maybe his theory about a deranged psycho wasn't so far off, but that still didn't answer where the simple knot of killing had spun loose. He fastened Terri's picture to one side, away from the women killed late at night.

As he hit the shower, his inner Jekyll and Hyde flip-flopped the cobblestone facts back and forth. The pulse-jet spray spattered his face. As the soap cascaded over his tightly squeezed eyes, Terri's blood covered face swam into a hellish apocalypse that scared the crap out of him.

*****

When Beth called the lake lodge caretaker's cottage, only one unreserved weekend was open. She booked it and wasted no time making lists of who, what, where and when. Beth hadn't forgotten the day she watched Gordie eye Terri Stanley crossing the main foyer, surveying looker Stanley from head to toe.

She said to Gordie, "Terri Stanley's got this new boyfriend."

Gordie mumbled, "And you want to make sure he's there." His eyes never left the TV.

Beth said, "You know what I mean."

"Yeh, I know what you want," Gordie grinned as he grabbed his crotch.

"I want her to feel welcome," she said.

"You want to check him out," Gordie guffawed. "You inviting Eric?"

"Sure." Beth came over to him. "We'll have the pool." He covered his hand with hers, squeezed his crotch and sweetly smiled.

"You're wicked," Gordie winced. He liked pain.

"I have good teachers," She said, giving him a kissy-kissy baby doll pucker.

She trailed her tongue down his cheek to his chin and the corner of his eye. They were nose to nose, eyes swallowing eyes. Nostrils flared as she inhaled the damp sweet heat of him and felt his crotch tighten. Her butch master smirk to Gordie's slave whimper, Beth loved to tease as long as it wasn't all tease and no action.

She said, "Stanley's kid is a hottie high schooler. Break him in, give the young colt a real test drive. Eric would enjoy being part of that."

"You like young ones." Gordie's eyes didn't move.

"Someone has to be first." Beth squeezed him harder.

"You are a dirty broad," he said and grabbed her shoulders. "High schoolers are jail bait."

"You've had your share of young meat that wasn't legal," she said, "strapped in the middle of those bedroom trains at those premed, pledge parties. About got your butt arrested." She gave a raucous laugh. "That would've put an end to med school, but you didn't care nothing about that."

"I didn't get arrested." Gordie licked her neck. "How'd you find out?"

"Deputies can be full of pillow talk. You're not the only one that goes for sloppy seconds, sweet things on their hands and knees between two deputies. Giving it away, bartering protection, while they work the freeway strip." Her hand got busier. "We might recruit some new faces, set up a video, party room—insurance if any parents make trouble about naked pictures of their kids." Her nails pinched a nipple. "Then there's Masters, all those tourists saying they're here for golf. Most could care less. They just want to have a good time. Columbia is always looking for new box cover faces."

Satyr Gordie mauled her tit. Beth let him play. Gordie was as gullible as any man.

Beth said, "Nothing like the first time, a bewildered look they never have again. Get them all juiced up with our party playthings. Their eyes roll back with the pain that hurts so good. We can train

him like we want. Why let someone else have firsts?" She was voracious.

She dropped to her knees. She craved a sex-fix, needed it badly the more she thought about the party. Gordie was soon sucking air.

She pulled away. "Eric can get our party favors." She stood and went to the phone. "Spike the mixers, have the Stanley kid flying high." She fed Gordie's walk-on-the-wild-side addiction.

Gordie gawked, "Why'd you stop?" His surgical scrubs were around his ankles.

He kicked off his scrubs, spun her around, yanked the neck of her dress loose, pulled her legs up around his waist and crashed into her. Mister straight-arrow, O.R. intern, cardboard clone was inspired. He couldn't wait for another of their night walks.

Beth clawed Gordie's head off one nipple, "First, I have to be sure Stanley brings that nice, tender son." She gave a sweet smile as she felt him inside her. "Before we finish, young Stanley will come begging for more." She wished Eric was here.

*****

At her desk the following morning, Beth brought up her e-mail, entered date, time, place and sent copies to each department head. She waited till the Stanley, T. receipt window flashed on her screen, then dialed Terri's office. When Irene answered, Beth said, "Terri in?" She was curt, not interested in Rozkovsky prattle.

Irene said, "Just a moment."

As she punched Terri's intercom, Irene thought how Beth had gotten snippety ever since she moved into the president's office.

"Yes?" Terri answered.

"Line two," Irene said. "Your favorite secretary."

Terri picked up, "Beth, I just opened your e-mail."

"Your son's invited," Beth said. "The ski boats will be there. The club house is in a cove. It's great for water skiing. The pool is great, too. You will be inviting that gorgeous hunk with the great body everyone's talking about, won't you?" She didn't let up. "Those strong, silent types have to be handled with kid gloves, but they are so appealing." She relished sinking her spurs into standoff Stanley. "'Specially ones that look that great." Beth's southern, bitchy drawl was way too

fake. "See you at the party." She hung up.

Terri had suppressed a delicious impulse to say she wasn't dating anyone, but she knew that would only interest Beth more. She wasn't surprised at Beth's grapevine, hen party busyness. Men were her hobbies; Craige was just another party favor. Once he met Beth, Terri could picture Craige's unapproachable aloofness locking into place. Terri hesitated whether to ask Craige, perhaps after supper. She found herself blushing. The quiet evenings were the times she and Paul kept for one another.

The day was gone. Lunch and five o'clock seemed only minutes apart. She called Craige but got no answer. She slipped into her jacket and skipped the elevator, she didn't want to run into Beth. She took the side stairs to the garage crosswalk, her footsteps on the cement fell with a spooky, hollow timbre she'd never before noticed. She thought about Beth's invitation as she threaded through traffic. Jeff was finishing up edging the lawn as she pulled into the driveway.

"That looks really nice," she said.

"Didn't take long. Craige's finishing up the backyard. We started this afternoon, soon as we got back from horseback riding," He continued. "Watered the horses at the lower rapids, then went skinny dipping." His bare forearm brushed a sweaty forehead. "We got it raked, the hedges trimmed and the cuttings bagged."

She was glad she hadn't forgotten defrost some meat. She washed and drained the romaine lettuce, sliced the carrots and tomatoes and diced the radishes. As she tossed the salad at the sink, she saw Jeff hurry around the corner into the backyard. The sprinklers came on, and Craige sprinted out of the rainbow spray, sunlight shimmering off his shoulders. Terri was glad Jeff enjoyed being around Craige. Looking at the two of them, she hadn't realized how much the adult had replaced the boy in her son.

"He's handling it better than you," she murmured.

As they had their coffee and dessert, Craige said, "Have to give you a rain check on the party. I've got a have-to-do that afternoon, which could eat a good part into the evening."

"Me too," Jeff said, trying the same tack with soccer practice. Craige made his stick, Jeff didn't.

*****

The next morning, Barry was enraged when he found Beth Pilgrim's e-mail.

"Didn't take her long to move up," he grumbled.

His mood darkened, and his secretary became more upset as the morning progressed. She couldn't seem to do anything right. Mr. Peters was impossible when he got like this. She cleaned off her desk, left midmorning and took two days' sick leave.

Barry fumed, "I'll show them." He chewed at the inside of his cheek. "Knowing her, she wiggled her butt, got them to throw this party and expected everyone to jump when she snapped her fingers." They all took him for granted. "They'll not treat me like they did him."

His wine cellar was calling him. Barry was in a seething frenzy by the time the hours dragged to five and hurried to his cloistered solitude. The great wooden door blocked the soothing, steady drip of water. He drew aside the mural drapes in his tabernacle sanctuary. The skull gleamed and basked him in its warmth. It eased the pain in his chest. He opened the cabinet, flung the moldy heads into the pit, and tugged down the handle. The water swirled and washed it all clean. He reached for the small vial. He would go to their party.

Later that week, he picked one up stumbling out of a corner bar. Made small talk and flashed some cash. The twenty-two-year-old begged for death before Barry quit with the knives. He shut off the electricity, split open the chest and held the beating heart in his hands. He flushed the whole mess away. He felt somewhat better, but the dull ache lingered behind his eyes.

*****

At the party, Beth spotted Terri and Jeff coming in. She made a beeline to them and gushed, "Great you could make it. Where's that hunk of yours?"

Over the booming crescendo, Terri said, "He couldn't make it."

"This must be that soccer playing son we've heard so much about." Beth forced smile.

"Yes," Terri introduced him, "my son, Jeffrey."

Jeff didn't miss it. Mom never called him Jeffrey unless it meant watch out. He could tell she didn't like this Beth person.

He pulled himself straight, "Pleased to meet you, Ma'am."

"My—" Beth said, the coquette batted her lashes.

In her world, "ma'am" was used for the wheelchair crowd. She eyed Jeff and knew Stanley Bitch had put her son up to that "Ma'am" bit. Her smile was harsh.

Beth said, "He is well-mannered." She turned to Gordie. "My husband, Gordie."

"Yea, Terri Stanley," Gordie said. "Beth's told me about you." He gave her a liquored grin. "All good."

Beth didn't like the way Gordie checked her out. Terri insulated herself with a silken, mother, grizzly reaction. Her mahogany eyes gave a razored look at this philistine plunderess.

"Nice meeting you," Jeff said. "I'm hungry." He was drawn to the smoking BBQ. "Mom, want me to get you anything?"

Terri said, "Not right now." She turned back to Beth and Gordie. "Teenagers are always hungry, and those desserts look luscious."

She couldn't resist the diet dig and caught the rankle in Beth's expression. She thought that ought to keep this pest at a distance yet knew it wouldn't.

"Terri, I want you to meet someone." She motioned toward Eric. "Eric Stompfer, this is Terri Stanley ... the one I told you about."

Beth was not about to be put off, didn't give a fuck what bitch mom thought.

Eric guzzled his beer and said, "Terri." He gave her his best imitation California-dude look.

"Eric," Terri remarked, "I don't believe I've seen you at the bank." She didn't miss Beth's look.

"I'm a med tech," Eric said, "with the county emergency service."

"Eric's in the navy reserve hospital unit, recently back from sea duty," Beth added.

Terri felt herself go pale. She thought of corpsmen in Paul's unit.

"You all right?" Beth asked. "Maybe something cool to drink?"

Terri said, "Perhaps a club soda."

"I'll get it," Eric offered and disappeared.

"If I didn't know better," Beth feigned a smile, "I'd say you were pregnant. Who could blame you with a big, strong thing around the house like you have?" She enjoyed her spiteful *tête-à-tête*.

Terri said nothing. This tawdry woman was worse than coarse. She

remembered a disgusted outburst from her father, "taste of a she-goat."

Eric reappeared. "See if this helps." He passed the frosty cup to her.

Through the triple doors opening onto the upper deck, Barry watched Beth work the party. His fingers fondled the vial in his vest pocket. He noticed the kid that came in with hawk-eye Stanley. Barry mingled and graded prospects. He decided against spiking the punch— too many eyes. He hadn't seen that stinking Garland Holton. He badly wanted to make him dance in the cellar.

Barry headed to the bar and ordered, "Water on the rocks."

"That all you having, Mr. Peters?" the bartender asked.

Barry said, surly, "I'm driving."

"I don't see the Missus?" The bartendar tried to make small talk.

"She wasn't feeling well," Barry said. "Touch of the flu." With that, he moved away into the crowd.

Barry discarded the bartender as a possible and ambled onto the deck toward the pool noises. He spotted Stanley's kid doing a clanging bounce off the diving board followed by a cannonball boom. It was past midnight when Barry meandered to the lower veranda. Down the steps, bodies on the dock shadowed in the glow from a dockside light. His nostrils flared when he spotted smart-ass Eric. This wasn't a good time to do him, but he sure wanted to take someone. He headed back up the steps. Chattering boozy magpies in the kitchen ignored him as though he weren't there, and there was a couple all over one another in the alcove behind the refrigerator. Barry spotted the rack of kitchen knives.

# Chapter 13

**N**ice evening," Barry said as he strolled out onto the dock.

Eric said, "Yeh—" He guzzled the last of his beer.

"Like wine?" Barry reached a second cup toward Eric. "I got this for someone. She left."

"Win some, lose some," Eric said. "I was about ready for a refill."

Eric gulped the cup empty. He didn't care what it was as long as it was booze. Barry took the empty cup and gave Eric his full one. The music boomed across the lake—the bleary-eyed all-nighter was in full swing. Several ski boats, a houseboat and some pontoons bumped and squeaked against the dock as Barry stared out across the murky, molasses swells of the water. He figured it still might be too strong. Off in the darkness, tree frogs and katydids sawed away, parents with children long gone.

"Warm night," Eric wiped his mouth with the back of his hand. "Think I've had enough." His words slurred.

A slow patter of wine from his cup legs dribbled into the water. Eric dangled off the dock, reached down, scooped water with the cup and splashed his face. Barry flashed a quick glance at the shaded silhouette next to him, hunkered swiftly to one knee and gave a quick look toward the empty dark steps toward the party. He thought of the hungry mural waiting in his cellar. With the knife in an iron-grip, his arm wrapped around Eric's neck, shoved the blade deep as his nostrils flared. He sought the sweet bouquet of blood as he felt the blade grate

bone. Eric gave a muffled grunt as bubblets spewed from one nostril. The body yielded against Barry, the oily gush looked black in a single, yellowish light at the far end of the dock.

"Could've done you better at my place," Barry muttered. He quickly stretched Eric on his back, split his pants and shirt and tugged them off. One shoe plopped into the water, floated for a moment, then slowly sank. Barry fingered the skin of Eric's hairless belly, gluttonous for the touch of raw flesh. He then rolled Eric out of his clothes. Eric gurgled as Barry eased the naked body face down into the water. He watched the carcass drift away, then splashed water on the dark stains. Barry felt better than he had all day. He puffed hard as he climbed the terraced steps to his car.

"Shit!" Beth muffled a whisper beneath the cover of one dockside boat. "I think he just killed that guy." She was no longer in the mood. "Let's get out here." She struggled into her swim suit.

"Think we ought to call the sheriff?" Larry asked.

"Forget that!" Beth snapped. "We're leaving." She rushed up the steps.

Gordie spotted them hurrying and couldn't wait to share the juicy details. Their last sandwich number had been fun. Beth didn't know all the tricks.

Eric's body settled, never made it out of the cove. Later, it rose to the surface like a bloated child's balloon and bobbed among shoreline snags about 300 yards from the dock, a distended blimp rolling in the gentle swells. Snapping turtles, furry critters, bottom feeders and other hungries gnawed one eyeball and socket bone-clean, stripped the top of the skull and left teeth marks along the neck bones. The left ear and upper neck were buried in the sand. The waxy, white, waterlogged arms and legs looked like wrinkled fence posts. The scalloped skin resembled soiled, off-white, satin, Austrian, puff drapes—the distended carcass was a disintegrating, biodegradable feast. Pretty-boy Eric Stompfer was no longer pretty nor human.

When Beth read the "unidentified body found at the lake" head-lines, she knew it was Eric. She didn't tell anyone, not even Gordie. She'd have to find someone else. Besides, Larry was great when he was in the mood.

*****

"Body's in bad condition. Been in the water for some time." Sheriff Paulie Shortson said to Gray. "Fred don't miss much, and I'd sure appreciate it if he could spare the time."

"Not a problem," Gray answered.

"I'll keep the area marked off," Paulie continued. "Don't want the kibitzers tracking around in what little findings we found."

Within thirty minutes, Gray, Fred and the team were on their way. With all the bailiwick bureaucracy, Gray had worked hard making cross-county collaboration the success it was. Any bruised egos, the bitching came to him, which stopped most of it.

As he hunkered over the no name corpse, Fred said, "Better do a full work up. Lots of postmortem changes." He looked at Paulie. "I'll have you a thorough dossier in case a grand jury needs it."

Drowning looked to be the obvious cause, but there'd initially been nothing suspicious about Sedgewicke either.

*****

Craige got up on the wrong side of the bed. Even a second cup of coffee didn't help. He cranked the morning away, at nothing, at everything, even the dog gave him a wide berth, but enough was enough. There was one source he kept turning in his head.

Instead of arguing with himself, it was time to stir into it. No matter where the juicy dirt was—college campus, social bigwigs, who was cheating on whom, business backstabs, real estate screw-yous, anything shady, walrus-rotund—chickenhawk ZB would know.

Zebulon Bergamot was manager of the underpass Valley Video since he was barely legal to drive and street trade long before that. Everyone in high school from bright-eyed preacher's kids to migrant families knew about the shady wonders shrouded inside "Den of Iniquity" Valley Video. Rent cheap cologne and sweat booths by the quarter-hour. There were mysteries to be mysteried, and adventures to be adventured.

The whole county knew poor, white trash, jelly-belly, precocious teen Zeb Bergamot was part-time whatever around Del Pingley's Valley Video. Rouged cheeks, purple-blue eye shadow, lip gloss with a spectacular pout, he learned the makeup trade at his momma's elbow. He had a head start in the family business with a whole lot of help

from Momma—curbside pickup, $50 for anything as long as Momma collected the cash. Scandalous Zebulon Bergamot carried the family bâton sinister legacy in his own grand fashion and would get in your face in a heartbeat.

Craige's rite of passage was the night he was allowed to sneak through the sacrosanct rear door of Valley Video with its unshaded, sixty-watt bulb glowing dull nite'n day, that is when the bulb wasn't burnt out, which was most of the time. It was easier to hide your face that way. He thought he'd finally "grown up." The narrow, smelly halls led him to XXX-video rentals for hunt club parties, football, and soccer bashes, naked pictures showing everything and things he didn't even know about—every position a body could get in; party gadgets; fancied, feathered getups; harnesses; whips; and hand, ankle and body chains. Even their Liberty weekend-after navy boot camp didn't come close to Valley Video. He couldn't wait to tell school buddies Darrell and Frank about his first Valley Video sojourn.

Craige worked odd jobs—a paper route, baled hay, mended fences and barn roofs to pay his share for a Pink Flamingo motel room and a rowdy, skin-flick weekend. After the beer and pizza runs, they never put their clothes on. He wasn't about to let his buddies outdo him. The girls drank them under the table, and Craige ended up puking his guts out after chugalugging a double six-pack of tall ones. They dropped him off home late Sunday morning.

Grannie knew what he'd done, puffed on her pipe and never let on. "A man had to do what a man had to do," she'd say, then putting her own kink to the Ingram family motto, "*Ainsi sera*—that's how it's going to be."

It had been worse. Before Craige was out of work bibbers, he'd learned another rule—you didn't mess around with namby-pamby, tubby Zeb.

Everybody treated Zeb like a sissy. Craige never razzed Zeb but others did. He might look like a sissy, but push Zeb the wrong way at the wrong time, and you got a bona fide eye-opener. There was an honesty about Zebulon. What you saw was what you got. He was trash to the core, yet in his own way, Zeb was bone country honest, sometimes ruthlessly so. Zeb looked life right in the eye and made no apologies.

You could say Zeb and Craige grew up but not together. Zeb

tagged after Craige every chance he got. It was flattering in a weird way. At graduation, when Zeb saw Craige in his Annapolis choker, dress whites, he thought Zeb was going to have a stroke. Craige didn't mind the attention. Zeb never came on to Craige and never made trouble.

One day, late that June after graduation, Craige happened to come upon a bunch of red necks badgering Zeb.

"Zebulon, you're a big, fat faggot who likes to suck cock," an overweight linebacker yelled.

ZB didn't flinch, "Don't you ever forget it, honey." His eyes narrowed. "And compliments won't get you outta paying for last night, you good-looking piece of shit." He then threw the footballer an outrageous kiss. "You left your daddy's plastic," he said and pulled out the credit card. "If you don't cough up the cash, I'll charge Daddy for the damaged tapes plus the extra booths you and your pals used, the ones where the girls weren't allowed in." He tossed his head and snickered, "Customers always got to pay, Sweety."

"Screw you, fuckin' faggot!" the linebacker snarled.

"In your dreams." Zeb didn't back off. "Sweet talk ain't gonna help." His smile fell away. "You're a closet case, claim to be straight. You're straight all right, straight to the nearest woodie. Don't care what you say, you still gonna pay."

The linebacker laughed and threatened, "I'll have the card cancelled."

"Go ahead," Zeb said. "Cancel the charges, and you sure enough won't like what happens. I'll put on my flashiest gown, gussy myself gaudy as all get out and show up where you work." With an eyelid flutter he added, "That ought to be a hit with your shop buddies. Keep givin' me lip, I'll do it anyhow, and if you still don't pay up, I'll show up at your momma and daddy's some evening for supper. That ought to make for a hellaciously fun evening."

"Gimme that damn card!" The linebacker grabbed Zeb by the throat.

That was a mistake. Tank top and gym sweats, barechest, checkout booth Ryan MuscleMeat moved faster than fast. Short, quick blows pummeled the snot out of smartmouth, gutty, football jock. He held him on the ground with one knee on his chest. Zeb tsk-tsked, knelt down and daubed the mashed nose with an immaculate hankie.

"Now that wadn't nice of you at all," Zeb tittered. "Pay now, honey, or I turn Flash here loose." He stood, hands on his broad hips. "Best to keep Zina Bea happy. Even someone as slow witted as you ought to understand that."

Zebulon got the money.

He ran a tight ship. He had lots of faults, but reading folks wrong wasn't one of them. He wasn't looking for rocket scientists when hiring and firing and never gave the powers that be an opportunity to pull Del's liquor license. Mouthy Bible Belt do-gooders often planted underage drug stoolies who bootlegged for a better court or jail rap. Del kept one eye on the local boys and their state capital flunkies. Vice raids never fared well. The charges of smut, prostitution and "clean up our town" never stuck. It was a money war for a slice of Del's action with worm-brained harass gimmicks for control of Deloma Pingley's franchise.

Zeb and Del were opposite sides of the same coin and a matched team, as tough as any of the wolf packs. ZB handled the meat, Del handled the business. The hired hunks had party-time mattress whirling duties but came in handy when an SOB decided to get muscle-ugly. Behind one-way mirrors, Zeb made sure Del's service stayed peaceful with plenty of the local fat bellies and saggy butts in topnotch center frame videos.

Grannie once said as she stirred her stew, "Mamie Bergamot's passel of kids ain't much. She's got a good heart, never had no upbringing, but you start behavin' like that, you'll ketch my knuckles across your bony head." Her cherokee eyes went blacker than night. "You an Ingram, sumthin' to be proud of. Goin' 'round behavin' beneath yourself ain't sumthin' an Ingram does, leastwise no Ingram what cares. But nobody ought not put Bergamots down jus' 'cause their no-count lout Bascomb Bergamot never married Mamie." She screwed the lid on two half gallon jars full of stew. "You take these and this fresh baked bread over to Mamie's." She wrapped the bread. "Them kids be powerful sick."

\*\*\*\*\*

Craige pulled into Valley Video's unpaved parking lot, parked and held his driver's license against the bulletproof glass with its small,

oval opening, while dumb-as-garden-squash, all-American steak and potatoes, desk duty, NewFace gave it the once-over. Par for the course, he did more looking Craige up and down than at the license. He buzzed the lock, and the inside security door snapped open. Once inside, Craige was the new face of the moment. It wasn't his first time being checked out here and in a dozen other Valley Videos. It never bothered him. Guys are always checking the competition. He had never understood men getting uptight when another man pays them the compliment of attention. He supposed it was a backwash spin on the moral majority conveniently never confronting their own monsters. Most 647A violations associated with child molestations are family, neighbors or live-ins. Valley Video often reminded him of other wild-time ports, rambunctious SEAL and raucous Marine binges.

Zeb swept forward. "Land's sakes alive! Lord have mercy, the dead have risen." False lashes aflutter, he asked, "Where'd the proverbial cat find your good-looking, sailor carcass?" His gargantuan belly smothered in an iridescent orange and lime chiffon, billowy phantasmagoria. "Craige honey, hot, hot, hot as ever," he said and grabbed Craige's hand. He held it that moment too long. "And still unattached I see." His buttery cheeks blended into his neck.

His puckered, pouty, ruby-purple lips gave Hollywood buzzes to both Craige's cheeks.

Loudly, Zeb shouted "Honey, just bring your sweet ass right on into my private office." He wanted everyone to notice.

A gush of cheap perfume and sweat flounced through the door ahead of Craige. The sofa creaked under Zeb's bulk as he pirouetted more into than onto the divan. He patted the cushions for Ryan to close the door and for Craige to come sit. The only unfeigned thing about Zeb Bergamot was the crafty, hog eyes that were never still, never missed one thing. Everything else was playtime drama.

"Now what kind of little'll ol' drink would you like?" Zeb asked, flicking his wrist.

Craige said, "Nothing, thanks." He took the large, overstuffed chair across from Zeb.

Craige ignored Ryan and another front desk Johnny Skeleton with their side-of-beef curiosity about him and Zeb. Craige had seen their lives in too many cities, skin trade cast-offs with short futures, smashed dreams, barren yesterdays and shambled, worn tomorrows. Zeb fluffed

his pompadoured, mauve wig, mindful not to break a long, pearl blue sheen fake nail.

Seldom out of cruise mode, Zeb said, "First time I ever noticed you was fifth grade." His appraisal loitered up and down. "You was in a fight during recess, beat the snot out of that punk. Remember that?"

"I got into lots of fights," Craige said.

With a put-on mope, Zeb said, "You never give Zina a chance to show you what I can do."

"Believe me, Zeb, I know what you can do," Craige said and chuckled. "Maybe it's because I don't like to be chased."

"Oooo, one of those who likes to do the chasing?" Zeb rolled his eyes.

"Something like that," Craige said.

Zeb's expression shifted to serious, "You never come around unless it's business." He reached for a Belgian, dark chocolate bonbon.

"I need information," Craige said.

Craige's words stopped Zeb's pudgy lips in midchew as he choked down what was left of the chocolate.

Zeb said, "Craige, honey—" His flighty pretense was gone. "That can be expensive and a whole lot dangerous." With a madam's curiosity, he asked, "What about?" Dirty or otherwise, money and information were interchangeable commodities.

"I'm not sure," Craige said. "Just a hunch. Where do I buy poison without anyone knowing?"

Zeb sputtered, "You sure enough are here on business." Cat quick, he continued, "What kind of poison you after?" He had seen Craige on a hunt.

Craige said, "Not so much the market as names."

"Names are even riskier," Zeb said. "Columbian kind of names?"

"No," Craige answered. "The tasteless kind of poison you don't buy from midnight pharmacies. Mixes with food or alcohol, doesn't take much."

"Ummm—" Zeb fell silent. "Where bodies disappear and scores get settled. Maybe we can help one another. Maybe you and Graysen know what's been happening to some of my best boys?"

Icicles stabbed Craige's gut. "What boys?" He recalled Gray's comment about possible unknown victims.

"Mostly weekend army trade, but not all of them. Some of my

locals just quit showing up. No call. Nothing. Dropped out of sight, like they never existed," Zeb said. "Word around the fort is they don't know nothing either." He flicked his tongue across his lips. "At first I thought they might've been arrested, but they hadn't."

"You file a police report?" Craige asked.

"Craige, honey, you got to be kidding," he said with a wicked laugh. "You don't often say dumb things, but when you do, it's a doozy." His ponderous belly shook. "It's truly refreshing to know there's a virgin-pure mind like yours in this sorry-ass world." Stone faced, he said, "File a police report? How long you think I'd be around if I started suckin' up to the cops? Some of them are crookeder than the ones in jail."

"You could've gone to Gray," Craige said. "You know you can trust him."

"Sure. I trust Gray but gone to him with what?" Zeb asked. "Come on Craige, get your head back in the real world. All I got is street talk. No one cares about the suspicions of a Nellie Queen or what happens to anyone in our twilight world."

"Gray's not like that," Craige said. "Sometimes suspicions can be the straw that breaks the camel's back."

Zeb said, "About drunk soldiers that fall off the world?" He shook his head as he continued, "I start running my mouth, and it wouldn't be long before I wasn't the only one catching heat. I have to draw you a picture to explain what that kind of noise would do for anyone look-ing for excuses to screw Del? Much less the trouble it'd cause Graysen. Yeh, they sing high'n mighty bullshit when elections roll around, but you let the wrong kind of questions get asked ..." he shrugged and didn't finish. "Mind you now, I'm not saying she sells anything. I've never been interested in her wares."

Craige asked, "Who?" He knew Zeb would know.

Zeb said, "Deep in your core, you're that rare breed who wants everything on the up and up." His gaze narrowed. "Plays by the rules, cain't be bought and won't be stopped."

"I don't always play by the rules," Craige said.

"OK, plays by the rules when it suits you," Zeb grinned. "You never let anyone control you. People can't get a handle on you, and that scares a lot of folks."

Craige said, "I was brought up to believe in myself. So were you,

and I've never heard you once complain about the choices you've made or the consequences."

Zeb had a pensive voice, "Moaning and groaning never helps." Among the pain were pleasant memories, Craige one of them.

"Holding a tight fist around what you believe is a rare thing nowadays," Craige said. "No percentage in being any other way. Sad how people sell themselves so cheap."

Zeb wistfully said, "Lonely too."

Zebulon's put-on fluff was gone. It was just he and Craige and times gone by.

Zeb said, "In this fucked up world, you're one of the few who never turned their back on me. You were never a close friend like I would've liked, and I'm not talking about getting your clothes off, but you never were hateful like some."

Craige said, "I'm not the only one in this room who scares people." Craige looked straight at Zeb. "'Specially the guys who aren't very sure about themselves."

"Yea, hunky jock types," Zeb said. "We know about them."

They both laughed.

"We're peas from the same pod," Craige said. "Accept the world, gutter to Nob Hill but demand respect on our own terms."

"Anyone ever tell you you're bullheaded?" Zeb asked.

"More than a few times," Craige affirmed and laughed. "But scrape off enough of my barnacles, about all that's left is a twelve-year-old kid that never grew up."

Zeb smiled. "Us sophomores thought varsity seniors were gods Well, maybe I thought you were a bit more godly than the rest. I never missed one of your soccer games."

"I know," Craige said.

With sad eyes behind the smile, Zeb said, "We had some good times." Yestermoments were sweeter in the remembering than in the living. He kept going, "Mama thought Grannie Ingram was one of the finest persons there ever was."

"Grannie was one tough lady, and so was your mother," Craige agreed. "They both faced life head-on, did what needed doing."

"Grannie Ingram always spoke to Mama any time she met any of us on the street," Zeb said. "But we came from different worlds."

Craige felt sad for Zeb, for the whole Bergamot clan who could

never be more than they were.

"Grannie knuckled my head more than once when I didn't behave, or worse, forgot," Craige said. "She had more love in one finger than most have their whole life. I always knew she loved me no matter what."

"That old woman could poultice with Indian herbs, draw out the poison, knew swamp medicines, which wild stuff to pick, what time of the year to gather and plant and brew sassafras tea to settle bilious, sour belly cramps," Zeb said. "She never needed a town doctor. I once seen her lance a cottonmouth bite on my sister's foot. She grew poppies for her own tonic, mixed corn squeezings, lemon and sugar and concocted a hot toddy that'd loosen a bad cough right up."

Craige added, "She'd soak sugar with her cough remedy, but it still tasted awful. I'm not sure it did any good, but it stopped the coughing, and you sure slept good. I can still hear Grannie hollering 'youngin,' git your hide outta my flower beds.' She tanned my hide for playing around those red-orange poppies she planted every year."

Zeb said, "Grannie brought her remedy to Momma that winter we got laid up with the catarrh. Nobody else cared. Grannie Ingram was a good woman." He sounded melancholy.

"If it wasn't for my Grannie, I wouldn't be where I am today," Craige said.

"Sallie Mae Drutherferde," Zeb said.

"What?" The name yanked Craige back to why he was here. "Where can I find her?" Craige asked.

"She's a bag lady." Zeb repeated the name. "She and Agatha Hutchers been on the street long as I've known them. Drutherferde comes from somewhere down near Blythe, south part of the county. When the weather gets bad, some of the local artists up on Artist Row let her and Agatha hole up in the empty lofts above their studios. The two got real scarce after that killing in the parking garage."

Craige leaned forward, elbows to his knees, "Think you could put me in touch with them?"

Zeb grinned, "Now ain't that neighborly." He pried his bulk off the sofa, his flabby underarms waddled. "Big, strapping sailor wants a favor from Zeb."

"I need your help," Craige said. "So does Gray."

Zeb snapped, "Dammit Craige, you know I don't like cops." He

abruptly turned all business. "Graysen's got his own snitches." His sparkly fluff and flounce bangles were forgotten. "Call me tomorrow. Even better, come back and see me."

Craige stood. "Thanks, Zeb."

Zeb rolled his eyes, "Lord God, you are one breathtaking man."

Craige headed past the neat rows of video cassettes in their numbered plastic boxes. As he crossed the parking lot, he spotted the white pickup with its law enforcement driver and vidcam recording faces and license plates of anyone coming in. There wasn't much privacy left in the electronic age. Someone was gearing up for another raid, more media slop served up to a guzzling public. Craige caught the red glow of his vidcam and smiled straight into the man's face to make sure he saw him. Let the fucker record all he wanted. He had a bone-deep detest of riffraff, legal or otherwise.

The call came early the next morning, right after Craige rolled in from Terri's.

He grabbed the phone. "Ingramme."

Zeb said, "Just get home from another night with that beauty from the bank?" He gave a dirty chuckle.

Craige asked, "There anything you don't know?" He ruffled fingers through his hair.

"If I didn't, this working girl might never get to see you," Zeb said. He turned serious. "Knowledge is power. Can kill damn quick and get squeaky clean away."

"That what happened to two women?" Craige asked.

He said, "Saying things like that over an open phone can get yourself and Zina hurt bad."

"It doesn't matter if it's bugged," Craige said.

"'Cause you got one of your fancy spy gadgets on it?" Zeb snorted.

"Hammerscape is one of my nasty gadgets I play with now and then," Craige said. "I modified it enough to block anyone I don't want listening."

"Same reason I'm on my limo phone," Zeb mused.

"Zebulon, your limo phone is a radio," Craige cautioned. "Don't matter if it is digital."

"You're making me feel re-e-al good," Zeb replied. "Meet me behind the old fireworks barn. Loading docks, your side of the river, twenty minutes."

"On my way," Craige said.

"Make sure you're not tailed," Zeb said. "Keep your eye peeled for a white pickup."

"The one in Del's parking lot yesterday?" Craige retorted.

"I figured you spotted that," Zeb said. "That's why I picked the old barn's big lot. No place to sneak, and no way to hide with a telephoto lens."

"Who else knows about this?" Craige asked.

"Just you and me and my driver," Zeb answered.

The tires of Craige's Jeep flung gravel as he took a hard left off the highway. Five minutes later, he spotted Zeb's burgundy limousine with its gaudy, extra wide, white sidewalls and smoky, monogrammed windows. As Craige pulled up, the driver's door opened. Ryan stepped out, dressed to the nines—requisite, Hollywood shades; special chauffeur's uniform; black, tux jacket; bow tie; trousers tailored thigh-strut tight; striking, black, Oscar de la Renta hand woven belt; black, patent shoes; no socks and no shirt. A classy image of a tan, bare chest and a six-pack, tight stomach—a Botticelli with muscles, a real attention getter that looked like living sex, the kind Zeb liked. He opened the rear door, and inside, Zeb wreathed in rose crinoline and purple taffeta.

Zeb said, "You got here fast enough."

Craige got in. Ryan closed the door and stayed outside. He slowly circled the car, never taking his eyes off the mile-long approach road.

Craige said to Zeb, "It's one of those things where time could make the difference."

Zeb said, "Sallie Mae didn't want to meet you." He put his flamboyant image away. "Says she's got bad feelings about this."

"This Sallie Mae hiding something?" Craige asked.

"Sallie Mae's always hiding. Among other things, she makes home brew, sells small amounts for spending money," Zeb said. "Feds have nosed around a few times. Sallie's a good person, never hurt no one. She thinks you're a plant." He chuckled. "Sallie Mae don't trust strangers, especially those cozy with homicide lieutenants, even if he is a good cop. That don't matter. In her world it's survive or get dumped in some ditch, while the parade passes right on by."

In that moment, Craige felt sorry for Zeb and his netherworld of concealed lives.

"We all have secrets," Craige said.

Zeb said, "There's secrets, then there's secrets." He stared through the smoky window. "Money talks, the golden rule, who has the gold makes the rules." He faced Craige. "It's not so much you I'm worried about. Promise you'll protect both of them. Old Lawton School on Walton Boulevard, behind the auditorium, dressing rooms below street level. Below that is a boiler basement. That's where they hole up. Seems the power's never been shut off." He laughed. "Sallie Mae said she had to fix her hair if she was receiving callers."

"I'll make sure I'm not followed," Craige assured him.

Zeb said, "You weren't followed here or Ryan would've spotted them. But you ain't exactly new at doing the sleuth bit."

"Neither are you," Craige replied and opened the door.

Zeb grabbed Craige's arm. "Be careful. I'd hate to see that body get messed up."

"Me too," Craige said. He sensed danger.

"They saw the killing," Zeb said, almost a whisper. "They were there that night on the way back to their basement."

"They saw who do it?" Craige asked.

"I didn't ask," Zeb said. "And Sallie Mae didn't volunteer."

# Chapter 14

Craige took Zeb's warning seriously. There were lots of things Grannie didn't like about the Bergamots, but Craige had never known Zeb to lie. As he drove away from their meeting, Craige couldn't shake a lurking foreboding that he ought to be suited in full battlefield gear, his frayed uneasiness clustered into apprehensive misgivings. In case he'd picked up an unseen tail keeping tabs on him, he headed in the opposite direction on a lightly traveled, country two-lane until he crossed the county line. He then took an unpaved, back road, which paralleled the interstate and kept one eye on his rearview mirror, backtracked twice and spotted nothing. As he headed for town on Harrington Boulevard, he re-sorted names and faces. He continued several blocks and passed the old elementary school buildings. Everything looked clear. At the traffic light he did a quick, right figure eight, circled the next five blocks, almost pulled a wrong-way on a one-way and ten minutes later pulled in behind the loading docks. When he turned the engine off, the noiseless quiet seemed eerily loud. His heart was pounding.

The battered, green, side door with its peeling, leprosy paint framed one small window with smudged shattered wire-glass. The door cracked just enough for a pair of bright, blue eyes to peek out at him.

A voice said, "That you Mr. Craige?" The grey head was hardly visible.

"Yes," Craige said. "Sallie Mae, that you?"

There was no answer, and she didn't come out. The door was left ajar, rusty hinges squeaked as Craige pushed against it and stepped into a vacuous, black void, the air heavy with a peculiar, stale warmth. He was more than queasy. It had the makings of a perfect ambush layout. Talk about the perfect setup. If Zeb hadn't OKed the time and place, he would've been out of there. Except for jumbled, grimy clutter and vague outlines in a trashed yawning interior, he could make out no details. As his eyes adjusted, Craige found himself facing two frail figures who'd been standing there the whole time.

"Sallie Mae?" Craige asked.

With a fragile movement Sallie Mae said, "Right here. A'gatha Ruth here's not too pleased about Zeb tellin' you where to find us."

"Don't like this a darn tootin'," A'gatha said. "Nobody's bizness." She was testy. "Plenty robbin' 'n 'killin' to be took care of 'stead of cops pokin' in folk's private matters. Botherin' folks what druther be left alone."

"I don't work for the police," Craige said.

A'gatha continued, "Fiddle-de-dee, who you think you're foolin'? Tain't a mite of difference twixt you and MacGerald 'cept he calls it what it be—cop." She had wizened, bottomless eyes. "Claimin' we make corn squeezin's." Her ire rose. "Don't try puttin' no lyin' to me. I know what the likes of you is after. Them bunch of scallywags wants you to help take away Sallie Mae's croup potions." She wiped her mouth with her hand. "That's what, you're after Sallie's makin's." She didn't care for him one bit.

"We been run out from lots'a places," Sallie Mae said.

"Lord knows, these old bones don't take up much room, and these empty buildings ain't no use fer nothin' much."

Craige interrupted, "Zeb told me you saw the killing in the bank's garage."

"Both of us seen it," A'gatha said. "What you want to know for anyhow? We ain't talkin' to no cops. Might as well git that out on the table right now. They throw us in jail, say we the ones what did it till we tell where our still wuz."

"You see who did it?" Craige asked.

"'Course we saw the man who done it," Sallie Mae said. "Didn't see no face, saw his big black car, the kind what rich folks drive." She

shook her head. "Lordy mercy, that poor woman didn't have no chance."

A'gatha nodded, "Skeer a body plumb to death. Gives me chill blains jus' thinkin' on it. Like some animal, like he wadn't mad, jes took o'nry mean pleasure beating her."

Craige asked, "You know it was a man?"

"Jesus my all!" A'gatha Ruth spit snuff juice into a paper stuffed big peach can. "You ain't much good at detecting if you cain't tell whether a body be man or woman. Maybe you need readin' glasses. Gettin' a mite blurry myself, but I don't have to see a body close-up to tell it was a man and sure didn't want that one close-up no how. Tell by the way he hit. He was hefty enough he didn't have to put much swing to it. Kept whackin'n'whackin', blood everywhere. Even after she mostly quit moving, he kept hittin'n'hittin', her legs just'a jerkin'."

Craige made a mental note to check with Fred if any clothing, gloves, anything showed DNA different from any of the victims.

"Awful!" Sallie Mae shivered. "We hunkered down so he wouldn't see us."

The filtered light framed Sallie Mae's dignified, wrinkled face, ancient beyond years with a proud reserve.

A'gatha said, "Even after the police got there, we never told them what we seen."

"You told Zebulon," Craige said.

A'gatha answered, "Only some of it after he asked if we'd talk with you." Wiry hairs puffed out form under her bandanna as she shook with each word. "Talkin' 'bout it gives me the night-blights." She threw a piercing glance at this stranger. "Ain't tellin' no cops." Big-eyed, she continued, "Cain't help what done happened, 'sides, night's full of haints out stirrin' to suck a body's spirit. No sirree, ain't tellin' no cops."

"Can you describe the car?" Craige asked.

"Done tol' you," A'gatha said.

"You get a license number?"

"Wadn't looking to read no plates," A'gatha said. "Wadn't gittin' near enough for that devil to spot us. We'd'a been next he put the evil eye to us."

Sallie Mae said, "Cops wouldn't'a cared whether such as us was

hurt or not." Her eyes shifted. "Most folks ain't bad by nature." Her words were now softer. "By the time a body find out which is which, it can be way too late."

"I'd like to ask you something," Craige said.

A'gatha snorted, "Told you, Sallie Mae. This un's no different, wants the crowfoot, be rid of somebody." She sneered, "Godless bunch. Tired of a wife, husband or boyfriend in the way, a partner you want to make go away? Like permanent?" She heeheed. "Jes like Bergamot said, crooked cops is all alike." She had a blizzard of distrust. "You wants to ask about the bane," she huffed. "Cops be worthless 'less you rich and important."

Sallie Mae asked, "That why you want the crowfoot? Zebulon told me you ask about who knowed the potions. Wantin' to buy or wantin' information?"

"Both," Craige said.

A'gatha Ruth gave Craige a gnarly, cagy, animal gleam. Sallie Mae was wary, too.

"This some cop trick?" Sallie Mae asked. "You doin' some rich dude's dirty work, maybe get shud of us out from this building." She shrugged. "Maybe get shud of us fer good."

Craige's only chance was to be straight up honest. He said, "I need to know about crowfoot."

A'gatha Ruth said, "Lots folks been wantin' to know about the crowfoot." Her rumpled, toothless face turned thoughtful. Zebulon never steered them wrong. They could trust him.

"Crowfoot's a mite tetchy," A'gatha said. "Mixes with anything you can swaller. Gives a body a real lift. Just a flit takes away the chest anguish, clears the head, breathing comes easier, but a pinch too much, your problems be all over. Kills dead."

"I brought some photos," Craige said. "Would you take a look at them?"

Sallie Mae's nose crinkled. "What fer?"

"I need to know if anyone in these pictures bought crowfoot," Craige answered.

"Why?" A'gatha snapped. "Tryin' to blame it on us?"

Sallie Mae said, "You 'spect us to tell?" She sidled a glance toward the pictures. "They done nuthin' agin us, and even if they did, why you buttin' in? Mouth shut, ears open. Only way to stay alive. Crowfoot don't kill people. People kill people. Cain't hep what on'ry folks do."

Craige said, "I'm trying to help catch the man you saw kill that woman."

Sallie Mae studied him. From the depths of the building came the steady patter of water.

Finally, she said, "Let's see them pi'tures."

Agatha Ruth peered over her shoulder as Sallie Mae flipped through them one-by-one. They then stopped and both women looked at him.

"This here one." Agatha Ruth pointed. "Never seen none of the others. Shifty-eyed type, bought the crowfoot some time ago. I suspicioned him up to no good, but the Lord didn't set me here to judge."

"Can I buy some?" Craige asked as he looked at the face of Nathan Marshall.

"What fer?" Sallie Mae asked, nodding toward the photo. "You gonna get rid of him?" She handed the photos back to him.

"He's already dead," Craige answered.

Sallie Mae sputtered, "Told you they was up to no good." She clutched her shawl tight around her shoulders.

"Shot himself," Craige said.

A'gatha sneered, "You mean that's what the police put out?" She grumped. "Don't mean it happened that way."

"He wadn't the one what killed that girl," Sallie Mae said.

Craige wasn't surprised. He didn't know Marshall well, but from what he did know, the man didn't have the mettle to use a bullet on someone, much less bludgeon anyone. Poison was more his style, but if Nate Marshall slipped crowfoot to Sedgewicke, Craige had no idea how he did it. None of it jived, which meant Craige hadn't looked in the right hiding places. He couldn't accept Marshall killing either woman, then putting a bullet in his brain. After Sedgewicke's death what changed that squeezed Marshall into feeling he had no choice? Craige could understand family pressures, but Marshall lived with that his whole life. Something else was going on, and the best guess was that there were at least two killers. It was a feeling Craige definitely didn't like.

Sallie Mae said, "The man what bought crowfoot was taller, didn't have the weight of the one did the garage killing. Man what done the beatin' was stockier, round shouldered." She reached inside the folds of her long shawl, came out with a neatly tied, small bag and dropped it

into Craige's palm. It reminded him of Grannie's asaf'ididy bag.

"I keep the crowfoot about all time," Sallie Mae said. "Take a little ever now and then to ease my rheumatiz, keep my system clean. Don't come around with no more questions." She was stern. "You won't find us less'n we wants it to be." Then to A'gatha, "Town's getting too big. Full of strangers what come'n'go, ones who don't keer a flap. Ain't neighborly like it onct was."

Craige scribbled his number on the back of an old business card. Even as he was doing it, he knew it was a ridiculous. These two had probably never used a phone.

"Here's my phone number if you think of anything," Craige said.

A'gatha prissed, "Oh, by all means, young feller." She puckered her wrinkly lips like she was getting ready to put on lipstick.

"I'll sure nuff have my secretary phone me an appointment." She fluffed scraggly curls.

"The police can protect you," Craige said.

They both gave him incredulous stares then looked at one another. A'gatha Ruth covered her mouth, squeaky laughs loosed in a high cackle.

A'gatha twittered, "Can and will be two whole, different things."

"Gracious sakes alive," Sallie Mae goggle-eyed at A'gatha. "He's not near as smart as I first figured."

"I appreciate your help," Craige said.

There was nothing else to say. As Craige snugged the outer door shut, he heard the metal burglar bar thud in place behind him. Big, black cars fit a lot of people.

*****

The rest of the week rolled by, gone too quick. Moving between Moccasin Hollow and Terri's place, Craige seemed to always forget something—belt, razor, tie, matching socks. More than a few have told him he lives in his own world and ignores reality. Maybe they're right. Nevertheless, trying to keep an eye out for Terri and Jeff, Craige rediscovered Moccasin Hollow's serenity all over again. There's a lot beyond Moccasin Hollow not to like. As much as possible, he kept it quarantined from beepers, cell phones, e-mail and answering machines. Not that he didn't have his fair share of toys, but playing ostrich with

one's head stuck in the sand can leave one's backside available for a 9/11 WTC surprise. He never liked those kinds of surprises, but that's exactly how he felt.

Craige woke up slowly. He was still half asleep when he rolled sideways into Terri's lissome nakedness, the sheet crumpled between us. All of the pleasant night came back to him. He'd forgotten that Jeff spent the night at Byrd's.

As Craige rolled onto his back, he said, "You startled the hell out of me. I must have been dreaming."

"I could tell." Terri snuggled closer. "About the investigation?"

Craige said, "It's really digging at me."

"I feel so good," Terri said, the covers slipped away. "I could laze away the rest of the morning." She stretched her arm across Craige's chest. "Would you like that?" Her hands moved lower. "Waste the whole day, just the two of us?"

Craige cupped one lovely breast, kissed it tenderly. He buzzed her silken touch with his tongue.

He said, "Would be nice." He felt like he didn't have a care in the world. They both wanted this. They both needed this.

She came against him, felt him between them.

She murmured, "Jeff knows."

Craige pulled her closer. "Stop with the guilt." And he gently kissed her. "Give Jeff some credit. He's a lot more mature than you think. He'll handle our relationship just fine. It bothered him at first that I was where his father should be, but you feel guilt about replacing Paul with another man also."

Terri said, "The house is so full of memories."

"Sell the house."

"Jeff would have a fit."

"I doubt that."

"It's the only home he knows."

"Good memories last no matter where you are."

"You'd never sell Moccasin Hollow."

"It's not the same. Moccasin Hollow has always been there. It's part of me, a part of my family, where I recharge. I didn't lose a wife or child. I'm not replacing Grannie with another face every time I wake up."

"You telling me there's never been other women?" Terri asked.

Her question came too close to the mark.

Craige dodged it with, "You know what I mean. I know how Grannie felt when she faced possibly losing it ..." His words trailed off as he kissed the pert tip of her nose.

As he kissed those wonderful lips, he wanted to repeat the night and kiss her all over.

Terri said, "It's as if I'm somehow betraying Paul." She shivered against him and added, "And Jeff."

"You'll always love Paul," Craige said. "You should. He's the father of a son you both love very much."

Craige hushed more words as he kissed her again, her eyelids, her throat, at first softly, then fiercely, almost violent, crushing the breath from her and feeling her respond. He moved over her, their tongues blistered skin to delectable skin. An awful longing somewhere inside him collided with the same from her. Passions loosed, sucking at the woebegone twosome of them. The exquisite bliss of the night helped each of them surrender each to the other again.

Terri felt powerless, swept away by the molten fire splitting her world. Everything swirled by this storm tempest—lightning bolts to places Paul and no one else had kindled. She'd almost forgotten how wonderful it was to be with an aroused, overpowering, fine-crafted male. She curved to meet him with the feverish skin of her frenzied body. Her resistance ebbed as she closed around his shoulders with her arms. She never wanted to let go. Her tongue stroked him; she felt him shiver and mouth sweet endearments against her as they rose against one another. He whimpered half-words in the abyss of his barbarous rampage through her. His need was as demanding as hers. Their bodies took their own direction as they deliciously plundered one another. Aurora ecstasy swept their lovemaking. Honeyed weariness drained them. They wrapped in one another. Terri sighed, every fiber in her body trilled with a palpable vigor, split apart with his magic. She thought of Paul and those times they'd talked about her finding someone else if anything happened to him. Paul's dreadful loss somehow softened, yet she could not quite catch the idea of loving two men at the same time. Paul's memory swept up in the whirlwind of Craige Ingramme, his massive onslaught so much like Paul's, carrying along her heart and soul.

Craige lost himself in this marveled delirium called woman. He

never wanted this to end. Nothing could have been better than last night but it was. Somewhere a phone splintered the stillness. He yawned and rubbed a groggy eye.

Terri answered, "Stanley residence."

Jeff was on the other end. "I'm staying for supper at Byrd's. Be home after nine. That OK?"

"That's fine," Terri said.

As they talked, Craige pulled the comforter around him, smelled the aroma of sunshine dried sheets and pillows and her. An added bonus had been getting to know piss and vinegar, young Jeff. Terri still saw him as a kid. Mothers often have that blind spot with their off-spring, but Jeff had become quite a young man.

Nature called. Craige got out of bed and stumbled toward the guest bath. The two bag ladies had plagued him the entire night. He brushed his teeth, and as he stared at his lathered reflection in the mirror, speculations danced his discontent. He paired Sedgewicke, Marshall and Holton in all manner of muddled knots, wondering if Holton had blackmailed Nate into getting the poison. If that was the way it was played, Craige sure as hell had skimpy to nothing evidence. He finished shaving and shoved blackmail to one side as he buried his face in a hot towel. His innards snarled at the prospects of murder making a clean getaway. He wished he had some idea what upset the apple cart. Was the McGiffern embezzlement a sideshow or the tip of an iceberg turned into swindle, gathering reasons that somewhere set off a nitroglycerin soufflé of murder?

Terri and Craige showered together, made love with hands, gentle touches, rough and hurried, doing everything with the hot water long gone. They then went out for dinner. Terri ate with a craven appetite. She bubbled with that special glow in a well-loved woman that seems to make the sun shine brighter. Craige was exhausted, but it was a good tired.

*****

Two mornings later, Craige sipped coffee on his screened breakfast porch and watched the early, somber sun stroke into dawn. He'd twisted and turned it, and even though it was a gamble, he decided it was time to turn the screws. He loosed his tried and true rule to pick a spot, any

spot, and go with it. He knew exactly what weak link to pick.

Craige had things ready by the afternoon. His penchant for appearances was Holton's Achilles heel, a chink he could pry against. He felt no remorse for planning to ram into Holton's private office. If Craige didn't put the fear of God into Holton's receptionist, Holton wouldn't believe him. It wasn't all an act. Craige sure didn't want Holton forewarned.

Craige put on his best gruff and stormed past a monumental aquarium that was a killing field of African blue cichlids that ate anything that wasn't meaner. It accomplished exactly what he wanted, plus the edge of surprise.

"I need to see Holton now!" Craige blustered.

"You were here previously." She was uncertain about this interloper. "He's in a conference," she said in her standard office put-you-in-your-place manner and reached to buzz Holton.

Craige leaned forward and stopped her hand on the phone. "I didn't say my name, and I don't want to be announced." He headed toward the door.

She got up and tried to get in his way.

Craige said, "Ma'am—" He was bloodthirsty, wintry polite as he mashed against her belly to breasts. "I don't wish to be rude, so don't make me force my way past you." It was not a bluff. "My grandmother taught me to be courteous to ladies, but you aren't going to stop me. I mean to see him, I mean to see him now, and I don't care who's in there."

Craige gave her an "A" for effort as she bellied between him and Holton's office door, their noses almost touching. He smelled her expensive perfume and wondered if Holton had bought it, wondered what else she did in addition to typing. She blinked and froze like a frightened doe caught in headlights. Craige pushed open the door and walked in. Garland Holton was startled. He gave a pleasant nod to the receptionist, shut the door in her face, locked it and found himself alone facing a very white-faced lawyer.

"What the hell's the meaning, busting in here like this?! This is a private office," he said, sallowfaced. "You got a search warrant?"

Legalese was his citadel, but he should've known better. He wasn't very good at it. His IQ had always hovered about two levels below absolute zero. Garland Holton wasn't very good at anything, but that

was just Craige's opinion.

"I'm not a cop, I don't need a warrant," Craige said over his desk and in his face. "I figure if you can twist the law to suit your purposes, why shouldn't I? Except this time I'm one step ahead of you, enough to dump your butt in hot water and let someone else make it stick." His fists were on the desk edge. "So up yours and screw you with the broomstick." Craige gave him his best stage smirk. Holton's cheeks became splotches of baby pink and coffin gray.

"What the hell you want?" Holton asked in a tone that was more beg than question.

Craige took his time, let Holton sweat and watched the droplets trickle down his cheek.

Finally, Craige said, "I've been digging through the McGiffern papers. From what little I've seen I have a good idea why you and your pals burgled a private residence to get hold of the originals. A half-assed attempt I might add that came up with zilch, but that doesn't keep it from being a felony. All sorts of bad things could happen to you on that count."

"You got no proof I had anything to do with that," Holton said.

Craige laughed and let Holton's fear get the better of him. It was exactly what Craige wanted.

"You were desperate to get hold of those records," Craige continued, "so you could bury your shady deals before the audit turns up a stink you didn't want anyone else to know about."

"You're blowing in the wind," Holton sputtered. "I don't know what you're talking about."

Craige said, "You're about as good at lying as you are at law." He tried not to enjoy this too much. "I doubt you'd know truth if it stood up and waved at you. If I wanted true confessions, I'd take you in some alley and wring it out of your seedy neck." After he let the room grow to thundering silence, Craige said, "I'm going to say this once, so listen good. You've let yourself get backed into a corner with bastards who decided it was safer to have Sedgewicke dead. We both know how much you can trust them."

"Sedgewicke died of a heart attack!" Holton gulped.

"That's what the death certificate says," Craige pulled out the copy and tossed it on his desk, "except that one. Keep it. Original of that is in a safe place, too. I underlined the part you'll find interesting."

Holton read CAUSE OF DEATH, then said, "This isn't Royce's death certificate." He looked at Craige with enough hate to kill.

Craige said, "Not the first one."

"What do you mean, not the first one?" Holton gawked.

Craige said, "I dug him up, had a thorough lab workup done." He wanted him to think he'd done it.

"That's against the law!" Holton yelled, half out of his chair.

"How 'bout that," Craige said with a bigger grin. "You know something, Holton, if Sedgewicke were still in charge, you amateurs wouldn't be stewing in your own shit. I know for a fact there's lots of McGiffern money involved in this, and I'll lay odds it's not the only account you've, shall we say, been working. Problem with your tidy scheme and offshore accounts is that Theosia McGiffern knew I'd make sure everything she wanted done got done her way. I probably know more about offshore accounts that you do. Someone get greedy, or did Royce want a bigger cut? Someone wanted to shut him up, because Royce found out their deals were being pulled behind his back. You ever consider that maybe the ones who killed Royce are tidying up their mess, and you've become the problem? Quickest solution, same as with Sedgewicke, get rid of anyone who knows too much. You and your shit birds made one, small miscalculation. You let me find out about you. Stupid move, letting that happen, but then you never were high up on the brain list."

Craige could almost hear Holton's ass slam watertight shut. He realized this piece of slime knew way more than was safe for him, and Holton knew if Craige knew, so did others. He didn't say more, too much could tip Holton how little Craige really did know.

Holton repeated, "I don't know what you're talking about." He wanted this pushy PI anywhere but here.

Craige figured up to now he'd hid behind the legal dodge of being ignorant of what was going on. He moseyed to the window, pushed aside the expensive drape and stared outside. Cornering a killer was dangerous. It was the last time he'd show him his back.

Craige turned and said, "Doesn't matter whether you knew or not. You're dumber than I think if you can't see you've been set up to take the heat for the whole thing." He got right in Holton's face and said, "You're not the one I'm after."

"What?" Holton gave a nervous stammer and coughed.

"You're in way too deep," Craige said, giving him a churchy smile. "Once they find out I've been to see you, you'll be the albatross that really worries them. They might dump their guts to the DA to save their hides, and if they haven't killed you, I'll have you right where I want. Your family ought to have a field day with this." He let out an ugly chuckle. "You think your family will pull your ass out of this once they see what Garland's gotten himself into this time? You've used up all your options. Nobody cares. What you think will happen when I pick up the phone and spread the word about how cooperative you've been?"

"That's a damn lie," Holton said.

"I know that, and you know that," Craige said. "They already know you're a crook, so who do you think will believe you? Of course you could meet with them. I can tail you or bug your phone. If I'm lucky, they'll kill you while I'm taping; then, I'll have the goods on them, save the taxpayers a lot of trouble. Who'd miss you? You dead would be a problem solved for the Holton Family." With his hand on the brass door handle, he added, "I believe your shabby line is, 'see you in court.'" Craige looked at the hunched figure behind the fancy desk in a plush office. Garland Holton didn't move. He'd made his choices. Let him roll in his own crap.

Craige nodded to the receptionist, "Have a nice day, Ma'am."

As Craige passed her desk, he wondered if he'd pushed a bastard too close to the edge. Garland Holten sat pale, breaths coming in short spurts, he'd warned them, but they hadn't listened.

# Chapter 15

**L**ong before Craige reached them, he spotted the tall, wrought iron gates with moss-covered, granite gryphons squatting on top of matching brick columns, their claws clutching the Preston coat of arms. He passed Tennessee Walking Horses, quarter horses, a cavorting, snorting bay stallion, an Arabian mare with her foal grazed the late summer lush green. Massive sprinklers sprayed rainbow arches to acres of grassy meadows. Old Pecans, Sweet Gums and White Oaks broke the slow rise toward the house. Ahead of him, the private drive with five manicured miles of white-washed, split rail fences, and at the end the white-columned, antebellum landmark of Willow Bend, the Preston estate.

It was impressive enough, but what got Craige's attention was the willowy figure of socialite Lavenia Lulalia Preston Sedgewicke. Lavenia Preston was from a prominent, old-line, colonial, philanthropic family and every bit as singularly cultivated as she looked. Like some regal dowager from another epoch, she stood waiting for him on the columned porch that ran along the front then wrapped around the house. The grand house made her look even smaller, but like some piece of delicate Dresden Meissen porcelain, she looked as though she belonged. The land had been in her family for generations, portions from an original grant from King George II. The deceptive illusion of her as a frail, little woman didn't match her formidable reputation, a Preston

hallmark and probably the reason they'd managed to hang onto what was theirs. Craige slowed on the curved drive, and as he got out, she came down the steps toward him. She extended her hand, the movement practiced, natural.

Her culture and decorum were personified as she said, "Mr. Ingramme, welcome to my home." Her words sounded with a soft, morning glory demeanor. "Do come in." She reflected generations of upbringing.

She carried herself as though having money was the most natural of expectations. Composed, with salt and pepper grey hair done in a casual, upswept style that gave her a pleasant but austere expression with soothing Robin's egg blue eyes, which brooked no impediment. Craige had rubbed elbows with Mrs. Royce Sedgewicke at numerous charity functions, and he was never able to fit her with a husband so opposite of everything she represented. It had to be one of those cases of opposites attracting.

Craige was curious what to make of her unexpected phone call and her invitation that he join her for high tea at Willow Bend—more of a summons than request.

She led him into a sitting room, which opened into a king's library, and motioned toward a Chippendale chair, which he could tell was an original.

She said, "Do sit down. Please excuse my imposition in asking you way out here. I most certainly appreciate your coming." She sounded patrician, cordial.

Craige said, "It was no problem."

"I suppose it seems a bit old fashioned, but it's unseemly for an unescorted lady to pay a visit to a bachelor gentleman," she said. "Besides, I'm not that familiar with Silver Bluff."

It was an unmistakable admission that Craige wasn't unknown to her. He wondered how much the world had lost in discarding such manners and refinement.

She said, "You must be wondering why I asked you here." She was candid in expressing herself.

"The thought crossed my mind," Craige agreed.

She said, "I want you to find out who killed my husband."

"With all respect, Ma'am, that's what the police are for." There was nothing timid about this one.

"Yes," her mouth tightened with a set smile that didn't veil a polished, flinty hardness. "We both know how very busy they can be."

"I assure you, Mrs. Sedgewicke ..."

"Lavenia, please," she interrupted. "They exhumed my husband's body and informed me after the fact." She gave him a weary look.

Craige said, "Yes, Ma'am."

Her steady gaze at Craige didn't budge, something more than pleasant yet not rude. From what little Craige knew of her reputation, this diminutive wife was no frail, shrinking violet.

"So unseemly," she said. "My sources tell me Detective MacGerald informed you about it, although that was not my reason for asking you to come."

Craige doubted anyone connected with the bank knew Lavenia Sedgewicke other than in black tie receiving lines, which was precisely the way she meant it to be.

She continued, "I made no official inquiries concerning the exhumation and don't intend to; however, I did let Detective MacGerald know how unsuitably inconsiderate his actions were."

Craige said, "I'm sure the Lieutenant didn't ..."

She said, "Graysen intended it to be exactly what it was. He had an autopsy performed and chose to let me know after the fact." She had a diamond hard countenance, which was proper. "That's one reason he's so good at what he does."

Craige said, "Gray was only doing his job."

"I'm sure." She said it in a tactful manner.

A butler entered carrying a polished silver, antique copper epergne tea service with a hand-painted rose and peony teapot and cups. Craige hadn't seen one since visiting Queensborough cousins when he was eighteen.

Craige said, "If Gray had waited, certain parties may have complicated the situation with court orders, preventing the police from proving your husband was murdered."

"Of course ..." Her gaze was steady.

She lifted her teapot and poured a steaming cup.

Holding the pot, she asked, "Would you care for some?"

Craige shook his head, "No, thank you."

"A renaissance man such as yourself is far too well-educated to accept the ends justifying the means. It's a treacherous philosophy,

quite safe in Graysen's hands but often misused in a world of men unlike Graysen MacGerald. Graysen is a good man, and he comes from a good family." She took a dainty sip of her tea. "The MacGeralds loved their children, gave them a proper upbringing which often overcame formidable obstacles. Graysen, perhaps, is at times too eager, bending corners when he shouldn't. He is a good friend of yours, which speaks highly of you. He's always had a touch of the devious, which I most certainly approve of, and he is probably one of God's truly honest people. Something one needs more of in your line of work." She made a slight frown. "I do hope Graysen doesn't let his job make him cynical. That can be so very unseemly. I can't abide it in myself and thoroughly detest it in others." Willowy fingers tilted her cup, its gold rim gave off blazing, little flashes. "Dreams tarnish so dreadfully easily, there are so very precious, and even fewer survive. Beleaguering Graysen is not the reason for my wishing to talk with you, but he is the reason I want our discussion to remain private. This is a parochial community, hardly anything goes on that doesn't become public one way or another. More so if it involves juicy tattle." Her cup settled ever so precisely in its saucer. "I want you to take something to Graysen for me." A slight stiffening gave away her nervousness.

There was no end for surprises with this one. If she knew so much about Gray, she must've known about her womanizing husband.

"Concerning your husband's death?" Craige asked.

Without a word she rose. "I shan't be long."

Craige waited. In the quiet room, slanted sunbeams streamed through the windows, backlighting the steamy wisps rising out of her cup. Waiting amid the chintz and damask refinement, he sensed she intended to protect Royce Sedgewicke. His gaze drifted about the room with its embossed first editions, original oils and water colors worth a potentate's ransom. Culture without gauche.

Lavenia Sedgewicke bolstered the long history of how much a good woman can do for any man, mediocre or otherwise. Her social position, as well as her money, had won it all for Royce Sedgewicke. Around him was the serenity and decorum of a world beyond high stone walls and iron fences as though nothing could ever affect it. This classy lady ran her world, covered her pain and got on with it. Craige gave credence to that not so uncommon rarity, a genuine steel Magnolia. Grannie would've approved of her.

She returned, "If you would …" She laid a ring of keys in his hand, "Please give those to Graysen. I'm quite certain he'll know what to do with them. Among those is a safety deposit box key. Its brass luggage tag is etched with a combination, probably for the old vault's main door."

"I've seen photos of the bank that stood on that corner," Craige said.

"An elegant building," she sighed. "Unfortunately, like far too many gems, age deemed it not worth saving, replaced I'm sure with something more utilitarian." It was unlike the way she felt. "Such a pity. There seems no end to the propensity for doing away with architectural treasures, and I might add, a few highly time-worn traditions as well. We treat our older people much the same. Younger generations lose so very much. At least a few of the old bank's finer accouterments were salvaged, for one the granite columns—elegant volute and ionic capitals recently incorporated into the new museum. It was intended to move the splendid, bronze vault door to the new bank until it was discovered they were built into the foundation. I suppose it was prohibitively expensive, but the bronzes are simply irreplaceable. Pity their splendid art is no longer accessible." She let out another sigh. "I seldom went to my husband's office, a fault in my character I suppose. Spouses who incessantly meddle in their husbands' affairs are so inestimably tactless. It's one thing to care, to be there when needed. It's something quite unbearably common to hover." She was accepting things she could not change. "I've known Graysen since he was in kindergarten. He's always been a hard worker," she continued with a modest smile. "There were escapades in his younger somewhat reckless days. He can be quite the scoundrel, which I'm sure so can you, or you wouldn't be his friend." She made Craige think of remembrances of yesteryear. "Graysen is a rarity in this contemporary society of little values." Her lips were thin. "I am quite certain Graysen had reason to unearth a grave belonging to my family. He knows it upset me, and perhaps I reproached him a bit too severely, but he should've at least had the charity to ask. If he deemed it important, I would've given my consent. I intend doing everything to help Graysen find who killed my husband. Oh, it almost slipped my mind. Graysen should be made aware that Royce kept an extensive collection of vintage Cabernet Sauvignon stored in the old vault. I'm sure those keys will be helpful."

"Other than yourself, does anyone know about the wine?" Craige asked.

"I have no idea," she said.

"Once your husband's will has been probated, then you could sell the collection," Craige said.

"I simply can't abide Cabernets. Horrid taste. If you would be kind enough to let Graysen know I wish to have nothing to do with that wine. Even though Royce had a penchant for bragging about it, I doubt he would wish it to be auctioned," she said, revealing disdain's lacy edge. "Perhaps it might be sold privately with as little fuss as possible, the monies given to one of your charities." Her delicate features were unperturbed.

The room grew quiet. Craige could hear the rustle of her impeccable, silk sleeves against the polished cherry wood. He had the distinct impression she wasn't speaking about the wine. He made a mental note to contact some of his navy buddies in St. Petersburg and Tel Aviv to ask them to check on Royce's business connections. He clutched the keys, all manner of likelihoods tumbling his thoughts.

She sat her cup down and, as she stood, said, "I appreciate your coming out and sparing me the drive. Such dreadful traffic."

"Gray will be glad to have these keys," Craige assured her.

A gentle smile lit her face as she said, "It's quite none of my business, but as a matter of curiosity, does Graysen still call you by your Sand Hill nickname?"

Her question caught him by surprise. Not many knew the Peadinger panhandle that Gray picked up from Grannie. Craige smiled, "He seldom calls me by any other name."

The Butler waited by the open door. Craige had no doubt that more than likely this imperturbable lady knew why her husband was dead.

She said pleasantly, "You have a good friend in the lieutenant."

Craige said, "I feel the same about him."

"Yes," she said, "I know."

As he drove off, Craige glanced in his rearview mirror at a half-light sepia vignette of her framed in the double entrance, wondering if worlds such as hers were more than illusion. He saw her step inside and the doors eased shut on a part of her life she meant to have nothing more to do with. The keys jiggled in the seat beside him. It didn't

surprise him that Royce would have a secret wine collection, but Craige couldn't accept it as part of what got Royce killed. He'd seen jealousy kill when it got the upper hand, and poison held a strong allure for a jealous woman, especially one who accepted her indignity in silence. Where divorce was not an option, murder was quite acceptable. If Lavenia Sedgewicke was using Craige as a pawn to mislead Gray, she was doing it damn well. Craige didn't like thinking she was Royce's silent partner and the brains behind this tango, but a few things she'd said dinged his curiosity about what else he might uncover.

*****

Garland Holton thought of all sorts of ways to get his butt out of Ingramme's meat grinder. He was convinced Ingramme was out to get him. Seeing Craige Ingramme dead was an option but not a very viable one with MacGerald standing in the wings. Arrangements had been going well. Most of old lady McGiffern's dormant accounts were so old no one knew about them, money wasn't doing nobody no good. Marshall was supposed to handle all the paperwork. Sedgewicke claimed it would be untraceable. It wouldn't be the first time Royce pulled a scam inside a scam, but the old fox had been right—a little bit at a time, a few stocks here, a few there, no one would ever know. Yet he never quite trusted Royce, but Garland never quite trusted anyone. He took out insurance, told no one and set up his own holding company, Gulf Oil Limited.

It worked better than he thought. He skimmed off the big deals so easily he wondered why he hadn't thought of it before—dipped out of CMA and other cash account turnovers, hedged the odds, played with a few international futures and stashed the spinoff cash in Gulf Limited. He had to be careful about Royce's personal contacts among those foreign conglomerates, some of the rake-offs used for hush-money payoffs, nothing new in the money-shuffle supermarket. It was his best layout yet and put him in the catbird seat. In Garland's world money wasn't a lever, it was *the* lever.

Then Royce ended up dead, and the word was out he was murdered, and Ingramme started nosing around. The more Garland tried to get a handle on that Carolina PI, the more brick walls he hit. He dug into Ingramme's background, found no axe handle to use against

the man but learned something incomprehensibly worse—rumors about Ingramme's fortune were true, the man could buy and sell the Holton family without putting a dint in his cash flow. A bastard country bumpkin, Ingram throw-off didn't deserve that kind of money, and it terrified Garland Holton. Holton's panic ate his peace of mind.

In desperation, Garland's next blunder was pure Holton swagger. He flubbed it bad when he tried brown-nosing his way into homicide for an inside look at the files. He never had a chance with Mabel. When Gray told him about Mabel's standoff with Holton, Craige chuckled. He knew his dodge and thrust had taken root. He'd sit back, see what popped to the surface and cross his toes no one else came up dead in the meantime.

Mabel had unnerved Garland. He saw things going beyond control. PI and cop had to know more than they were telling besides his hired goons nearly getting caught in the Stanley house. Dragon's teeth sprouted about other things Ingramme might dig up.

He decided a reverse ploy would twist things in his favor, made the tape, edited it a last time, rerecorded to a clean original, and he'd take it to Ingramme.

He'd followed Craige several times during the next weeks. Ingramme was sleeping over at Stanley's every night. Envy rippled his groin, wished he was banging a looker like her. Ingramme and Stanley were working together. Someone was out to make him the fall guy, and Ingramme was doing their dirty work. He wasn't about to rot in prison, better to cut a deal with the DA before it came to that. With his legal savvy he could pull it off. His mother always told her bridge club how smart her son was.

Already halfway to noon, Garland stewed about it the rest of the afternoon. He didn't like to think about facing Ingramme. He knew he was walking a fine line. He had to make sure it came out his way. He bit the bullet, and with a last hesitation, he reached for the phone.

Craige answered, "Ingramme."

"Garland Holton here," he said. "I got a tape I want you to hear."

It wasn't so much his call that was the surprise, as his buddy-buddy demeanor. Craige had seen him in action a time or two. It was too much of a turnaround for a small change artist, but he was curious what he was up to.

Craige asked, "What's on the tape?"

"A threat I received at home," Holton said.

"In the mail?"

"On my answering machine."

"Only a fool would pull a dumb trick like that. Tapes leave a voice print."

Craige's distrust roared wide open. Holton wanted something, knowing anything he gave Craige would go straight to Gray. There is nothing to lose by stringing him along.

Craige said, "You need to report that to the police."

"Police ask questions. I don't want the hassle."

"Which means you don't want the police involved."

"The media could pick it up from a police report."

"And police reports are public record, and you don't want Grandmother to know."

Craige didn't miss Holton's short intake of breath at his crack about his grandmother. Craige wasn't about to let him off that easy. Besides, if Holton didn't want Gran'ma knowing, then it wasn't on the up and up, which fit the Garland Holton he knew.

"You're investigating the Sedgewicke case," Holton said.

Craige said, "I'm looking into it, but there's a big difference between me and the police."

The man was too damn agreeable. This whole conversation smelled fishier than a backwater dead crab.

Holton said, "Will you listen to it?" It was his ploy to make it work.

"All right."

"I'll bring it out."

Craige didn't want Garland anywhere near Moccasin Hollow. Lucky would eat him alive. Craige's first impulse would be to let the dog have him, feed his leftovers to the gators, except it might be bad for the gators.

"I'm on my way into town," Craige said. "I'll stop by your office. Warn your secretary."

Holton said, "She won't forget you." He gave Craige a fake laugh.

"Few people do," Craige said.

When he got to his office, Craige nodded to the receptionist and walked right past her. Holton was unbelieveably cooperative. Craige felt the urge to keep his back to the wall. He listened to the tape,

rewound it and listened again.

Then Craige asked, "You recognize the voice?"

"No," Holton said.

"Whoever made that has to know voice prints can be used as evidence," Craige said. "Sounds like some type of harmonic muffle in the background, maybe a cheap recorder. You make a copy?"

"This is a copy," Holton said. "I didn't want to chance the original getting messed up."

Craige said, "You keep the copy." He popped it out of the player, handed it to him. "I'll take the original to Graysen."

Holton sputtered, "Homicide?" His eyes grew big.

Craige said, "It is a death threat. Gray ought to know about it." Craige BSed right back at him.

Craige couldn't believe he was so doorstop dumb. His first impression was he'd faked the tape, but Craige would find out more by pretending to go along. Let the squirmy bastard stew in his own juice, Garland Holton was afraid of something, and he wanted the details.

Craige said, "Would've been better if you'd've let the police pick it up. That way, in case there's ever a name to go with it, it'll be verified with their date-time mark as having come from the plaintiff." It was his own touch of legalese. "From your own experience, you know it's best to protect evidence from being questioned in court. Keeps everything on the up and up."

Craige figured his crack would needle him. Besides, other stinks he didn't know about might stir to the surface.

"You take it," Holton said. "I trust you."

"You sure?" Craige asked.

He nodded. Craige grabbed an envelope off his desk, dropped in the cassette, licked it, dated it, folded and stuck it in his pocket. Craige didn't speak to iceberg secretary as he left. He headed for his lunch meeting with Gray at Morningshine Deli.

*****

Holton's change of heart didn't set right with Gray either. They'd both seen their share of the shell game.

"Mud crawlers don't change," Gray said. "Holton's scared. He's hedging his bets unless he'll say who made the tape."

"My guess is he made the tape," Craige said.

He dropped the ring of keys on the table and jangled the second set in his hand.

Gray said, "What you plan doing with those?" His eyes were at Craige over the top of smudged glasses.

"The fewer people who know about these keys the better," Craige said. "If you use them, there's no way some reporter won't snag onto the story."

Gray said, "I don't like surprises."

"Neither does the DA and neither do I," Craige said. "For right now, I'd like to keep this between Lavenia Sedgewicke, you and me." He jiggled the keys. "Odds are, Holton doesn't know Royce's wife had these."

Gray started to say, "You keep your set, and—"

Craige interrupted, "I know, you don't want to know what I'm doing unless I find something."

Gray nodded, "Meantime, I'll see what's in the deposit boxes and seal any contents as evidence. Theosia's money could be right under our noses."

"I doubt it," Craige said.

"You would've made a first-rate larcenist," Gray said.

"There's some who think I am, but you got to admit it gives one the edge in the survival business," Craige replied. "I'll say one thing for whoever planned this, stealing from the bank and hiding it in the same bank was a good plan until poison messed up the playhouse."

"Why do I think you're right about not finding money in any safety box?" Gray sipped his second cup.

"Holton's running scared. His scrawny neck is next," Craige said. "Wouldn't be the first time we've seen a shadow dancer trip themselves up." He gave him the cat-ate-the-canary look. "Even if Holton wanted Royce dead, he doesn't have enough guts to slip Sedgewicke that glass of wine. I don't think he knows who killed Holton. If he did, he'd either already be dead or hiding evidence for protection."

"Blackmailing a killer can get tripwire tricky, even worse if we're dealing with a psycho," Gray said. "If Holton knows who's behind this, he's juggling nitro and that never works."

Craige asked, "You haven't filed the second autopsy report, have you?"

"Not yet. That way neither Mabel nor Fred will have to lie about knowing what's in it. Craige, be careful. There's parts of this poker hand that haven't been dealt."

Gray's remark prodded memories Craige had never liked remembering.

Craige said, "Last time you said that, our CTU team was dug in on that screwed-up nightfire recon exercise." The ugly details flooded back as he gazed into the bright glare from the street. "It was a low tide beach. It crawled with sand crabs and incoming mortar rounds passing all around us. Darrell was my backup. If he'd have listened, he wouldn't have died."

"I remember," Gray said quietly.

They seldom spoke about it. The scars receded but never went away. They paid their checks.

In the parking lot, Craige said, "I'll catch you later."

Gray drove off. Craige walked the few blocks in the direction of the bank. The dry September briskness felt good, firing his blood with an agitation, which wasn't all from the weather or the investigation. Terri was no small part of things tugging at him. He turned into Antapolsky's Mercantile, bought a brass key ring and strung the keys. He didn't want any of them to get lost.

Late lunch customers were thinning as Craige pushed through the glass double doors into the bank's grand marble and paneled lobby. He stopped at a service counter and pretended to fumble with deposit slips as he surveyed offices along the main floor. With sublevel foundations being sunk during the bank's construction, entrances to any old tunnels connecting previous buildings either collapsed or were sealed up. He took the side exit and couldn't help noticing the rails of the old spur glistening in the afternoon sunlight. He had always had a thing for trains, especially steamers. He even tossed around the idea of getting a private rail car—maybe some day.

From across the street, he stared back at the reflective exterior of the bank. It would be like Royce to move the entrance to his vault-wine cellar from an inside staircase to the old bank's rear exit, then renovate and lease the old building. He pulled out the ring of keys and tried several. His heart skipped a beat when one slid in. With an easy twist there was a faint click, and the door opened. He wanted to explore the levels below, but he first prefered to reconnoiter unfamiliar

turf. He wanted to look at county records, see if there were drawings or surveyor's maps of the early layouts. He locked the door and walked toward Riverwalk. Like a surreptitious prowler more comfortable with the night, once he was familiar with a layout, he favored the dark; it was less noticeable.

*****

Gray received his court order.

"I'm not so sure I ought to let you do this," the vault receptionist said. "You'll have to sign this." She pushed the signature card toward him.

Gray said, "It's legal."

He scribbled his name, briskly thumbed previous sign ins and saw only Royce's signatures. He followed her into the vault as she fitted both keys. Gray could tell that it wasn't heavy by the ease the long, flat box slid out.

As he handed her a copy of the court order, Gray said, "I want you to stay. You're my legal witness." He lifted the lid and wasn't surprised when he found no cash. He used his pen to edge up the random papers— Sedgewicke's expired passport but no current one, a mini-cassette, a small pocket notebook and several folded, worn stock certificates with Arabic lettering beneath a logo. The only words in English were tall black letters that read, GULF OIL LIMITED. Beneath that was a small partial vial of pale yellowish powder. A lump choked his throat as he gingerly rolled it back and forth with his pen. He had an odious feeling he was looking at what killed Royce Sedgewicke. Fred would have to check the glass for prints. If it was poison, he finally had a method to add to too many opportunities. Now it came down to motive. He carefully lifted the cover of the passport and could make out some visas. Fred would get the rest.

"This lock box is sealed," Gray said as he locked it and took both keys. "No one is to have access unless they have badges certifying them as members of the homicide department."

Gray was hardly out of the building before Garland Holton knew he'd been into Sedgewicke's lock box and ordered it sealed. Holton was positive all their secrets lay inside, and worse, Gray had used a key instead of having it drilled open. Everyone at the bank had been looking for Royce's keys.

Holton muttered, "Damn Stanley bitch!" The corner of one eye

quivered as he popped a mouthful of antacids.

Before the morning was out, Garland wasn't the only one who knew. Barry overheard secretaries on the elevator talking.

The brunette said, "They had a court order." She hardly gave Barry a desultory look.

The other one said, "I'll bet that twisted the old harpy's tail in her cage. She guards that vault like it belonged to her."

"She'll fume if they didn't ask her permission," the brunette giggled. "The woman ought to get a life." The elevator doors opened, and they got off.

Barry knew they were watching.

# Chapter 16

The streets were empty. A vague uneasiness was still prickling at Craige as he parked on Front Street near Riverwalk and headed toward Seventh. It wasn't so much fear but more like one of those nightmares that wakes you up in the dead of night. You're afraid but not sure of what.

A knot of rowdy teens tumbled out of a '47 pickup with a new red paint job, a bold white racing stripe and a Georgia bulldog pennant flying off a whip antenna. They headed for the amphitheater and were soon out of sight. He cased the adjacent streets, window-shopped the area for out of place bodies who didn't belong, then turned into the alleyway with the keys ready.

A soft click and the door swung inward. Once inside, Craige made sure the door caught behind him. His muscles were as tight as a violin string. The soft interior smelled stale and mildewed. The narrow shaft from his penlight swept walls, floor, ceilings, across stacked old furniture, water-spotted, sagging cardboard boxes and heaps of moldy newspapers. He centered the light on recent repairs to the handrail, then flashed it down the steps. Bright dust specks glided lazily through the beam of his light. Below him, in the circle of light was the immense vault door. Its bronze surfaces were barely perceptible in its own time-warped obscurity. He felt as if he glimpsed into some long-buried pharaoh's final sanctum. He cautiously moved down the stairwell one step at a time. At the bottom, he let his fingers caress the smooth

brass. Brass had always been his favorite. In the hands of an artist the alloy could almost breathe alive. Royce was the only one supposed to have been there, yet the ornate metal handles and embellished combination dial were dust free. Someone else besides Sedgewicke and his wife knew about this place. Several names came to mind.

Craige checked the aged tarnished surface of the combination dial, its pointer on the same number as the last one engraved on the metal tag Lavenia Sedgewicke had given him with the keys. Apparently the combination was never reset. He thumbed away most of the grime from a portion of the glass face covering the time clock, its sweep second hand frozen in some forgotten past. The old vault made an ideal temperature-humidity controlled wine cellar, yet he couldn't accept that this penchant for privacy was part of what got Royce killed. Craige would go for guiltier secrets with no more proof than a very dead Nathan Marshall having purchased crowfoot poison and the faceless "who" he bought it for. Any one of Royce's banking associates could have reasons for wanting him dead, reasons they didn't want anyone to know, and a number of those same people hadn't been at the banquet. It was a small detail Craige would make sure not to overlook. Royce's death didn't have to involve only bank employees. He'd been around enough mayhem to know even the mildest of rabbits could kill under the right circumstances. Hoping he'd find more answers on the other side of the vault door, his eyes roamed other junk—neglected partitions, a broken chair and a smelly rat nested desk. Most of the stuff didn't seem to have been touched since the bank closed.

Craige's eyes darted to two big, brass padlocks to one side of the vault door, one above the other. They reminded him of old railway switch locks, which fit the bank's early history. Brass keys on the key ring matched the locks and opened each with a dull click. The locks likely secured the inner cage door now standing open inside the vault, the bars matted with cobwebs.

A yawing, unlit pernicious void seemed to lay beyond the vault door. The blackness swallowed the beam of his penlight as though it was some opening into the underworld. Craige spotted new breaker boxes but decided against trying the switches. He didn't want a burst of light being seen from the street. He flashed the light into the inky nothing and caught dull outlines of wooden racks lined with dust covered bottles, the ocean of vintage wine hoarded with a banker's

obsessiveness. He swept the light further. He could barely make out dim outlines of row after row of neck-down dusty burgundy bottles, empty cases stacked along the walls, the racks, which filled the vast underground grotto, all of it carried down the narrow stairs a case at a time. From what little he could see, there was enough wine to drown a proverbial army, queue after queue. There was more wine than a dozen Royces could consume in a lifetime. He lifted a bottle, wiped its label, then another and a third, all the same—Napa Valley Rutherford, Caymus Vineyards cabernets. This label had triple-A collectibility ratings (sauvignons were some of the world's greats) and these special selections kept in expensive French oak for forty-eight months. He could almost taste the tart black grapes of the first picking, but cabernets were never on his list of preferred dry reds.

Craige almost missed the heavy, planked door at the far end. He yanked its iron strap handle hard, but the door didn't budge. He examined the jamb closer. It looked old except for the fresh cement, sawdust and a couple of new screws on the floor. It had been replaced and not too long ago. With his ear to the door, he picked up the faint muffled gurgle of running water. None of the keys fit the double-keyed dead bolt. His light trailed up to the beams and across the ceiling. The walls of century old bricks were made on-site, all part of the original substructure foundation of a spectral world forgotten beneath busy city streets.

He recalled old maps of colonial Fort Cornwallis, the Hamburg railhead across the river from Charleston, then downriver to Savanno Town. He had to be far enough below the streets to be near the original river edge, under part of the levee. He wondered why Royce replaced a door in a metal frame at the river end of the vault. Royce probably sealed off any old wharves or docks still down here. That would explain the recent filings and the sawdust.

Near the end of one rack Craige stumbled against an open case with the same clustered grape label. He scooted it out, found it full except for the one open bottle next to the box, odd that an open bottle would be down here. The label struck him as different. He reached for a bottle off the rack. The labels were different, but both were from the same winery, one a draped grape cluster instead of a single splayed flat grape leaf.

He thought of his friend Pierre Fonds, a French olympic national

rower and the wine quarterly article he had seen in his apartment. They both enjoyed good wine. Pierre was a topnotch wine connoisseur and kept an excellent small selection of his own. Each time he made a trip home to France, he brought back some hardly known labels. That day, Pierre had pegged an article to the front of the fridge. It was a review of vintage years, scheduled release dates for open sales, standard vintages which wouldn't be released followed. At the top of the list was his latest acquisition.

Pierre, thrilled with his purchase, said in the king's English with his accent, "Ah, Monsieur … You are one of the few who esteems the pleasure of a superior wine. I work double shifts to support my hobbies, rowing and the unending search for the perfect wine."

He went to the small pantry in his efficiency apartment where two bottles lay side-by-side.

"Let us celebrate," Pierre said, reaching for the corkscrew.

Craige said, "Pierre, you paid a small bundle for this."

Craige was familiar with the label. Pierre liked Cabernet Sauvignon, this label was one of the few with a good aftertaste.

"Of course." Pierre answered and popped the cork. "For a special occasion." He sniffed its bouquet. "Quality is best seasoned when shared with a friend." He poured two glasses. "To your health, my friend." After checking with several wine shops, Craige found Royce's label was only available by special order. In some shops, not even that.

"No demand for it," one owner said.

Craige was convinced a good portion of Royce's vintages had never been offered on the open market. He got a stronger light and returned to Royce's cellar. The case of Caymus Estate was out of place. Royce wouldn't confuse Caymus Estate with his Rutherford special selection. Maybe he kept the cheaper stuff for clients and hadn't racked it because he didn't care whether it turned or not.

That's when the thought hit Craige—what if Royce wasn't the one who put it here? Craige hadn't given it much thought when Lavenia Sedgewicke handed him the keys, but Gray's remark about different MOs kept bumping his suspicions and what the wife might not have told Gray or him. He didn't like the thought of her being an accomplished black widow, giving him the keys to throw off suspicion. He hated it when suspicions took him where he didn't want to go. He couldn't pin down why he trusted her.

He kept remembering Grannie saying, "Trust your feelin's." Lavenia Sedgewicke came from landed aristocracy with a code of living—values she would never break. In her world, jealousy wasn't a motive for murder. Behind four walls, she might deball the bastard, but she had too much class to air dirty laundry in public.

The case of Caymus Estate kept meddling with Craige's mind. He took a handkerchief, reached into the case, lightly set the cork on the opened bottle, and with two fingers, he picked up the opened bottle lower on its neck where most seldom grasp a wine bottle. He avoided the rim in case anyone mouthed the bottle, telltale traces of saliva could yield good DNA. He made his way back up the stairs and realized this wasn't the first time he'd pulled a dumb stunt by not letting at least Gray know where he'd gone.

\*\*\*\*\*

Jeff hunkered over his algebra assignment, his advanced college level course was tougher than expected. He liked his teacher, but she pushed them hard, and SATs were coming up in 6 weeks. Jeff hated his future being judged on one day of opscan widgets everyone had to jump through. Mom had enough to think about besides trying to save up for his tuition.

Last year at parent-student awards night, grads from their tri-county school raked in scholarships, one in soccer, two in rowing. He meant to snag one and pay his own way. He enjoyed soccer, but he wasn't sure he could keep up with soccer, rowing and his grades.

He was glad today's practice had been canceled after last weekend's playoff against a school everyone said couldn't be beaten. His thigh still ached, but he wasn't about to let Mom know it kept him awake last night. There wasn't another game this week. He'd hit the gym and spend some time in the whirlpool. He understood Mom hovering, wondering when she would see he could take care of himself.

At first, he paid no attention to the noise, the newspaper usually came about this time. When the second thump came, he got up, went through the family room to the foyer entrance door, stepped out and checked the yard, behind the rhododendrons and next to the steps. He saw no paper but saw that he'd left the garage door open. Mom would raise a ruckus, especially since the break-in. He couldn't blame

Mom for being jittery, wanting all the doors and windows locked. He crossed the drive, headed back inside, made sure the front door was locked, pushed the button that brought down the garage door and heard it thud shut. He never noticed the crumbled wood chips at the bottom of the door.

Back at his desk, he fiddled with the radio, fingers played with his pen and glared at his open book and the neon blue flutter of his Art Deco timer. He rubbernecked outside at the autumn-blotched leaves. The house was too quiet. He got up, stripped off his baggies, pulled on his black bike skins and adjusted the crotch till it was snug. He then grabbed his favorite loose cotton gym trunks splashed with crimson valentine hearts, big black letters "Luv Me" scrawled across the butt. He grabbed his baby blue tank top, floppy high tops sans socks and the garage opener.

"Good bike ride and a cold shower," he mumbled. "Get through that friggin' chapter after supper."

He rolled his bike out of the garage and made sure the garage door was down. He buckled his feet into the peddle straps and headed for the dirt road between the canal and the old dam. The late afternoon was cooling. The old Mule Road's tree-lined bike trail on top of the levee was the best biking trail around. The dirt shoulders were good for jogging if he changed his mind. He didn't like jogging on hard pavement. It made his calf muscles sore. It might be good to split his workout, leave the bike on Olmstead Bridge, jog around the lake, pick up the bike and be back home before Mom got in. He coasted to a stop at the bridge, leaned over the weathered cement guard rail, watched a Green Heron give him the eye, squawk a protest, then wing away out over the river. Most of his buddies favored wet suit water skiing this Indian summertime of year, but Jeff liked biking. He pushed off and peddled toward the park where seesaws and jungle gyms were loaded with kids.

The Mercedes slowed. It was concealed in the roadside tangled overhangs of thick wisteria. The car came from nowhere and straight toward him. Jeff realized too late that the driver had no intention of passing. He jumped but not quickly enough. The crunch of the bike's rear wheel and the jolting blow came together. His head thudded against gravel and dirt. The breath was knocked out of him. He tasted grit and blood. It hurt to breathe, then nothing.

Barry leaned over the crumpled youth. He had wanted to take the kid at the house, but a bunch of yelling brats were playing across the street. So he parked the next block over, then walked back. The kids were gone, the open garage waited. He took a tire tool off the wall, pried open the utility room door and slipped inside just as a sheriff's patrol car cruised by. He moved into the hall with the ivory handled straight razor in his pocket. He planned to slit the kid's throat while he was at his desk and leave the headless corpse as a present for Momma to find. He toyed with setting the goggle-eyed head in the middle of the gore soaked carpet or dragging the bloody stump all over the house, paint the carpets with long crimson streamers, leave her with another dead man in her life or make it a threesome by adding country bumpkin Ingramme to his collection. Just then the kid came out of his room, and went out the front door. Barry slipped out, thirsting for the slick oily feel of flesh on the knife. He had wanted to watch the dying eyes as he sliced the throat. When he saw Jeff leave on the bike, Barry hurried to his Mercedes, followed and waited till they were in a secluded stretch. He saw the kid stop at the bridge, gunned the vehicle and felt it hit.

He nervously glanced around to see if anybody saw him. Jeff groaned with blood coating his lips. Barry pulled the bike away. The blue tank top and gym shorts were torn where the front bumper had slammed bike and rider. He duct taped Jeff's wrists and ankles and put strips across Jeff's mouth. He searched the ground, didn't want to overlook a shoe or wallet or anything that might have fallen off. He rolled Jeff over, grasped him under the arms—the kid was heavier than he looked—tumbled him across the back floor and felt for a pulse. He didn't want him dead just yet. He covered him with a blanket. It would be a kicker if he could make Momma watch. Barry absentmindedly rubbed his crotch. Maybe he should get a bigger cooler he thought as he eyed the strong legs, chest, face and the full head of hair. He could keep the whole body, a perfect trophy. Maybe keep him alive till he could redesign the refrigerated cabinet or maybe taxidermy and there'd be no need for a cooler. He would take him to the cellar right now.

He opened the trunk and lifted the crumpled bike, the twisted rear wheel jammed against the lid. He yanked and shoved. He knew the bike could be disassembled but didn't know how. He jerked it out

and mashed his thumb. He tried several angles, which made his hands greasy. He couldn't stand the feel of grease and grime on his hands under his impeccable manicure. It refused to fit. That's when he noticed his broken headlight.

He muttered, "Screw this shit."

He glanced over the bridge railing. Down the briar and weed cluttered embankment, rip-rap boulders dropped sharply toward the snarled, blackberry bog. He tugged the bike toward the railing and froze in mid-toss because of the unmistakable growl of a heavy truck grinding its way up the levee road toward the "ROAD WORK AHEAD" area. He was out in the open, didn't know which way to do what. Through the overgrown trees, he could see the cab and bed of the heavy vehicle lumbering right toward him. He dropped the bike, hurried to his car and flung gravel as he spun away, the crumpled bike left in the middle of the road.

The truck driver saw the sedan move off in a big hurry and figured it couldn't be kids. The car was too fancy. More likely a couple sneaking around on their husband and wife, didn't want anybody to see them. He stopped and climbed down from his cab. He didn't want to mash a kid's bike. He was in no hurry to get to the gravel pit. Trucks in front of him were lined up four deep. Give 'em time to dump, he thought, and get out of his way. He wouldn't have to wait. He wondered why that guy threw the bike down. He looked at the bent rear wheel. He saw nothing unusual about one more abandoned piece of trash near the old river dump. A lot of lazy good-for-nothings were bringing their old refrigerators, washing machines, mattresses, rolling cast-offs down the levee. He had watched that TV program on rain forests.

Environment nuts could bitch till birds quit flying, but wouldn't stop trash from being dumped in the river. When he reached to move the bike, he saw the blood smeared on the handle bar and the broken headlight glass. His bushy John L. Lewis eyebrows scowled. He climbed in his cab and reached for his CB mike.

*****

It had been one of those days, one nit picky detail after another. Terri felt as tired as though she'd spent the day spring cleaning. Craige

had called right after lunch and said he wouldn't be free till close to eight. It would be just she and Jeff for dinner. She did a quick grocery shop stop on her way home, pulled into the garage and gathered the groceries.

She called out, "Jeff, I'm home."

She got no answer. She put the milk and eggs in the fridge and turned on the tea water.

She mumbled, "I'm going to hide those earphones before he ruins his hearing with that loud music."

She dropped her jacket across the sofa, pulled her blouse out of her skirt, kicked off her shoes and walked into her bedroom.

She called again, "Jeff?"

After she started her bath water, she stuck her head in his room. His desk lamp was on, books open. He was probably at Byrd's. She'd have time for a hot soak.

She gave it no more thought till she was drying her hair. The microwave timer dinged, bamboo steamer puffed away at the broccoli. It had been over an hour. She picked up the phone and dialed Byrd's house.

When Marlene Stone answered, Terri said, "Marlene, this is Terri. Tell Jeff dinner is about ready."

"He's not here, Terri," Marlene said. "He stopped by after school, but he left right afterwards. Hang on a minute, let me ask Byrd."

As she waited, silence mushroomed Terri's thoughts with a tremor in the pit of her stomach.

Marlene came back, "Terri, Byrd said Jeff left about three. Is anything wrong?"

Terri said, "His book bag's here, but he's not." She tried to be calm. "I'm sure he'll be in soon."

"Call me back if you need anything," Marlene said.

"Thanks Marlene, talk to you later."

Terri went back to the garage and saw the bike was gone.

She went back to his room, his jogging shoes were gone too.

She felt relieved and aggravated at herself for being so silly. She poured a cup of strong tea and stared into the backyard as she sipped. Paul could let time slip away, too. Like father, like son.

*****

211

As eager as he was, Barry drove around till late dusk. He stopped for gas and made sure Jeff hadn't worked loose, the tape in place. He made sure to stay under the speed limit. It would be dark soon.

*****

Another hour passed. Terri tried to reach Craige, no answer, and his answering machine didn't come on. She fought a rising anxiety and whether or not to call the sheriff. After another thirty minutes, Terri looked up the number for the police and the GBI. She wanted answers, no matter how silly it might be.

# Chapter 17

Jeff could tell he was propped against a wall or something. The place smelled moldy, his side hurt, his head throbbed, and he couldn't seem to focus. Things looked weird—blotchy with smeared outlines. His wrists and ankles were twisted, and he could feel a strap around his neck. His mouth was taped. He noticed a shape moving, like a man in a dark suit.

Barry's forehead and neck were beaded with sweat while admiring his handiwork.

"Got a real prize," he mumbled to himself. "Play this right, and I can add Holton to the other three."

Barry checked Jeff's feet and ankles and made sure nothing worked loose, then pulled back the curtain from his mural and admired his artwork. He thought of his assorted blades and all the tricks he wanted to do once he had Holton down here. A little imagination and he could make it a real production—get the kid a partner, have them perform and make the mother watch. He smiled big, turned off the lights, locked the door and left.

In the sticky blackness, sleek, shiny roaches darted about, their hairy antennae seeking blood's scarlet juice. Sewer rats squeaked. Their noses wiggled, and their whiskers flicked. They sniffed and licked flea infested newborn crap in the corners. Their gleaming, beady eyes searched as they emerged from crevices into the sodden grotto beneath the street.

\*\*\*\*\*

Terri gripped the phone. The sinister, gravelly voice in her ear filled her whole world.

"You want to see your son again, don't call the police."

"Who is this?" Terri demanded. "What have you done with my son? Where is he?" She struggled to control a rising panic.

The soft click in her ear left her holding a dead phone. This couldn't be. Frightened, confused and not knowing what to do next, it seemed the whole déjà vu nightmare was in front of her all over again. The paralyzing numbness of Paul's death and then Jeff. Her life was no longer hers. Only fear and the dreadful silence were left after the voice. She was terrified she might never hear anything more, Jeff gone with no reason, just gone. Her wide, horrified eyes stared back at her from the hall mirror. Her world was spinning upside down. Had this been the person who'd come into her home, taken their peace of mind, taken Jeff? Somewhere in the swirl of confusion and fear, she struggled to contain a mother's rising frenzy.

\*\*\*\*\*

Barry was so excited that he held down the hook on the pay phone for a moment. The Stanley woman made an easy pawn—he didn't know why he hadn't thought of it sooner. He would bag the whole nest of them. Revenge was sweeter than he thought it could ever be, and that somehow made it better.

His finger released the phone hook. He dropped another coin and dialed Holton's office.

When Garland answered, Barry said, "It's about time you started doing like you were told."

"What're you talking about?" Holton asked. "How did you get this number?" He was as afraid to ask as not to.

"From Royce's computer," Barry laughed. "But let's not begin our association with you trying to let on that you care." The old snub ate him. "Treating me like I don't know what's been going on."

"What's this about?" Holton said.

Barry heard the click as Holton turned on his tape recorder.

Barry said, "Record this all you like." He sounded indifferent. "Won't do you any good. You're still acting like I'm one of you idiots that milked old lady McGiffern's accounts and didn't cover their ass. Maybe someone should let the police know where to look." He giggled. "I'd like to listen to you explain why your name is everywhere, claiming you didn't know anything about it." Hot hate enjoyed the taste of being in charge.

Holton quickly said, "We can split it. Fifty-fifty, right down the middle. Auditors will never spot the transfers."

"Is that what Royce said?" Barry inquired.

"Assets aren't stateside," Holton said. "They're under investment umbrellas, never listed with the trust. We can withdraw as much as we want. Auditors will never know, even your wife doesn't have to know. You could live like a king. You can have it all."

Barry said, "Your fat, oil friends in Vienna think they're real sharp at covering up things." He wanted Holton to sweat. "Maybe I'm being unkind. Why not keep the whole arrangement rolling along like it is? That what you want?" Barry looked down at the paper in his hand and at the scribbled name he'd found in Royce's files, the one that surprised him. "You're going to sign a few releases." Barry paused, then said, "Keep it the way I want, or I'll make sure you're the first to go down." He then added, very softly, "Grandmother doesn't like nasty publicity, and I'll make sure she finds out long before it hits the papers." His tone never wavered.

"You sonofa—" Holton started.

"Now, now—" Barry interrupted. "Let's not ruin our nice chat. We're getting along so well."

"I do the work and you walk," Holton said. "That the way it's going to be?"

"That sums it up pretty good," Barry agreed. "Makes a nice arrangement, don't you think? I can't truly claim all the credit. All I did was learn from a master. With Royce out of the way, why should I take chances? You've done a splendid job. Gulf Oil Limited has made extraordinary gains." He knew he'd hit the soft spot.

Holton demanded, "Who told you about Gulf Limited?"

"You ask dumb questions," Barry said. "For a supposedly educated man, you're a cretin." He added insult to truth. "There's no secrets with computers. You don't know how many times I wished I'd never

heard of your family. That's changed. Your scheming family has come a long way downhill with a worthless offspring like you. This gets out, your grandmother will skin your thieving ass. So much for loyalty among blood kin. When Grandmother is gone, the Holtons will be what they always were—buckra white trash." He enjoyed the dig.

"What do you want?" Holton said.

"That's more like it," Barry said. "And I want to hear more of the same. You're right, I do want something. You'll do what I say or pack your bags. Run as far as you can because I'll ring phones and mail letters, tell everything I know." He enjoyed threatening this milksop namby-pamby. "You're nuts if you think I'm letting you off the hook with this."

*****

Terri knew she wasn't thinking clear. She dialed Craige's number again. Still no answer. She tried desperately to push fear away and clear her head, but it only seemed to make it worse. There had been nothing familiar about the voice. After she hung up, the first instinct was to call the sheriff, yet something told her not to. If only Craige were here. He would know what to do.

She murmured, "He might kill Jeff regardless of what I do."

Her mind reeled, her knuckles clenched white, and helplessness rose in tidal surges. Without thinking, she found herself in the garage. She knelt at Paul's foot locker, the gritty concrete ground her knees. She carefully unwrapped the downy silicone cloth; its glossy blue, polished surface gleamed like new. Those times on the firing range seemed only yesterday with Paul showing her how to reload the clip.

Paul had said, "Make sure the bullets are seated so it won't jam."

She remembered how Paul steadied her wrists, his voice calm in her ear told her to keep both eyes open. Most of her first shots missed the target. By the time they finished, the bull's-eye was well-tattered.

Paul whispered close in her ear, "You're a natural." He bought her a .38 that same afternoon. "I want you to have a revolver. They don't jam."

They made uncivilized, ecstatic, unrestrained love that night.

She looked down at the revolver and wondered when Paul had last touched it. She forced herself to consider whether she was being ratio-

nal. Jeff's face swirled through her thoughts and swept away any doubts. She didn't care about rational, she cared about her son. She meant to do whatever it took. She found two empty clips, two full ones and below them, in plastic holders, the untarnished .38 shells. Terri clutched the gun and bullets, closed the lid and went back inside.

Craige still didn't answer. She forced herself to sit quietly and tried to be calm. She felt very alone by the phone. With the gun in her lap, each passing second nagged at the thin edge difference between Jeff living or not.

In a desperate lament, she muttered, "Craige, where are you?"

*****

"You saw nothing else?" the deputy asked as he scribbled notes.

The truck driver shook his head. "Didn't see nobody except the driver. Didn't get a good look at his face, but he acted kind'a peculiar when he saw me, and that's what made me suspicious. He climbed in a black car in a big hurry ... spun rubber. Wanted to git gone fast. I didn't recognize it as a kid's bike till I stopped. That's when I saw the blood, got on the CB and called you all."

The deputy examined the bike. "We'll put out the word to the garages about a damaged front paint job and broken headlight." He collected pieces of broken glass. "So far there's no 'missing persons' reports fitting the general description." His fingers rubbed away oily dirt on the bike. "There's a number engraved on the bike frame, maybe we'll get lucky if it's registered."

The driver said, "Somethin' fishy going down. Nobody hauls ass and leaves a bike unless they're up to no good."

"I got your phone number in case we need to get hold of you," the deputy said.

*****

Holton was as jumpy as a fox as he waited on the riverfront Overwalk. He was too scared to ignore Barry's demands. He was afraid to leave and, at the same time, afraid to stay. The crowds were sparse. In the arch below him the large green-and-blue banner flapped in the breeze. Garland felt like his heart stopped in mid-beat as two cops walked by.

For an instant, he had the appalling premonition Barry was playing him, and they were coming to arrest him. His entire world filled with a consuming, ever-widening crisis.

From directly behind Garland, Barry said, "You're acting guilty as hell. You got to get rid of the Stanley woman. She knows too much. She won't turn this loose."

Garland stammered, "What?"

His hands shook as he lit a cigarette. He took a couple of quick puffs, crushed it out harder and harder. He didn't want to look at Barry.

"God!" Holton's voice quivered. "I wished I'd never heard of Theosia McGiffern." He wondered what Barry meant. "Terri Stanley's not the only one that knows."

"So Ingramme knows," Barry sneered. "What's one more body?" His words were pleasant.

"What?" Garland said.

"Cheaper by the dozen," Barry answered. "You might as well do him, too."

"What are you talking about?" Holton said. "You been talking with that private eye sonofabitch?"

Holton was certain Barry somehow found out about his little tape shindig with Ingramme.

"Ingramme wouldn't know me from Adam," Barry laughed. "But it's a thought."

Holton said, "You're going to hire someone to off Ingramme?"

"And bring in an outsider?" Barry laughed again.

To Garland it sounded more like a growl.

"With ideas like that, it's no wonder your ass is in hot water," Barry said. "Bringing someone else into your screwup isn't very bright, but I'm curious. How did a spoon fed sniveler like you manage to get where you are?" He smirked as he said, "I've been wrong about you. You're a lot more stupid than I thought. You and your country club group think the world owes you. I got no problem with letting all of you do the work."

It finally hit Garland.

"You killed Royce," he said.

"Slick way though, in his own wine," Barry chortled. "What was done to Royce could be done again."

218

"Nobody knew he'd been poisoned," Garland said.

"Some think the wife did it," Barry said. "Now there's a lady, but how would you know? Look what you married."

"I wouldn't talk about other men's sorry wives," Garland interrupted. "What reason would Royce's wife have to want him out of the way?"

"Maybe she didn't care if he left her home while he bed hopped girlfriends to Atlanta, Europe, ski vacations, the South Pacific and Australia," Barry said. "Word is she preferred that. She never traveled with him. The night he died was one of the rare times they were seen in public together. Scuttlebutt is she was planning on filing for divorce."

"I don't buy that," Garland disagreed. "Not with her."

"Only with people like us?" Barry asked.

Barry hated Holton that much more for his snobbery. The hate boiled hotter because Holton had hit close to home.

"For a woman, being scorned is sometimes enough reason," Barry said. "Men prefer a gun, bomb, arson. Sends a louder message. Women have always preferred poison. It's personal, and murder is always personal."

Barry looked at this turd. He couldn't wait to show him Royce's collection. Once he chopped off Holton's head, he'd piss on it just for pleasure. Let Holton and Mama Stanley watch while he used the knife on the kid, then do Holton.

Barry said, "Haven't decided how you're going to do Stanley, but you're going to do it while I watch."

Holton gulped, "What do you mean watch?" He tried to swallow, but his throat was parched. "That wasn't part of the deal."

"It is now," Barry scowled. "And you'll do it. After the others, what's one more going to matter?"

"What others?" Garland gawked.

Barry said, "Parking deck, airport, few more you don't know about." He laughed at this little man. "Now you get to share the fun."

"Police said the killing in the garage was about drugs." Holton cringed. "I don't believe you."

"Who cares what you believe," Barry said.

Garland didn't believe this; Peters had to be lying. Embezzlement was one thing, this blackmailing, pudgy dormouse was nuts. He bragged

about killing people and calmly discussed killing more. He tried to light another cigarette, fumbled and dropped his gold, monogrammed cigarette case on the ground.

Barry said, "First, we bring the Stanley woman here."

Holton looked around, "Here!" He questioned the open spaces and no cover.

"Why not?" Barry said.

It would be a real charge making Garland do it out in the open.

"What—" Garland stammered.

Barry said, "She screwed it up for you."

"Royce didn't have to die," Garland said.

"You have no idea why Royce died," Barry said. "Doesn't matter. Why not have fun?" The shark was in a feeding frenzy. "I want to watch you do Ingramme's woman. Wouldn't you like making him watch, knowing he was next?"

Garland felt cornered at ground zero in a nitroglycerine situation. Taking the tape to Ingramme had been a mistake. His brain said run, call Barry's bluff, but he couldn't think of any place left to run. He pictured what would happen if he went to the cops with no proof. Garland Holton had no idea what to do. He couldn't keep from thinking how this would look splashed across the front page.

"Let's you and me make us a phone call," Barry said, giving Holton a good ole boy slap on the back.

*****

Terri sat staring at the pistol in her lap. When the phone rang, she let it ring several times, half afraid to answer.

Finally, "Yes?" her voice trembled. "What have you done with my son?" she continued in an angry burst.

Barry said, "Nothing compared to what I'll do unless you do exactly as I say."

"Is he all right?" she asked. "I want to talk to him."

Barry said, "You're not being very nice." He crumpled the handkerchief around the mouthpiece.

Terri snapped, "Kidnapping my son isn't nice." She gripped the phone so tight her fingernails drew blood.

*****

Craige tossed his jacket over the kitchen stool and glanced at the clock over the sink. It was way later than he thought. He noticed the answering machine message light flashing. He punched replay, then saw he hadn't put in a new cassette. It had been a tiring trek hot-footing across three counties, musty courthouses, cross checking records, backgrounds, marriage licenses and death certificates. He ended up with mostly loose leads that went nowhere, leads that didn't mesh and some that weren't leads to begin with.

He played with the house key Terri had given him. Over the last few days he'd caught himself worrying more about her. He admitted to himself he cared for her, afraid of the guilt if he let something happen that could be prevented. Pictures came to mind of body bags on lonely stretchers, and the clear sound of medevac choppers carrying the bags away. He decided to call her, let her know it could be a good hour before he got there. He sort of liked the idea of knowing she would wait up for him no matter how late he was. Her smell had lingered in her thoughts all day. It wasn't only skin and lathered sheets with her, it had become much more. Waking with her this morning made him realize he'd almost forgotten what it was like to watch someone he cared for next to him in bed, the intimate niceness with no hidden reasons. She slowly woke in the hollow of his arms. Somehow she'd put all his built-in alarms at ease, and it had left his steel core un-guarded.

At Grannie's grave Craige remembered girding a gut-wrenching resolve never to let love get that close again. Grannie's death had re-newed the loss of his parents with an ache deeper than he wanted to ever have again. Terri was not one of his girls-in-every-port, and it had been a long enough list. None of them came close. Terri Stanley had somehow slipped through his barricades, and he found himself trust-ing without questioning. It was a good feeling.

This morning, her sand dollar, doe eyes smoldered close to his, growing wide as they did wonderful things to each—things he didn't want to stop. When she sat up, the sheet slipped away. Her exquisite Pietà breasts emerged and her nipples hardened in the cool chill of their cocoon room. Her delicate fingers tousled through his hair, while the lovely strands streams of her hair singed molten scorches across his

chest. She smiled at him. She disarmed him, and he reveled in her. They lost track of time again. He couldn't shake that special first night they made love. It was lust yet much more, a bewilderment he couldn't pick through, one he seldom experienced. Maybe he was horny. Maybe a lot of things, but the doing was more than simply incredible.

The chimes of Grannie's grandfather clock broke his fixation. With Jeff in the house, tonight could be a sofa night, but at least they wouldn't be alone. Craige fixed his espresso and forced himself back to his pegboard with its snapshots, rearranging them several times. Lavenia Sedgewicke beneath Royce, Nathan Marshall beside Royce, Holton next to him. He made two black, felt-tip-framed, two-by-three squares for Agatha Ruth and Sallie Mae and a third for Zebulon. He set a copy of Eric Stompfer's morgue snapshot next to those of the female victims. Every face on the board had at least a passing connection to the bank except Stompfer and that was only because he was at the party. He tossed the envelope of bank employees on the table and looked at Ben Harrell's photo.

Just because he put the move on Terri didn't make him a killer. Harrell loved to play the women but didn't rate high in the smarts department. Testosterone ego was about all he had and that wasn't much. He had a mean wife who'd threatened several of his rent-a-chippies. He thumbtacked his photo underneath Holton's. He'd re-learned too many times to not disregard the improbable. Harrell may have nothing to do with Royce or the McGiffern mess, but philanderers are never dependable in any situation that required guts.

He tacked several missing person reports Gray had copied for him concerning Zeb's boytoys. Zeb was into a lot of things, but Craige couldn't fault him for being a loner. He was guilty of that himself. He bent the law but never broke it, and he wouldn't mess with something like this. Kill yes, maybe to protect Del, Craige's ego quickly suggested, and him.

As Craige studied the montage of faces, the thought hit so scalding sharp that he felt silly. No matter how he paired, repaired, sorted and grouped, these faces that looked back at him had lives that would make them amateur at killing, except one. Maybe more than one or maybe none of them. He glared at the board and decided to sleep on it. He'll rework it again in the morning, maybe he'll get a different perspective then.

Craige thought again of last night, falling asleep on her. He'd give her a call, tell her he was on his way. He tried her number again. It wasn't that late, and it was a school night. He thought it odd why neither Jeff nor Terri were home. He was thinking like a lonesome husband.

He called Lucky, "Been ignoring you? Might take you over there with me if this keeps up." He decided to play fetch with him.

Craige washed out his water bowl, dumped in more food and watched him wolf it down as he grabbed his jacket and car keys. His mind's eye regrouped the photos as he drove.

He pulled into Terri's drive and the first thing he noticed was the darkness of the house. Inside, the house was more still than it should've been. He checked the garage, her car was gone. No Jeff, no Terri. That's when he found the note taped to the refrigerator. In Terri's handwriting were seven numbers circled in red in a hurried scribble. It had to be a phone number. She's probably at one of her friends or with Jeff. He took off his shirt, shucked his pants and decided he might as well shower while the bath wasn't busy. The shower massage was thudding his skull when something in his brain jarred him. His eyes snapped open into stinging suds. The number was Jeff's phone to take with him when he and Byrd were going on overnight, camping, hunting, doing guy-things, a flat tire, accident or needed a pickup. Terri had gotten it two weeks ago. Shampoo was streaming out of his hair. Why that number? Why on the refrigerator? Why now? He was beginning not to like the possibilities. She put it there because she knew he'd see it!

"Damn!"

Craige flung back the shower curtain. Soap was everywhere and water sprayed wildly while sloppy, wet footprints hurried to the kitchen. It *was* Jeff's number. He snatched it, rushed into the den where the base unit sat empty with another note. His blood shrieked to a frozen halt when he read the words "Pendleton Park." His head swam, late at night, miles from the house, miles from the bank, miles from the airport, miles from everywhere. It was a deserted place Terri would never go to at night, not with what had gone down during the past few weeks. The bottom of his stomach did a falling elevator bit. This was somehow making a murderous sense. Terri headed into something. He grabbed the phone and called Gray's unlisted home number.

# Chapter 18

As instructed, Terri parked where she'd been told—away from street lights and near the open BBQ pavilion. She stayed in the car and made sure the front passenger door was unlocked. She was running on adrenaline. She chewed at her lip as she tried to make herself sit quiet but fear boxed out everything. She knew Jeff was being used as bait for her. She prayed Craige found her note. Unless he called the number she'd scribbled, no one knew where she was. She and Jeff could become another unsolved fade-out.

She reached behind her seat, brushed back the navy raincoat covering the gun and phone, the coat almost invisible on the floor. She slipped her hand underneath, touched the cold metal of the weapon and, for a moment, questioned if she could really shoot someone. Her fingers fumbled the phone's keypad, pushed power, then recall for the number she'd programmed and pressed send. She had a moment of angst, afraid she could've pushed the wrong button. She knew she was being watched. She couldn't pull it out and be sure but was relieved when she heard the muffled burr of its rings and thanked her lucky stars she'd recharged the day before yesterday. She snugged the coat around it to shroud its display.

She played mind games to keep her eyes off the dashboard clock. She thought of little things she wished she'd done, wondered if she'd ever see anyone she loved again. She couldn't stop her thoughts about Jeff. She refused to accept the awful dread that he could already be

dead, if that was the reason the voice wouldn't let her talk to him. The lump in her throat got bigger and tighter. Tears were for later, if there was a later. She had done exactly as ordered. She was convinced it had to be the same one who broke into the house. Her stomach was queasy. She clutched her hands in her lap, then clenched the steering wheel. She waited in the dreadful, empty, dark night.

Terri was startled at the sharp snap of the passenger door as it opened, and the hunched figure got in.

"Drive!" the muted voice commanded.

She didn't recognize the voice except it wasn't the one who called. This one was more afraid than she, and that frightened Terri even more.

"Where's my son?" she asked.

"For God's sake, just drive," he almost begged.

Terri said, "Where?"

"Just drive," he hissed.

"You're not the one that called," she said as she started the motor. "Who are you? Is my son all right?"

"So far," he replied.

Her throat clutched, "What do you mean so far?"

"Will you shut up and drive?" he pleaded. "He might be watching. You'll get both of us killed."

Her heart hammered. "Who's watching?" she asked as she eased into hardly any traffic.

He said, "You don't want to know."

"You have my son," Terri said. "I want to know."

Terri fought against a rising relentless fury. She wanted to bury her fingers in his eyes, claw him blind, hurt him and tear the words from him. Her mind raced, grabbed at any straw and played a desperate mother's impulse.

"You have children?" Her voice was as calm as she could make it.

He murmured, "Yes." He turned his head away.

Terri caught his fleeting reaction, a chink she might use.

"Would you want this to happen to them?" she asked.

"I don't want this happening to me," he snapped. "Turn left at the next light."

Crowding him, she continued, "You didn't answer me."

"It's all mixed up," he said as he wiped his face.

He was her only hope, and Terri could see he teetered between useless and a complete breakdown.

"We should call the police," she said.

"No!" His head jerked toward her. "We can't!" he exclaimed with terror. "We have to do exactly what he says. He'll kill all of us if we don't."

Terri smelled her own fear, her mind ran like the wind of a summer storm.

"If he's that dangerous," she said, "he can't leave any witnesses, including you." She was afraid to ask but did, "Is my son dead?"

"I told you he wasn't," he answered.

Terri said, "What do you expect me to think when I'm forced to wait in the middle of nowhere at night." She refused to let up. "Then a total stranger who's holding my son gets in my car, takes me to God-knows-where." Her determination was tighter. "Why should I believe anything you say? My son needs help, I need help. Please, let me call the police."

"He'll find out," His head drooped and shook back and forth.

Terri said, "Not if you don't tell him."

"You don't know him," he said.

Terri's fury swelled, "You're using my son and me to bargain for your life." She halted at the funereal look on his face. "He's going to kill Jeff, isn't he?"

Holton started to say, "I didn't—"

He knew she could never understand. He'd never had to fight for anything, and he had no clue what to do except what he was told.

Terri kept driving, instinct the only card in her hand.

*****

"She's left the handset on," Craige said, dogging other possibilities.

Gray said, "Best hope we'll have is the tower that carries the signal, and pray her phone doesn't disconnect before we get a fix."

Craige's muscles ached fromt he spring-loaded tension of the SEAL blood-beast that raged inside him. Somehow, somewhere, he'd left a cornered killer with no out, and it could cost Terri and Jeff their lives. Thieves seldom killed.

Craige didn't know why he picked that moment to remember the work order he'd seen on the counter in Terri's kitchen. It was a customer copy for activating Jeff's new phone. Craige was aggravated for not thinking of it earlier. He reached for his phone.

When the operator answered, Craige said, "We need a trace on one of your mobile handsets." He gave her his name, surety bond and permit number.

The operator said, "I'm not allowed to do that unless it's an emergency."

Craige said, "Lady, this is an emergency." He bit down hard on his temper.

She said, "You should've told me that! Perhaps you should report this to the police."

"There's lives at stake. We don't have time for bullshit." A warrior volcano's built inside Craige. "I'm saying this once, so listen, or I'm coming over there to rip your guts out."

"What!" she said startled. "What did you say?"

"You have my name and my investigator's number." Craige tried to find a calm that was long gone. "The homicide lieutenant is here with me and your flimflam could cost a woman and her son their lives." He was shouting even though he knew he shouldn't. "Report me to whoever you want, but put a trace on the goddamn number before we lose the connection, or by God I'll see the DA charges you as an accessory, and I'll bloody hell personally make your life a vacation in purgatory." He glanced at Gray's I've-seen-this-before expression.

"Well, I never—" she huffed.

Craige said flatly, "Check the number. And do it now."

"I've already done that," she said brusquely. "It's busy."

"Cut in."

"There's no one talking. It's simply ringing."

"Ringing to what number?"

"A downtown bank," she said acidly. "I can't disclose that number, but the party placing the call should know no one at a bank will answer at this time of night."

Craige's thoughts raced faster. It had to be Terri trying to tell him where she was.

"Can you trace where the call originated?" Craige asked.

"Is this some kind of joke? Are you drunk?"

She was convinced this rude man was probably a womanizing, overweight, cigar smoking ruffian who thought all it took was a license and a seedy office. He probably carried one of those cheap little pistols. She would certainly report him. She wasn't about to be treated with such disrespect, after all she was simply doing her job.

"God—" Craige muttered. "Can you locate where the handset is?"

He ground his teeth and wondered where they grew these people. Craige knew neither his agitation nor his language helped.

"My equipment only designates which tower is being used," she told Craige in her officious monotone. "And that will work only as long as the set transmits."

Craige turned to Gray, "How about radio finders? Could they locate it?"

"It's a long shot," Gray answered. "We don't have the equipment, but we might borrow some from the signal corps at the fort if they got it aboard the base. You're sure banking a lot on the handset batteries. No telling how long it's been ringing, and if the batteries are weak, we'll have to be right on top of it to pick it up."

"It's the only shot we have," Craige said.

The operator broke in, "The transmitting tower is the new one on Old Pond Road. The unit didn't dial in on roam so it's likely within a three-mile radius of that tower. If it moves, the signal will transfer to one of the towers in the south part of the county or across the river if it travels north. Further south, the Sylvania tower would pick it up."

Craige said, "Thank you. Gray, there's no need for us tailgating one another. We can cover more ground if we separate. I'll check Terri's office."

Terri had to be alone when she scribbled the note he found. If she met someone, they might be still with her, and she couldn't talk.

Gray said, "I'll contact the fort."

*****

"Pull in there." Holton pointed.

"Is my son here?" Terri asked.

She didn't like the desolate look of the dimly lit store front win-

dows nor the empty shopping center parking lot. "I've got to blind-fold you," Holton said, pulling a hunter's bandanna from his pocket. "I'll drive from here on."

"No!" Terri recoiled.

Not nearly as calm as she pretended. She didn't want him touching her. In the same instant, she realized she had no choice. She trembled as he knotted the blindfold behind her head and made sure it covered her eyes. When she caught a glimpse of his face, Terri remembered he was the one always flirting with the ditzy redhead in accounting. She'd heard fragments of kaffeeklatsching gossip about Garland Holton. She heard him get out, the car door close and hers open.

"Scoot over." He said as he helped her to the passenger side.

The car edged forward, Terri tried to get some idea of turns, bumps, smells or street noises. It was hopeless. She didn't have the faintest idea of their direction, except they never took the freeway. They crossed a railroad track, and their speed never got above thirtyish. The car slowed, jostled over a speed bump and stopped. She heard the clanking grind of a garage door open, close, then the engine turned off, and her door opened.

Holton said, "Come on."

"Where are we?" Terri asked.

He gripped her arm. Terri groped for something to steady herself and thought of the gun and the phone. He led her through a creaky door. She caught the smell of mildew, the hollow echoes of their foot-steps and the faint gurgle of water. It had to be one of the old mills or warehouses, a perfect place to get rid of bodies.

"Watch your step," Holton said. "There's steps down in front of you."

A different voice said, "Well looky here—"

The blindfold came away, and Terri found herself staring at the smirking face of Barry Peters. She had never liked him. She thrust away her fear and doubted she or Jeff would live to see tomorrow.

*****

From inside his glass cubicle, the flash of headlights caught Security Guard Lon Hurstwood's attention. He thought the car was turning around, then saw it wasn't. He wondered why anyone would park

at night in that weeded-up alley, then saw the car's lights shut off. He thought it was a bunch of horny kids looking for a quickie place. No wonder AIDS was out of hand, sex is too free nowadays. Nobody been in that old bank since the new one opened, and the last time he'd seen a switch engine along that siding was years ago when the flatcars brought that load to the downtown lumber yard.

Lon shrugged. This was his first late shift rotation, and it looked to be a long night. He plopped down in his creaky chair in front of the row of black-and-white monitors, opened his thermos and refilled his oversized cup with steamy chicory coffee. The cup was almost to his lips when the figure appeared across the street hurrying directly toward him.

Craige burst through the glass door, "Has Terri Stanley gone up to her office in the last hour?" Craige said as he showed his ID.

Lon rose out of his chair and said, "No, she could've used her key to the outside door on four and gone in from employee parking." He pressed "talk" on his two way, and said, "Jim, gimme a come back."

"Yeh?" a voice answered in a fuzz of static.

"Jim, where you at?" Lon asked.

"I'm on six," Jim answered.

"Anyone with you?"

"Yeh. We're making rounds. Why?"

"We got a PI down here. Says his name's Ingramme. Wants to know if Mrs. Stanley is working late. You seen her since closing time?"

"Not seen anybody," Jim said. "She that widow lady that works in trust?"

"Yeah." Lon glanced at Craige.

"There wasn't no lights in those offices when we made rounds," Jim said. "We hadn't made our second sweep on four, but that yellow car of hers ain't in her space. You want us to check the offices?"

"I'd appreciate it," Craige said.

Lon looked at him and asked, "What's going on?"

"I need to find her ... her son's missing."

Lon brought the radio to his mouth, "Jim, check her parking spot. If it's still empty, see if she took the stairs and went to her office. Check her office then give me a call on the radio when you finish. We don't want any surprises."

"Roger," Jim answered before the connection went off.

Time seemed to stretch forever for Craige.

Lon asked, "Coffee?"

"No thanks." Craige paced harder.

"Lon?" Jim's voice crackled. "Come back."

Lon replied, "You find anything?"

"Nothing here—no car, no lights, everything locked up tight," Jim confirmed. "Funny thing though. On first rounds we heard a phone ringing in her office and it's still ringing."

"Phone?" Lon was puzzled.

Instantly, Craige said, "Tell him not to pick up!"

Had Terri used the phone to tell him where she was? Craige's thoughts were scrambled. If she wasn't in her office, then where?

Lon frowned and said, "Leave the phone be, don't answer it." He lowered his radio and asked, "What's going on?"

Craige said, "Stanley and her son may have been kidnapped."

Lon's jaw went slack. "You call the police?"

"They know," Craige assured him. "Can I borrow your phone?"

Lon punched an open line, "That'll get'cha outside."

Craige dialed Gray's mobile and listened to rings that seemed to go on for a lifetime.

Finally, Gray answered, "MacGerald."

"Any luck?"

"Fort's got a crew on call. Take about an hour to get the equipment set up."

"An hour!" Craige yelled.

Terri and Jeff's chances slipped away with every tick of the clock.

Gray continued, "They're meeting me in the courthouse parking lot. I'm headed over that way. You still at the bank?"

"Everything here's quiet, too quiet." Craige hated feeling so helpless. "Security here at the bank hasn't seen anyone. They checked her office. Her phone was ringing but no Terri."

"I'll wait for the equipment," Gray said. "Once it's rolling, I'll meet you there."

*****

Barry wondered which of them this bitch was in cahoots with. It didn't matter, they all had to go.

231

Barry said, "Have fun on the ride?"

Terri snapped, "Where's my son?"

"Back there." Barry pointed to the closed door.

Terri glanced around. "Where?" Then, like the avenging Goddess Juno she said, "I want to see him."

"Still giving orders." Barry dropped his smile. "You aren't ignoring me now."

Terri didn't care what he was talking about or what this creep wanted, but she'd play along. Every nerve in her body felt like it was on fire. She meant to see Jeff, refused to even consider his being dead.

"I want to see my son," she demanded. "Now!"

Barry mimicked her, "I want to see my baby. Right now!"

He sneered at Holton. "Think we might let her see him?"

Beyond hope, Garland said, "Why can't we just let them go?"

Barry's eyes blazed a slivered hate at Garland—just one more puke he despised. He moved close to Garland's face. He could see the tiny, webbed blood vessels in the whites of Barry's eyes.

Barry said, "I never understood why Royce put up with you." He spit the words. "But he liked his toadies close by." He nodded toward Terri. "With her out of the picture, they got nothing."

"They had a court order to take the files," Holton whimpered. "Wasn't anything I could do about it."

"They got a court order," Barry parroted Holton. "You were stupid for not getting rid of those papers in the first place, but better you than me."

Terri couldn't believe what she was hearing. A dreadful winter clutched at her heart. She wished with all her might Craige were here. She recalled Craige saying it had to be an inside job. She looked around at this dreadful place. She had to gain time, had to be careful. Peters was unpredictable and dangerous—she'd have no second chance. She flinched when he stroked her arm with the back of his hand, his touch like an electric shock. Terry could smell his garlic breath.

"Right this way," Barry said as he tugged open the heavy wooden door. "Apéritifs await."

The dirt and grime clashed with the startling white table cloth and the tall, lighted tapers in crystal holders—serenity in the midst of chaos. Then Terri saw Jeff.

Terri screamed, "Jeff!"

"How touching," Barry smiled.

"For God's sake Peters, we don't have to do this." Holton shook.

Barry said, "You have a point." He faced Holton. "We don't have to do this. What do you suggest, counselor?"

"What?" Holton stammered, confused, terrified.

Barry said, "You said we don't have to do this." He gave Holton a lifeless smirk. "How do you plan to keep two kidnap victims from running to the cops?"

Holton's throat worked. "Just turn them loose." He couldn't make more words come.

"You never could do anything right." Barry's face turned macabre. "Besides, that's not what this is about." Spit frothed at the corner of his lips. "I want you to do the kid."

Holton was petrified. He saw Terri brushing hair from Jeff's forehead and tug at the tape across his mouth.

Barry turned toward Terri and brooded. "Get away from him."

The skull in the mural dazzled sarcophagus gray above the huddled group buried in the catacombs beneath the streets.

# Chapter 19

Craige paced back and forth in the mezzanine of the bank. Time was running out, which made waiting for Gray worse. Each second stretched to what seemed like hours, fighting haunted bogeys of mistimed ambushes paid with someone else's blood. He felt helpless, unable to fight off a sense of a no-win situation. He watched the hands of the clock move past the witching number twelve. Fists rammed in his pockets, he battled to keep a lava-hot fury from overriding survival instincts. He clung to the slender hope that the time of death of most of the victims had been in the early-morning hours. His body screwed hair-trigger tight, all the while knowing it made little difference.

The guard broke his train of thought when he said, "I hear MacGerald's a decent cop." He slurped coffee from a stained cup.

"Yeah," Craige answered, barely listening.

The guard slurped again. "You know," he continued as he rocked back on the heels of his boots, "odd you'd be looking for Mrs. Stanley's car on the same night."

The remark stopped Craige in mid-pace. The guard had his complete attention.

"What did you just say?" Craige asked.

The guard said, "She drives that snazzy looking sports car." He swirled his cup. "Sure would like owning something like that. Canary

234

yellow, nice color, classy little number. Never seen another one like it, and that's the funny part 'cause earlier tonight I saw another one just like it. Ain't that some coincidence? Spot something you don't see much, then see two on the same day. Happens that way I reckon."

The guard's words rumbled through him like a Richter 10 earthquake.

Craige made his words real slow, "You saw a yellow sports convertible like Terri Stanley's?"

"Sure did," Lon nodded. "Something like that stands out. Drove right down the street. I didn't think nothing about it when you first asked. I knew it wadn't her when it stopped over yonder. With her parking slot up in the deck she's got no reason to park there." He pointed with the fist holding the cup. "Drove right into that garage."

Like an AWAC radar, his eyes narrowed and skimmed the whole street in a single sweep and into the dark, narrow alleyway.

Lon frowned. "Now that I think about it, I don't remember no garage in that alley. I used to play on those old loading docks, but by golly, it looks like it's sort of been fixed up."

Like an arrow, Craige was out the door, across the street and knelt and angled his head to catch light reflections off the old rails. They looked red-brown in the saffron glow of the street lamps, but he could barely make out imperceptible tire tracks in the grit covering them. He felt dull-witted. He could've kicked himself. It was a flawless disguise straight from his own playbook, the unseen in plain sight. His skin was pincushion prickly and his tongue sticky as he hurried to the garage door and glued himself to it. He could smell fresh treated wood, latex, paint and joint sealer. He searched edges, the bottom and any opening he could find to get a grip to pry it open. His heart banged inside his chest for what he didn't want to find on the other side.

The door fit tight. Craige put his shoulder into it and shoved. It didn't budge. He made a quarterback dash to his vehicle, grabbed a flashlight and Royce's keys off the floorboard. He went back to the garage door and  pressed an ear against it. There was a muffled electrical hum from some kind of motor, diesel, air conditioner, maybe elevators. It didn't sound like a car. Fear smacked him hard—what if it was Terri's car with her inside, engine running, pumping out monoxide, maybe already dead because he'd pussyfooted around. Rage churned, caution evaporated, adrenaline whisked full throttle, he'd had enough what ifs.

Craige shouted "Hurstwood" as Lon crossed the street toward him. "Get back out of the way!" He fired up his RV.

He hollered, "What?"

Craige snugged his seat belt as tight as he could get it, rolled down his window to get as much glass out of the way as possible, lined his high beams directly on the door, jammed his foot on the brake, down-shifted, engaged the four-by transmission and felt the gears sync.

He leaned out and yelled again, "Lon! Get back across the street." Craige's engine revved to max.

He braced his head against the headrest and yanked his foot off the brake. The vehicle lurched. Lon must've thought he intended to use the front wench to force the door until he heard the full growl of pedal to the metal and saw Craige's tires squeal blue smoke. He quickly scurried out of the way. The speedometer was pushing sixty-plus. Craige threw a forearm across his face just before the roaring impact. The door splintered, frame and support beam came down and electrical wiring tugged loose. He felt the crunch of his front end to rear bumper. Through a cracked windshield and debris, he caught flashes of white hot metal and parts of a golden car arching and yellow paint flecks flying through the air. He swallowed his fear that anyone might be in the other car. His RV had bulled through. The yellow trunk lid buck-led and caved inward. His hood rumpled crooked, and he heard the screech of his radiator, grill and fan grinding together. Steam spewed, the engine coughed then died. Part of some cinderblock wall crumpled, the garage door track crashed down above his head, and its light bulb burst with a luminous blue-white fizzle. He threw a shoulder against his jammed door, creaked it open and climbed through the rubble. Broken glass showered everywhere, dust and bits of plasterboard sift-ing down. The side of Terri's car canted a crazy angle.

Lon's jaw dropped, "Gawdamighty!" He was dumbfounded.

Craige shouted, "Call Lieutenant MacGerald, tell him I found the Stanley car."

Craige ripped open Terri's car door, relieved to find nobody inside but in the same instant knowing he didn't know where she was. Had she been here at all? Was this another dead end he'd pay for with her life, likely Jeff's as well? He rummaged the front floorboard, the glove compartment, console, underneath the demolished seats—no note, no phone. If she took it with her, why was the car here where no one

would see it? He then had the sickening thought of the Savanno's turbid whirlpool and its devouring waters. Had she or Jeff been taken on the Riverwalk overlook, bound, gagged and thrown over. He pictured a floating corpse with crawdads and turtles chewing and pulling off stringy chunks of water-bloated meat. He was more afraid than ever for the two of them. He buried his grisly guilt of too little, too late. Instinct rejected the impulse to check along the river in an undergrowth of muck and moccasins. With some eerie certainty the river wasn't the place, he didn't consciously think about searching her car again but found himself doing it. His hand rumpled behind the mangled driver's seat, snagged the coat and blanket. His fist closed and tugged to find the winking greens and ambers in his hand—blinking digits of Terri's office number. He clutched it. It was his only link to her. For a moment, he listened to the phone on the other end still ringing as his eyes roamed the bank's tall spectral outline. Was she trying to tell him where she was? He imagined her bound and gagged in a locked closet or office, stripped naked, abductor doing as he pleased. Shivering more from excitement than the damp night air, Craige brushed gravel and wood fragments off his face as he crossed the street toward Lon.

"You all right?" Lon asked stupefied. "You sure 'nough wrecked that door."

"You have a flashlight?" Craige asked. "I just busted mine."

"Here—" Lon said and passed a heavy duty 12v lantern toward Craige.

With Royce's keys clutched in his grimy fist, Craige faced the bank. His gut said "no," then he looked toward their two cars in their corkscrewed ruin, at the old bank building, then down at the keys in his hand. He thought of all the interlaced mismatched pieces. The cellars below the old bank were big enough for a stadium full of screaming people. He flicked on the hand torch Lon gave him, centered its broad halogen beam in a bleached bright circle on the door beyond Terri's car, scrambled over fallen beams, shoved the key into the lock and watched the door open. Craige swallowed sticky, thick spit. His stomach knotted and his muscles trembled. The beam of light danced life into the catacomb, cavernous, black abyss. It beckoned him toward the grotesque, billowy, ghostly phantoms that seemed to move on their own. The hollow deadness around him echoed in the cave-like nothingness.

Craige called over his shoulder, "Lon?"

"Right here," Lon yelled back.

"You get hold of the lieutenant?"

"Sure did. He's on his way."

"You stay up there. I want someone to know where I've gone."

"Where you going?" Lon squinted into the dark pit.

"Down there."

*****

In the cellar, the muffled thud was more a far off grind.

Holton winced, "What was that?"

Barry threw a ferocious scowl toward Terri.

"Stay here." Barry handed the ice pick to Garland. "She make any trouble, kill the kid."

The door thudded shut behind Barry. Holton gawked at the pick in his hand. He heard the clank of the bolt shoved to place and wished he were with Grandmama, she'd make everything all right.

*****

The air was heavy. Craige's nose picked up smells of old, wet rot as he swept the beam along the hand-rail, wall, floor and ceilings, taking each step carefully. His ears searched for giveaway sounds that would tell him he wasn't alone. He bumped against a stack of cardboard boxes and mildewed, rat-chewed bank ledgers piled on grimy marble floors. His light swept the huge, open, bronze, vault door. The outside world seemed to be some other place and time. It left him with the sensation of being in the dungeon oubliette of some great castle. He flashed the beam ahead of him. Its brightness stabbed beyond the corridors of wine and centered on the far door. No reason to think anyone would be down here, but everything else about tonight hadn't made sense either. He seethed with a wordless bitch at himself, had his first impulse been right? Was Terri in the bank? Was that what she was trying to tell him with her phone? He pushed his foreboding aside, distracted with that instant too long … the blade struck.

*****

238

Lon paced the street—on the curb, then off, hands in his pocket, then out. He looked up and down the street, checked his watch, eyed the smoking wreckage of the cars and looked up and down the street one more time. It seemed a long time since that Craige fella had gone inside. He wondered when the cops would get here when headlights burst in his face. Lon waved his hands for attention. The unmarked car pulled up, Gray climbed out and glanced toward the wrecks, Craige's radiator still spewed.

Lon said, "You the guy Ingramme had me call?"

"Lieutenant MacGerald." Gray flashed his badge. "Where is he?"

"He said for me to give you this." Lon reached for Terri's phone and gave it to Gray. "Found it in that yellow car yonder, said to tell you it's ringing in Mrs. Stanley's office in the bank. We checked, and she isn't there. We're still searching the rest of the building."

*****

Terri watched Barry leave. She heard the door lock as she turned to face Holton and saw tiny quivers break across his face.

"He's insane." She refused to panic. "He's going to kill all of us."

The door suddenly shoved open. Barry dragged Craige's limp form. He dumped the body face down on the damp bricks, bright fresh blood soaked around the handle that obscenely jutted from Craige's back.

Terri clutched her mouth, shivered and gave a muffled, "Oh God."

Her last hope was strangled. She glanced toward Jeff, then to Craige and thought of Paul. Was she going to lose everyone she loved? She had to do something.

She looked at Barry, "What have you done?" Her words were strangely calm.

With a blaze of hate, Barry said, "That's what he gets for poking into other people's business. Simpler this way." He jabbed a semiconscious Craige with his foot.

Craige's shoulder and side ached. He picked up indistinct voices, heard someone groan, then realized it was him. He tried to clear his head, make his way through a woolly fog that spun him in some half twilight world. He couldn't make out where he was, but he thought

he heard Terri's voice. He coughed and tasted blood. It hurt to breathe. He must've cracked ribs during the crash through into the garage.

Barry said, "Holton, get me that roll of duct tape on the shelf."

Garland meekly hurried to get the tape. Barry jerked Craige's wrists behind his back and wrapped them and his upper arms. He snickered as he wiggled the bloody handle.

A bolt of dull pain shot through Craige. His mind reeled in some steamy desert tent with a bunch of smelly, smirking faces with their bamboo slivers.

Barry giggled, "Leave that right where it is." He jiggled it again. "Keep a troublemaker like you from getting ideas. Give you something to really groan about before I finish." He took no chances with this one.

Terri knew she had only one chance. She watched Barry, his attention on taping Craige's wrist.

She whispered to Holton, "There's a phone in my car."

"Phone?" He had a glazed look.

"I left it on in my car," Terri said. "Once they find it, they'll know where we are."

Holton's eyes darted toward Barry. "No one's going to look down here."

She said, "All you have to do is tell Peters about it. If he doesn't go, he'll send you. Then you can get the police." She gave Holton a desperate look as Barry came toward them.

Afraid Barry meant to kill him now, Holton whined, "She left a radio phone on in her car."

Barry said, "I never met a lawyer who wasn't a liar."

Terri backed toward Jeff and screamed, "You promised you wouldn't tell!"

Barry's face was an unmovable mask and found he liked her this way.

Barry looked at Holton, "Go make sure the street's empty and check her car." He pointed the knife. "I'll start the kid. Her too if she makes trouble."

The door jarred shut behind Garland. Terri knew she was alone and slowly backed toward Jeff. In the stygian gloom, Barry fixed her with a hollow-eyed scrutiny, fist tight around the gluttonous handle.

"I've had enough of you," Barry said.

The primal mother raged with a demon strength in her. She knew he was stronger, her odds next to nothing, but all she needed was one good crotch shot, claw both his eyes and ram her nails brain-deep into the sockets if she could. Terri didn't care what he did with the knife. He wasn't getting to Jeff as long as she had a breath left.

"Leave my son alone!" The time to beg was gone.

Barry could hardly control himself. Offing Holton would be a disappointment after this woman. A silly grin ate his face. He edged forward another step, then another.

# Chapter 20

As the door thudded shut behind Garland, he sagged against it, his head throbbed, and he felt like puking.

He didn't want to think about what lay on the other side. He wished he knew nothing about this, wished he was anywhere but here, all out of wishes. He tottered like a zombie between the strangling rows of wine. He couldn't go to the police without involving himself. Each step on the stairs creaked like a crack of doom in the obscure dimness.

Gray shouted, "Craige! You down here?"

The sound of MacGerald's booming voice rattled Garland Holton, rooting him to the spot. He didn't want to face the cops, didn't want to face Peters, wanted to run, run anywhere, upcountry Georgia, Cumberland Island, any island, further, as far as he could get to a place that never heard of Holtons. He was in a bug-eyed daze as saber flashes of light crisscrossed ceilings, slashed steps, walls and came closer. He was numb to the moist, warm urine soaking his crotch.

Gray grumbled, "Got to be a light switch here somewhere ... Hurstwood!" He yelled up to Lon. "See if you can find a breaker box."

"Here's one," Lon yelled back.

There was a clanking thunk of metal against metal. Long rows of fluorescent tubes hummed and flickered into life, illuminating two startled men, face-to-face in the dazzling, blue-white brilliance. A gape-mouthed Holton left with nowhere to run.

Gray hunched, jungle reflex, and said, "Hold it right there!" His Smith & Wesson Airweight .38 steadied.

"He made me do it," Garland sniffled. Holton's arms shot up.

Gray slammed Holton against the wall. Holton's knees wobbled, his eye quivered. He didn't hear, didn't see, didn't do much of anything. He was submissive as Gray patted him down and as the cuffs clicked his wrists behind his back.

"Spread 'em," Gray ordered. "Where's Ingramme and the Stanley woman?"

Gray frisked Holton, pulled out his wallet and flipped it open. Gray's eyes darted back and forth. He could feel they weren't alone.

Gray said, "On your stomach." He continued, "I asked you a question." His eyes skimmed the shadows. "You budge, I'll hogtie you, leave you on the floor for the rats."

Gray stepped over Holton, attention fixed passed to the vault toward the far door. He should've heard from Craige by now. Gray eased up to the door with his feet braced and weapon at the ready. He slid the bolt aside. The hinges grated.

Gray flung it wide with a swift step inside and met the astonished faces of a half-naked youth, one frightened woman, Craige on his stomach—hands bound—and a man knelt over Craige. He glared at Gray with hate-filled eyes.

In a ready-to-fire stance, Gray commanded, "Police! What the hell is this?" He put his attention on Barry. "Get away from him! Over there, and don't even twitch or you'll be dead before you can blink." Into his shoulder mic he requested, "Get an ambulance to my location."

*****

Gray's knee was pressed to the back of Barry's neck. He taped Barry's hands and feet, then cut away Craige's shirt and examined the knife.

Gray said to Terri, "Rip strips off his shirt and wad the rest into a pressure pack for when I remove the knife. Craige, it doesn't look like it hit a major vessel, but it's deep and this isn't going to feel good."

Craige said, "Go ahead."

Terri had the pack ready, Gray got a firm grip, a quick pull, and it

was out. Gray let it bleed to flush it, then tied the pack and used masking tape to keep it in place.

"How's it feel?" Gray asked.

"I've had better days," Craige muttered, nauseated at the bone-deep ache. He fought a buzzing wooziness, felt lightheaded and ready to let someone else take charge.

"There—" Terri snugged a last knot. "That should hold till we get you to the ER."

She looked at this dirty, wonderful man. Relief and fear were side-by-side in a dam about to burst. She wanted to sit down and have a good cry, and that was exactly what she was not going to do, but it was neither the time nor the place, at least until she got home. She wanted to be away from this brooding inner sanctum of death, its restless spirits locked forever in the diffused light that strained through street grates high in the curved ceiling. She could never erase memories—that dreadful pit, the macabre mural and the horrifying emptiness in Barry's eyes. Yet, in spite of everything, she felt a tinge of sadness for such a tormented soul, relieved he was no longer loose in her world.

"You OK, Mom?" Jeff said, rubbing his side.

"I am now," she said as she hugged her son.

Gray came through the door. "Ambulance is on the way." He knelt next to Craige. "You doing OK?"

Craige took a short breath. "Helluva private stock." He looked toward the racks of wine. "Royce never had enough, and it all comes down to this."

Terri checked the sling. "I kind of like you depending on someone else."

"You mean depending on you?" Craige looked at her.

"Something like that," Terri answered.

"Guess I'm slow catching on to lots of things," Craige said.

Somewhere inside Craige, a shy, eleven-year-old liked having her hold his hand. Gray helped him up and Terri slipped her arm around his waist. As Craige stumbled past the racks, his foot knocked over a couple of bottles, and one rolled out. He grunted, leaned down, picked it up and recognized it as the same out of place label he found the day Lavenia Sedgewicke gave him the keys.

Craige muttered, "'77 and '78 Estate vintage, probably picked during '76, same year Royce upped his Caymus orders." He lifted

another bottle. "This isn't Royce's, must be from the cases he used for the banquet." He shook his head. "Royce didn't want to use his good stuff or risk the caterers ripping off some of his premium wine."

Then it hit Craige why the label bothered him.

"Clustered grapes," Craige said. "Gray, this label is different from the poisoned bottle you have in the evidence locker."

Gray examined the bottle.

Craige continued, "Rutherford first growths have a single, green, grape leaf logo."

It made wicked sense. He reached for one off the rack and compared the labels.

He said, "Cuvée '86 grapes were bottled sometime in '84." Craige rolled the bottle in his hand. "Royce bought only special selection."

He thought of Peters back in the cellar, juggled what didn't fit with what he suspected and didn't like one bit where it hung. Right then, he knew Gray had the name of one killer, but not the one who killed Royce.

"Killing Royce during the banquet couldn't have been spur-of-the-moment," Craige said. "Everyone knew Sedgewicke had a heart problem, and his killer counted on that raising no questions. Royce must have taken his keys home before you had the box sealed, and the killer had no way to get rid of the evidence. What Peters didn't know was someone besides himself had been down here. Royce carried the poisoned bottle in himself. Everyone else was served different wine."

Gray asked, "You think the killer was at the banquet?"

Craige said, "All the hungry courtiers were there—board members and department heads—it was a command performance. They were afraid not to attend."

Gray said, "You change your mind?" He looked surprised. "You think she did it?"

"No," Craige said. "But talk about fate's caprice. Royce brought his own wine made a perfect way to target him, especially if we're looking at this the wrong way around. Suppose Royce found out who was pulling a money shuffle on him with the same accounts. He couldn't expose them, but he might've set up his own scam. He took small dose of the poison to make it look like attempted murder, then pinned it on whoever he wanted. With his heart he either miscalculated, or someone miscalculated for him."

Terri murmured, "It's frightening how you can be around a Peters or a Sedgewicke and never suspect."

Craige said, "That's little consolation to the victims or those left to deal with the pieces." He put his good arm around her.

"What Barry did makes no sense." Terry was relieved to be with Craige.

"It made sense to Barry," Craige said. "Psychopaths live by their own rules, which make impeccable sense to them. They keep an eye on every detail. If they perceive a threat, real or otherwise, they can kill at the drop of a hat. Some enjoy it. Let's get out of here."

Craige's shoulder hurt like hell, but the pain melted away as he closed her within his arms and bent to her. For that moment it was just the two of them. He didn't care who saw as he kissed her. He knew how near he'd come to losing both her and Jeff.

"Let's go," Gray said.

Craige clutched the damning bottle in one hand as Gray shoved the massive vault shut on a world of broken vanities. Maybe it was the light or the way he held the bottle that caught the barely discernible, slivered groove between the glass and cork, but it hit him—Sedgewicke's medical history was only part of how crowfoot got into his banquet wine. Peters may have intended killing Royce, and hid his murder with decoy dead bodies. Terri's operation had tossed a monkey wrench into more plans than Barry's.

"I be damned!" Craige mumbled. "Two bottles were poisoned before the banquet, the one Royce drank from and this one. Both dosed with a syringe. The needle track is visible along the side of the cork." He gripped the one in his hand. "The one Royce drank from was poisoned after he brought it from his wine cellar."

"Why poison both bottles?" Gray was confused.

"The killer noticed the difference in the labels and couldn't use the Cuvée. Sedgewicke would've spotted the wrong label. The second bottle had to be poisoned the night of the banquet." Craige was aggravated with his own blind spot. "Royce didn't keep his keys in his office. He kept them in his deposit box. Barry used a master key to raid Royce's box for whatever he could find—bearer bonds, cash, negotiable securities. What he found were documents implicating Holton plus the poison, but he didn't know he wasn't the only one using a master to get to Royce's keys. Those sets of smudged prints Fred found

on the safety box are likely two sets, Peters and Royce's killer. Sedgewicke carried his poisoned bottle into the banquet. After the autopsy and word got out Royce had been poisoned, Holton realized he'd been set up. Barry also knew he wasn't the only player in the game, but he had a perfect setup. Rob the robbers, let someone else take the fall. Barry likely blackmailed Holton, probably meant to get rid of him along with you and Jeff. Talk about irony. You upset everything. What no one figured was one classy lady just doing her job."

"Ambulance finally made it," Gray said.

Craige climbed into the rear of ambulance, onto the stretcher, the door slammed behind him and the driver's door openned. It felt good to lie down until he found himself faced with the one person they had ignored, an ER face mask and head cover and the very nasty end of a .38 revolver.

"You talked to Mother's doctor," the voice was no longer sweet. "Once you got chummy with Mz. Know-it-all Stanley and Royce's wife gave you the second set of keys, I knew you'd put it together." Her lilac, southern drawl was gone. "I watched the Stanley house ever since you started sleeping there." Her blood red lips had a thin gash. "Stanley left in a real hurry. I followed her and our dimwit lawyer. Saw him bring her to Barry's sick party pit."

Craige said, "Your diabetic mother is a registered nurse, gives herself insulin injections and has access to a ready supply of tuberculin syringes with needles just the right size to punch through a wine cork."

She said, "Ah yes—" Her face was vicious. "Dear mother, who knew every time sweet daddykins came into my bedroom … such loving parents. I was just one more 'get me another cup of coffee' girl. Everyone wants something, and as long as I provided the services, I could get whatever candy bar favors dirty, old men were willing to give me. Being trash isn't limited to the size of one's bank accounts. I never forgot a single one of them."

"It wasn't difficult to pick up what you needed from a nurse's station supply cabinet," Craige said. "You covered your tracks pretty well, but it won't be hard to check."

"I should've taken care of you before now, but tonight was a chance to get rid of the whole lot—you, Stanley, Barry and Holton." She hated Terri Stanley for having everything she wanted. "Men are stupid. You all think from the waist down. Give it to you, you'll do any-

thing." Her beauty—callous, ugly. "Royce promised me a condo on Amelia Island, a new Jag and charge cards. Him and his damn wine. He liked having me with him on trips but didn't want to be seen with me anywhere in this town, didn't want his snooty wife to know." She felt no remorse. "He said I wasn't good enough for their high-and-mighty country club. You didn't catch me with any syringes or the poison. You got nothing; you can't prove a thing. I'll make sure you're tied nice and firm to the stretcher." She started toward him. "Drive you somewhere and finish the job."

"Put down the weapon," ordered Gray at the window. "I don't want to shoot a woman, but I will if you force me. I thought it kind of odd when the ambulance was delayed, then arrived with only one Tech. I'd forget Jamaica. Federal agents have had those bank accounts under surveillance since that last sizable cash deposit."

She flung a look of pure malice toward Craige as Gray cuffed her and escorted her to the waiting patrol car. Craige hated to think she was right about men and women who get hooked in their own trap, believing moist silken skin and satin sex is every man's lure. He had seen too much ass backed by too little sense, trip up hell-bent weirdos too many times—a few of those times his own. Men and women aren't the same. They weren't made for the same job, but they sure fit to-gether nice. Her tread worn plumbing wasn't her flaw. Beth Pilgrim types plan their conniving one-night stands with their legs over too many shoulders, leaving precious little for the plumbing to do except wash and wipe and get back to scheming.

Terri said, "You think the charges will stick?"

"Gray has enough evidence," Craige assured her.

Craige watched the police car drive away. Beth Pilgrim hadn't used the word "great" once.

Printed in the United States
17855LVS00008B/32

Poison at the Pinnacle

ISBN: 0-9744668-6-7

Published by

TurnKey
press

2525 W Anderson Lane, Suite 540
Austin, Texas 78757

Tel: 512.407.8876
Fax: 512.478.2117

E-mail: info@turnkeypress.com
Web: www.turnkeypress.com

# POISON
## at the
# PINNACLE

**Hawk MacKinney**